BAD MOON RISING

Sheila Quigley started work at fifteen as a presser in
Hepworths, a tailoring factory. She married at eighteen and
had three daughters: Dawn, Janine and Diane and a younger
son, Michael. Recently divorced, she now has eight grandchildren, five boys and three girls, and every Saturday and
Sunday can be found at a football match for the under tens
and under fifteens.

Sheila has lived on the Homelands Estate (at present with
her son and two dogs) at Houghton-le-Spring near
Sunderland for thirty years.

ALSO BY SHEILA QUIGLEY

Run for Home

BAD MOON RISING

Sheila Quigley

CENTURY · LONDON

Published in the United Kingdom in 2005 by Century

1 3 5 7 9 10 8 6 4 2

Century
Random House Group Limited
20 Vauxhall Bridge Road, London SW1V 2SA

Random House Australia (Pty) Limited
20 Alfred Street, Milsons Point, Sydney, New South Wales 2061, Australia

Random House New Zealand Limited
18 Poland Road, Glenfield
Auckland 10, New Zealand

Random House (Pty) Limited
Endulini, 5a Jubilee Road, Parktown 2193, South Africa

Random House Group Limited Reg. No. 954009
www.randomhouse.co.uk

A CIP catalogue record for this book is available from the British Library

Papers used by Random House
are natural, recyclable products made from wood grown in sustainable forests. The manufacturing processes conform to the environmental regulations of the country of origin

Typeset by Palimpsest Book Production Limited,
Polmont, Stirlingshire
Printed and bound in Great Britain by
Mackays of Chatham plc, Chatham Kent

ISBN 1 8441 3434 2 (hardback)
ISBN 1 8441 3435 0 (trade paperback)

For Margaret and Danny Burgess, my parents who adopted me at nine days old when no one else wanted me. Sadly they died before I realised my dream, but I know that somewhere they are watching and are very proud of me.

Acknowledgements

Once again, thank you to Susan, Kate and Darley. Without these three the dream would have never come true.

Thank you also to Ron for a lovely detour to Stonehenge, and Alex for my constant stopping for a ciggie and not a moan in sight.

Also to everyone at Random House – and let's not forget the receptionists, a great crew.

And last, but only because I can't fit everybody on top of each other, Darley's girls. Gems, every one of you.

Prologue

The little boy watches the other children playing. They are in the park and it is a bright sunny day with only the faintest hint of a far-off cloud. Mother said earlier that it might, or might not, rain by teatime and he puzzles over what this contradiction really means.

He longs to join in the game the others are playing: Mother is talking to another lady about things he doesn't understand and it is really dull. Every now and again they laugh and Mother's face goes a funny red colour and then she glances at him, frowns, and shoos him away. 'Go and play, now. This isn't for your ears. Go and play.'

He doesn't know what isn't for his ears, only that it has something to do with that thing called sex. He doesn't know what sex is either, only that it makes Mother go red and funny and then she doesn't want him around. And he wants to play, he really does. Only they won't let him. The big girl called Jessie whose mam is talking to Mother called him a little freak and a mammy's boy. And then her brother Simon started calling him names too and made all the others join in.

And Mother won't listen.

He sidles up to her, his arm resting on her knee. Jessie and Simon's mam, who has the same skinny lips that her children have, stands up and calls to her children before saying goodbye to Mother and walking away. Jessie pulls a face at him behind her mam's back and he quickly looks at Mother's face, but she is looking away.

Then Mother takes hold of his hand and he feels happy until she starts speaking in that cross voice she sometimes has.

'Really,' she says, tugging hard on the hand she holds and hurting him, 'you've got to start mixing with the other children.'

'But Mother –'

'What did I tell you? You're to call me Mam like the other kids do, at least when we're out.'

'Mm-mam. Sorry, Mam.'

She relents then as she always does and bends down to cuddle him to her chest. He is truly content then: he doesn't really want the other kids with their silly games, he never has. He just wants Mother. Or Mam.

Smiling, he puts his free hand in his pocket and rubs the red button which fell off Mother's cardigan between his finger and thumb. The button will go in his box with all the other things. He already has a special place for it. Yes, it will look nice next to the piece of black hair he picked up from the floor when Mother had her hair cut by Jessie's mam.

1

The girl's long dark ponytail swishes from side to side as she struts along the Broadway. Her white high heels make a loud tapping noise in the deserted street, scattering the tiny night creatures that infest every human habitation.

Scantily clad, in a short red top and even shorter black skirt, she shivers as she crosses the road and heads towards St Michael and All Angels church. The church has towered over Houghton-le-Spring since the thirteenth century, but there is evidence of an even earlier church on the site. On a moonless night like tonight it harbours many dark corners.

It's two o' clock in the morning. It's early October and winter's chill has arrived with a vengeance. There's frost on the ground but something special in the air because Houghton Feast is just a week away, and for many the celebrations have started early.

The girl stumbles slightly, having left the nightclub with more than one vodka under her belt, but she rights herself, and starts to walk a bit faster. She'd had two or three offers of an escort from the local studs but had announced to all her intention of going home alone. Proclaiming loudly that she'd had enough of men. *Bastards, the fucking lot of them.*

She loves Houghton Feast though. As her nan tells her every year, it's been celebrated in Houghton since the middle ages, and was established as a feast of dedication to the church. By custom it takes place on the nearest Friday to October tenth, when the lights are switched on by the Mayor of Sunderland and the locals are treated to a tattoo, complete with bagpipes, after which the fairground opens. On the Monday after a weekend of celebrations a huge ox is roasted in the rectory field which lies between the rectory and the police station.

But there's more to it than that: the feast, the tattoo and the fair may be the official story but everyone knows Feast time is a chance to let go, to go wild, to let off steam. It's like a get-out-of-jail-free card letting you off the hook for things you've wanted to do but not dared all year round. For most of this week and at the oddest hours imaginable, the fairground travellers have been pulling onto the field and the excitement is building. She can almost taste it.

Feeling a sudden cold breeze she rubs her bare arms, but the vodka is a good insulator and will keep her warm enough, for the moment. She heads for the almshouses that lie directly behind the church just as a huge truck with rearing wild-eyed carousel horses painted on the side hurtles through the Broadway. A minute earlier and the driver would have hit her. The horses would have ended up on their heads with blood on their hooves. Shivering, she walks faster still.

To the right of the almshouses, the stone steps will lead her to the bridge over the dual carriageway, then on up to Hall Lane where she lives with her two-year-old son, Dillon. Dillon will be fast asleep – just as well, because the baby-sitter is probably stoned out of her mind. She grumbles to herself about the fiver she'll have to hand over for having

Dillon minded, especially since she hates that cheeky twat Simone.

Fancy fucking name for a cheap tart. But she'd been the only one available on short notice and after five days and nights cooped up with Dillon, she'd been desperate to get out.

Winter nips at her exposed shoulders, breathing down the nape of her neck, and she wraps her arms around her body. The cold air should be sobering her up but instead it seems to have the opposite effect and in a fit of vodka-fuelled animation she starts to sing, her voice – poor even when she's sober – sounding remarkably like that of the black cat which streaks across the path behind her.

The cat is not the only warm-blooded body behind her tonight, but she hears nothing above her wailing and the rhythmic tap of her shoes. When the fingers creep round her throat, she's still singing . . . But only for a moment.

Too late, realisation pierces the alcoholic fog. The hard rough fingers tighten their grip, digging with relentless cruelty into the soft delicate flesh.

She's struggling now. Fighting for her life.

The heel of her left shoe snaps, her ankle turns but her brain, struggling for oxygen, does not register the pain.

The cat sits on the fallen gravestone of some eighteenth-century industrialist beside the path, watching with the dis-interested air cats save for humans, as she grows weaker and weaker and slides quietly to the ground, his hands still at her throat in a deadly embrace.

She manages one quiet, pathetic little cry into the dark as the cat, unconcerned, turns tail to hunt the mice foraging for food in the almshouses' bin.

So easy she slips into death, and how peaceful she looks. The last thing she sees in her mind's eye is the smiling face of her infant son.

2

Detective Inspector Lorraine Hunt of Houghton police shot one long slender arm out of the pale green quilt and pressed the alarm button barely a second before its strident buzz pierced the silent morning.

Eyes still shut, she groaned, turned over and, burying her face in the pillow, muttered, 'Shit, Shit, Shit.'

She'd known as she'd closed her eyes the previous night that today was not going to be a good one. No way. Now, six hours later, she was doubly certain. The thought of facing Dakis, her solicitor, turned her stomach.

At least, she mentally crossed her fingers, John was doing nothing to stop the divorce. She couldn't wait to be officially rid of him.

And her day wouldn't get any better after she'd seen Dakis. She was down to go to Houghton Kepier school to talk to a class of sixteen-year-olds there about drugs and while she was happy to do that – the drug problem in Houghton was spiralling out of control and anything they could do to stop it getting any worse was worth a try – she wasn't happy about having to take Constable Sara Jacobs along for the ride. Much as Lorraine tried, she just couldn't make herself like Sara – she had disliked her on sight and Lorraine always went with her instincts. The woman rubbed her up the wrong way, but it was more than that: she was almost unhealthily ambitious, spending more time greasing up Clark, their boss, than out on the streets doing her job – and Lorraine knew Sara would stab her in the back at the first opportunity. There was nothing wrong with ambition – Lorraine knew better than most that as a woman in the police force you had to be doubly determined to get anywhere, and she'd fought hard herself to get to Detective Inspector – but there were some things you shouldn't stoop to. And she wasn't ever entirely sure Sara realised that.

Rolling over onto her back, she flung the quilt off and forced herself out of bed – and the thought she'd been trying to dodge ever since she'd woken up slyly drew itself on the blackboard of her mind.

Today Luke Daniels comes home.

Sighing, she moved to the bathroom, showered, decided on her navy pants suit. Sexy as well as smart. *Woah, slow down girl!*

She scowled at her reflection in the mirror as she put her long blonde hair in a french plait.

Why would I want to look sexy? I don't give a flying fuck if Luke thinks I look sexy or not. Why would I?

She shook herself, added a minimum amount of make-up to her face, just enough to highlight her already fantastic bone structure, gave one last tug to her white blouse, and headed for the stairs.

On her way down she heard laughter coming from the kitchen, and with a smile she guessed who it was. Her mother's best friend, her godmother, Peggy. Who must have spent the night.

Peggy had buried two husbands and divorced the third – swearing, as the ink dried on her divorce papers, that she was finished with men for ever. Mavis, who never had a bad word to say about anyone except Lorraine's soon-to-be-ex-husband John, pulled a face behind Peggy's back every time she said it.

Finished with men, they're all the bloody same. She always seemed to make it sound like the thirteenth commandment, but it seemed that what she was actually finished with was marriage. As far as Lorraine could see, Peggy had run through more men than ever since declaring she was finished with them – she just wasn't going to make the mistake of getting hitched again. And it seemed her new policy agreed with her – she looked glowingly healthy. Though that might be down to the fact that she'd only just got back from five months in Spain. Lorraine smiled wryly to herself for Peggy's trip had started out as just a two-week holiday – until she'd met Juan.

She'd breezed in late last night like she'd never been away, full of stories about Juan – who she seemed now to have abandoned – and the commandment had rolled off her tongue as if it were gospel. Shaking her head but smiling, because it had always been so easy to love Peggy, Lorraine walked into the kitchen to find the pair of them drinking tea.

Mavis, teapot in hand, smiled at Lorraine. 'Cup of tea, pet?'

Mavis was Lorraine's mirror image, apart from a few lines round her mouth and the corners of her blue eyes, and the fact that Mavis dressed as if she were still living in the seventies. Peggy on the other hand was small and round, with bright red hair that came from a bottle. She wore it twirled around the top of her head in a vague style all of her own.

Mavis repeated her question, successfully drawing her daughter's eyes from Peggy to herself.

'Sorry . . . aye, Mam . . . Er, make it a quick one, will yer please?' She needed to be off.

8

Peggy tutted. 'Yer'll end up with stomach trouble if yer not careful, Lorry. I don't know, yer've always been the same. Quick this, quick that . . .'

'Good morning to you too, Peggy.'

Mavis laughed, before adding, 'Why don't yer have an egg or something, pet?'

The thought of an egg or something turned Lorraine's stomach. 'Tell yer what, Mam, let's just forget it, eh? I really haven't got the time.'

The truth was, the nerves had made her stomach distinctly edgy, but she could see Peggy gearing up to have another go about her eating habits – and Peggy could go on for ever, so long that by the time she was finished she'd always forgotten what she'd been on about in the first place. Lorraine knew Peggy meant well, of course she did – she'd come out of her three marriages childless and had always treated Lorraine more like a daughter than a god-daughter – but she felt too jumpy to deal with a lecture today. *I've grown up with two mams*, she realised. *One permanent, one breezing in and out like an over-zealous absent dad.*

Quickly, before either woman could say anything else, Lorraine kissed them both and was out of the door and into her car in a blur of movement that left Mavis and Peggy staring at her dust. She swore she could hear the pair still tutting a full half mile away.

The trouble with moving back home at thirty years old was that her mother, God bless her, had started to treat her as if she was still a gawky teenager, and the last few years out in the big bad world on her own had never happened.

And now Peggy was back. Lorraine sighed inwardly. In Peggy's eyes she was probably still only three years old.

Jesus, the fact that I'm a Detective Inspector doesn't seem to impress either one of them.

The traffic was building up because of the huge lorries

pulling onto the rectory field. Once Lorraine had loved this time of year, a Feast in every sense of the word. Even now the sight of the lorries brought to mind the sugary sweet smell of candyfloss, the burnt caramel of toffee apples, the blackened charcoal of cheeseburgers, and, best of all, roasting ox. Back when she was at school, you could see the teachers getting more and more desperate as the Feast approached and their pupils got more and more excitable. By the day before the Feast no one even bothered trying to keep the kids under control – they were too excited themselves.

Saturday had been her favourite day, she'd loved the carnival parade with fancy floats where people dressed up in themed costumes and threw sweets out to the crowds. Marching bands and pipe bands from all over the place . . .

Lorraine pulled herself out of her memories. That was then, when she was a kid with not a care in the world; this was now, and she was responsible for the safety and well-being of the whole town.

The Feast seemed to get bigger every year, drawing people from all over Northumberland and Durham – last year they had even arrested a pickpocket from Nottingham of all places. Cheeky bastard. She smiled, remembering how Luke had nicknamed the culprit Robin Hood.

But pickpockets were the least of it. The world had changed so much since Lorraine was a child, and since joining the police she'd seen some sights she'd never be able to erase from her mind. Gatherings like Houghton Feast left people drunk either on alcohol or on high spirits, and that made them careless. She knew that – all the police knew that – but it was because the thieves and cheats and worse knew it that latterly the Feast had meant trouble. It brought out the best in people, but also the worst, and the worst was getting nastier. Last year a woman had been attacked; the year before a man had been stabbed in a fight and lost one eye; and the year before that a girl had driven to her death over a cliff, too drunk to know what she was doing. What on earth would they be clearing up this year? Well, she'd find out soon enough.

Finally arriving outside of Dakis's office, fifteen minutes late for her appointment, Lorraine noticed a bunch of teenage boys hanging about. Mostly she was willing to give kids the benefit of the doubt, but not the bunch that hung around with Lance Halliday.

Seeing the weight he'd put on made her groan out loud. The creep had gone inside as skinny as Dakis himself, but he'd obviously spent his time body-building in the gym, and now he was surrounded by admirers.

Flaming hell. She shook her head in disgust. *We spend God knows how many man hours catching the little creeps, then once they're locked up they spend day after day transforming their weedy little bodies into huge lumps of muscle. Bastards gain more knowledge than they had when they went in, and come out stronger than ever.*

Lorraine chewed her lip. Lance Halliday was rotten to the core and his sister Julie was as bad if not worse. The pair were the product of a couple of useless dopeheads who had let them roam the streets since they could walk, and long before they had been able to talk.

The favourite pastime of the brother and sister duo was preying on the old and frail who couldn't fight back. Both had been banged up more than once for their hobby. Julie, ten months and four days older than her brother, was easily recognised by her shaven head, and the biggest green eyes Lorraine had ever seen. But it wasn't their size so much as the utter coldness in their luminous depths that made you catch your breath. Lance was just as unmissable, tattooed from head to foot in the most revolting scenes imaginable. Lorraine had told Carter, who had eagerly joined her team

11

five months earlier, more than once that Halliday's skin should be outlawed.

Grabbing her handbag and quickly giving the inside of the car the once over – *'cos that creep'll be in if there's even a used toothpick he can sell* – she got out. Like a hawk going in for the kill, Halliday's shifty little eyes were drawn to her. Recognising her instantly, he scowled, drew back and immediately moved his gang off down the road towards the centre of Houghton. Lorraine watched him go.

'Damn the friggin' idiot do-gooder that's let him back on the streets. That's all I flaming well need,' she muttered under her breath, although she felt more like shouting it out loud. 'Especially now, with Houghton Feast round the corner.'

Sighing, she headed for the solicitor's door, knowing full well that she would only get half the extra police she'd asked for.

An hour later, and sick to death of listening to Dakis's interminable explanations, Lorraine threw her bag into the car and started it up. So that was it – her marriage was pretty much over. And what a waste of time it had been. She was an idiot to have trusted someone like John in the first place. But she wasn't going to make that mistake again.

When she arrived at Houghton Kepier – on time, but only by the skin of her teeth – she shook her head and frowned at Sara's panda car already parked there. *Talk about bone idle, the station's just across the bloody road, for Christ's sake.* But, shaking her irritation off, she was strictly professional when she tapped on the police car window where Sara was sitting reading what looked like a report. Sara jumped in surprise, and Lorraine noticed with interest how hastily Sara shoved the papers in her hands into a black briefcase at her side before jumping out of the car to greet her boss. Much shorter than Lorraine, Sara was petite with short dark hair and the top of her head barely reached Lorraine's shoulders. She always made Lorraine, who was usually comfortable with her height, feel awkwardly tall, and as Lorraine quickened her pace so that Sara had to almost jog to keep up, she knew she was doing it out of irritation rather than a need to hurry.

As they entered the classroom, a tall gangly boy who seemed to be all elbows and knees was on his way out, and his right elbow accidentally knocked against Sara's right breast. Realising what he'd done he blushed to the roots of his dark-brown hair and mumbled his apologies, but he'd been seen by three other boys who laughed loudly. Not a great start. But Sara went up a few notches in Lorraine's eyes when the smaller woman turned her face towards the laughing trio. In moments they had quietened down, and the two officers made their way to the front of the classroom to be introduced by the teacher.

Mr Bentley had been teaching at the school when Lorraine had been a pupil. She remembered he'd looked ancient then. Must have been in a time warp for the last seventeen years or so.

Beaming around the class as if he was solely responsible for Lorraine's success in her chosen profession, and not forgetting to tell the class that he had once been one of Lorraine's teachers, he introduced her and Sara, then stepped back to stand beside the blackboard and left Lorraine to it.

Looking around at the expectant faces, Lorraine could see that half had knowing smirks she'd dearly love to wipe off. The week before Houghton Feast, and kids still got fidgety as it approached – not a great time to have a serious talk about drugs. Ripples of restlessness eddied around the room as some played up to impress their peers, while the rest looked either bored or totally clueless. And Lorraine knew enough

13

about kids to know for certain that quite a few of the seemingly innocent would be in truth far worse than the ones who were trying to look tough.

She recognised a few of the kids – Emma Palmer had had a bit of trouble with her stepfather a couple of years ago but he'd moved on, thank God; Barry Hamill was a tricky one – family of seven and a single mother who didn't have the time or money to deal with three kids, let alone six; and a cheerful wave from the back drew her eye to Jamie Wilson.

'All right, Inspector Hunt,' he called with a grin. 'Come to read us our rights?'

'That's right, Jamie,' she smiled back. He was a good kid – got into the occasional bit of trouble but wasn't ever guilty of anything more serious than a bit of excess energy. 'Going to have a little chat about your right to grow up somewhere other than a young offenders institution.'

The class laughed, and Lorraine knew the banter with Jamie had woken them up and got her off to a good start. And she'd better do what she'd come here for, so she put thoughts of Dakis, Luke, Sara and the Feast out of her mind and started to speak.

When the bell rang for the lesson end, Mr Bentley was clearly astonished at how well his class had behaved. Lorraine was a good speaker – clear and precise but young and open enough to get through to some of the kids in the room. As they left, she prayed that what she'd had to say might stop some of them from trying that first joint, or spliff as they were now calling them, which Lorraine knew often proved the gateway to hell.

Sara, after her good start shutting up the giggling boys, had lapsed into sulky silence, seeming utterly cold and bored with the whole business. *Silly cow*, Lorraine thought as they were waved off by Mr Bentley – and Jamie. *It might not be the most glamorous bit of the job, but if we can get through to this lot it'll make all our lives that much easier a few years down the line.* But if Sara couldn't see that for herself, there wasn't much Lorraine could do about it.

Shrugging off her irritation, she turned the key in the ignition and pulled out.

The police station was only round the corner from Houghton Kepier, and by eleven o'clock Lorraine was standing outside her office, dreading going inside. No point trying to ignore the fact of Luke's imminent return any longer. When she'd sent him to Scotland on an exchange with the Strathclyde force three months earlier she'd known he was a good candidate for the swap – but that wasn't the main reason she selected him. The main reason she'd chosen Luke was that she and Luke had got too close. They'd worked together on a tough case and she'd found herself looking for him at her side, missing him when he wasn't there. It was just as she'd found out about John's betrayal, and she couldn't deal with her feelings for Luke. Couldn't deal with the idea of having feelings for anyone – she just needed to be by herself.

But now Mackenzie had gone back to Strathclyde and that meant Luke would be back here. Today.

What if he's in my office?

What the hell do I say to him?

Had a good time in Scotland sounds so lame.

'Oh, fuck it,' she muttered as, taking a deep breath, she pushed her door open and walked in, breathing a sigh of relief to find the place empty.

But she didn't even have time to take her jacket off before a breathless Carter came hurrying into the room. Carter was ginger, the real carroty kind of ginger, the summer sun had put freckles upon his freckles, and he was puffing pinkly in excitement.

'Boss.'

'Yessss?' Lorraine said suspiciously.

Confident he had her full attention, he blurted out his news. 'There's been a dead body found.'

3

Doris Musgrove was seventy-two years young, most of the time, but today she was feeling her seventy-two summers and then some. Her grey hair was badly in need of a perm – but although she'd already made two appointments she'd forgotten to keep them.

She was of medium height, with blue eyes, and before the grey had taken over, her hair had been a beautiful dark auburn. She remembered the way she used to look as she ran her fingers through a fringe that kept flopping into her eyes, then laughed at her own vanity as she caught sight of herself reflected in the shop window. She had been an outsize customer since giving birth to her first-born.

Julie had taken one breath, then died. A year later Doris's second daughter, Shirley, had followed in her sister's footsteps. Chocolate was a great comforter, and as an addiction it beat drink or drugs.

Sometimes Doris daydreamed about Julie and Shirley. In her dreams they were both happily married with grown-up children. A boy and a girl each. She even had names for her grandchildren, who would visit every day.

Each time she envisaged her imaginary family she left them with a deep sigh, then as the dream faded she thanked God for the miracle he had presented her with on her forty-third birthday.

Her boy Jacko.

Doris smiled to herself as she took a tin of corned beef and a loaf of brown bread out of her basket and put them on the Co-op checkout belt. She would love to have bought a nice piece of steak for Jacko, but she was pink lint today. Thank God Jacko would be bringing potatoes and fresh fruit home from the market, where he worked on the fruit and veg stall. The job had been a blessing in disguise in more ways than one.

'Hi, Doris,' Katrina the checkout girl said, breaking into Doris's thoughts.

'Hi, yerself,' Doris grinned. She'd known Katrina and her family, who lived in the next street to her on the Seahills estate, for years. 'How's the bairns?' Katrina had twin tearaways.

'Same as ever, Doris, and driving me more round the bend every day. Boys, who'd have them!' Katrina wore small round gold-rimmed glasses that always seemed to be tilted to one side, and they gave her a rather drunken look as she scanned the goods. 'How about your lot? Your Melanie doing all right?'

Doris beamed at the mention of her granddaughter, Jacko's only child. 'Good as gold that bairn is. Good as gold, God bless her. Reading away to herself in the library while I do the shopping – I'm just off to pick her up.'

Melanie had been the second good thing that God had given her in this life: a beautiful granddaughter she could help her son raise. Doris held firm to the belief that all good things came from God and all bad things came from the

18

devil. Moneylenders in particular were the devil's spawn, and as such could be ignored every now and then – especially when times were hard, which in Doris's life had been quite often. But Melanie definitely came from God. As had Tom – Doris's husband, Jacko's father and a fine man, who had died near enough to Jacko's fifth birthday, leaving her to bring the lad up alone. She prided herself that she'd done a damn good job.

'She looking forward to the Feast?' Katrina asked as Doris paid.

'So excited she can hardly sleep at night,' Doris grinned, and her thoughts turned to the carnival parade the following Saturday afternoon. The Seahills had recently started a residents association and the committee had decided they would have a float on the parade. A vote, their first as a committee really, had been taken amongst great excitement; Arabian Nights was to be the theme and it was just amazing how pretty old net curtains looked when freshened up with a bright dye.

Melanie was in blue, which matched her colouring perfectly.

My but she was a bonny bairn.

And Doris knew that she would look just splendid on the float. Some of the teenage girls had gone for it in a big way, clamouring for an excuse to show off their belly button rings.

Doris sighed, they grew up fast these days. She would keep a good eye on Melanie – *she* wouldn't be roaming the street like some of the little vixens.

No way.

The thought of Melanie growing up took some of the brightness out of her smile. Then she mentally shook herself. It would be years before Melanie grew up, the bairn was only eight years old for pity's sake . . .

'Doris? Doris?'

With a shock, Doris realised she'd got so involved in her own thoughts she'd completely forgotten where she was.

'You all right, love?' asked Katrina, looking worried.

Doris gave herself a little shake. 'Just fine, pet. Sorry – off in a world of me own.' And she laughed it off, although she was uncomfortably aware it wasn't the first time her mind had wandered. And it had been doing it more and more lately.

Just then the St George Cross flags in the dump bin beside the counter caught her eye. 'Oh, great,' she clapped her hands. 'How much are the flags?'

Doris was rugby mad and never missed a game on the telly, and the forthcoming clash with the All Blacks was the highlight of her life at the moment.

'Ninety-nine pence. Penny cheaper than the pound shop.' Katrina grinned at her, managing to look more drunk than ever.

Doris just had to have one. Rummaging in her purse she found enough coppers to make the ninety-nine pence. Grinning triumphantly she held out her hand. 'I'll have one.'

She left the Co-op feeling dead pleased that the carrier bags were free, else no way would she have been able to afford the flag and that would have been really embarrassing.

God would it not. Katrina was a nice enough lass, but she was also a damn good little gossip and the last thing Doris wanted was the whole of the Seahills thinking she couldn't afford a measly little flag. No way.

Outside Doris breathed in the sweet autumn air. It was such a lovely day that it bucked her spirits right up and made her feel better than she had an hour earlier. She decided to walk down, save the seventy pence bus fare.

Shocking, she thought as she passed the new library. Seventy pence for a ride less than a mile meant that if she rode up to Houghton every day and rode back, she would be spending nine pounds eighty pence a week.

Mind-boggling.

But it was good to know that even if she had a pocket full of money she was pretty fit and able to walk, not like some of her poor friends who were crippled with arthritis.

As she walked through the Homelands, crossed the road and entered the Seahills, the first person she saw was Christina Jenkins who lived across the road from her.

Christina was the same age as her Jacko – about twenty-nine, though with her slight figure and young face she could easily pass for twenty – but she and Jacko had always been friends. He'd always been kind to her – she'd needed it, particularly when her mother had died in that horrible accident – and Doris had always hoped at the back of her mind that her and Jacko would get hooked up together. Jacko would have looked after Christina, and Christina would have been a sweet wife to Jacko. But after her mother's death Christina had retreated into herself, and silly Jacko had missed what was under his nose and ended up with the bitch of bitches. Melanie's mother.

Doris pulled a face every time she thought of the woman, she couldn't help it. She tried to change it into a smile for Christina but when she saw the girl step back she realised she was too late. Christina obviously thought Doris was pulling a face at her.

Quickly she spoke, 'Hello, pet, off to work are yer?' She smiled encouragingly because Christina, although very pretty with big dark eyes and long raven hair, was also very very shy. Any other girl would have been proud of her looks – would probably have become a bit on the big-headed side – but not that one. No confidence at all.

Christina mumbled something as she hurriedly passed by.

Oh dear, Doris thought, looking after her. *I've upset the poor lass now.*

Turning, she nearly bumped into Trevor Mattherson,

another one of her neighbours. Trevor had been born with a purple birthmark that covered half of his face and Doris sometimes wondered whether that was one reason he'd never strayed far from home: people round here knew him and so they didn't see the mark any more, they just saw him. He'd lived alone since his mother had died, but he kept himself busy giving cheap lifts in his car to most of the people in the street and he'd proved a godsend when Jacko had had his bike smash. She'd been back and forth to the hospital so many times she almost counted the nurses as family and Trevor had asked for nowt but the cost of the petrol.

'Careful, Doris, yer nearly knocked me into next week,' he said as he steadied himself.

'Sorry, mate. Going somewhere nice?' It was rare to see Trevor on foot.

Trevor shook his head as he side-stepped past her. 'No, no, er . . . see yer later, Doris.' Then he walked away.

Whatever's the matter with him? Doris shrugged, if he didn't want to talk there was nowt she could do about it. Strange bugger Trevor, always was – one day full of the gab, the next anybody would think he hardly knew yer, let alone spent weeks ferrying yer to visit yer son. But people were allowed their moods, she supposed, turning to her own house.

But as she put her key in the lock her whole body stiffened as if she'd suddenly been freeze-dried.

'Jesus Christ.'

She'd only gone and left Melanie sitting in the library.

Jacko Musgrove strode up the street, long lean and swarthy. The black patch over his left eye had been part of his face since his nineteenth birthday, the result of his motorbike skidding on ice and hurtling into Newbottle off-licence through the large plate-glass window. Luckily for everyone who'd fancied a drink that night, it was past closing time. The left side of his face was fairly covered in a mass of criss-crossed scars.

If he were asked to pick the worst day of his life though, he'd not choose that one. No, it would be the day his young wife Kay had walked out on him. That had been the day their baby daughter Melanie was diagnosed with cerebral palsy. Kay had not even waited around long enough to find out that Melanie's cerebral palsy was considered to be very mild, and only really affected her right leg causing her to have a slight limp. Sometimes when she was tired the limp was very noticeable, but other than that Melanie was very bright and quite capable of holding her own with her peers.

When she was a week old, Jacko took his baby girl home alone and did everything the doctors told him to and some of the things they hadn't. He was constantly updating his knowledge of the terrible disorder.

Jacko often told people that he had been born under a bad moon.

And it was rising again, because Jacko was fearful that his mam was going senile. It was just small things really – misplacing her door keys or her purse, forgetting to turn out the gas when the kettle had boiled – but small or not, they seemed to be happening more often of late. Only yesterday he'd caught her going out to the shops in her slippers. It was starting to seriously worry him and he planned to try to catch Christina tonight to ask her about it. Christina worked in Houghton library and there must be some books written on the subject – somebody must know something that would keep it at bay for as long as possible. He needed his mother the way she was. For Melanie's sake, and for Doris herself. But mostly for his own sake. Mostly because he loved her.

He'd watched Mr Felton who used to have pigeons go that way. Night after night as kids, he and his mate Beefy had sat with the old man up at the pigeon crees listening to his war stories. The old man told a hell of a tale and many a time he had Jacko and Beefy going. It had fairly broke Jacko's heart the night old Felton had recognised neither one of them. And then one day Felton's daughter had told them that something was wrong – they'd sussed that out for themselves already, but they hadn't understood the words she'd used. Senile. Dementia. Alzheimer's.

A few weeks after that Felton had been taken away, eyes watering and mouth dribbling, to the hospital, where he'd spent the next two years in what Jacko had always hoped was a happy enough world.

It was not going to happen to his mam.

Not if he could help it.

He turned the corner, two carrier bags filled with fruit and veg, one in each hand. His boss had dropped him off at the Beehive pub – best not to rub it in people's faces that he had a bit of extra income. They all knew like, but if it was kept under cover from the jealous ones, nobody really minded. Yer sharp learned who to trust.

Tomorrow he was in charge of the stall because the boss was going away on holiday and he'd been instructed to get a couple of lads in to help. He knew just the two he could trust: Robbie and Mickey. Good kids the pair of them.

He was three gates from his own house and wondering if he could stretch to a pint or two up the club tonight when Doris came bustling down the path.

Sensing that something was wrong, Jacko lengthened his stride reaching Doris, who hadn't noticed him, a split second before she turned to go the other way.

'What's up, Mam?'

Startled Doris jumped. 'I er, I . . .' She stared at him, unable to complete her sentence.

Jacko was becoming worried. 'Where's our Melanie, Mam?'

'I, er . . .' She looked away, her face flushing a deep pink. 'I left her at the library.'

'Yer what!' Jacko shouted.

Doris cringed, 'It, it was such a nice day and, and I walked down and I just forgot, that's all. I'm going back for her now. You wait, she'll be all right.'

Jacko sighed. He knew in his rational mind that Doris was right, Melanie would come to no harm in the library, but the thought of his daughter abandoned sent chills down his spine. He took a deep breath. She'd be OK, of course she would. And it was no use shouting at Doris, she did her best. She might not be herself right now but he'd no idea how he'd have coped without her after Kay's disappearing act. During the pregnancy he'd been, to his shame, rather detached. He'd let Kay get on with it and so when Melanie was born, when in the moment he first saw her he realised that she was and would always be the centre of his life, he'd not been well equipped to cope. And that was even with a wife to help him – once she'd buggered off he hadn't known what to do.

But Doris had picked up the pieces: she'd shown him how to feed and bath Melanie, how to look after her. She'd got him through those first difficult weeks of sleeplessness and worry, and if he was honest she'd got him through the last eight years. She looked after Melanie when he was at work, she kept her clean and tidy, and she did all the things a girl needs a mother to do. When she became a teenager in a few short years' time he'd need her more than ever.

'Go in the house, Mam,' he smiled reassuringly at his mother to hide how urgently he needed to get Melanie back – to see for himself that she was safe and sound. 'It's OK. I'll go up for her.' He looked round the street and spotted Trevor's car. 'I'll get Trev to give us a lift up.'

'He's not in.'

'But the car . . .'

'I saw him going that way.'

'Christ, has he finally grown some legs . . . Here', he handed the bags to her, now desperate to get up to the library and get Melanie back before she realised she'd been forgotten. But then suddenly, behind him –

'Daddy.'

Gasping with relief at the sound of her voice, Jacko spun round. Melanie. She was obviously in pain, but grinning at him, and hurrying as fast as she could up the street. Jacko blinked tears of joy out of his eyes as he dropped the bags and ran to her. Picking her up, he hugged her then spun her up onto his shoulders.

'Thank God,' Doris muttered as she bent down to pick up the potatoes that had escaped from the bags; one or two were making a bid for the gutter but she caught them and straightened up as her son and granddaughter reached her.

'So sorry, Melanie love.' Doris patted Melanie's arm.

'It's all right, Nana.' Melanie patted her back.

Together, Melanie still on his shoulders and Doris bringing up the rear, they went into their home.

4

Lorraine left her car and jumped into the panda with Carter who, always eager to impress, sped off with a screech of his tyres, earning himself a severe glare from Lorraine.

'Where?' she demanded in a clipped voice.

'Near the dual carriageway, boss. Apparently it's on that grass verge under the bridge. If yer ask me it looks like a jumper.'

Lorraine gave him a sharp look which said very clearly: *don't rush to conclusions.* 'How come the body wasn't found till now? It's nearly midday for God's sake.'

Carter shrugged. 'I suppose people were whizzing past that quick they must not have noticed her? If they were in a hurry, like. And Sanderson reckons you couldn't really see her from the road.'

Two police cars guarded the roundabout that led onto the dual carriageway which curved around St Michael and All Angels, then wove its way to Sunderland, via Doxford International Business Park.

Carter brought the car to a halt. Incident tape had already

been stretched over the area and forensics were busily at work. A shell-shocked, shaking young woman sat in a squad car with her head between her knees, clearly trying not to pass out. Presumably she was the woman who'd found the body – Lorraine was pleased to see that Sanderson, one of her most trusted officers, a man who'd been with her since the beginning, was taking her statement. Walking over to the tape, Lorraine nodded at the two men, Travis and Dinwall, who were also part of her own squad.

'Scottie's on his way, boss.'

'Good.' There wasn't much they could do before the pathologist turned up, but Lorraine lifted the tape so she could slip under it, and walked over to the body. 'Jesus Christ.' Lorraine had seen many bodies in the course of her career, but even she blanched at this. The woman had obviously fallen from the bridge above, and her body was shattered.

Carter gulped and quickly looked away, barely managing to hold onto his bacon and eggs. Suddenly finding something very interesting near his panda car, he walked back towards it. Even Dinwall, the joker in the pack, was unusually quiet.

It was Travis who broke the silence. 'We'll need Scottie, but it looks to me like a clear-cut suicide.'

Carter grinned, pleased to hear someone else making the same mistake he had, but a sharp look from Lorraine subdued him.

'Jumping to conclusions, aren't you, Travis?' Lorraine's tone was mild, but the rebuke was clear. If they started making their minds up at this stage, before they'd had a chance to look properly at the crime scene and evaluate the evidence, they'd make mistakes. And mistakes were dangerous. Travis looked suitably embarrassed and Lorraine asked him, 'Any idea as to who this is?'

Travis shook his head. 'Don't think I've ever seen her around. Might not even be a local.'

Lorraine nodded. That was a possibility, there were a lot of strangers in town. She stepped smartly to one side when she felt someone touch her shoulder, and looked relieved a moment later to see that it was Scottie.

'Hello my lovely.' He smiled at her.

Scottie was a big man in every sense of the word, with a mane of thick black hair. Body hair, looking like a thousand spider's legs, peeped out of the top of his collar and the cuffs of his shirt. He was seldom seen without his assistant Edna, who still worked beyond her retiring years out of an almost maternal devotion to him. Lorraine was never quite sure who had adopted whom.

He knelt down and ran his eyes up and down the body. After something like five minutes he rose and looked up at the twenty-foot wall which edged the boundary of the church's land. Slowly he swung round, taking in every detail. From where the body lay, the footbridge from Houghton to Hall Lane could be seen.

Lorraine raised her eyebrows in an unspoken question, but he shook his head.

'Sorry, Lorraine, don't think I can give you a simple answer. Not yet, anyway. She could be a jumper – she's close enough to the bridge – but I'm going to have to take a closer look at her.'

Lorraine looked sharply at him. 'What are you saying?'

'I'm saying I'm going to have to take a closer look. It just doesn't look quite right to me.' He kneeled next to the dead woman and pointed. 'See those marks on her neck? Those ones?'

Lorraine nodded.

'Look to me like strangulation.'

Lorraine's heart sank. Murder. 'I did wonder. Look at her clothes – she's all dressed up for a night out. High heels, the lot. And look at her make-up – lots of it, but quite smudged, she'd definitely put all that slap on a good few hours before she died. That's not an outfit you wear to kill yourself.'

Scottie nodded sadly. 'I could be wrong of course, could be anything – could be old marks from a boyfriend who just likes to play a bit rough – but I need to find out the cause of death before I can tell you anything more conclusive.' He looked up at her. 'Sorry, love, I know that's not what you want to hear.'

Lorraine shook her head. 'You're right, it isn't. We've got the Feast coming up and not enough folk to police that as it is – last thing we need is a murder.' She sighed. 'How long? How long till yer know?'

'I'll do the autopsy today. You'll know as soon as I do.'

Scottie turned to the ambulance men, who had just arrived. 'Take her in, boys.' Bearing a stretcher, they moved past Lorraine and Scottie to begin the grisly task of transporting the body to the morgue.

Scottie, Lorraine and Carter were watching the ambulance pull away when a car Lorraine recognised instantly drove up.

She felt herself flush right from her toes. *Oh God, it's him.*

Carter beamed at the sight of Luke. ''Bout time an' all, isn't it, boss.'

Not wanting to sound churlish she muttered, 'Yes, of course.' Then, turning, she held out her hand. 'Hello, Luke.'

Luke took her hand, only for a moment, and then Carter broke the spell.

'How was Scotland, Luke?'

'Good, lovely place but there's nowt like being home, is there, Scottie.'

'No, yer right there. Anyhow,' Scottie patted his coat pockets, looking for his car keys, 'time for me to be going back. See yer later then, Lorraine.'

'Yeah, Scottie, no problem.'

'And good to have you back, Luke.'

'Thanks, Scottie, it's good to see yer,' he replied and turned to Lorraine. 'So what's going on? I got to the station to find you were all out here – all except Sara of course.' He grinned, and Lorraine knew exactly what he was thinking: Sara was too ambitious to risk getting caught up in something as basic as a suicide. She found herself instinctively smiling in response, slipping quickly back into the easy, close relationship they'd always had, but caught herself. That wasn't how it was going to be this time. This time round she wasn't going to forget she was his boss.

'Well it's a bit early to tell what we've got,' she said, noticing Luke's grin turn to a frown as her tone became businesslike. 'Could be a jumper but Scottie suspects it might be something more than that. Traffic police are desperate to get the dual carriageway open again, but we'll have to cover all possible bases in case Scottie's suspicions are right, so we'd better get going.' Turning, she called the team together and gave her orders – two to check the bridge for evidence, four to check the road, two to start asking questions in the area and hunting down any passers-by, and Sanderson to finish taking the witness statement. Then she said over her shoulder to Luke, 'My office.' And got into the panda car.

Carter, who'd clearly wanted to talk more with Luke, moved in double quick time to the car. On the way to the station he said, 'I wonder if the dual carriageway's still on consecrated ground.'

Lorraine looked at him. 'What the hell makes yer wonder that?' A moment later she wished she'd never asked.

'Well,' he said enthusiastically, 'as it happens, in 1315 a man called John Sayer was fleeing from a party of Scots, and he only went and climbed the bell loft and fell over, smashing his brains out on the path, and the church had to be granted

31

absolution for the accidental shedding of blood in its walls.'

'So what . . . ?' Lorraine looked at him with raised eyebrows.

'Well, I just wondered if the land by the road was church land, and if yer still had to get absolution, that's all.'

'I swear, Carter, I don't know where the hell yer get it from.'

Carter opened his mouth to tell her, thought better of it, and drove into the police station yard. Luke was already there and waiting for them in the office.

Lorraine walked round the desk to her chair, opened the top drawer of her desk and rummaged around until she came up with a pencil stump. The pencils were substitute cigarettes and if she didn't lay off them pretty soon she'd be suffering from lead poisoning, which was probably only marginally less dangerous than cancer.

Just look at him, she thought as the pencil made its way to her mouth. *Thinks he's the centre of the universe just like the bloody lot of them*. But still her heart skipped a beat at the sight of him.

Luke coughed. 'Well, boss.'

Carter looked nervously from one to the other.

Lorraine couldn't help but notice how incredibly pleased Luke looked to be back. She gave him a quick begrudging smile.

No need to let him think I'm that pleased to see him.

His smile widened, showing a glint of gold against his nearly-black skin.

Then, seeing that Carter was in the process of opening his mouth to start babbling again, she quickly said. 'Sorry, I was just thinking . . . Pull up the chairs, we haven't got time to mess about.'

If Luke was disappointed by her rather frosty welcome, he kept it to himself.

'Not talking Scottish yet, Luke?' Carter asked.

Lorraine frowned at him, he could be such a tit at times. Not seeing the frown, Carter went on.

'Glad to be home I'll bet though, aren't yer? Scotland's a great place, all that heather and that, but there's nowhere like home, is there, Luke?'

He couldn't miss the loud thud the book made as it hit the desk. Knowing instinctively that it was meant for him, he glanced quickly at Lorraine, and this time he didn't miss the frown nor the way it quickly changed to a strained smile when her eyes darted from him to Luke. Getting the message, Carter shut up.

'Well, we've had a reasonably quiet summer, Luke, apart from a few stabbings. They all seem to be carrying knives these days.'

Carter nodded. 'Aye, it's been pretty quiet.'

'I wish the fuck you'd be,' Lorraine snapped.

'Sorry, boss.'

Luke hid his grin behind a cough. It was great to be home. He'd missed the intimacy of station politics – it was never the same when you were the outsider, only there for a few months – he'd missed Carter's overexcitable enthusiasm, and he'd missed Lorraine's sharpness. Actually he'd missed more than her sharpness, but now wasn't the time to be thinking of that.

'Here, Carter,' Lorraine fished her keys out of her bag, 'would you go and get my stuff out of the car please.'

'Sure, boss.' Carter sprang to his feet. 'Catch yer later, Luke,' he said as he was going out the door.

'Yeah, later.'

Lorraine made a big show of shuffling the papers around on her desk. She'd been dreading this moment.

In as bright a voice as she could muster, she said, 'So, Luke, was Scotland all right?'

'Aye, beautiful place, but all the same I'm glad to be back, boss.'

She fiddled with a pencil. 'Just got back this morning, didn't yer? Would yer like a day to settle back in then?'

'Not really, boss. I'll start tonight if yer need me.'

That was the trouble, Lorraine mused. She didn't need the distraction, but she really did need Luke, he was one of the best coppers in Sunderland and Newcastle put together. Aye and Durham an' all . . .

'Boss, boss . . .'

Lorraine jerked back to the here and now.

Damn.

'Sorry, Luke, I was just thinking about the poor girl we've just seen.'

He smiled at her.

Don't do that.

She tried to smile back, but because she was gritting her teeth it came out as a grimace.

Wondering what he'd done, Luke got up. He opened his mouth to speak when a sudden loud explosion caused them both to duck.

'Jesus,' Luke said a moment later when they had straightened up.

Lorraine moved quickly to the window, followed by Luke. They watched as a group of youths hanging round the courtroom door fled every which way.

'Bloody kids,' Lorraine said.

'Fireworks. They seem to start earlier every year.'

The group of boys reassembled, some of them laughing, others looking nervously about.

'Getting louder each year an' all. And bloody cheekier, to throw them in here. There's a couple of rival gangs up at court this morning.' She smiled. 'Carter's first big collar, he'll no doubt spend the rest of today and all next week

34

boring your socks off with the details, so I won't spoil it for him.'

Luke smiled, 'How's he doing?'

'Carter?' Lorraine's smile was genuinely warm. And Luke marvelled at how it lit her whole face up.

'Actually he's doing great. A bit over eager, sometimes he makes yer want to tear yer hair out. But he'll make a damn good copper. Oh, and beware: at the moment he's heavily into local history.'

'Aye, he told me when I phoned him the other week, he's joined the local history group.'

Lorraine groaned. 'That's where it's coming from.'

'Afraid so.'

It was then that Lorraine realised just how close Luke was standing to her. Rather self-consciously, she moved quickly over to her desk and silently thanked God when the phone rang. She snatched it up, said hello, then listened for a minute.

'OK, sometime tomorrow then, bye.'

Looking at Luke she said. 'That was Scottie. There's problems at the lab – bloody government cost-cutting – and things are so backed up there he won't be able to do the full autopsy till tomorrow morning.' She paused for a moment to rein in her temper. What sort of friggin' world was it where caring for the dead, where finding out whether they were dealing with a killer on the loose or just one tragic girl who couldn't take it any more, wasn't enough of a priority to give the pathology lab the funding it needed. She took a deep breath, swallowing her anger. 'So,' she continued, 'you may as well go home and settle in. OK?'

'Yeah, right.' Feeling as if he'd been dismissed, which in fact he had been, Luke left.

Lorraine sat down and rolled her head around. Her neck was stiff and every muscle seemed tight; the kinks were a long time coming out. She'd been hoping she'd have time to go to her karate class this evening which always helped her to work though any stress. But making time for it now seemed very unlikely and it looked as though she'd have to rely on sorting the tension in her neck out herself.

Just when she thought she was making some progress, Carter came in bearing news.

'There's a woman missing from Hall Lane, boss.'

'Photographs?'

'Aye, I think it's her. Diane Fox.'

He passed a folder over. Lorraine quickly opened it and a pretty young woman with long black hair smiled out at her. She was holding what looked like a very happy little boy.

Lorraine felt the sadness that always came when a victim was identified. Whether she'd been murdered or just hadn't felt able to take the stresses and strains of her life any more, one fact remained: this young woman had had a lot of living yet to do. And with a queasy feeling in the pit of her stomach, Lorraine transferred her gaze over to the toddler, a handsome little boy who would now grow up without the love of his mother.

Well we can't bring her back for yer, pet, but I'll do my damnedest not to leave yer wondering.

He manages to get out of school before the rest of them: he's become quite good at that.

Not because they chase him or bully him for they mainly ignore him. But because if he gets down the beck first he can find a way to watch them.

He knows for a fact that Chris Mandel was telling lies about Julie Winters. She'd told him to sling his hook when Chris tried it on and had stomped back up the beck saying she'd tell her mam.

Jake Forbes, though. Wow. He hadn't told enough about Kelly Jackson.

He ducks down in the long grass as he hears them approaching. He is just starting to prepare himself, giddy with excitement, when he feels something brush against his leg.

Kelly Jackson has her knickers down now but he has to tear his eyes away to see what's touching him. It might be a snake, he knows that there are snakes in the beck.

It's a cat.

Bastard.

He grabs the cat and although his body is puny for his thirteen years his hands are big and strong. More than strong enough for a kitten's neck and he squeezes and squeezes until the creature goes limp. For a long time he stares at the dead cat lying in the grass.

When he finally looks up, Kelly and Jake are gone.

Angrily he jumps up and begins to kick the dead cat. 'Your fault, your fault,' he repeats over and over again.

5

Mickey Carson, his black curls in need of their usual trim, quietly closed the door behind him.

They were at it again.

Bloody hell, he kept out of their way as much as possible, had done for a long time now – he much preferred the chaotic family of his best friend Robbie Lumsdon – but he had to touch base sometimes, if just for a change of clothes. And as usual his mam and her husband were at each other's throats.

Why does she put up with it?

Shaking his head at his mam's stupidity, he began to walk along the street.

'Oh, no,' he groaned, 'not Fran.' He felt a blush begin in his toes and he just knew that by the time they were face-to-face he would be the colour of an albino's worst sunburn.

Fran had lived next door for as long as he could remember and he'd been madly in love with her since the day he'd hit twelve, which meant – after a moment's calculation – for roughly a third of his life. *Jesus!*

But there was no dodging her – God, she was nearly on top of him.

I wish.

The picture of his wish caused his face to burn even more – *she'll think I've fell in the bloody fire* – as Fran, in tight white jeans and, despite the chilly weather, an even tighter white T-shirt that hugged every curve, came alongside of him.

'Hi, Mickey.' She smiled that plump-lipped smile that practically had him drooling.

'Hi, Fran,' he grinned at her as he prayed at top speed, Please make her be in a hurry, please don't let her stop. Just keep her moving right on, God.

But stop she did, her magnificent breasts bouncing in her T-shirt.

He prayed again, this time for rain. A good solid soak in seconds, a downpour. That would do it. He glanced at the sky – well wouldn't yer guess, not a cloud in sight.

It took an heroic effort on his part to drag his eyes away from what they clamoured for as she spoke.

'So, how yer doing, Mickey? It's ages since I've seen yer.' She looked him up and down.

Were her eyes lingering longer than necessary down there? *In yer dreams, kiddo.*

She smiled again, that delicious Fran smile, and he felt his knees go weak.

'Great,' he managed after what seemed an age.

Christ, she'll think I'm the village idiot.

'I'm just great,' he gushed. 'Me and me mate Robbie are starting work on Chester-le-Street market today, just for a week though, 'cos the bloke who owns the stall's on holiday, like.' He tried hard to stop babbling, but it was really hard. 'Just for the experience yer know. If, er, if we like it we might start our own stall up.'

Now where the fuck did that come from? he thought, suddenly tongue-tied.

But she was impressed. 'Hey, go for it, Mickey. What yer gonna sell?'

Oh, God . . . 'Er . . . Umm . . .'

She waited.

Don't help me out none, he thought as his eyes of their own accord found their way back to her breasts. Then, without thinking, he blurted out, 'Women's underwear.'

Fran laughed and clapped her hands. 'Cool, Mickey. I can just see yer now, waving a pair of black laceys in the air.'

Mickey stared at her, his head tilting further and further to one side in amazement as his imagination ran riot. The picture of Fran in black knickers and black bra very nearly overwhelmed him.

'Yer'll soon be rich yer know,' she went on, becoming quite excited by the idea, 'selling knickers and things. Oh, and remember to get plenty of thongs – they are so in. A girl can never get enough of them. Especially slinky silky black ones.'

She winked at him, and for a wonderful moment Mickey thought she was flirting with him. Then she continued: 'Ta-ra then, kid, catch yer later.' And she was gone, leaving him practically sucking the air to taste her perfume.

His heart sank. *Kid* . . . What a fucking let-down. Couldn't she see he was all grown-up now? Eighteen, for Christ's sake . . . *It's not as if she's an oldie herself, she's only twenty-two! But she always makes me feel like I'm seven or something.*

Why does she do that?

From elation to depression is a very short trip, but by the time Mickey reached the Broadway he was back to his usual good-natured self.

Looking up at the church clock, Mickey saw he had a good twenty minutes or so before he was due at Robbie's house. Turning, he scanned the Broadway in case there was anyone else around to pass the time with. It was a common meeting place – a large paved area in front of St Michael and All Angels church which, Mickey's mam told him, used to be guarded by the four lions: the Red Lion pub on its right flank, the Golden and White Lions on the left, with the Black Lion bringing up the rear. Only the Golden and the White remained. And they didn't look like they'd be guarding anything in the near future, save maybe the cash the regulars squandered on booze night in and night out.

No one was around. So Mickey decided to chill out for five on one of the benches facing the church before going on down to the Seahills. The wintry sun bathed Mickey in its weak light and he closed his eyes and lifted his face. Lost in thoughts of Fran, his back to the park, he didn't see Dave Ridley until the man was sitting on the seat next to him.

'Jesus! What the hell happened to you?' Mickey said, staring at Dave's face. The whole of the left side was an angry mixture of purple, black and blue, with red thread veins running every which way, giving the whole a marbled effect.

'Shh,' Dave whispered, looking frantically around. Then, swinging his head back to a throughly mystified Mickey, he stared at him for a moment as if judging whether he could trust him or not. Apparently liking what he saw, he leaned forward and said in a conspiratorial tone, 'It's them over there.'

Mickey looked 'over there', which seemed to be in the general direction of the Golden Lion.

Yeah, he thought, them over where? At least twenty or so people were passing back and forth, minding their own business.

Knowing better, but unable to resist, Mickey said, 'Them over where?'

'Them bastards man.' Dave kept gesturing with his head across the road.

Still none the wiser, Mickey held his hands up. 'OK, Dave, spill the beans, and speak plain English 'cos I haven't got a clue what the hell yer on about.'

Dave gave a huge world-weary sigh, and spoke as if he was speaking to a nice but very dim person. 'Them bastards, man, them in the nash.'

The social security building was behind the Golden Lion, and could not be seen from where Mickey was sitting.

'Ehh?' Mickey looked with open disbelief at Dave.

'Aye,' Dave was adamant. 'Them bastards . . . I know it was them that done it. The twats hired a fucking hit man.' He stopped speaking and looked nervously around again.

'A hit man . . . The social!' It was all Mickey could do to keep a straight face.

He'd known Dave since as long as he could remember. It was well known that Dave had been an alcoholic since his teens but now it looked like, twenty or so years since he first started hitting the bottle, the poor bugger had finally lost the plot.

'Shh, lad,' Dave went on. 'Keep yer gob shut. I'm telling yer it was them. I was necky to one of the rotten sods the other day, 'cos the greedy bastard wouldn't give us a crisis loan. You'd think the fucking money was his . . . So I told him to fuck off and stuff it where the sun don't shine. And the bastard looked right upset when I threw the fucking loan forms all over the place and stamped on them.'

He pointed to his face. 'I called him an ugly fucker an' all, so I know it was them that done this.' He nodded his head in total agreement with himself, even though it must have hurt.

Mickey found himself staring at his shoes. No way could

he trust himself to look Dave in the eye and keep a straight face.

But Dave wasn't finished. 'Aye,' he went on, glaring across the road. 'The sly bastard was waiting over the bridge last night,' he scratched his head, a look of bewilderment entering his eyes. 'Or it might have been early on this morning. Or the day before that, I can't remember much. Anyhow, whenever it was I was on me way home from me mate's house. We had a game going, yer see. First time I've won anything in ages an' all, but the bastard fairly clobbered me and took the fucking lot, put the boot in an' all, dirty bastard. Tell yer what, I've got a good mind to put a fucking claim in, that would fairly sicken them wouldn't it? Let the whole world know what they're up to, aye.'

He paused for a moment looking over at the Golden Lion, then he was off again. 'I know it was them fuckers what hired the hit man . . . Yer don't know what goes on over there, kiddo, believe you me. Keep away from the whole fucking lot of them, they all work for the fucking government yer know, and yer know how sly that lot is.'

He shook his head harder than ever and Mickey winced. Then Dave bent his head forward and whispered. 'That's how come people all over the country are going missing. Aye that's right, I've got it on good authority. Trust us, mate. The fucking government's having them knocked off, so they don't have to pay so much dole out. You'll see.'

Mickey nodded seriously so as to be polite, then slid off the bench and hurried away. He hardly made it to round the corner of the Britannia and out of sight before he burst out laughing. And it took a few minutes and one or two curious looks in his direction before he got himself under control enough to head off in the direction of the Seahills.

Five minutes later he was turning into the bottom of the estate with an unwipeable grin on his face when Kerry,

Robbie's eldest sister and about as feisty as feisty could get, ran past him.

Kerry was as dark as her younger sister Claire was fair, and seriously into running. Mickey didn't miss the fact that Kerry was at long last catching up to Claire in the breast department, even though she was two years older than Claire. But both sisters took his fancy. He wondered for a moment if he was a serial fancier, then shook the thought off.

He waved at Kerry, and felt elated when she smiled and waved back.

Robbie was waiting at the gate for him. They were to go down to Chester-le-Street market and learn the ropes off Jacko. Cal, another friend who worked at the old folks' home, had promised to give them a lift.

Mickey hitched himself up on the wall next to Robbie. 'All right, mate? Just seen your Kerry – nearly run me down, she did.'

Robbie laughed. 'Aye, there's not much stops her. Since she won the big race a couple of months ago it's all she thinks about.'

'Mate, it's all she thought about even before she won,' Mickey pointed out. And then paused before adding, 'She all right then?' The Lumsdon family had had a terrible time earlier in the year – Claire had been kidnapped and Kerry had been attacked. They'd all come out of it alive – and as for their mam Vanessa, it'd been the making of her, she seemed to be off the booze for good – but it had been touch and go for a bit, and things like that had to leave their mark.

But Robbie smiled awkwardly. 'Yeah, seems fine. And our Claire's doing well an' all. Thanks for asking.'

Relieved, Mickey changed the subject and told Robbie about mad Dave. When Cal arrived five minutes later in an old beaten-up red Escort that should have seen its last rusting place years ago, the pair of them were laughing heartily.

Escorts were not Cal's kind of car. He much preferred the newer sportier types, especially if they were sleek and black. But he'd also wisely decided that he preferred to be on the outside of a jail. So, until he found his vocation whatever that might be, and made his first million, he was doing just what the judge ordered, namely behaving himself and leaving other people's cars alone.

Cal was big, blond and had a sunny disposition to match his good looks. His old ladies at the home where he worked would go ten rounds with Tyson any day since he'd arrived on the scene – he'd breathed fresh air into their stale little world.

'All right, guys?' He asked as he drove away from the kerb. In the back Mickey nodded as he watched Claire come out of the house. God, but she was getting bonnier every day. He tried a little finger wave, but she must not have seen him. *Damn.*

In the front Robbie said, 'Fine, but me mam's not feeling so good, she's just had a coughing fit.'

'A coffin fit!' Mickey yelped. He thought the world of Robbie's mother, Vanessa.

Robbie and Cal glanced at each other and burst out laughing.

'What?'

'Not that kind of coffin, yer dip stick.' Robbie mimicked coughing. 'That kind.'

'Ohh, I thought yer meant . . .'

'We know what yer thought, Mickey.' Cal grinned at him through the rear view mirror.

Grinning back, Mickey settled down in his seat for the ten-minute journey, pleased that it was a nice day, and thinking alternately about Fran, Claire, and Kerry.

After parking the car under the beady eye of an eighteen-stone traffic warden, who immediately checked the time on the ticket, the three of them made their way to the market where Jacko was waiting for them with a ten-strong queue who were starting to get restless. Spotting them, he gestured for them to hurry round to the back of the stall.

Over the years Jacko had done a number of fiddle jobs to help get Melanie whatever she wanted, but this one he'd been at for a couple of years and he loved it especially in the summer. The wintertime though, that was a whole different ball game: freezing cold, wet, and business was only half as good. But he had to stick it; the interest was rising on the Disneyland trip he'd taken Melanie and Doris on last year, and this week's money was already pigeon-holed for Houghton Feast.

'Right, lads.' Jacko threw an apron at each of them. 'Get on with it.'

'I'm only stopping five minutes,' Cal said with a grin. 'Gotta take Betty and Lady Jane for eye tests, see yer later.'

'That should be fun,' Robbie replied dryly.

'Talk about being thrown in at the deep end,' Mickey muttered as he and Robbie tied the aprons on.

'About time an' all,' complained a very fat middle-aged woman with no teeth in, who looked like she'd been poured into the lime green mac she wore. 'Right. I want half a pound of tomatoes, half a cucumber, and a bag of new tatties. Oh, aye, and give us a small turnip . . . I've been standing here that flaming long me bloody feet have practically took root . . . Oh and I'll have a pound of sprouts an' all. I don't want none of them apples, 'cos the ones I got last week were bloody well bruised to death.'

Fascinated by her many chins wobbling with each word she spoke, Mickey scratched his head and said, 'Come again?'

She curled her lip at him, but before she could gather steam for another tirade, Robbie handed her a carrier bag. 'That'll be three pounds forty, love.'

Grumbling to herself about the price of food these days, she counted the exact money into his hand, took her bag and wobbled off.

'Show-off,' Mickey said.

Laughing, Robbie turned to the next customer, nodding goodbye to Cal as he headed back to the car. 'What'll it be, love?'

This woman, charmed by Robbie's smile, was much easier. 'A pound of potatoes and some of those beans please.'

Robbie reached out for the potatoes and – spotting a customer who looked just his type – Mickey decided to give it a try himself. 'All right, darling. What you after?' he grinned, thanking God his voice hadn't cracked as he addressed the pretty blonde girl hovering at the outside of the stall.

'Just a couple of pound of apples please,' she said with a smile.

'Yer sure that's all you want?' Encouraged by her smile, Mickey decided to try his luck. 'Slim little thing like you, yer want feeding up you do.'

The girl blushed prettily, and in that moment Mickey decided this could well be the job for him.

They were kept busy for the next two hours. Twice Robbie noticed a couple of lifters who belonged to Houghton hovering around the stall and warned them off with a shake of his head, surprised that they would even come near a stall where Jacko, who was nobody's fool, worked.

Things quietened down around late morning though, and the three of them took a well-earned break, perched on a sack of potatoes.

'Thanks for doing this, lads,' said Jacko. 'Couldn't manage alone – all those angry women wanting their veg! Bloody terrifying!'

Mickey laughed. 'Yer right. Wouldn't want to cross that lot.' Looking across at the other side of the market, he saw a familiar figure disappear down an alleyway. 'Oh Christ,' he groaned, 'there goes that mad Dave again.'

'Where?' asked Jacko. 'What mad Dave?'

'Dave Ridley,' said Mickey. 'Saw him this morning and I'm telling yer, the booze has finally got him. Swore blind that the Social had set a hit man on him.'

'A hit man?' Jacko asked in astonishment.

'That's right. Looks to me like he's been mugged – his face is all cut up – but he reckons a hit man was waiting for him on the bridge a couple of nights ago. Mad bastard. And yer know another thing –'

But Robbie and Jacko never found out what the 'other thing' was, because the friendly bustle of the marketplace was suddenly pierced by the sound of screams coming from across the road. Simultaneously, they all smelt smoke.

'Christ, it's the chippy,' Robbie yelled as he jumped up, quickly followed by Mickey and Jacko.

The fish shop, which also had an adjoining restaurant, was directly opposite the stall. Smoke was already billowing out of the door and windows and hanging heavily over the building in the calm morning. Mickey would swear later that it was also pouring out of the bricks. The sound of the crack-ling, spitting fire taking control of the building made his blood run cold.

People were screaming as they fought their way out of the door. A ten-year-old boy slipped and fell in the stampede, and only missed being trampled on by a quick-thinking skin-head who pulled him up and out of the way. Jacko ran to call 999 while Robbie and Mickey bolted across the road.

As they reached the shop door, the metal shutters came down with a resounding crash that set everybody off screaming again.

Mickey ran over to a man who'd just dashed out and stood, bent double, coughing his guts up on the pavement.

'Hey mate, is everybody out?' he asked urgently.

It took the man a moment to catch his breath, then he turned to Mickey. 'The waitresses,' he said huskily. 'Two of them. And a woman with a baby.'

'Fuck. A baby?'

'Yeah, a little one. Can't be more than a month old.'

Mickey and Robbie glanced quickly at each other, listening to the terrified screams coming from those trapped inside. They could hear the baby now, picking up the fear in her young mother's voice and obeying an age-old instinct, adding her own tiny cry to the mêlée. Then all three men threw themselves to the ground just in time as the front window blew out, followed by a long tongue of orange yellow fire, scattering glittering shards of glass everywhere.

There was no getting in where the window had blown out – the flames were too hot. The only way in was through the front door and, scrambling quickly to their feet, they reached for the shutter. Together, they got their fingers underneath and tried their hardest to heave the shutter up. But it stubbornly refused to budge. A moment later Mickey and Robbie were shoved aside by Jacko, who got a firm grip and with one gigantic effort managed to yank the shutter halfway up.

'Help them out, lads,' he said, legs planted solidly and muscles bulging. 'Quick, I don't know how long I can hold the damn thing!'

Needing no urging, Mickey and Robbie bent down and went inside. The place was filled with smoke but they could just make out three women huddled around the doorway. Robbie took hold of the two waitresses and helped them under the shutter, while Mickey helped the young woman who was tearfully clutching her baby to her breast.

They were about to help them over the road when one of the waitresses cried out that there was someone else inside. An old man who'd been sat in the corner. He was eighty-ish, with a pair of walking sticks, and there was no way he'd got out already. Mickey spun round quickly just as Jacko was about to let go of the shutter.

'No,' he screamed, hurrying over.

Jacko froze. 'What's the matter, mate?'

'There's still somebody inside,' Mickey yelled as he ducked back in.

'Jesus Christ. Be quick.' Jacko's veins were bulging in his neck with the effort of keeping the shutter up.

Quickly Robbie led the women across the road, all the time looking back for signs of Mickey. With each second he became more and more worried for his friend and he could hear Jacko moaning with the effort of holding the shutter up.

Then, suddenly, Mickey was out, half-dragging and half-carrying the old man across the road.

With a gigantic sigh of relief, Jacko let the shutter fall, stepping smartly to the side as it came loose from its moorings and crashed down to the path. The noise could be heard clear across the market.

The fire engine arrived a few moments later and soon had everything under control. The three heroes walked back to their stall amidst a thundering round of applause, and many pats on their backs.

'Jesus, Mickey,' Robbie said, as they slumped back down on the sacking. 'You took so long in there, man, I thought yer were a goner.'

'Aye,' Mickey grinned as he wiped his soot-streaked face. 'I thought I'd had me chips an' all!'

6

Lorraine looked from the poor broken body on the autopsy table to Scottie, and saw the sadness in his eyes. Shaking her head, she moved over to the smoked glass window.

What a mess, she thought, taking a pencil out of her pocket. The girl lying there was so young, so pretty, she had a beautiful kid waiting for her at home . . . she'd had so much to live for. For a moment Lorraine couldn't decide what she was hoping for in Scottie's verdict. You never wanted it to be murder – that meant there was some bastard out there responsible, and if he'd done it once he'd probably try it again – but, looking at Diane Fox's body, Lorraine found it hard to hope for a verdict of suicide. *What have you got to kill yerself for?* If a young girl like this thought there was nothing left for her, what did that say about the world they were all living in?

For a moment the only sound in the morgue was Edna as she slapped sticky labels onto glass test tubes containing samples of the victim's body fluids.

Then Scottie coughed into his handkerchief. He had the

damn flu, as he'd told Lorraine three times in the five minutes since she walked in. Earlier Edna had practically pushed two flu tablets down his throat with the warning that if he didn't stop whingeing she would personally shoot him.

'Right, what have yer got for me?' Lorraine asked finally.

Scottie sniffed then, realising that he was going to get as much sympathy from Lorraine as he had from Edna, said, 'She was definitely dead before she hit the road.'

Lorraine sighed, and realised she'd been holding her breath. 'So we're looking at murder?'

'That's right, love. The perfect beginning to Houghton Feast,' he added dryly.

Lorraine chewed the end of her pencil then slipping it back into her jacket pocket, asked, 'So, what killed her?'

'Asphyxia,' he answered.

'Strangulation. Your instinct at the scene was right?'

'I'm afraid so. You see those bruises on the front of her neck? The disc-shaped ones? They're the marks left by finger-tips. So the killer strangled her with his hands rather than by tying her or anything. But all the signs are there: the poor lass's heart's enlarged, her veins are engorged up here above where his hands went, and there's clear enough evidence of cyanosis.'

Lorraine looked more closely at the body and, yes, her lips were slightly blue.

'Plus the tongue and larynx were elevated, and I found haemorrhaging around the eyes. It's pretty straightforward.'

'And definitely a male killer, I assume?'

'Yer know as well as I do, Lorry, yer can't be definite in this business. But yer need to be a deal stronger than your victim to kill like this – a woman probably couldn't have done it. And the psychology's all wrong. Women don't tend to strangle – particularly not if they're attacking another woman on a deserted street.'

'That makes sense.'

'Aye, an' he'll likely be taller than her too, going on the angle of the primary pressure. You're looking at a man who's at least six foot two, bearing in mind how high her heels were.'

Lorraine nodded. That was a start. 'Did it happen at the bridge? I've had a team of people checking the area and they found nothing out of the ordinary up there.'

'I'd have thought so. Time of death would be between twelve and three o'clock early morning. The broken bones and the bleeding look like they came post-mortem, but there won't have been much of a gap between death and her hitting the ground.'

'So that's how she came to be where we found her? He attacked her on the bridge then pushed her off?'

'Looks like it. He came up on her from behind.'

'Are yer sure?'

'Look here.'

Lorraine moved back to the table as Scottie gently moved the girl's head and shoulders, and the rest of the body made a sickening slap as it turned over.

Scottie pointed at two round bruises at the back of the neck. Then he placed his thumbs over the marks. They fitted exactly and the rest of his fingers easily encompassed her neck.

Lorraine nodded. 'So, he's come up on her from behind. He could have spotted her in the nightclub and maybe asked her for a dance, she rejected him and he followed her out? Or he could have been lying in wait for just about anyone, and this poor bugger was it.'

Scottie shrugged. 'Sounds good to me. We didn't find anything under her nails so the poor woman didn't even get the chance to struggle much – there was a fair amount of alcohol in her bloodstream so she'll have been too inebriated to fight back. But it means we've got no DNA for yer I'm afraid.'

'Damn.' That was a blow – even assuming they found the killer, it would be that much harder to prove his guilt in court without a DNA match. Jurors had watched so much about DNA matching on the telly that they pretty much expected it. 'Well we'll have to cope without. At least we know who the poor woman is. Or was.'

'Yer do?' Scottie asked, and Lorraine felt suddenly guilty that she'd forgotten to tell him. Scottie took great care of the men and women who crossed his table – she'd even known him attend their funerals.

'Yeah, she's called Diane Fox. Reported missing yesterday. That's what I meant about the nightclub: she'd been out dancing but left on her own by all accounts.' Lorraine sighed. 'Single mother as well – she's got a baby son. I suppose I'll have to send her parents along to officially ID her.' She looked sadly down at Diane's lifeless body. No parent should ever have to see their child like this.

Josh Quinn tightened the last bolt on the waltzer with a vicious twist. He hated this job, hated this life, hated the fair, hated Houghton Feast. In fact, Josh hated the whole world and everything and everybody in it. Up to and including himself, whom he hated more than anything or anybody else.

Out of the corner of his eye, he noticed three schoolgirls who were obviously playing the nick to hang around the fair, even though the Feast didn't start for nearly a week. They were watching him. He knew what they could see from that angle would fairly please them – get their horrible little hearts going like the clappers, with feelings they were probably too young to understand. A good-looking gypsy boy with a profile that belonged in films.

Yeah, that's me all right.

Fucking horror films.

He smiled, but it held no humour. His smiles when they came rarely did.

Josh decided it was time to give them a little treat. Really set the blood flowing through their adolescent veins. Enough so it would be a long time before any of them played the nick again.

Slowly, gaining as much effect as he could, he turned around and, curling his lip to maximum effect, stared full on at the three girls.

Only one of them had the grace to blush and quickly look away. The dark mousy-haired one in the middle, no beauty queen herself and never likely to be, actually gasped out loud.

Ha, as if that was a fresh reaction.

The third girl, still staring, nudged her friend in the ribs before she pulled a thoroughly disgusted face. Then, as if on cue, all three turned and ran off.

Josh laughed, a harsh vicious bark that was loud enough for them to hear as they ran through the gates. He stared after them for a moment, then threw his wrench down and stormed off to the caravanette he shared with his uncle.

'Fucking bitches,' he muttered as he reached the American tourer. Going in he slammed the door behind him, hard enough for the tourer to shake.

Percy Quinn, Josh's uncle, a tall thick-set man whose dark hair had decided to go South before he'd reached the tender age of twenty-five, had been watching. Sighing heavily to himself, he carried on hanging the golden-furred teddies with the red bows around their necks along the posts that held up the shooting gallery.

Josh was his dead brother's son, and he had been horribly disfigured in the fire that had taken the lives of his mother, father, and three infant sisters.

Before the fire Josh had been a very handsome sixteen-year-old, with dark brooding gypsy looks. Now, five years on, there were still more bad days than good. The bitterness that had changed the happy teenager into a very depressed and sometimes suicidal young man, was wrapped tight around him. Sometimes Percy thought he was shrink-wrapped in misery.

In the first year after the fire, Josh had twice tried to take his own life, and he'd tried again at least once a year since then. October was always the worst month. Percy had kept away from Houghton Feast for three years running, thinking that it was something in the area that set him off – although the fire had happened at the Newcastle Hoppings. It could have been past memories of the good times the family used to have here when Josh was just a lad and they'd rested up for a full year. But truth be told, wherever they went it was always the same. Come October, he kept a very good eye on Josh. They had been in Houghton for three days now, and this was the fifth time Josh had stormed off to the caravanette.

The teddies finished, Percy jumped over the side of the stall which had recently been painted in bright yellow with swirls of blue and red, then made his way over to the cara-vanette. Percy had never married so the blow of losing his brother, sister-in-law and three nieces had been very hard. He had other family, but most of them lived down South on static sites, apart from one great-uncle in Scotland and the two maiden aunts who lived in the local static site at Grasswell.

Not many travelled like the old times, but he and Josh liked the open road, and off season they headed wherever the wind took them. As a child Josh had loved Cowboys and Indians, so when the old caravanette had died on them near South London last spring, Percy had deliberately picked an

American tourer that came complete with Red Indians in full feather headdress painted on the sides.

Taking a deep breath he opened the door. There was no sign of his nephew, but Percy didn't need radar ears to hear the snuffling coming from Josh's bedroom.

He shook his head, *When was it ever gonna stop?*

In the last five years Josh must have been stared at a thousand times or more, and each time he had laid himself wide open, almost as if he enjoyed the pain and the following self-pity.

His face wasn't so bad.

At least not when you got used to it.

Percy had figured out long ago that it was the contrast that was so shocking. When you came upon the bad side first it was enough to make you wince, but come up on the good side, then the other . . . well, it certainly took your breath away.

When anyone stepped into the tourer, they were always surprised at how neat and tidy the place was. But it was all down to Josh, on his own Percy would have quite happily lived in the large trailer that the waltzer was stored in. His needs had always been simple and his wants few. A couple of good meals a day, and somewhere, anywhere to lay his head.

He knocked on Josh's door. 'Are you all right, son?'

He was greeted with silence. Well, nothing new there. He tried again, then heard Josh curse softly to himself before he said, 'Yes, yes I'm fine. Just go away.'

Percy shuffled awkwardly outside of the door. He'd been hoping Josh would come with him today. 'I, er . . . I'm going over to visit with the aunts for an hour or so . . . Do you fancy coming? It'll be a change.'

'No.'

'But they haven't seen you in a long time now, Josh, and

every time we come to Houghton they expect you to visit with them . . . They'll be sitting there with the best china out, and it won't be for me.'

'I'm not coming.'

Percy grimaced. The aunts, both of them almost house-bound, would give him a hard time again.

He tried once more, knowing that the two old biddies genuinely wanted to see Josh. 'Certain you won't change your mind and pop out for an hour?'

The answer he got was something large and heavy rebounding off the door.

'Suit yourself,' Percy muttered.

A few minutes later he left the tourer and headed towards Houghton town centre; the aunts loved flowers, they might go easy on him if he took them a bunch each.

Josh waited until his uncle was well away before coming out of his room. There were tear tracks in the dust on his face. Slouching out of the tourer, he slammed the door then moved off in the direction of Houghton Park.

'What are yer looking at, son?'

Quickly he puts the binoculars back in their case. 'Nothing, Mother.'

'Nothing?'

'Oh, just a bird. I thought it was a rare one, but it's just a common sparrow.'

'Birds! Yer always watching birds. That's all yer ever do: day in, day out, yer watch birds.' She sighs, the deep self-indulgent sigh of someone who believes herself to be a martyr. Then adopts her wheedling tone, 'Will yer put me tea on now, son? Not too much tonight, eh. Just a few chips with that nice piece of gammon yer got at the shops earlier.'

'Yes, Mother.' He moves towards the cooker, his mind still on the girl he'd been watching through his binoculars. The same little beauty he's watched for five years or more.

7

After a clear crisp day, a heavy sea fret on the Northumberland coast rolled inland making it the sort of night when you need a pair of gills instead of lungs. Above the fret the nearly full moon was hidden by dark clouds.

Samantha Dankton, in a right strop, stormed out of her mother's home and into the night, slamming the door hard enough behind her for it to shake the foundations of the house.

Samantha had a pretty face, but up close she looked older than her twenty-five years. Her long dark hair hung limp and lifeless but would soon be frizzed to death in the dampness. After four abortions her plump body was starting to change and sag. Her temper however was the same one she'd possessed all her life. And tonight it was fairly up.

It was the same every time she came to see the bastards empty-handed. Her old witch of a mother and that ponce of a brother Brian. Different when she was bringing bags of food in for the fat bastards though.

Oh, aye. No questions asked as to where the money had come from to feed the fat twats.

No not then, they just scoffed the lot like the pair of fat fucking lazy pigs that they were.

Different ball game tonight though, 'cos I've got nowt.

And people were talking about her.

That bloody saint Brian had heard them in the White Lion. They were calling her the number one bike of Houghton.

Wow fucking wow.

That was an old tale, and her brother needn't pretend he'd never heard it before.

He's been growing fat for years on my fucking earnings. Bastard.

The gate slammed as hard as the door had and she made her solitary way up Tulip Crescent.

So the neighbours are talking, are they?

She blew warm steamy air out of her lungs into the cold damp night as she shook her head in amazement.

As if they hadn't been talking for years. Fucking Seahills, nowt but a fucking gossip hole.

I hate the bastard place and every fucker in it.

She glared at the windows of the houses as she passed. Smug bastards some of them. Liked to pretend their muck didn't stink. She spat in the garden of number forty-six.

'And your man's no great fuck, Mrs high-and-mighty Mandy Cooper, with yer fancy fucking fountain and yer ugly daft fucking garden gnomes. Who the fuck do yer think yer are,' she muttered, coming to a halt beside the waist-high wall and staring vehemently at the Coopers' front door.

'And he's a tight twat an' all,' she shouted, getting angrier by the minute. 'Daft bastard thought he could have a freebie last week, well fuck him and fuck his freebies.'

Bending over the wall she picked a stone out of the rockery and threw it at the nearest gnome, and was instantly rewarded with the satisfying sound of it breaking into a dozen pieces.

'There yer go.' Content for the moment, she fastened the

top button on her red duffle coat and moved on, muttering to herself, 'Proper Houghton Feast weather.'

The thought of Houghton Feast cheered her up some.

Come Friday she'd be rolling in it.

Aye, the bastards would want to know her then all right, bike or no bike.

Well, fuck them. They can bastard well starve to fucking death for all I care. Friday I'll be laughing, then the bastards will be sick as chips. All those strangers in town, made a canny penny last year all right.

A few hundred quid in four days wasn't bad, even if she'd have to put the extra time in. She did the maths, she'd put her price up at Christmas after a weekend at a friend's in Newcastle, figuring if the Geordies could afford another fiver then the Makams could an' all. So this year it would be twenty quid a punter – got to take inflation into the equation.

Some of the pros her mate knew racked forty or fifty quid a time in. 'Aye, but,' she muttered out loud to herself, 'they've mostly got beds, not sharing a house with an old cow and a whole fucking brood of her kids. A stand-me-up behind the Blue Lion in the pissing rain's not exactly a luxury hotel.'

She shrugged, decided she'd go for it and try for twenty-five.

Why the fuck not?

Her mind made up and fivers parading in front of her eyes, she smiled and, forgetting for the moment her fall-out with her mother and brother, moved at a quicker pace into the dark night.

Passing Grasswell fish shop a few minutes later, she debated on a bag of chips, then changed her mind. A cup of tea and a cheese sandwich would tide her over until the morning. Besides, her feet were fucking killing her and she was bone tired, the last thing she needed tonight was to stand in a flaming queue.

Spotting Andy Turner through the window as she passed, she gave him a little wave, wondering if he felt in the mood, but he made his intentions clear when he didn't return the wave and turned away from her.

Shit, if she hadn't been so tired she would have took time out to stamp her foot. He and Pam must be on speaking terms again.

Andy was one of her best punters – he and his long-term girlfriend Pam, long-term as in forty years, were forever falling out, and if Andy didn't get his leg over at least every other day then there was hell to pay.

Feeling spiteful she prayed for Pam to be struck down with a septic fanny, as she turned into her street. Noticing that the street lights were out yet again, she tutted. The street was pitch black and she lived near the end.

Grasswell was a tiny place on the road from Houghton to Newbottle; it consisted solely of a few terraced streets and a fish shop, plus the garage at the top of the hill and the allotments on the other side of the road. A few chinks of light showed around some of the windows, but not many. Certainly not enough to give off the sort of illumination that a person might see by.

She felt a rush of anger again, *Damn that Harry Crow.*

It'll be him all right, just 'cos the lamp-post's outside of his window he moans and groans that it keeps him awake, so the rest of us have to risk life and limb every time the crazy bastard smashes the light and blames the kids, just to keep the twat happy.

Aye why, wait till I see him in the morning.

Trailing her fingers along the wall as she went easy in case she tripped over a toy one of the Farlowe brats were keen on leaving about the place, she made it to her front door.

Her key, when she finally found it in her pocket, fitted smoothly into the lock. It turned easily. She was about to enter her small domain, when diamond-hard fingers grabbed her throat from behind.

Such force was used in that first squeeze that she didn't even have time to gasp or to fight for another life-giving breath. The pressure built up immediately and her brain, rapidly starved of oxygen, gave up the unequal struggle.

The small thud her body made on landing was negligible, as was the faint sound that followed of something being dragged down the street to the waiting car at the bottom.

Over in Newcastle, the last light went out in Jake's bar on the quayside. Hammerman, so named because of his fondness for clouting people who owed him money and wouldn't pay on the back of the head with a hammer, calmly closed the door behind him.

Inside, he was anything but calm. Tonight's takings had been low, and today's collections had been abysmal.

Especially in the Houghton area.

The bastards think 'cos it's Houghton Feast they don't have to pay. The cheeky twats.

Maybe Stella's going soft on them.

Stella was his right-hand woman – and much as he depended on her, he couldn't honestly say he understood her. She was a mass of contradictions – although the same could be said of most women. Most women he'd ever encountered, anyway.

On the surface, Stella was fearless and fearsome. Big and blonde, she worked out every day and was as strong as most men. Plus of course there was the added benefit that people didn't expect a woman to be as tough as she was – which meant she could be trusted to bring the lolly in. She'd been bouncing on the doors in Sunderland when he'd first met her a couple of years ago, and the attraction had been mutual.

But as he got to know her better, he came to realise that

there was another side to her. A side she kept hidden from him. Stella was determined that he'd never see inside her life, and she'd nearly managed it – except that Hammerman had decided to surprise her one night shortly after she'd first allowed him to seduce her. And when he'd walked into her house and seen the photos of her daughter – and the empty bedroom neatly laid out as Amanda would have liked it – he began to realise why Stella was as she was.

Three years earlier, when she'd been living in Houghton, Stella's only daughter had walked out of the house one night and never come back – and Hammerman, hard man as he was, could imagine how that would feel. He had kids of his own. Although his little angels had no idea what sort of job daddy did, and his wife thought he was an insurance collector. 'She's right,' he often laughed with his friends, 'she doesn't know just how right she is.' But if anything happened to his kids . . .

'Hey, what yer waiting for?'

Hammerman realised he'd been lost in thought and glared down at Stella, waiting in the car for him. Looking at him, she felt the usual mix of attraction and revulsion – but after Amanda's death it had been so long until she'd been able to feel anything at all, that even revulsion was worth something. She could tell by the glint in his eye as he looked at her and the stiff way he held himself that she was in for some bruising tonight. But she didn't mind the violence. She always fought back – and every time, it was like fighting back at whatever had taken Amanda. Although each time it got worse, and each time she felt that flicker of fear she knew she was messing with something that could destroy her.

Stella started the car.

'Back to yours,' Hammerman said, staring out the front window. He kept calm longer than she'd expected and they were nearly across the bridge when he blew.

'Fucking bastards!' he screamed as his fist hit the passenger-side dashboard. For the dashboard, which had been abused time and time again by Hammerman's fist, it was the last straw. It simply crumpled in on itself leaving a gaping hole.

'What the fuck yer doing, yer crazy bastard! Yer'll fucking well pay for that.'

'No, them fuckers from Houghton'll fucking pay for it. Think I'm a soft touch.' He turned his glare on Stella, 'Unless you're not doing yer fucking job properly.'

'I am doing me job. I can't help it if some of them are never in, can I?'

'Tell yer what, I'm gonna have to make an exhibition of somebody, else they'll all think I've gone soft, then the fucking lot'll be taking the piss.' He thought for a moment, then a sly smile crossed his face. 'And I know just the fucking pair an' all.'

Stella shrugged, relieved that whatever he had planned had quietened him down.

8

Doris counted the small stash she had in the back of her purse. She'd been putting two pounds away a week for Houghton Feast for the last six weeks and Jacko had given her his last tenner yesterday to add to it. Now where in heaven's name had she put the bloody tenner?

Melanie entered the room to find Doris on her hands and knees sifting through the cushions on the settee.

'What yer looking for, Nana?'

'Nowt, pet, but I'll find it.'

Melanie looked puzzled for a moment, then shrugged and said, 'Can I take Jess for a walk? I asked Dolly and she said it was all right if you said it was.'

Preoccupied, Doris nodded. Dolly Smith and her son Jason lived just four doors up from Doris, and Melanie had a big soft spot for their dog, Jess.

'Great.' The little girl clapped her hands. 'See yer later, Nana.'

Outside Melanie, who already had Jess on her lead and tied to the gate, bent over and stroked the small black and white collie. 'We're on, Jess. Now, where should we go?'

Jess thumped her tail. She loved to be walked, anywhere was good to her.

Still surprised that Doris had agreed so readily, Melanie started to walk up the street, Jess happily waddling beside her. She'd expected her nana to say no because she was well and truly in her bad books, and her much-anticipated trip to Houghton Feast was looking very dodgy now. She wished she'd never looked under the stones on the rockery now. It was only 'cos she was bored.

Everybody else had been at school, but because her leg was playing up this morning, Dad had said she had to stay off. She hated it when that happened, but Dad wouldn't let her take the pain tablets to school. And anyhow, it had eased off ages ago, sometimes it did that.

So she'd looked behind the stones for snails and found a needle.

And God how her nana had shouted at her when she'd carried the needle into the house! 'How many times have I told yer never to pick them bloody dirty stinking things up?'

Then Nana went outside and raked around the whole garden to see if there were any more, and all the time she'd been shouting at the top of her lungs about 'Dirty druggie bastards'.

Mr Skillings who lived next door had come out to see what all the fuss was about, and he'd agreed with Nana, but he'd winked and gave her a handful of sweets. Jelly babies. Mr Skillings always had a pocket full of jelly babies.

She knew Nana was right, she never should have picked the needle up. But she'd just forgotten, that's all. Now, if Nana stayed mad enough, she might not be able to go to Houghton Feast and she just had to go, especially this year, 'cos she was on the float. And if she missed it all – the parade, the bagpipes at the beginning, the candy floss and the fair – she'd just die.

Ohh, Nana wouldn't be that nasty.

Melanie stopped for a moment at the top of the street.

Which way should she go?

She looked at Jess, stroked her again as she said, 'She might forget, Jess.'

Jess wriggled with pleasure.

With a new and eager hope that Doris would forget all about the horrible stinky needle, Melanie and Jess turned right at the corner.

Josh was taking a break from yet another row with his uncle, who seemed to understand nothing at all about the way he felt. The way he had always felt, the way he would feel for ever. He had wandered into the park, and he was sitting staring into space running the row over in his head, trying to see if it had been his fault again – but he really didn't think it was.

He knew Percy thought that he wallowed in his misery, that he relished the grotesque shock of the burns on his face, but that wasn't how Josh saw it at all. The burns were part of him, part of his history – a physical reminder of his lost family – and that was why he refused the skin grafts, why he refused the plastic surgery. And anyway, it was none of Percy's fucking business anyway – it was his face. And his life. If he didn't want to go to see the old aunts, if he wanted to stay a loner, how could Percy blame him? Getting close to people just led to getting hurt – and Josh knew that better than most.

He was just deciding that he definitely wasn't in the wrong, when a small girl with a fat black and white collie on a lead came into view. The girl, sweet faced with dark auburn curls, was singing as she sat on the bench facing him. She finished her song, 'Swing Low Sweet Chariot', and smiled at him.

For fuck's sake.

What the hell does she want, applause?

And what did she want to go and sit there for?
There's a whole fucking park.

He half rose to move, then changed his mind. He'd been here first, why should he move for some brat with a mouldy old dog. Mouth settled into a scowl, he sat back down.

She was staring at him, like they all did, whatever fucking age they were. He did what he'd done countless times to horrible nosy little brats, he pulled a face that was bad enough to give them nightmares, that usually had them screaming their horrible little heads off.

This one however was different.

The little creep's actually smiling at me.
And the fucking dog's wagging its tail.

Taken aback, Josh said in a harsh voice, 'It's rude to stare, kid. Or were you never told that?'

Josh was further surprised when, instead of being even more frightened off, the girl stood up and, dog in tow, crossed the small path between them and sat on his bench. He noticed she had a slight limp, but the bad leg didn't seem to hurt her.

Not shy either.

Josh moved right to the end of the bench. This brat must be soft in the head, sixpence short of a shilling, his mother used to say. Then the spear stabbed him, like it did every time he thought of his mother, even after all these years.

'Hi,' Melanie said, holding out a small hand. 'I'm Melanie, who are you . . . ?' There was a pause as Josh failed to reply. 'Have yer been crying?' she continued.

'What the fuck's it got to do with you?' Josh snapped, ignoring her hand. *Cheeky little bastard.* 'Anyhow, surely you've been warned about talking to strangers. For all you know I could be an axe murderer, or even worse.'

'What's worse than an axe murderer?'

'You taking the piss, kid?'

Melanie shrugged innocently. 'No.'

Josh glared even harder, this time curling his lip, but Melanie went right on smiling.

'I've got thirty-three china dolls and every one's different.'

'Wow,' Josh said unenthusiastically.

Unperturbed, Melanie went on. 'Yer don't live round here, do yer? I know 'cos yer talk funny.'

'I think you'll find when you get out in the big wide world, kid, that it's you lot up here who talk funny.'

Melanie giggled. And for a moment Josh nearly did something he had never done in years. Smile. The kid's laugh was certainly infectious. But Josh's smile muscles were frozen. Frozen in time and that was the way he preferred it.

'Does that hurt?' She didn't point at his face, she didn't have to, they both knew what she meant.

'Mind your own business,' he snapped. 'For fuck's sake, you have got to be the cheekiest brat in the whole fucking world . . . Jesus.'

'Sorry . . . I am sorry, truly honestly . . . I only asked 'cos it looks really sore.'

Slowly Josh raised his hand to his face and touched it. Something he rarely did. His skin felt like it looked, rough and puckered. The touch brought a host of painful memories. Memories that he kept as tight a lid on as possible.

Angrily he turned on Melanie. 'Fuck off, kid. Go on, just fuck off. Who asked you to sit here anyhow? Who even wants to listen to your stupid noise?'

Melanie sighed. She'd heard worse from the lads in her street. Shrugging daintily, she said quietly, 'Sorry.'

Somehow that simple little word that was uttered a million times a day and mostly meant nothing at all, sounded different when Melanie said it, and Josh knew she really meant it. He calmed down, and grudgingly found himself nodding at her, accepting the apology in the spirit it was given.

'I've been to Disneyland in America,' she announced, abruptly changing the subject the way children do. 'Me dad took me and Nana. Have yer ever been?'

Josh had, Disneyland Paris. But Disneyland, like a lot of places, opened the memory box up. He knew he shouldn't have given the brat the time of day, she'd only caused him more grief than ever. He hated memories of places they'd been as a family, because in memories he could see faces, his parents' faces and his sisters' faces.

'Mind your own business, kid,' he replied curtly, though not as roughly as before. 'I don't even know why I'm wasting time talking to you anyhow. You're just a stupid kid.' Standing up, he shuffled off in the direction of the fairground.

Melanie watched him go. She felt so sorry for him she could cry. With a little sigh, she stood. 'Come on, Jess, we better be getting home in case we get wrong again.'

Melanie was so busy feeling sorry for Josh and worrying that she'd hurt his feelings real bad, that her mind blocked out the pain signals her leg was desperately trying to force on her. She didn't even realise how badly she was limping on her way home.

Percy was helping his old friend Tom, the owner of the waltzer, to take the black waterproof covers off. There was one left to go and together they lifted the cover.

Percy's hands were doing the work, but his eyes and his mind were on the tourer. He was surprised that Josh got out of bed this morning, because some days his nephew just didn't bother to clock in to the world. Sometimes it lasted a day or two, other times a week or two. He didn't eat, or change his clothes, he just lay in bed all day staring at the ceiling.

The doctors he'd seen over the years had each diagnosed deep depression and had prescribed any number of different pills that either made Josh a complete zombie or had no effect at all. It had been a while since such an episode had occurred, but Percy had noticed that there always seemed to be a reason, although sometimes it could be something completely trivial that set him off. After what happened with the schoolgirls Percy was expecting an episode at any time.

It had been a mistake coming back to Houghton: he knew it deep in his bones. Josh had been acting differently; he'd been elusive and even quieter than usual, disappearing off for hours on end and then, just when Percy really started to worry, storming back into the tourer and locking himself in his room. Percy had no idea where he'd been the last few nights – 'just walking' Josh had said. And that couldn't be a good sign.

Perhaps he'd ask Tom if Josh had said anything to him – or if he'd heard any gossip from anyone else. But just as Percy opened his mouth to put the question, bearded, barrel-chested Tom screamed as loud and as piercing as any woman. Shocked, Percy dropped the cover, looked at Tom, then looked quickly down to where Tom, his eyes on stalks, was staring.

Lorraine looked at the array of chewed pencils on her desk. She had to have a tab, the taste lead left in yer mouth was even worse than tobacco.

The craving for tobacco, plus the first day of PMT, had her irritability level set at dangerous. Five months on from giving up and the craving was no better than on the first horrible day; a friend of hers had told her just the other day that after abstaining for nearly six years she could still snatch one out of someone's hand in passing. Although the friend had hastily added, when she'd seen the look of pure horror on Lorraine's face, that it only happened occasionally.

'Jesus,' she said to the pencils.

Her right hand rested on the autopsy report of Diane Fox.

Strangulation. A vicious strangulation at that. And what made her particularly nervous was the barefacedness of the attack – pushing a body off the bridge up by Hall Lane? Anyone could have seen him.

She looked from the pencils to the papers she'd already studied.

Who?

Why?

Scottie had put time of death between twelve and three, which fitted with everything else they'd been told. The babysitter Simone, a right stroppy little cow, had 'fallen asleep' – which Lorraine assumed was code for passed out cold – some time before twelve o'clock, having arrived at about eight to look after Dillon. She'd expected Diane back about two-ish and so had settled in for the duration – and had been woken up at six in the morning by poor Dillon crying for his mother. Who was never coming home.

Lorraine gave a sigh and picked the sheaf of papers up once more. Maybe if she looked again she'd see something that hadn't been there before. *Fat chance.* She knew what was there: absolutely nothing. She'd gone through them time and time again and to date the only thing of note was that the heel of one of Diane's shoes was still missing. And that had probably snapped off when she hit the ground and meant nothing. Strange they couldn't find it, though.

She turned to the witness statement by the young woman who found the body. No help. Mid-twenties, just off to do a bit of shopping, looks over the bridge and there she is. Never seen her before. Never even seen a dead body before, poor cow. And clearly not a suspect.

They were still interviewing everyone who owned to having been at the nightclub but, save for a lad who'd shared a dance or two, it was pretty much a dead end. A request for information had gone out on local radio and in the local press, asking people who'd been in the area at the time to get in touch, but Lorraine knew what the odds of that coming to anything were: slim at best. Particularly at that time of night, there wouldn't have been many people around and those who were out on the streets were probably too half-cut to realise where they were and what they were doing, let alone come forward with useful information that might help her track down a murderer.

And family? Well the old rule was that you look for a killer close to home – most murder victims knew their attacker – but no obvious suspect had materialised so far. Her father didn't fit the physical profile – probably not strong enough to carry out the attack, and in any case he was only five foot eight-ish so too short according to Scottie's report. Her son's father was in prison so that ruled him out – there wasn't about to be a tug-of-love over little Dillon – and she didn't seem to have any particular boyfriends. It was obvious from what her neighbours said about her that she wasn't exactly a stay-at-home type, but there was no one regular man they could identify. Which left Lorraine with . . . nothing.

The door opened then and Luke walked in. He was wearing jeans and a lemon Nike T-shirt. For a moment Lorraine's thoughts were off the cigarettes and on to how nice he looked, but only for a moment. When she looked at his face, she sensed trouble, and instantly she was all business.

Luke wasted no time in telling her just how bad the trouble was. 'Another body, boss.'

'Oh, shit . . . We haven't even began to unravel this one yet. Where?'

'The fairground. In one of the waltzer cars.'

'Jesus, he's really not trying to hide it, is he? A bragger do yer reckon?'

Luke shrugged, 'Looks like it. Could be a show-off. Or

I'm sure the psychologists would tell us that subconsciously he wants to be caught.'

Lorraine gave a wry smile. 'Or he's so cock sure that we'll never pin it on him that he couldn't care less where he leaves them.'

'He sort of tried to disguise the first. Leaving her by the bridge like that could have made us wonder about suicide – or just a drunken mistake.'

'Yeah, but he wasn't exactly subtle about where he dumped the body. Could have left her out in the hills and she wouldn't have been found for months. Either he's not thinking straight or he's pretty sure of himself. Either way, he's way over the line.' She shrugged into her jacket.

A few minutes later they were walking across the show field, the air heavy with the smell of last night's hot dogs and fried onions – although the rides wouldn't start up until the Feast officially opened, the food stalls had opened for business as soon as the fair arrived. Dodging around the coconut stall, the hot dog van, and the high carousel brought the waltzer into sight. Lorraine looked at the carousel horses – she'd always found something rather frightening in their stare, and had refused to ride them when she'd been a kid.

The first person she saw when she reached the crime scene was Sara Jacobs ordering everyone around. Lorraine frowned. That wasn't right – she'd put the woman on the school patrol. She was still annoyed by how detached she'd seemed at the drugs talk, and hoped Sara might learn something if she was stuck at the school for a few more days. What the hell was she doing here?

'Hi, boss,' Sara said confidently, as Lorraine and Luke reached her. Before Lorraine could ask, Sara rushed on, 'I was in the park when I heard this unearthly scream. I mean you had to hear it to believe it. I rushed down as fast as I could and found these two men.' She pointed at Percy and Tom.

Percy and Tom were standing side on to the two detectives and had not seen them arrive. Tuning Sara Jacobs's irritating whine out for a moment, Lorraine studied them. The smaller man was thick-set and stocky but his skin was a sickly grey, and he looked desperately ill. He kept shaking his head as if he could not believe what was happening to him. The larger man seemed to have distanced himself from his friend, and he was staring across the empty patch of field in front of them that led to the caravans with a puzzled look on his face.

Lorraine followed his gaze, and saw a young man walking towards the caravans from the direction of Houghton. As he got closer, Lorraine could see that one side of his face was terribly disfigured. He went into a large American tourer and closed the door behind him. The man who'd watched him continued to stare at the caravanette.

Lorraine walked over to the waltzer, but told Luke to make sure she got to speak to the taller man herself. Something was seriously bugging him. Something to do with the younger man.

But did it have anything to do with the murder?

The waltzer was covered, as Lorraine had expected, with the ubiquitous police tape. And this time Scottie was there before her. He looked up at Lorraine's approach, and gave her a sympathetic grimace. 'Sorry, love, this ain't gonna make your life any easier.'

He stepped back to allow Lorraine nearer the body, and she dipped under the tape to take a look.

All of sudden, she felt a horrible sense of déjà vu. A young woman. Long dark hair – though loose this time rather than in a ponytail. A lot of make-up, and dressed up to the nines – though in a different way to Diane Fox. Diane had been out to have a good time. This woman looked . . . like a professional. But what Lorraine found herself staring at, what she couldn't look away from, was the marks on the woman's neck. Disc-like bruises. Just like those on Diane Fox's throat.

Fuck. A serial killer. On my patch.

'Scottie. Is it what I'm thinking?'

He nodded. 'That's right. Same MO. I'll have to do the autopsy for time of death and so on, but my guess is that it's going to be a case of what you see is what you get.'

Lorraine sighed deeply, took one last look at the broken woman, and stepped back over the tape just as her mobile rang.

'Hunt,' she said sharply.

'Lorraine, it's Clark.' Oh, fuck, that was all she needed – her boss sticking his nose in.

'Yes, sir.'

'I hear another woman's been found. Is it . . . does it look like it's linked to the Fox woman's death?'

'I'm afraid so. I've just talked to Scottie and seen the body: there's no doubt, I'm afraid. We're looking at a serial, sir.'

Clark gave a heavy sigh. 'Right, Lorraine, we're going to have to play this one carefully.'

Play this one? What the hell was he talking about? Two women were dead – it wasn't a game.

'How do you mean, sir?'

He clicked his tongue impatiently. 'Come on, Lorraine. You know what I mean. Houghton Feast is about to begin, it's the biggest event of the year – and we can't afford to have it go belly-up. You've got to play things down. Keep your investigations discreet.'

'But, sir, I was going to suggest a press conference to ask for –'

'Are you not listening to me?' he raised his voice sharply. 'A press conference is the last thing we need.'

'But, sir, we've got a killer on the loose in the area. We have to let people know.'

'And we will let them know – news like this always spreads – but we're not going to alarm them any more than is necessary. Understood?'

'Yes, sir.' Lorraine knew that tone, and knew she was banging her head against a brick wall.

She pocketed her phone and turned round. 'Luke,' she called him over, and Sara Jacobs came bouncing alongside. *Christ, hasn't Jacobs got any sense at all? A woman's body lying ten yards away and she's the picture of happiness because she found it.* She gave Sara a hard look which seemed to make her remember what was appropriate, and then gave them the bad news.

'It's the same killer.'

'What?' Sara gaped. 'The same as –'

'Yes. The markings are the same as on Diane Fox's neck. Unless we've got two stranglers in the area – which seems pretty damn unlikely – it's the same man, and he's killed twice now. Once late evening or in the early hours, and I'm guessing we'll find that this girl was killed late last night or early this morning – same principle.'

'What do yer want us to do, boss?' Luke asked, and Lorraine felt a rush of relief that he was there. Thank God she had someone she could trust. Sanderson was great, but Luke had better instincts and a quicker mind.

'Interview everyone on the site, find out where they were last night.' She thought for a moment and decided that ignoring Clark's orders was more than her job was worth in this case. 'But hold off putting out an information request just yet. If we send out alerts on two dead girls in three days we'll just spark a panic. News is gonna get out – it'll be all round Houghton within the day – but we don't want to alarm people more than we have to. So be careful, be tactful – and round up Sanderson, Carter, Dinwall and Travis to help yer.'

'What about me?' Sara asked eagerly.

*Damn. I can't send her back to the school patrol now –
it'll look too much like sour grapes as she was first on the
scene.* 'Work with Luke please, Sara. There'll be a lot of
interviewing to be done.' And with that, Lorraine walked off
in the direction of the tourer which had so intrigued the taller
of the two men who found the body.

Mickey and Robbie had walked into Houghton to catch the
bus for Chester-le-Street. They had opted out of going in
with Jacko because he was off to the cash and carry to
replenish the stall which meant leaving home at six thirty in
the morning. So seeing as mornings were always pretty slow
anyhow, Jacko had told them not to come in until after
dinner, when things quickened up a bit.

Passing the Britannia, they turned right and entered the
Broadway. Council trucks with hydraulic lifts were everywhere as the workmen put the finishing touches to the lights,
which would signal the start of the Feast when they were
switched on.

It was Robbie who first noticed that none of the workmen
were actually up the lifts – instead they were in huddles
talking to groups of people.

'Oww, what's going down here then?' Robbie said, looking
at Mickey with raised eyebrows.

'Dunno, but I'll sharp find out. Hey,' he said stopping at
the first group of people, 'what's the matter, guys?'

A small man with tiny wisps of greying hair brushed across
his scalp, turned from the huddle and said importantly,
'There's been a murder.'

'Never.'

'Ohh, aye. Found a young bit lass on the waltzer, of all
places. That ride will never be the same again. Reckon it's
the Houghton Ripper, that's what I say, like.'

One of his workmates, a young man with thick glasses on,

broke in. 'She was strangled, dip stick. So how the fuck can yer call him the Houghton Ripper?' Looking at Mickey he pointed his forefinger at the first man's head and drew circles in the air.

'Well, yer know what I mean. Bloody horrible, it is. And there was that girl found by the dual carriageway.'

'Was she strangled too? I thought she jumped.'

'Well the police report didn't say, did it. Just asked people who'd been in the area to come forward.' Mickey and Robbie were all ears but a bigger man who they guessed must be the foreman called the men back to work and they moved on in search of more news.

As they walked towards the bus stop, they bumped into Vanessa, Robbie's mother, standing with Dolly Smith and a couple of other women.

'Not safe to let yer bairns out. Not if some daft bastard's strangling everybody in sight,' said a bleached blonde with a toddler in a pushchair.

'Yer right there,' Dolly agreed.

'What's the coppers doing? That's what I say,' her friend, another blonde, added. 'Who's gonna be next, eh? Well, I'm not bringing me bairns to the Feast and that's a fact. Not unless they've caught the bastard. Fucking coppers, pile of shite if yer ask me.'

'Do they know who the poor girl up at the fair was?' Vanessa broke in.

'Not a clue, love. Fucking useless. But I did hear that the girl by the dual carriageway lived up Hall Lane. A friend of mine knew her – Diane, she was called,' the woman with the toddler answered. 'Had a little son, about the same age as my Simon.' She reached down and ruffled her child's hair affectionately – to his evident annoyance.

'And how did she die? Was it an accident or was she,' her friend lowered her voice, 'strangled too.'

'Dunno. But I'd put money on her being killed. Too much of a coincidence otherwise, isn't it?'

Robbie took advantage of the small pause as they all contemplated the idea of two murders in Houghton, to break in. 'Will yer be able to manage the shopping today, Mam?'

'Why aye, son. Youse two get going. It's not good to be late yer know, that's called taking the piss, especially as yer've only been there a day or two.' She smiled at Mickey who grinned back at her.

'Aye, we're going now. See yer.' He winked at Dolly.

'Begone yer little creep,' Dolly snapped, but laughed a moment later.

At the bus stop, Robbie said, 'Yer'll have to get the fares, Mickey, I gave me mam yesterday's dosh.'

Mickey froze, then shook his head. 'Fraid not, mate. I . . . er, I thought you might get them.'

'Why would I do that?'

''Cos I've got nowt left.'

'What!'

'Aye, I called in at the prize bingo on me way home last night and had a session with the bandits.'

'Yer didn't.'

'Aye, ah did.'

'What we gonna do then?'

'Thumb?'

Robbie shook his head. 'We might as well walk, nobody's gonna give us a lift. Not these days, and especially seeing as there's a bloody murderer about.'

'OK.' Mickey sighed. 'We can't let Jacko down.' They set off in the direction of Chester-le-Street, which lay through Chiltern Moor, Fence Houses, past Lumley Castle, and was at least a four-mile walk.

'So what were yer doing playing the bandits?'

'Well, it was like this see, I was just gonna cross the road when that idiot Lance Halliday and his gang of dopehead creeps came round the corner. And there wasn't a bloody soul in the street, so he would have had a carnival with me . . . Not that I'm frightened of him, like.'

Mickey puffed his chest out and Robbie smiled.

'So yer thought the safest place would be in the prize bingo.'

'Aye, and the price of protection's gone up. The flipping bandits took every penny I had.'

'That'd be right.'

They walked on in a comfortable silence until, a couple of minutes down the road, Robbie piped up. 'So when was it you saw that Dave Ridley, Mickey?'

Mickey thought for a moment. 'Must have been Saturday morning, I suppose. First day we helped Jacko on the stall – the day of the fire at the chippy. Why?'

Robbie's eyes were wide with excitement. 'Well think about it: he said the man from the social attacked him on the bridge up to Hall Lane, and that's where that girl was killed last week.'

Mickey looked sceptically at Robbie. 'Or where she had an accident; or where she did herself in. You don't want to be believing all the gossip those women spread.'

Robbie nodded, unconvinced, and the two boys walked on in silence.

They had just reached Chiltern Moor when a car beeped at them. Robbie looked quickly at Mickey. 'You thumbing?'

'Ner, look it's Trevor.'

'Yeah great.'

Trevor pulled over, and the boys jumped in.

'Where yer going?' Trevor asked, pulling back into the light traffic.

'Chester, we're on the market with Jacko,' Robbie explained, and was surprised when Trevor said, 'Yes, I heard.'

Looking at Robbie, Mickey shrugged. He wasn't that surprised, the folks on the Seahills got to know everything.

'Have yer heard about the murders, Trev?' Robbie said. 'I'm surprised you're still giving out lifts with a killer around.'

There was a moment's hesitation before Trevor replied. 'Aye, shocking, eh. But I figure you two boys probably aren't gonna be a danger.' And he gave them a grin.

'But it could be anybody yer know, Trev,' Mickey said earnestly. 'Could even be our Robbie.' He turned to Robbie. 'How about it, then? Where were you last night?'

'Me? What about you,' Robbie laughed. 'It might be you.'

'The boy's right, it might be you,' Trevor said, staring at Mickey for a moment in his rear-view mirror.

'Ner,' Mickey shook his head adamantly. 'I know it's not me.'

Robbie nudged Mickey in the ribs, and changed the subject. 'Is it all right if we slip yer a couple of quid the morn, Trev? 'Cos we've got nowt until tonight.'

'Aye. No probs.' Trevor knew Robbie wasn't going anywhere.

When they reached Chester-le-Street. Mickey had the door open and was scrambling to get out before Trevor had properly stopped.

'What's the matter with you?' Robbie said as Trevor pulled away.

'Ah don't like him.'

'Why?' Robbie looked sideways at Mickey. Mickey mostly liked just about everybody – he even liked Robbie's psycho sister Emma, and nobody liked Emma, she didn't even like herself.

'Dunno. I just don't.'

Melanie and Jess were on their way up for another visit to the park. Melanie felt so sorry for the man with the poorly face that she just had to see him once more and when Doris said she could take Jess out again she knew exactly where they were going to go. She started to sing. 'Sweet Chariot' was a favourite of her and Nana.

Sitting on the tourer steps, Josh heard her coming. He shook his head in wonderment. Her voice was so sweet and clear it sent shivers down his spine and washed away the nastiness of the last couple of hours – the police had made no bones about suspecting each and every one of them of killing the girl Percy and Tom had found, and he'd seen the woman who seemed to be in charge talking to Percy for ages. He had no way of knowing the singing was the cheeky kid back again, but it was her face that came to mind, and he wasn't surprised when she limped onto the rectory field, the dog at her side.

Of course the little nuisance spotted him almost at once. *Not in the mood for her*, he groaned, and was about to jump up and go when she started waving.

Josh looked quickly around – *good, no one's noticed the little creep, they're all too busy*. He decided to ignore her and go inside, but suddenly it was too late: the little creep had moved as fast as she could and now she was here.

What the fuck was it with this kid?

'Hi,' she beamed up at him as if he was the most important person in the whole world.

Grudgingly, Josh said hello back.

Melanie sat down on the step next to him, and started rubbing her leg, while Jess flopped down on the ground.

'Make yourself at home, why don't you?'

'Thank you.'

Josh raised his eyebrows. He didn't think the kid was stupid, but obviously sarcasm was lost on her. 'You, er, you sing real good.'

'I know.'

'Oh, you know do you.'

'Course, I can hear other people sing, can't I?'

'And you reckon you are better than them?'

'Aye.'

Josh shrugged, there was no answer to that, the kid was right. 'Fancy a cup of tea?' He was joking, the first in a long time, the very last thing he intended was to make her one, but when she declined the tea and asked for pop, he found himself jumping up and filling a glass with lemonade.

'Here,' he said gruffly a minute later, as he thrust the cold glass at her.

She gave him a dimpled smile and Josh replied with a lopsided one of his own, also the first in a very long while.

Melanie noticed how one-sided his smile was, but she didn't ask why, guessing rightly that it was the scarring on the side of his face that caused it. Instead she sipped her pop then, looking around her, said, 'I can't wait for Friday. Especially when they switch the lights on, and even more especially when the rides start.'

'Who brings you up to the Feast then?'

'Dad and Nana.'

'Not your mum?'

'Oh no. I don't have a mam. Everyone at school says she wanted to send me back on account of my funny leg. Look, see?' And Melanie matter of factly stretched her toes out for Josh. 'But I think Dad an' Nana stopped her – they must have, mustn't they? But I don't care. I don't need a mam in any case.'

Josh felt a lump in his throat as he looked across at the slowly growing show field.

'You, er . . . You don't have to wait until Friday for the fair, if you don't want to.' As he heard the words come out of his mouth, he couldn't believe he was saying them.

Melanie stared wide-eyed at him, then followed his eyes. 'Yer mean . . . ?'

'Yeah, why not . . . Come on, they'll be trying some of the rides out soon, you can come on with me.'

'Great. Jess can watch.' Melanie jumped up and grabbed hold of Josh's hand. For a brief second Josh froze, no one had held his hand in a long long time. Then he sighed. Today seemed to be an unusual day, and he was not completely sure he liked what was happening.

Taking a deep breath, he steadied himself and, still unsure if he was doing the right thing or not, walked over with her to the carousel horses.

9

Melanie had made it to school the next morning only to be sent home with the rest of the kids at eleven o'clock because the heating had broken down. And so she and Suzy sat on Suzy's steps with their heads together – one auburn, one fair – debating whether or not they should go up to the park and watch the fair being put up.

'Nobody will know,' Melanie said.

'Yeah, but if we get found out we might miss the Feast,' Suzy replied, even though she was dying to go. A moment later she added, 'Should we?'

'No, better not . . . I'll just die if we get grounded.'

'Me an' all.'

'We'll have to keep it top secret if we do.'

'Better not tell our Emma then.'

Melanie looked at Suzy. Both girls grinned at each other as they said in unison, 'Come on then.'

Because Melanie couldn't really walk that fast it took them nearly twenty minutes with numerous stops to reach the show field. Both girls were already excited and couldn't wait for

Friday night, but as they went in the back way past the swings, the closer they got the more their excitement grew.

'Ohh, look.' Suzy clapped her hands.

With only a few days to go the field was buzzing as the big shows were erected. Wide-eyed, both girls watched the action from behind the fun house. In one corner half a dozen men were busy with the Meteor, a huge circle where people stand up and pay for the privilege of practically having their guts wrenched out. In the opposite corner the Helter-Skelter was being erected by another group of men.

Melanie looked around the field, her eyes resting on the cordoned-off waltzer. She pointed towards it. 'Look, Suzy, that's where that woman was murdered,' she said in a loud whisper.

Not a hundred per cent certain what murdered actually meant, Suzy nodded seriously, then replied importantly, 'I know. It's a good job there's another waltzer, isn't it.'

Melanie nodded. She liked the waltzer, but Dad didn't, and he would only let her go on with him and last year he'd been sick. So a ride on the waltzer this year was looking dodgy.

She sighed from her shoes. 'Is your costume for the float finished yet?'

'Aye, Sandra made it.'

'Ohh, can't wait.'

'Can't wait for what?' a deep voice that Melanie recognised said from the gathering shadows behind them.

Both girls spun round. Suzy gasped – seeing Josh's face was a shock. Her mind suddenly buzzed with warnings from her mother.

Don't go away from the door.

It's not safe out there.

And then she'd said something about a bad man being on the loose. Suzy began to back away.

Josh looked down at them. 'I thought it was little miss

motormouth,' he said, but this time his expression wasn't as ferocious as his words.

'Hello,' Melanie said brightly as she smiled at him, then added to Suzy in a matter-of-fact voice, 'It's all right, Suzy, he showed me round the fair the other day and let me go on the rides. Oops!' she clapped her hand over her mouth. 'But I wasn't supposed to tell – promise you won't tell either? Honest, he's a friend.'

'Presumptuous little brat aren't you,' Josh said, almost smiling. He hadn't realised he was Melanie's friend.

'What's that mean?' Melanie asked.

Never once taking her eyes off Josh's face, Suzy inched closer to Melanie.

'It means . . . Never mind what it means, brat. Anyhow, you should go home.' He looked over and saw his uncle walking purposefully across the field towards them. Damn. He'd got in enough trouble yesterday for taking Melanie on the rides; if Percy caught him with her again today he'd go mental. 'Go on, you'd better go,' he said, rather more forcefully than he'd intended.

Suzy began to shake with fear as she nibbled on her fingernails.

'Go on,' he repeated. 'Get yourselves away from here, it's not a good place to be this year.' Leaning towards them, he raised his hands in the air, wriggled his fingers, and went, 'Booo.'

Suzy screamed, and tears of fright sprang to her eyes. Unperturbed, Melanie laughed.

'Mel, I want to go home,' Suzy pleaded, tearing her eyes from Josh and looking frantically round for a means to escape.

'It's past dinner time,' she went on, thinking fast, trying to find the right words that would get Melanie out of there. 'They might be looking for us. If they find us here we'll get real wrong. An' we'll have to miss the Feast.'

'OK,' Melanie said, hearing the fear in her friend's voice but not understanding why she was scared. She knew Josh wouldn't hurt either of them. 'Come on then . . . Bye,' she said to Josh, as she took Suzy's hand and led her confidently past him.

Josh watched them go, a slight smile playing on his lips. The kid had some nerve, you had to give her that.

Turning round to wave at Josh, Melanie noticed the smile and how different it made him look. Much nicer. She smiled back.

Josh tutted, then begrudgingly he nodded to her.

When she was out of hearing range, Percy materialised at Josh's side. 'Josh, I don't think this is wise, son.'

'What?' Josh asked, his voice sharp and his face pulled into a deep frown.

'You know what I mean. You're a grown man. And grown men do not have eight-year-old little girls for friends.'

'Says who?' Josh demanded defensively.

'Says everybody . . . It, it's not natural.'

'It's not what?'

Percy took a deep silent breath. He knew damn well Josh had heard him the first time, and he also knew that his nephew knew exactly what he was going on about.

'Not natural,' he muttered, his voice low, trying to stave off the inevitable. 'People will talk.'

'People will talk.' Josh spat the words out. 'And everybody round here knows exactly what natural is, do they?' Josh's voice was nowhere near as low as Percy's and it was rising all the time. 'Dirty-minded sods.'

'Josh, you'll have to get rid of her . . . she's a nice enough kid, anybody can see that. Voice of an angel. Had old Mimi nearly in tears yesterday with her singing. But you have to tell her to stop bothering you.'

'She's not bothering me.'

Percy could see the flush starting on Josh's neck, a sure sign that Josh was about to lose it. But Percy pressed on. 'You know I'm right, Josh.'

The explosion came. 'Fuck you. Fuck you and fuck them.' And, with that, he ran off towards the park.

'JOSH,' Percy shouted, forgetting himself and attracting the attention of Rosie and Will, who ran the hook-a-duck stall.

Percy smiled quickly at them, but he'd seen their raised eyebrows and the way their collective eyes had followed Josh. That's all he needed. *Them two love nothing more than a good gossip, and the pair of them are past masters at Chinese whispers.*

Lorraine, smart in long black jacket and black trousers with a pink shirt, stood at the front of the incident room facing her officers. Behind her the board held pictures of the two murdered women, and each murder scene. A photograph of Diane Fox in life, smiling broadly with her son in her arms, had been pinned to the board soon after she was found. Now, just four days later, another woman's smiling photo sat alongside it. Samantha Dankton.

Lorraine's suspicions had been right – she was a pro, and a well-known one at that. She'd spent the evening at her mother's and they'd rowed. Then when her mother phoned her the next morning to give her what for, she hadn't been there. When she'd gone round there was no sign of her daughter. She'd heard the gossip about the body found on the waltzer at lunchtime, but hadn't thought anything of it until, twelve hours later, she still hadn't been able to get her daughter on the mobile she carried everywhere with her. Finally she called the police – and they had the identity of the second victim.

Lorraine looked around the room. Luke sat on the desk

slightly behind her, and Carter stood at the other side. Detective James Dinwall sat slightly too close to Sara Jacobs. Lorraine sincerely hoped she was misreading the vibes that were radiating off the pair of them. Dinwall had been married to his wife Beth for three years and they had a one-year-old son, Liam. Lorraine remembered their wedding day, and Liam's christening day.

I'll have to separate them.

She'd seen office flings before, and picked up the pieces afterwards as well.

What a cat that Jacobs is.

Tut, tut, remember girl, it takes two to tango.

Sanderson noticed her staring at the pair who seemed oblivious to her attention, and coughed loudly.

Lorraine blinked quickly, then clapped her hands. 'Right, guys. It seems that we have a double murder on our hands at the worst possible time.'

'So they're definitely linked, boss?' Sanderson asked.

'Looks that way. Same MO, the victims are the same physical type, no DNA on either of them I'm afraid but the law of averages is against two stranglers suddenly striking in the same area.'

Heads nodded round the room. Dinwall, tearing his eyes away from Sara Jacobs for a second, said, 'House-to-house, boss?'

'If yer were paying attention you'd have known we haven't even got that bloody far, Dinwall.'

'Sorry, boss.'

Lorraine curled her lip at him, then picking her stick up she proceeded to divulge the small scraps of information that had already been gleaned about the two women. Although Samantha Dankton was a prostitute, Diane Fox wasn't – so it wasn't a case of someone picking off hookers. 'Though, Carter, you'd better have a check with some of the pros and see if there's been anyone odd hanging around.' No obvious connections had materialised between the two women so it looked like an opportunistic killer, but the build and hair were similar so that could be a factor. They'd already pinned down some sightings of Samantha – Andy Turner said he'd seen her outside the Grasswell fish shop at about half eleven and Scottie's best bet on time of death was between eleven and two so that gave them a good time frame.

What wasn't yet clear was where Samantha had been killed. Scottie reckoned Diane had been strangled only a few minutes before being pushed over the bridge, but Samantha was a different matter. It seemed certain that her body had been moved. Andy had seen Samantha walking in the direction of her home, which was where her mother said she was going. So how did she end up in the waltzer? Had she changed her mind and gone to the fairground in search of a punter? Or did this point to the murderer being one of the travellers? The first death had certainly coincided pretty neatly with the fair's arrival.

Lorraine turned her mind back to the briefing. 'One last thing. Samantha's missing one of her earrings. Could be that if we find it, it'll give us where she was murdered. Or could be that it's still in the grass somewhere round the waltzer. Dinwall, I want yer to look into it. OK guys, anything I've missed?' She looked up. 'Yes, Sanderson.'

'Sounds silly I know, but there's a bloke down in Houghton reckons he was mugged by the social last week.' A ripple of laughter spread around the room. 'No really . . .' Sanderson flushed. 'Sorry, that's not what I mean. Obviously he wasn't mugged by the social, but something did happen to him – his face was cut up bad. And I'm pretty sure it happened on the same night Diane was killed and up near Hall Lane.'

'And when did all this come to light?' Lorraine said sharply – she shouldn't be finding out about this now for God's sake.

'Just something I overheard. He came into the station rambling – bit of a drinker, yer know – and tried to report it to that new young lad on the front desk. But he was so sure it was the social that I think the lad gave him a flea in his ear and sent him on his way.'

Lorraine sighed. 'And do we know who this bloke is?'

Sanderson made a note. 'I'll find out.'

'Right. Good. Anything else?' Lorraine hoped not – they needed to get out there and get working. 'Yer know what you're doing?' A murmur of agreement floated round the room. 'Right then, well go and do it!'

Primed and ready to go, the team filed out one by one. But when Dinwall passed, hot on the heels of Jacobs, Lorraine beckoned with her finger for him to stay behind.

Christina Jenkins had worked in Houghton library since the day she'd left school. She was now twenty-nine, and far far prettier than she realised. A domineering father, who still had a tight hold over her, made certain that his little girl dressed as dowdily as possible. Belly button rings! Christina wasn't even allowed to wear earrings. If Stan Jenkins had thought he could get away with making his only child wear a chastity belt he'd have ordered one years ago.

Christina's mother had died a horrendous death on Christina's sixteenth birthday. Mown down by a double-decker bus, her injuries had been so bad that it was over a day before she'd been identified and then only by the clothing she wore.

That she'd been on an errand for Christina, her father never let her forget.

Christina's midnight black hair, the same colour as her eyes, was scraped back off her face and worn in a tight bun at the nape of her neck. She wore a dark brown calf-length skirt that used to belong to her mother – Stan had never emptied his wife's side of the wardrobe – and a grey polo-neck jumper. She was tall and slim with a good figure, but her only hobbies were ceramics, cooking and reading. She had one piece of jewellery and that was her mother's wedding ring, which her father made her wear on her wedding finger – he said it would warn men off, that otherwise they'd think she was easy and available. And Christina, with no mother to guide her, always thought her father knew best.

She had lived at number thirty-seven, Tulip Crescent, just across the road from Jacko Musgrove, since the day she'd been born. In the last eight years she'd spoken to Jacko perhaps a dozen times, even though she'd gone right through school with him – and they'd sort of been friends. But since her mother had died Christina had hardly spoken to anyone.

Jacko's mother Doris was the exception. Doris would not be ignored, plus it was a long way around Doris – easier to talk to her, or rather just to listen. But it was always good to know that she did have someone out there if she ever needed them.

And little Melanie of course; no one could ignore Melanie. Christina often daydreamed that Melanie was her little girl. She loved the colour of Melanie's auburn hair, and her pretty laughing brown eyes. Much better than her own eyes, that were so dark you could hardly see the little black bits in the middle.

Christina would have loved to have been pretty, and to have a nice figure, and perhaps to be able to dance. She had never been to a party or a dance, nobody had ever asked her. Not that she would have gone.

She had to look after her dad.

Not for the first time, she wondered how anyone who was

as ill as he claimed to be could smoke eighty cigarettes a day and drink at least eight or nine pints every night.

Tonight was her only night out in the whole week, and he grumbled about that.

Would his supper be on the table when he got in?

Well it had been up until now.

She chided herself for being so sarcastic. Her dad was very good to her, he always had been.

Didn't he tell her so often enough?

Didn't he give her a roof over her head, and three square meals a day?

Didn't he take nearly all of her pay to provide it?

She sighed. What was wrong with her tonight?

Then she remembered how surprised both of them had been when she'd stuck to her guns about her once a week ceramics class at Shiney Row college.

She'd been coming for four weeks now and thoroughly enjoyed it. The people in her group had only ever heard her speak once and that had been on the very first night. It had nearly destroyed her, giving her name to nearly twenty people – she shivered now at the very thought of it.

She'd mastered the art of working in the library, mostly by doing the jobs on the computers or stacking the shelves. The regulars and her colleagues knew her well, and if she was ever called on to work at the front desk, they respected her silence, perhaps guessing that for her, panic was never very far away.

Christina fastened her red wool coat as she passed through the college gates. It had started drizzling again, another damp foggy night, and she'd left her umbrella at home. The tutor had rambled on a bit this evening, and she had a feeling that she'd missed the hourly bus. When she saw no one at the bus stop, she knew it had already gone.

If it had been the middle of the day, she would have crossed over the old railway, through Russel Woods and would have been home in no time at all. But on this dark drizzly night, Houghton Feast weather all right, she was faced with God knows how long a wait for the bus, or a brisk walk along the very badly-lit road.

She opted for the road.

Five minutes later she came to the part of the road that Russel Woods came down to. She shivered and tasted the dampness on her lips, then she heard soft footsteps behind her.

Unconsciously she quickened her step, and it seemed to her a moment later that whoever it was that was following her, did the same.

Not meaning to, but unable to stop herself, she quickly looked round. Not five yards away there was a man. His head was down and his shoulders were hunched up against the weather.

Of course his head's down, it's drizzling.

It means nothing.

But she couldn't stop the fear tingling in her blood as he seemed to increase his stride with every step. Looking forward again, she frowned. She had reached the part of the road where one of the lights fizzed and buzzed, threatening to go out at any minute.

Please don't, she silently prayed.

Her heartbeat speeded up and tiny little pricks of fear hit her spine, right in the middle of her back. She was frightened now in case her legs gave way. She knew that if the light went, then she'd just crumble.

To her immense relief the light held and she was fast approaching the next one.

Won't be long now.

She'd soon be home and putting Dad's baked potatoes in the oven.

Then, suddenly, the man was abreast of her. She held her breath, then he was past and innocently wishing her a 'Goodnight'.

She breathed, realising that for a while she had forgotten to exhale.

Tension easing out of her shoulders, and chiding herself for being so silly – the man had a perfect right to be here, the same as she did – she set her sights on home.

Not far now.

The man was out of sight and over a slight rise in the road when she was grabbed from behind and pulled nearly to the ground.

She screamed, but her cry was quickly cut off. Rough hands circled her throat. Her legs buckled beneath her, ready to give up the fight before it had barely started.

For a moment she thought the lack of oxygen was causing her to see stars, then she realised, with a small well of hope, that it was the headlights of a car coming towards them. Quickly, as if panicking of their own accord, the hands left her throat. She sucked a much-needed lungful of air in as the hands grabbed under her arms and she was dragged into the woods.

Branches stretching every which way threatened to have her eyes out, she winced time and time again as she was repeatedly scratched. She tried to cry out, but the pressure of his hands on her throat seemed to have choked her voice. She was so frightened she thought her heart was going to burst right open.

Why was he doing this?

She'd always been a good girl. Never brought any trouble to the door.

She always did as she was told.

Then another deeper thought from a part of her mind that she kept subdued. Why are you letting him?

He's gonna kill me.

The realisation hit her hard.

Suddenly, from somewhere, something that had been suppressed and hidden deep inside of her since the day her mother had died, rose to the surface.

NO.

This was not gonna happen

She was gonna stop it, right here and now.

Kicking out hard with her right leg, she caught her assailant on his shin.

He grunted, then punched her hard, spreading her nose over her face. Then quickly again, this time because she tried instinctively to duck, he caught her ear causing an instant dizzy spell.

She felt a bit sick, then even more so as she tasted the blood from her nose that was fast pouring down her throat and threatening to choke her,

She felt the darkness beckoning to her – in there she would be safe and warm, no one could reach her, no one could hurt her. Slowly she began to retreat, almost welcoming the feel of her attacker's hands round her throat once more.

Then the stranger in her mind rebelled. Her fingers, equipped with long sharp nails that she'd always been secretly proud of, gripped into his ankle gouging deep holes that burned immediately.

Now it was his turn to scream.

Letting go, he drew back his foot, kicked her as hard as he could, and snarled his satisfaction when he felt and heard at least a couple of her ribs snap.

The stranger, new to the world and its cruelty, could take no more. Slowly it retreated back to where it had lain dormant for the last thirteen years, and Christina closed her eyes.

*   *   *

Allan Greve's mother had sworn from the day her son was born that he could hear a fish fart from half a mile away. At twenty-seven Allan's hearing was as acute as it had always been, but tonight it wasn't something he'd heard that made him stop. Rather, it was something he wasn't hearing.

Christina Jenkins hadn't recognised him, but he had certainly recognised her.

Who wouldn't. She was bloody gorgeous.

He spun round to be greeted by an empty path. Of the delectable Christina, there was no sign.

Surely she's not gone across the fields?

It's be like trying to walk through a swamp in this drizzle. Frowning, he strained to hear.

He froze . . . Was that a scream?

Then he heard sounds he couldn't put a name to.

Puzzled and more than a little apprehensive, he walked back to the last spot he'd seen her. The sound came again, and this time he identified it as a sort of thrashing, dragging noise. Then there was a definite grunt, which came from somewhere to the right.

'Christina, is that you?' he said loudly.

Then, shouting, 'Christina, are yer all right?'

Dead silence. Even the night seemed to be holding its breath.

He shouted again. This time he was answered by the sound of somebody thrashing their way through the trees.

Christ, Allan thought, scrambling his way up the verge and into the woods.

He cupped his hands round his mouth and yelled again. 'Christina, love, are yer all right. . . . ? Shout if yer hurt, pet, so I can find yer.'

He stayed silent, the seconds ticking by, but there was no answer.

Shaking his head and convinced that something had happened to her, Allan moved deeper into the woods.

His hearing might have been acute, but his night-time vision was no better than anyone else's. He finally found Christina by falling over her.

10

Doris watched the kettle boil, remembering years back when her own work-weary mother used to say, in that high nasal twang that set yer teeth on edge, 'A watched kettle never boils.'

Well this one was boiling its arse out.

Better turn it off, if there's no teabags there's none. None that I can find anyhow, though I wouldn't put it past our Jacko to have hidden one or two for himself.

She sighed. As long as Melanie had her milk. *I'll pop along Dolly's later on, get a cuppa then.*

The pounding on the door, a moment later, made her twitch in her skin – even though she'd been expecting it. She hadn't thought it'd come this bloody early though – folks were barely outta their beds.

'I know who yer are,' she muttered as she made her way along the passageway to the front door. There was no one it could be except for Hammerman.

'I'm not in,' she shouted.

'Very funny,' came back the answer. 'Open the fucking door.'

'There's no point 'cos there's no money so take yer filthy gutter mouth outta here.'

There was silence for a moment, but Doris didn't kid herself that he'd gone.

'Doris.' Doris groaned, he'd brought his sidekick, Stella.

'What.'

'Why don't yer open the door so we can talk? I'm sure you don't want the neighbours to know our business.'

'Why not, half of them's in the same boat as I am.'

'Open the door, Doris.'

'Can't.'

Doris heard them talking amongst themselves, then Stella asked, as if she was concerned – like hell she was – 'Why can't yer open the door, Doris?'

'Cos there's a bloody murderer about. Haven't yer heard? And you just might be it.'

'Open the door, yer silly old bag,' Hammerman shouted, losing his patience as he pounded his fist on the glass.

Doris prayed for it to crack so he could slice his veins in half, but the devil looks after his own. No such luck.

'I've told yer. There's no money. Are yer deaf or what? It's Houghton Feast for Christ's sake.'

'Where's Jacko?' Hammerman demanded.

'Like I'm gonna tell you, yer great creep,' Doris muttered under her breath, then said loudly, 'He's got a job away, some-where down the country to pay you off, yer greedy scumbag.'

'I don't believe yer. He owes and you owe, and I want paying, so stop taking the piss, yer old bag.'

'That's the second time yer've called me an old bag.' Doris was becoming very agitated. How dare he, with a mother like he had.

'Doris . . .'

Not her again.

'What?'

'I've left some pop and sweeties on the step for Melanie.'
Like I'm gonna fall for that old chestnut.

'Aye, right, she'll get them later . . . Oh and if I remember rightly, Mr bloody Hammerman as yer calls yerself now, it's yer own mother that was the bag. I remember her tarting herself up and flaunting herself down Hendon docks. Hussy, that's what she was, a dirty stinking cheap hussy. So there.'

That was it, Doris was having no more. Turning, she stormed back down the passageway into the kitchen slamming the door behind her.

Outside on the step Hammerman was livid, purple-faced, as he marched down the path with Stella in tow.

'The cheeky old bastard, for two pins I'd strangle the old twat.'

Stella shrugged. She was on a percentage, which meant if they didn't collect it in, she didn't get paid, and already this week had shown very poor returns. She knew though that Hammerman would be back, the old woman had tried his patience too far with her cheeky gob. She felt sorry for Melanie, stuck with the old bat all day. Shouldn't be allowed.

They climbed into the car and drove off into the next street where they had four other calls. They had been at it an hour already and it was only half past eight now. Hammerman was determined to catch everybody in this morning.

Stella really had left Melanie some pop and sweets on the step, she brought them every week. There was something about Melanie that made your heart go out to her, poor little mite.

If she'd looked up at the bedroom window as they'd walked away she would have seen Melanie's worried little face staring at them.

Lorraine sat at the breakfast bar brooding over her corn-flakes. She'd had no choice this morning, everything had been ready and waiting for her when she'd come down a few minutes ago after a restless night. She stirred the remaining few flakes round and round, praying that the strangler would be satisfied with two women – but she had a very strong hunch that this business was far from over.

'Penny for them, love,' Peggy said, leaning over her shoulder and practically falling in her face.

'Mind yer own business, Peggy darling . . . And where's yer best friend this morning?' Lorraine looked around the kitchen for her mother.

'She's having a lie-in, so I made breakfast for all of us.' The last eight words made it very clear that breakfast wasn't optional.

Lorraine pushed the bowl to one side and put the plate of bacon and eggs in front of her. She'd eat nothing more for a month if she swallowed this lot, but she would have to make the effort – though she knew that if Peggy didn't find a new love soon, then flat hunting would be the order of the day. She'd liked living back with her mam, and it had been a huge relief to have her around when the nasty business of the divorce had first started, but living with her mam and Peggy both was just too much.

And where was her mam, anyway? 'She never lies in.'

'Well she is this morning.'

'Why?' Lorraine insisted.

'There yer go, being the detective. Can't yer just shut up and eat up.'

Lorraine did, at least for long enough to swallow some bacon and one of the eggs.

'I'm going in to see her.' She wiped her mouth with the napkin, threw it on the plate and walked down the passageway to her mother's bedroom.

Peggy tutted. 'I knew what she'd do.'

Lorraine knocked lightly before walking in. Mavis was

sitting propped up against the lilac pillows with a cup of tea in her hand.

'What's the matter, Mam?'

'Why nothing, pet,' Mavis said. 'What makes yer think there was anything wrong?'

'The fact that you're lying through yer eye teeth, Mam. For one thing yer sitting there as white as a ghost, and Peggy in there is about as bad a liar as you are.'

Mavis sighed. She'd known this would happen and had prepared a speech, but faced with Lorraine's agitation she'd forgotten it.

Mavis's sigh made Lorraine look sharply at her mother. 'Come on, Mam, yer beginning to seriously freak me out here. What's wrong? There's nothing you can't tell me.'

'Honestly, love, I'm fine. Just thought I'd take it easy for a change.' But the look on Mavis's face told Lorraine she knew she'd been caught.

'Mam please, yer frightening me now. What is it?'

'Sorry, love,' Mavis paused for a moment to gather her thoughts. 'It's just, just that I have this er . . .'

'What?' Lorraine said impatiently, desperate to get whatever her mother was hiding out in the open.

'It's just a silly little lump on my breast, that's all.'

Lorraine felt as if the breath had been knocked out of her. It took her a moment to speak. 'That's all! Mam, how can you –'

'It's nothing to worry about, honestly,' Mavis tried to calm her daughter. 'Dr Mountjoy says he's eighty per cent certain that it's just a cyst or something like.'

But Lorraine could hear the wobble in her mother's voice, although she was completely unprepared for what came next.

Mavis burst into tears.

'Jesus, Mam.' Lorraine crossed the room in a second and, sitting on the edge of the bed, she put her arms around her mother and cuddled her. Stroking her hair, Lorraine could feel Mavis's slim body shaking with silent sobs.

'You're not telling me everything, are yer? Please, Mam, how long?'

'It's only a few weeks, love. It's in my right breast, very very tiny.' Mavis looked down at the offending breast as if she still could not quite believe it had let her down in such a drastic way.

Lorraine felt herself go cold all over, as if she was sitting in a warm sunny room and someone had opened the door to winter. The women in her family had a tendency to breast cancer. Her grandmother, an aunt and an older cousin had all succumbed to the dreadful illness. On the other hand, she told herself trying to bring a little optimism, quite a few of the Hunt women had lived full lives without ever feeling the dread that a strategically placed lump brings.

She squeezed her mother's hand.

Mavis squeezed back, then said, 'I didn't want to tell yer, pet. There was no need for yer to worry, not until we knew for certain.'

But Lorraine was worried, worried and hurt that Mavis hadn't confided in her.

'So when were yer gonna tell me?' She hadn't meant to sound so abrupt, and winced when she saw the pain in Mavis's eyes.

'Sometime this weekend, love . . . I go into hospital next week to have the lump removed and tested . . .' She made a feeble attempt at a joke. 'I may bring it home in a jar, yer know, put it on the window sill.'

'Mam.'

Mavis smiled, 'Honest, Lorry, it is frightening, but Dr Mountjoy's practically convinced it's nothing.'

'The great Dr Mountjoy has X-ray eyes now I suppose.'

Standing up, Lorraine paced to the window. Outside, Peggy was hanging washing on the line.

Lorraine spun round. 'That's why Peggy's here isn't it, she hasn't fell out with her new amour at all, has she?'

Mavis nodded. 'I had to tell somebody, and my instinct was to protect you. Yer've had it bad enough this year, pet, there was no need to tell yer until everything was sorted . . . And Peggy's good for me, yer know that.'

'Oh, Mam.' Lorraine could barely swallow past the lump in her throat. 'Yer sure now that Mountjoy thinks it's gonna be OK?'

Mavis nodded, 'Eighty per cent.'

'Well . . . With odds like that.' Lorraine smiled, but mentally she crossed her fingers; cancer in the family must surely knock a big wedge off the eighty per cent. But, if this was the way Mavis wanted to play it . . .

'I'm still a bit angry with yer, Mam, that yer wouldn't of told me first, but I want yer to know, I'm in your corner.'

Mavis smiled. 'I knew yer would be, pet.' She lifted the covers and got out of bed. 'Really, yer know I don't even feel poorly, just a bit washed out from the worry. It's Peggy who won't let me do anything.'

Linking arms with Lorraine she walked down the passageway and into the kitchen. 'So, pet, how's that big hunk of a man?'

'Clark? He's fine.'

Mavis laughed, 'Yer know fine well I don't mean Clark.'

'Carter?' This time Lorraine laughed.

They talked around the subject for the next ten minutes, then Lorraine had to leave for work, but she did so with a heavy heart.

Cancer, her mam might have cancer, she thought, over and over as she drove to work.

'Time they had a fucking cure,' she muttered as the police

110

station came into sight. 'Instead of pissing around and grabbing millions for useless remedies and expensive treatments that never work.' She slapped the steering wheel in frustration over and over, with the palm of her hand.

No, she thought, turning into the yard and beeping at a bunch of school-kids who were already late, and sauntering over the road without a care in the world. *Gotta think positive.*

It will not be cancer.

No way.

She got out of the car, and locked it – not out of habit but because last week some cheeky little rat, on a dare or a crack trip, had had the nerve to come into the station car park and steal Clark's car. His face had been a picture.

Melanie stood in the garden looking up at the sky. Behind her back her fingers were firmly crossed. Just days to go now. She'd been careful not to stand on any cracks in the path: *Stand on a crack break yer nana's back.* Best of all, she'd seen two magpies together, and that meant really good luck. Now all she needed was a black cat and it wouldn't rain at all. Even if the weatherman on the telly, and Nana's hips and legs, said it would.

Her own leg wasn't so bad either today, but the school was still closed and Suzy was at the dentist.

Dad had really stretched her toes out last night, and although it had hurt at the time – she winced when she remembered just how much it had hurt – it was always better the next day, for a while.

'Got yer!'

Melanie shrieked as strong hands grasped her from behind and whirled her high in the air.

'Dad! Nana said that you'd already gone up the market, that I'd missed yer.'

'I did, pet, but after I dropped Robbie and Mickey off I came back to see whether my favourite girl mightn't like a trip down the library, what with there being no school or nothing. What d'yer think?'

Melanie nodded vigorously – she loved the library.

'OK, I'll give yer a lend of my library card an' all so you can choose a good lot of books to bring back. An' tell yer what . . .'

'What?' giggled Melanie, really pleased that she'd have this unexpected time with her dad.

'Promise not to leave yer there like Nana did, neither!'

Jacko had left the boys to open up the stall partly because he did want to spend some time with his much-loved daughter and to check that last night's exercises had helped ease the pain of her leg. But finding Doris trying to make tea without any tea bags that morning, when a full box stood right in front of her on the counter, had reminded him that he desperately needed to work out what was wrong with her. He'd decided there and then to take a couple of hours off and make the promised visit to the library. It was there that he'd found the books which taught him all about Melanie's condition and how he might help her and Jacko was convinced that it was the place to try to solve the puzzle of Doris's growing absent-mindedness.

Arriving at the library with Melanie, he left his daughter happily browsing in the children's section, but when he asked for Christina at the desk he was told that she hadn't turned up for work. Disappointed, Jacko did his best in medical reference but had to finally admit that the whole subject was just too large for him to tackle. He knew deep down that he needed to get proper advice.

As he sat with his head in his hands a small set of fingers crept in to grasp hold of his and he felt his heart lift. Gathering Melanie to him in a huge hug he told himself that as long as he had her, there was nothing he couldn't face.

'Shall we go now, Dad? I've chosen.'

Jacko smiled to see his daughter clutching a pile of books with one on the weather, which she must have found in the adult section, at the very top.

'Aye, pet. But tell yer what, let's see if we can't find something a bit more interesting fer yer than that one, eh?'

11

A couple of hours later, having dropped Melanie clutching her precious books outside the house, Jacko was back at work on the stall and already serving his twentieth customer. He put the money for a dozen blood oranges in his apron pocket, then looked up to see the man he'd just served staring at him.

'Can I help yer with something else?' Jacko asked.

The small pot-bellied man smiled at him, and it was a cold smile that at once had Jacko on edge.

Then he laughed sarcastically before saying, 'I don't think so. And after today we won't be helping you. Yer've been what yer might call caught red-handed.'

He pulled a badge out of his pocket, and with a mean smirk shoved it in Jacko's face. Jacko's heart sank as he read the logo and the name that went with it.

The blood-orange man was from the social security.

Jacko groaned. 'Shit.'

'Aye, and you're right in it.'

'Look,' Jacko spread his hands wide, keeping a calm,

friendly smile on his face despite the panicky feeling growing in the pit of his stomach . . . 'I'm only helping out for a few days, while the gaffer's away on holiday, like.'

'Tell that to the guys who have to listen to yer sob story. My job's just to catch yer . . . So consider yerself caught.'

Turning, he grinned at a blond man who was standing at the second-hand book stall opposite. Jacko had noticed him ten minutes or more earlier, but had never dreamed he was from the social security.

Sly bastard. Pretending to be a book lover. He'd even heard the bastard ask Pete, the stall owner, if he had an original copy of *The Lord of the Rings*. The git greasy twat.

'Here, come on now . . .' The attempt at friendliness over, Jacko was panicking openly now, fighting to keep tears of defeat out of his eyes. The very last thing he needed was to have his benefits stopped. Not with the debt he was in. Not with Melanie to look after. Not with Doris in the state she was in.

Shit, shit, shit.

He would beg if he had to, the twat must have a heart somewhere. 'There must be some way round this, mate.'

'I'm not yer mate,' the man said harshly.

But Jacko never heard him, his mind was in overdrive. Christ, how the fuck was he gonna manage?

He was behind with everything.

And some of the people he owed money to . . .

Oh God. He shook his head. Hammerman was getting nastier by the week, and there was no knowing how much longer Jacko could stall him.

Thinking that maybe the man had not heard him properly, he tried again. 'Yer can ask the gaffer when he gets back. He'll tell yer, I'm only helping . . .'

The man had heard it all before and was totally unsympathetic as he said, 'Sorry, only doing me job.'

Sorry? The grin on his face told Jacko he was far from sorry. 'Ohh, that's all you lot ever say. Fucking parasites, the whole bastard lot of yer.'

'I think yer'll find, sir, that you are the parasite.'

Jacko leaned forward. He felt like grabbing the little creep by his throat, but thankfully some last drop of rational thinking stopped him: the last thing he needed was an assault charge against him. Instead he said, as sarcastically as the man had earlier, 'Didn't yer know that some parasites is good for yer . . . ? Anyhow, go on fuck off. I hope yer fucking nose falls off. Bastard.'

And the man smirked and for a moment there was silence between them.

'What's the matter Jacko? He giving yer some grief?' Mickey asked, glaring at the man as he and Robbie arrived back from the sandwich van with cups of tea and a plate full of bacon sandwiches.

Robbie gave the man a quick once-over – he'd seen him somewhere before and then it came to him, but before he could put the tray down and drag Mickey away, the man clocked him.

'And who might youse two be then?'

'Tom and Jerry,' Robbie said, as he and Mickey turned and took off to hide behind the material stall.

'Never mind,' the man was cocksure as he took a small camera out of his pocket. 'Twenty-six snaps, all of you and yer mouse and cat friends, OK? We'll sharp find out who they are the minute they come in to sign on. Or off.' Turning, he looked at his friend and shrugged. 'Whatever the case may be.'

Now Jacko was really angry. 'Are yer gonna stand there and gloat all day, yer prick? Or are yer gonna do us a small favour and tell us who the hell grassed?'

'Why would I do that?'

'So I can have a friendly little word with the horrible bastard,' Jacko replied through gritted teeth.

The small man leaned forward, knocking a stack of green apples over. He ignored them as they tumbled off the stall. 'I've answered harder questions.'

Jacko was about to explode, his hands gripping the metal stall, when the man said with another one of his cocky smirks, 'Next time yer decide to play hero, make sure yer mug doesn't get in the papers.'

Jacko gasped. Shit. The story on the chip shop fine. Heart beating wildly, he stood open-mouthed as the two men walked away.

That was it. He was fairly banged to rights.

There was no way of getting out of this one.

No giro in the morning. Shit.

Lance Halliday flipped open his top-of-the-range mobile, and putting it to his ear he listened intently for a minute. A slow smile full of spite spread over his face.

His sister, guessing it was the call they had been waiting for, matched his smile. 'When?' she asked, as he put the phone back in his pocket.

'Now.'

She clapped her hands in anticipation, then snatched the bottle of vodka from Dan, and took a large swig. Dan, a Goth whose chest was covered with last night's vomit, and who called himself a wall artist, watched her guardedly from under hooded lids.

They were sitting on a seat next to the pathway in the middle of Russel Woods. The seat was covered with graffiti – Dan was a regular here. Slowly, almost pleadingly, he raised his hand up for the vodka.

'He coming?' Julie cocked her head to one side and asked her brother.

'No, leave him, he's wasted.'

With a sly smile she held the vodka out to him, and just before Dan's hand went round the bottle she dropped it. The fire in Dan's eyes was the most emotion he'd shown in over a year.

'Bitch,' he said, moving as fast as he could to rescue the bottle which had fallen on the grass, and was quickly regurgitating its contents. By the time he'd picked it up, Julie and Lance were already on their way.

Doris took the cheese and onion pie she'd baked out of the oven. The crust was a lovely golden brown, and the smell tantalising.

'Ooh, if it wouldn't burn me mouth out I'd have a piece now,' she muttered. Her mouth watering, she put the pie on the kitchen bench to cool. *Melanie and Jacko will love this.* And for a moment she felt utterly content. Then memories of the darkness which haunted her more and more frequently came rushing back: the missing hours, the missing days, the gaps she tried to pass off as simple absent-mindedness. But she knew there was more to it than that – she knew common forgetfulness, and she knew this wasn't it.

She sat down heavily. *And what'll happen if I'm not around?* Who would look after Melanie when she needed to stay home, with Jacko working every hour he could to provide for her? Who would make sure she never felt her mother's betrayal? Who would give her all the help and guidance only a woman could? *I'm just gonna have to pull myself together. I'm needed round here, and that's that.*

She stood up again to turn off the oven, and a moment later she grunted, the centre of her back blossoming with a burning pain.

Oh, God, please no.

Not a heart attack.

She whimpered with fright. Her husband had died alone – and it was both a guilt, and a fear she'd lived with for years.

Then she heard a high-pitched giggle behind her and spun round. A boy not quite a man, and a girl not quite a woman – one equipped with a folding pole, the other with a base-ball bat – were slowly moving towards her. Towards the open kitchen door.

She looked down and saw the stone at her feet, guessed that the girl had thrown it. Thankful that she wasn't at least at this moment about to drop down dead from a heart attack, she said angrily, 'Get out. How dare yer come in here off the streets. If it's money yer after then yer haven't got a snow-ball's chance in hell.'

They just stared at her.

'Go on, go . . . Now. Before my son gets home and gives yer both a hiding!' Their silence was beginning to scare her. And there was something in both of their eyes which set off serious alarm bells. No actually, now she looked closer she realised that it was that there was nothing in their eyes. Just a cold twin vacancy. Doris's heart was pounding so loud that she thought both of them must surely be able to hear it.

Then the boy leapt forward, and punched her right eye. Doris felt the skin split, and a moment later she was blinded as blood poured into her eye. At the same time she felt the baseball bat pound into her left arm.

They're gonna kill me! flashed through her brain and then, hard on its heels: *No they're fucking not. Aye why, I'll go biting their fucking ankles if I have to.*

She shook her head to clear her vision, then threw herself at them. The girl, a slip of a thing really, was easily knocked to the ground by Doris's bigger bulk. She screamed in anger and amazement. The boy however, muscle-bound as he was, proved a much more dangerous enemy.

He laughed. 'Lie down, yer stupid old bat.'

'Up yours!' Doris screamed, lunging for him. Her own son had never talked to her like that and she was having no punk off the street thinking he could. Ready and waiting, Halliday slapped her and she spun round and tripped over the girl who was just getting up. Banging her head on the side of the pantry door, Doris was out of it in moments.

'Come on you,' Lance snarled at Julie, 'yer stupid cow, before somebody comes.' He grabbed Doris's bag from the bench, but tipping it out he found nothing but some old bus tickets, a set of keys, a photograph of a smiling chubby-faced little girl, and a bottle of paracetamols. Cursing, he kicked viciously at the bench sending the just baked pie flying across the kitchen floor.

'Here, yer'll need these.' He threw the tablets at Doris, and they spread out over her prone body like confetti. 'Hammerman says he wants his money,' he added, but couldn't tell whether Doris was together enough to hear him.

His sister stood awkwardly and watched, angrily rubbing the top of her leg where Doris had caught her, until Lance grabbed her arm, spat at the old woman who lay broken on the floor, and the pair of them fled into the street.

Lorraine carried the bunch of flowers, white and pink dahlias, into the house. They were for Mavis, just a small show of her love and support.

Hearing voices from the sitting room and expecting just Mavis and Peggy to be in there, she was surprised to find Luke sitting with them. Seeing her, Peggy, who was behind Luke when he turned to look at Lorraine, blew him a kiss. Lorraine frowned at her and Peggy grinned.

'Hi, boss,' Luke said, standing to greet her. 'I missed yer when I got back from talking to Samantha's family, so I thought I'd find you here.'

Lorraine looked up at him. 'Anything?'

'Well they're seriously upset that their only source of income has gone and got herself killed, but I don't think there's more to it than that. Though they're a pretty nasty pair.'

Lorraine nodded and handed the flowers to Mavis. Wondering why Luke was here.

Must be to see Mavis.

She frowned. *Don't say he knew about Mam before I did an' all. Jesus.*

'So what yer after, Luke?' Her voice was abrupt and Mavis looked strangely at her.

Luke wondered briefly what he'd done, before saying quietly, 'There's been another girl attacked.'

'Shit . . . When, in broad daylight?'

'No, last night.'

Lorraine frowned, 'Last night,' she echoed. 'And attacked, rather than . . .'

'Yes, boss. She's alive – though only just. Only thing is,' he looked at the ground rather awkwardly, 'Sara Jacobs took the call and she's sorted it herself.'

'She what!' Lorraine spat.

'Aye, Carter rang me as soon as he found out.'

'The cheeky madam,' Peggy said. 'Yer want to watch out for people like that, Lorry, she'll be having your job next.'

'Fat chance.'

Luke thought there might be something in what Peggy had said, but he kept it to himself as he went on, 'Law of averages says there must be a connection, but Carter's had his nose to the ground and found out that Sara's adamant that there's not.'

'Is she now? Why's that? How badly hurt is the girl? Any bruising around the neck?'

'She's in Sunderland Hospital. Alive, but very poorly. A

broken collarbone, cracked ribs and some deep gouges on her face and neck, but that's mostly off of the trees and the undergrowth – she was found up in Russel Woods. Allan Greve found her – and yer know how thick the trees are up there. There's no bruising as far as I know, but she's out cold so we'll have to wait till she comes round.'

'Yer seem pretty well informed,' Lorraine said wryly. She'd bet Sara hadn't kept Luke up to speed of her own accord.

'Carter had a look at the notes.'

'Good for Ginge,' Peggy interrupted.

Lorraine looked at Peggy as if she wasn't there, then said. 'Right, come on. We'll pay her a visit. You do have a name for her?'

'Aye, Christina Jenkins. She –'

'Christina! Oh no!'

This time Lorraine looked properly at Peggy. 'What's that? Do you know her?'

'Course I do. She's Stan Jenkins's daughter. Lives up on Tulip Crescent. The one whose mum had that horrible acci-dent years back. Sweet girl. She –' and Peggy burst into tears.

Lorraine knelt down beside her. 'Now, Peggy. I know yer upset but I need you to tell me anything you know about Christina. It might help us catch whoever attacked her.'

Peggy looked up at Lorraine through tear-stained eyes. 'I know, love. And I didn't even know her very well – it's just such a shock. I, er . . .' she thought hard, '. . . I don't know what to tell you. She was a quiet girl, kept to herself. Worked at the library and never went out much as far as I know. Pretty little thing, though. Dark hair, nice face.'

Lorraine looked at Luke and knew he was thinking the same thing she was. Diane and Samantha had been dressed up to the nines, faces covered with slap – hair aside, it didn't sound as if Christina fitted the pattern. Maybe Sara was right in thinking this attack wasn't linked to the stranglings. But the only way they'd find out was by getting down to the hospital sharpish.

After they had gone Peggy, having recovered from her crying fit, looked at Mavis. 'Made for each other, them two.'

'Aye, but our Lorraine's the only one who can't see it.'

As Jacko, Robbie, and Mickey were on their way home from the market, the right front tyre on the van blew, just past the Shiney Row roundabout.

'Shit . . . What the fuck else can go wrong?' Jacko muttered as he managed to keep the van straight, and gently steer it into the side of the road.

'Got a spare?' Robbie asked.

'Aye, such as it is.'

The three of them jumped out and went round to the back of the van. Jacko took the spare out.

'Jesus,' Mickey gasped. 'It's as bald as a coot.'

Jacko shrugged, 'It'll have to do guys.' He rolled the tyre round to the front and in minutes they had the spare on the van. Wiping his hands on a rag, Jacko climbed back in. 'Just got to call in at the doll shop, then we'll be home in no time.'

'The doll shop?' Mickey looked confused.

'For Melanie,' Robbie explained. 'But Jesus, Jacko, how many dolls has Melanie got?' he added, glancing sideways at the three teenage girls wearing very short skirts who strutted along the street beside them.

'Well, she's not been too good this week yer know, her leg's been playing her up, poor bairn. And this doll's special – it's a collector's one, and I've been paying for it in instalments. Today's the last one. It's a surprise. I have to get it, man, Melanie's gonna love it.'

'Can yer eat it?' Mickey asked, confused. Jacko had just got cut off by the social and he was buying dolls?

Jacko groaned. 'I wish.'

'What we gonna do tomorrow when we have to sign on?' Robbie wondered out loud.

'God knows,' Mickey mumbled, his head in his hands.

'We'll think of something,' Jacko said. 'Don't worry, man.' He didn't let on to them that he was worried sick himself. And that his mind had been in a turmoil all day. Figuring out bad solution after bad solution then resigning himself to the bald fact that there was no solution.

Twenty minutes later, they turned into their street and got the shock of their lives. All thoughts of the dole and where the next penny was coming from left their minds instantly.

Jacko's house was cordoned off by police tape, and an ambulance was standing by.

Doll in his hand and his heart in his mouth, Jacko jumped down from the van. Leaping over the waist-high wall he landed on Doris's immaculate lawn that nobody, under sentence of death, was allowed to step on, and ran into the house.

'Melanie!' he shouted. 'Mam!'

For God's sake, which one is it? Please let them be OK.

'In here, Jacko,' he heard Dolly Smith say.

He hurried into the sitting room. 'What the . . .'

Doris was surrounded by two large policemen and two ambulance men – one of whom was even bigger than the largest policeman, the other a small wiry man with a grey goatee beard, who was trying to stop the blood which was flowing freely from a large cut at the top of his mother's eye.

'Christ, Mam. What the hell happened?' He had not missed the angry black and yellow bruising down her arm.

'I was attacked, son . . . In me own home.' Doris was near to tears.

'Shocking if yer ask me,' Dolly Smith said from the corner, where she was drinking a cup of tea. 'Nothing's sacred any

124

more, when an old woman can be attacked so viciously in her own home. Especially in broad daylight. Eeee.'

'Who, Mam?' Jacko felt a burning white rage inside, he slapped his fist in his hand. 'I'll kill the bastard, just wait till I find him. He'll never walk again, that's for sure.'

'I'll pretend I didn't hear that,' the larger of the policemen said.

'Yer can pretend what yer want. 'Cos I guarantee yer'll not catch the bastard. That's if yer even bother to look.' And besides, Jacko already had a horrible feeling he knew who was behind the attack – and him getting his social cut off wasn't going to make things any better.

The policeman was about to come back with a retort when he saw his partner frowning at him. Getting the message, he closed his mouth.

Jacko turned back to Doris, and kneeling down in front of her he took her hand. 'Who was it, Mam?'

Doris looked deeply into her son's eyes. She tried to shake her head but the ambulance man stopped her. 'Don't you move, love.'

Staying obediently still, she looked at her son. 'Kids, Jacko.'

'Kids? What do yer mean, kids? Big kids as in eighteen or whatever, or little kids . . . Not that it fucking matters, either way somebody's gonna pay.'

'I think I might have seen them around, but they don't live on the Seahills, Jacko.' And she started to get agitated again.

'OK, Mam,' Jacko soothed her. 'Just chill, we'll get it sorted. Did they say anything?'

Doris looked confused. 'What do you mean?'

'I, er . . .' How could he ask what he needed to in front of the policemen? 'Can you remember anything they said?' he tried again. If the attack had come from Hammerman, he'd have wanted to make sure his message got through. But, looking at Doris's bewildered face, Jacko realised he'd have to wait to get the whole story out of her.

Then, as sudden as an unexpected bucket of water in the face, he realised that Melanie was nowhere to be seen.

'Where's Melanie?' he asked, looking around the room.

'Who's Melanie?' one of the policeman asked.

'My daughter.'

The policeman shook his head. 'How old?'

'Eight,' Jacko felt that familiar panic rising in him again. 'She's eight. I dropped her back here this morning after we'd been up the library.'

'Never seen any kids the whole time we've been here. Dolly Smith phoned us, she was coming to the hospital in case you weren't back – that's if we ever manage to get your mother there. Tough old bugger, isn't she.'

Jacko didn't need to be told just how tough Doris was, he knew. His main concern now was Melanie.

'Mam, listen love, yer've got to concentrate.' He winced, then gritted his teeth when he looked at her face.

Bastards. Nasty, nasty bastards.

Doris looked confused for a moment, then she pushed the ambulance man's hand out of the way. 'I don't know, son, it, it seems ages though since I saw her. I'm sorry, I should have took better care.' Doris's face crumpled and she started to cry.

'It's all right, Mam. Please don't cry.' Biting his lip Jacko looked around. *Not now. Please don't let her have one of her turns now.* He stared at the settee for a moment as if Melanie might suddenly materialise from underneath the cream-coloured cushions singing at the top of her lungs, like she usually did.

The ambulance man, who was still trying to stop Doris from losing even more blood, didn't know any Melanie and wasn't one bit bothered about her whoever she was. His only concern was his patient and her refusal to go into hospital. As far as he could judge, the poor old bugger needed at least eight stitches in her eyebrow. He turned to her son.

'Look, man, yer've got to talk some sense into her. She's got to get to the hospital. At her age she can't afford to lose this much blood; she needs stitches, and a tetanus injection, very soon.'

Jacko, his mind on Melanie, stared at the man for a moment until his brain caught up with the situation then, turning quickly and practically marching, he went into the hallway and grabbed Doris's blue coat from the peg, noticing with a pang that Melanie's coat was missing.

Back in the room he said, 'Come on, Mam, stop messing about, eh. If he says yer have to go to the hospital then that's where yer going. No arguing.'

'But . . .' She looked around her in confusion. 'But what about Melanie? If yer can't find her I'm not going anywhere. The poor bairn might be hurt somewhere.'

Ignoring for the moment the stab of fright that pierced his heart at the thought that Melanie might be hurt, Jacko gently took hold of his mother's arm, and began to help her up. Until he got Doris shipped off to the hospital he couldn't start to search for his daughter.

'Come on, Mam. I mean it. I'll find our Melanie, and anyhow,' he forced himself to sound optimistic, 'we're probably worrying for nowt. She'll just be playing somewhere and have forgotten the time, the way kids do, they're all like that. So stop worrying and leave it to me.'

Doris sighed. The problem with her Jacko was that he could be as stubborn as she was once he set his mind to it. Deciding that she had no choice, because her eye was throbbing like hell now and the blood was getting on her nerves, she moved to get up and the blood began to flow again. Knowing when she was beaten, Doris allowed the ambulance man and her son to help her on with her coat. But she flatly refused to get on a stretcher or sit in a wheelchair. The ambulance man, pleased to get her moving, waived the rules and gave her his arm.

Dolly Smith slipped her coat on. 'I'll go with her, Jacko, you just look for the bairn.'

'Thanks, Dolly, yer a gem. I'll get through as soon as I can.' He paused for a moment. 'I take it yer haven't seen her at all, have yer?'

Dolly shook her head. 'Sorry, love, never seen her all day. Try little Suzy Lumsdon, the pair of them are nearly always together.'

'Aye, I'll do that.'

Jacko watched the ambulance leave, then turned to Mickey and Robbie who had hovered outside and caught up with what was going on from the neighbours. 'Where the hell can she be?'

'I wouldn't worry, Jacko, yer know it's not the first time,' Mr Skillings said. 'Remember a few months back when yer got the police and she'd fallen asleep behind Vanessa's settee.'

'Aye,' Mickey laughed. 'Though how she did's a mystery with all the racket in there.'

'Then there was that time her and our Suzy went missing last Easter, and the little buggers were found up Penshaw Monument rolling their Easter eggs. The coppers laughed about that one, didn't they.'

'Why aye, lad. Yer worrying about nowt.' Mr Skillings nodded wisely.

Only slightly mollified, Jacko said, 'OK, I'll give her half an hour, but first I'll just have a talk with Suzy, if yer mam won't mind.'

'Course she won't.'

And together the three of them crossed the road and went into Robbie's house.

He turns the key in the lock as quietly as he can and then creeps inside the dark house.

'Mustn't wake Mother,' he whispers. 'Ohh, no. Mother needs her beauty sleep. Mother'll be cross.'

Climbing the stairs on tiptoe, he freezes when one gives out an almighty creak. But it's OK and moments later he is safely in his room.

Reaching up, he lifts one of his boxes down from the top of the wardrobe and gently eases off its lid. 'All my treasures safe,' he murmurs. 'Oh yes, all my treasures safe.' He takes a plain blue hair ribbon out of his jacket pocket and is just about to put it in the box when he hears the querulous voice from the bedroom next door.

'Is that you? Where have yer been all this time? Where have yer been? I've been calling and calling an' I badly need the bathroom an' all.'

He leaves his bedroom, shutting the door firmly behind him. 'Now, now, Mother,' he calls soothingly as he makes his way across the landing. 'I've only been downstairs. I must have had the telly up loud 'cos I never heard yer.'

Going into Mother's room he almost gags at the smell of age and decay but manages to stifle it.

'I'm here now, Mother. Yer little boy is here to look after yer, so he is.'

12

Lorraine stifled a yawn as she and Luke arrived at the hospital. They walked across to the entrance, Lorraine nodded once to the security guard, and they took the lift to Christina's floor in silence.

His boss seemed preoccupied with something and Luke couldn't help thinking how beautiful Lorraine looked even when she was distracted and in the middle of a case that was keeping them all awake at night. He loved her hair in a french plait, loved how after a few hours, tiny hairs at the nape of her neck and beside her ears escaped, creating a sort of glow around her face.

He'd hated being in Scotland – not that he had anything against the country, nor the natives. One was beautiful and the others were really friendly. He'd just missed Lorraine – more than he ever thought he would.

But had she missed him?

He'd not had much time to question Carter, but in their occasional phone calls Carter had never mentioned anything at all that would give him hope. Even though he'd skirted round the issue once or twice.

Reaching Christina's room, Luke stepped back so that Lorraine could enter first. She gave him a little half smile, and Luke devoured it.

The woman on the bed was still unconscious. Her long dark hair fanned the pillows. Dark circles under her eyes made her look even paler than she was, and the hospital-issue white nightgown did not help any.

A bald-headed man, somewhere in his middle fifties with a huge beer belly that was only just restrained by a scarlet checked shirt, sat in a chair by her bedside.

'What do yer want?' he said sullenly. 'She's been seen by enough bloody doctors to last her a flaming lifetime. And she still hasn't woke up.'

'We aren't doctors.' Lorraine took her badge out.

'Ohh, you lot. I've already spoken to your boss. The little dark one.' He smirked, looked at Luke. 'Women in power, eh. Anyhow, she knows everything I know now, so there's no reason for me to be speaking to underlings.' He turned back to his newspaper, dismissing them at once with the gesture.

Uh oh, Luke thought. He looked at Lorraine, and was amazed at how much she had kept her cool.

'I am sorry, sir,' she started politely, 'but you have been misinformed, or drawn your own conclusions. Constable Jacobs is not my boss, nor is she the boss of this gentleman here. And so,' she leaned forward, and said ever so sweetly, 'I'd appreciate it if we could run through a few things right now.'

Stan Jenkins looked both Lorraine and Luke over, and shook his head. 'No, fuck it. I'm not going through all that bollocks again just for your fun. If Jacobs wasn't the boss, I want to talk to the person who is.'

'Well that,' Lorraine said, rather less sweetly, 'would be me. My name is Lorraine Hunt. Detective Inspector Lorraine Hunt. And unless you cooperate, I will personally have your arse off that chair so fast it'll take the skin off.'

Jenkins looked like he was going into shock, 'Yer can't talk to me like that, you're a a a . . .'

'Would woman be the word you're looking for?' Lorraine stated, with a quizzical expression. She'd run into his type before – men who either refused to believe a woman could be in charge, or just refused to deal with them. Full stop. She recognised the look in his eyes as he stared at her – disbelief, dislike and quite a lot of distrust.

'Aye, that.' He wriggled in his chair, the buttons on his shirt threatening to pop at any minute.

'Got a problem with women . . . Sir?'

'Ner, I just . . .'

'What was it you said? "Women in power." You didn't sound too happy about that as a concept.'

'Yes, well, I . . .'

'You what, sir? Strong women make you nervous, do they?'

'No,' he looked thoroughly uncomfortable now. 'It's just that . . .'

'They should be barefoot and pregnant? Is that the phrase yer looking for?'

Red-faced, Jenkins finally managed to heave his bulk out of the chair. 'I'll report yer for harassment if yer not careful. That's my daughter in that bed, I don't need the likes of you and especially not him coming in here and making threats.'

Especially not him? As Luke had said nothing yet, the only thing Jenkins could be objecting to was the colour of his skin. Lorraine was fed up, what this bigot needed was a good bop on the nose, but getting into a fight wasn't going to get her anywhere.

'It's your daughter's welfare that we're here about, sir,' she said tightly. 'Hers and maybe others' as well. So if you could just answer some questions, then we can get on with the business of finding him. OK, sir.' She was quite pleased with herself, it had taken a lot of will-power not to poke him with each word she'd spoken.

Jenkins stood eye to eye with Lorraine. It took him a few moments to realise that he could not bully her like he bullied his daughter and had bullied his wife before her.

'What do yer want to know?' he said sulkily, still not acknowledging Luke's presence in the room. He obviously disliked blacks even more than women.

With a smile, Lorraine said, 'Luke will be keeping yer company until your daughter wakes up. I don't think you, or constable Jacobs, have realised that your daughter may need protection.'

'What do yer mean?'

Lorraine paused and looked over at Christina. She was so battered that it was hard to tell whether an attempt had been made at manual strangulation – she'd need Christina awake and talking to tell her that, and until then there wasn't any precise link to the other deaths. 'I mean,' she said carefully, 'that the attacker may well choose to find your daughter and finish off what he started. Think about it: chances are she can identify him, in which case both of you are at risk.'

For the first time Jenkins actually looked properly at Luke, as if weighing him up. After a moment he seemed satisfied that Luke's tall muscular frame was adequate enough to defend him if necessary. Begrudgingly he shrugged and said, 'Whatever.'

Lorraine signalled with her head for Luke to follow her into the corridor.

Once there, she said, 'Get what yer can out of him, Luke. I doubt he's got anything to do with it – he's a bully and a bigot, but if he was going to attack his daughter I don't think he'd drag her out into the woods to do it. But still . . .'

'And what about the other deaths?' Luke asked. 'What do you reckon? Is this the same man?'

Lorraine chewed her lip. 'It's too soon to know – we need her conscious – but my money's on it being the same man. I'm not a great believer in coincidence. And if it is, she's been damn lucky to escape.'

But before Luke could answer they both turned to the sound of high heels tapping up the corridor.

Luke smiled at the small dainty woman, in the very high heels, whose long brown hair hung in a plait down her back. Sandra Gilbride. A legend on the Seahills estate – and someone both Luke and Lorraine had got to know quite well when the Lumsdon girl had disappeared a few months back.

'Hello, Sandra,' Luke said with a smile, and Lorraine echoed him.

'How is she?' Sandra gestured with her head above the colourful spray of flowers she was carrying.

'Know her well, do you, Sandra?' Lorraine asked.

Sandra thought for a moment. 'Tell yer the truth, I don't think anybody knows Christina that well. She's a quiet lass, that one. I'm really just the messenger from the committee, we bought these flowers for her out of the funds . . . Is she all right?'

'She will be,' Lorraine said, mentally crossing her fingers, 'but she's asleep now . . . If yer want to take the flowers in, I'll wait here and we can talk on the way out.'

'Fair enough. Not much point sitting about talking to the walls, is there.'

'Yer could talk to her father.'

The face Sandra pulled told Lorraine everything Sandra thought about Stan Jenkins.

Five minutes later, having left Luke sat by Christina's

bed for the duration, the two women were on their way outside.

'So how many years have yer known Christina?' Lorraine asked.

Sandra shrugged. 'I think I must have been about fifteen or something when she was born.'

'So yer've known her all her life?'

'Aye. She was born on the Seahills, same as me.'

'What sort of woman was her mother, can yer remember?'

'Quiet.'

'Quiet, is that it?'

'More or less. I don't think anyone knew her particularly well. She spoke if she saw yer coming, but she never stood outside talking with the other women, while us kids were playing in the street. Usually, hello was all yer got.'

'Why was that do yer think? Shy?'

Sandra shrugged. 'Can't really say, yer'll have to ask some of the older ones – Dolly Smith, Doris Musgrove, they'll know better than me . . . but that Stan's a right bully an' I'm damn sure he always was. Anyhows, she got run over by a bus when Christina was just a kid. And the talk is that her dad blamed her for it.'

'Blamed who? Christina?'

'Yeah.'

'But that's ridiculous. Why?'

'Can't remember, Doris'll tell yer best. She's practically the only one Christina really talks to. Actually, Christina's just like her Mam like that. Hello if she sees yer and that's about it.'

'OK, Sandra,' Lorraine said with a smile, realising there wasn't much more to be discovered here. 'Thanks.'

She hadn't found out much about Christina, and bearing in mind the fact that Sandra usually knew everything about everybody, that probably meant there wasn't much to tell.

But one thing Lorraine knew for sure: Christina had nothing in common with Diane Fox or Samantha Dankton in terms of her lifestyle. So if she was a victim of this marauding bastard, then what exactly was the link?

Jacko was frantic. He, Mickey and Robbie had searched everywhere. Suzy hadn't had much to say for herself – she hadn't seen Melanie all day – but she seemed quieter than usual and Robbie had wondered whether there was something she wasn't letting on about. He'd tried his best, but all his coaxing couldn't get another word out of her.

And it didn't help that Jacko also had to make frequent trips home to see if Doris was all right. When she'd finally come home, sometime after seven, with eight stitches in her eyebrow, it was all Jacko could do to stop himself from punching holes in the wall.

Doris had given him a very good description of the pair, and Jacko had been shocked and disgusted to find that a girl had been one of them. He'd find them all right, there couldn't be that many totally tattooed freaks with a bald girl as a partner knocking about. He had his contacts.

Doris had been very reticent with the police though, and it wasn't until she was back home that she'd told Jacko that she thought the horrible little swines had been sent by Hammerman. Just as he'd thought.

But that was against all the rules, only the lowest of the low could do what had been done to Doris. And they would suffer, oh would they suffer. That he guaranteed . . . But first things first. Doris was safe and warm at home; Melanie, on the other hand, was still out there somewhere and might be in danger. It felt like she'd been gone hours. The policemen who'd tended to Doris had said they'd file a report and send someone back out, but as the day wore on there was no sign. He'd left Doris phoning to chase them up again and now, under a swiftly darkening sky and a baleful moon, he was back desperately searching for his daughter with half his mind on Melanie and half on what he would do to Hammerman and his sidekicks when he caught up with them. He couldn't believe that Melanie's disappearance had anything to do with Doris's attackers. And yet . . . maybe she'd seen something? Or maybe they'd snatched her as they left? Jacko's mind swung backwards and forwards imagining the worst.

After three full circuits of Russel Woods, Newbottle, Grasswell, the Homelands and the Seahills had thrown up nothing, most of the neighbours had joined in. Every bin and every backyard on the Seahills had been searched. Jacko and Mickey were on there way to the Seahills corner shop – nearly everybody had ran out of batteries and the night could only get darker.

'Hope Mr Stanhill lets us tick them on?' Mickey said. ''Cos I've got nowt left but shrapnel.'

But Jacko's thoughts were elsewhere, until a moment later when a panda car came shooting round the corner.

'About bloody time an' all,' Jacko shouted when he saw them. He stuck out his arm and flagged them down. The panda car stopped and a tall thin policemen got out.

'Have yer come about me bairn?' Jacko asked anxiously. ''Cos I'm outta me mind with worry here. We've searched all over the place and there's no sign of her anywhere.'

'Jacko Musgrove?' The policeman said, with a Middlesbrough accent.

'Aye, it's me bairn Melanie, she's been missing ages. The copper who came to see me Mam said he would report it. That was fucking hours ago, where the hell have yer been? And don't say yer've had to come all the way from bloody Middlesbrough? For God sake.'

'A very busy time in Houghton at the minute, we've been drafted in.'

'So what's so special that it takes yer hours to respond to a missing call about a kid.'

'Well, sir, it seems –' He flicked open a small notebook. 'Melanie Musgrove. Your daughter, I suppose?' He looked at Jacko with a raised eyebrow.

'Aye, get on with it.'

The policeman raised his other eyebrow, then said. 'Well then, as you'll know it seems she has a habit of going missing and then turning up practically under your nose.'

Jacko was stunned for a moment. 'What?'

'She and her friend were found rolling Easter eggs up at Penshaw Monument back in the spring after you pressed the panic button, is that right, sir?'

Jacko nodded.

'And then a week or so after that you reported her missing and found her napping behind a neighbour's settee?'

'Yes,' Jacko interrupted, 'but that was different. She'd never stay out after dark like this, and –'

'But, sir, you must see our position. You'll understand why it wasn't a top priority for the Houghton police – what with the Feast starting soon and all.'

Jacko's shoulders slumped in despair. 'Aye, I might have panicked a couple of times, but yer never know with bairns do yer? And it's better to be safe than sorry.'

'And look what happened to my friend Robbie's sister!' Mickey broke in, unable to hold back any longer. 'She got kidnapped round here just a few months ago, and she nearly died!'

'I know that, son,' said the policeman sharply. 'But that's hardly likely to happen twice in six months, is it. And of course she hadn't done a runner before. Look, we'll keep an eye out for her, honest, but if she turns up phone us at once.' Then he got in his car and slowly drove off.

'I suppose that's what yer call keeping an eye out,' Mickey

said, watching the car resentfully as it disappeared round the corner into Daffodil Crescent. The policeman couldn't have made it more obvious that he thought Melanie was nothing more than a tearaway, a bad kid who made a habit of causing trouble and wasting police time. God, the truth couldn't be more different!

Jacko nodded, 'The cheeky borough bastard.' He looked up the empty street that had been searched over and over, and bit his lip to control a sob. It was pitch black now, and Melanie had never been out in the dark this late before.

He pictured her alone and frightened. The temperature had gone down with the sun, and her leg would be giving her some gyp now all right.

Please God, he silently begged, *please let her be safe. Please bring Melanie home.*

Then he brought his fist down on the wooden gate of number ten, never feeling the splinters that pierced his skin and oblivious to the blood that ran down his hand.

What fucking God.

There is no God.

And fuck him if there is.

A proper God wouldn't let kids go missing, not with all the fucking nonces and creeps out there, just hovering around like fucking wolves waiting for bairns.

'Would yer, yer bastard?' he raised his bloody fist to the sky as the sob he'd been holding back finally escaped, bringing with it a flood of tears.

Hastily he swiped them away.

'I'll tell yer this,' he raged as Mickey, his heart aching for Jacko, stood with his head down. 'If yer are up there, vengeance won't be yours like yer goody two shoes preach. It'll be fucking well mine. I swear I'll kill the bastard who's got her.'

13

Melanie had her eyes tightly closed and was feeling nice and comfortable in the after-effects of a cosy dream in which she had a cream-coloured pony called Clover, with a brown star on his head. She and Suzy had been taking turns riding him, and she had a nice straight leg that never hurt or stiffened up so bad that her toes curled underneath.

Slowly she stretched her arms above her head. Her left plait caught under her shoulder and the action pulled her head back. Flicking it out with her right hand, she then snuggled deeply into the pillow trying to find the dream.

A moment later her small face creased into a puzzled frown, and she froze.

Something was wrong.

Something was badly wrong.

Her senses stretched to the limit.

What was it?

Then she had it.

The smell!!!

This was not her pillow. The smell was all wrong.

Nana put lavender sachets in the pillows, but this pillow didn't smell of lavender. It smelt musty and old.

Quietly, in case there was somebody there, somebody bad, she sniffed.

Slowly her memory returned, and she whimpered in fear.

She didn't want to open her eyes. She wouldn't open them.

Closed was safe.

Closed meant yesterday had never happened.

The minutes ticked by, until she could bear it no longer. Trembling with fear, she opened her eyes and screamed.

Luke rolled his neck from side to side, trying to get rid of the stiffness. He'd spent most of the night in what had to be the most uncomfortable chair in Sunderland hospital. Jenkins, after hours of almost complete stony silence, had gone home sometime after three.

He sighed as he looked at the still form of Christina. He'd checked on her as often as the plump but very pretty brunette nurse had through the night, but there had been no change.

Lorraine had promised to send a uniform over this morning so that he could go home and grab a couple of hours' sleep, but in the meantime he could hear the tea trolley on its way.

Thank God for small mercies, he thought as he moved over to the window. From here you could see over the rooftops of the city. Earlier he'd watched a fantastic sunrise, and thought of Lorraine.

His thoughts now echoed those of earlier.

Should he ask her out?

How about flowers first?

Women love flowers.

What if she laughs. God, that would be mortifying.

What if she says no?

He could see her now, telling him to go and sling his hook.

If she says no, I'll die and beg to go back to Scotland.

He sighed. He wasn't shy or frightened of women, but he loved Lorraine so much that he couldn't bear the dream to end. Once she said no that would be it. And he'd lose her friendship, which would be the worst thing of all.

He turned back to Christina. She was lying in the same position she'd been in all night.

Only this time her eyes were wide open.

Mickey had slept on Robbie's settee. Something woke him and he opened his eyes to see Emma staring down at him.

At least she's not spitting, he thought – Emma wasn't the most sociable of the Lumsdon clan – as he smiled and said, 'Morning, Emma.'

'Yer look daft,' Emma said, before sticking her tongue out and turning her back on him.

Mickey shrugged, it was more or less what anyone expected from Robbie's red-headed younger sister, whose sole function in life seemed to be to torment the rest of the household, and just about anyone who came into it. A moment later, the whole Lumsdon tribe descended on him.

Mickey sat up as Robbie, who'd obviously been up for a while, thrust a glass of milk at him. Mickey swallowed most of it in one gulp.

'Heard anything?' Mickey asked, handing the empty glass to Darren, Robbie's only brother, as he passed on his way into the kitchen.

'No,' Robbie said. 'But that copper what's been patrolling all night called by. Dolly took him a cup of tea.'

'Melanie mustn't have turned up then. God, Jacko'll be going spare. He was bad enough in the early hours this morning when we finally gave up – but at least the police are here now.'

'Aye, I know.'

'What time did youse lot get in last night?' Vanessa asked,

as she came into the room with a cup of tea in her hand. Knocking Mickey's legs to the floor, she sat down next to him.

Mickey couldn't help but notice how much better she looked these days. Her hair was shiny and she had colour in her face, she'd even put a little bit of weight on. Not that he'd dare tell her that, she'd swallow him whole in one gulp if he even suggested it. But five months ago the cup would have held vodka lightly laced with tea. Now she went to weekly AA meetings and had improved one hundred per cent. 'Sometimes after three,' he answered with a smile, when he realised she was staring at him and waiting for an answer. Even at her worst Mickey had always liked Vanessa.

She took a sip, then said, 'No sign of the bairn.' It wasn't a question but a sad statement. She gave a shiver. 'I know how poor Jacko must be feeling.' When Claire had gone missing, Vanessa had been distraught.

Mickey shook his head. 'And Doris is in a right mess.'

'I know, love, but the doctors say she's going to be OK and that's what really matters.' Vanessa tried to sound reassuring, but if the rumours were true – if Doris's attack had something to do with Hammerman, and the money Jacko owed, then they weren't out of the woods yet. Why aye, and what with the attack on poor Christina Sandra had told her about, yer had to ask what on earth the world was coming to. *Now come on, don't think like that.* Didn't do anyone any good to get gloomy. She pulled herself together. 'And Melanie'll turn up,' she told Mickey, praying that she was right. 'She's a good kid, and she's not daft neither.'

Mickey could only nod – that was more or less what everyone had been saying to Jacko last night.

'So, what we gonna do today, Robbie? We've got to sign on. Then we still have to go on the market 'cos Jacko can't get there and we can't let him down.'

Robbie pulled a face. 'Beats me. We can't go down the social 'cos yer can guarantee that slimy bastard will be standing guard over the door, with his bloody pictures in his fat sausage fingers just looking for us . . . And we don't need to go down the stall till later: Jacko got in touch with old Nick last night, he used to work there before Jacko. He's gonna go in and set the stall up and work it until we get there.'

'D'yer reckon sausage fingers'll be back at the market today?'

Robbie shrugged. 'I doubt it, he reckons he's got the three of us banged to rights.'

Mickey sighed. 'Rock and a hard place, mate. Rock and a hard place.'

'I've got an idea, boys.' Vanessa snapped her fingers. 'Yer gonna love this.' Putting her cup down on the cracked coffee table, she disappeared into the kitchen, leaving Mickey and Robbie to frown at each other behind her back.

The two shaven-headed youths walked warily into the social security office and took their place in the queue to sign on. Both kept their heads down, and when it was their turn at the desk, both avoided looking at the man behind the desk checking everybody out. Ordeal safely over, the pair, trying as hard as they could not to run, headed outside.

A couple of minutes down the road, and safely out of sight, Mickey leaned against the wall as he heaved a gigantic sigh of relief and blew air out of his cheeks. For a minute back there the pot-bellied bastard had stared at them and he'd thought they'd been rumbled.

'We made it, Robbie. I told yer it was a good idea of yer mam's.' He ran his hand over his smooth scalp. 'Doesn't feel half as cold as I thought it would. Don't yer reckon?'

Robbie, feeling his own scalp, grinned, 'Yer right, I might

just keep it. Anyhow, we'd better be getting a move on, poor old Nick will be sick as a chip by himself.'

They jumped on the bus and twenty minutes later were behind the stall putting their aprons on.

'About time an' all,' Nick complained, spraying spit all over the place. Mickey kept his head down so that Nick, who was toothless, couldn't see him grinning.

'Did yer's get away with it then?'

'We think so . . . Are yer certain he won't come back again today?'

'Ninety per cent, son. What would be the point, he's already caught yer once. They can't stop the dole twice, can they?'

'Do yer think the gaffer might set us on permanent like, Nick, if we lose our dole money.'

'He would if he could I suppose. But the markets don't make what they used to yer know, not with all the car boots that's about now. Fairly ruined the markets, the car boots have.'

'Ohh.' Mickey polished Nick's spray off the apples.

'Yeah, yer looked right interested in that bit of information, Mickey.'

Mickey grinned, then ducked. He'd spotted the fat lady in the lime green mac. 'You serve her, Robbie, she fairly did me head in the other day.'

Lorraine sat at her desk, fiddling with a colourful assortment of chewed pencils. Carter had been prattling on for half an hour about Houghton Feast, but she'd let most of it go over her head. Her thoughts were bouncing back and forth like nobody's business. From the poor murdered girls – and the frightening fact that there might be more – to Mavis and praying that Dr Mountjoy was right. From wondering if Luke really did like her, and what to do if he didn't – or worse, what to do if he did – and then back again.

146

'Some people think that the Feast started with Barnard Gilpin, otherwise known as the apostle of the North. But others say it goes way further back than that, I think they're right, way way further back . . . Did yer know that Barnard Gilpin was knocked down by an ox in Durham marketplace in 1583 and that's what finished him off? Sixty-six years old he was. His tomb's in St Michael's Church, but yer know that don't yer,' Carter nodded to himself. 'Everybody in Houghton knows that . . .'

The phone rang, bringing Lorraine out of her reverie. 'What did yer say, Carter? Tomb? Amazing, yeah.' She smiled at him as she picked the phone up.

Carter nodded eagerly, and Lorraine held her hand up to restrain his outburst.

'Right, I'll be right there,' she said after a moment. Putting the phone down she stood. 'That was Luke. Christina's woken up. We may finally get somewhere today, so cross yer fingers she's got something useful to tell us.'

'Oh, right.'

'I'll be at the hospital if anyone wants me, Carter, so keep yer eye on things.'

'Right, boss.' He knew the things he had to keep his eye on. Jacobs and Dinwall. Jacobs was in the doghouse with Lorraine again for failing to contact her when the call came in about Christina's attack, and also for making the naive assumption that just because Christina was still alive her attack wasn't linked to the murders. She'd known the stranglings were Lorraine's case, and had been so keen to lead her own enquiry – particularly after the frustration of being first on the scene when Samantha Dankton was found but having to give way to Lorraine's seniority on that one – that she'd jumped the wrong way. Carter was glad he wasn't in her shoes.

Just as Lorraine was reaching for the door handle, the door

opened and Sanderson entered. He held a slim folder in his hands. 'Kid missing, boss.'

'Oh, Christ.' At the worst possible time an' all, she thought, taking the folder off him. Quickly she flicked through the couple of pages.

'She seems a bit of a wanderer.'

'Aye, her dad's had us out once or twice. I think he's a worrier. But this time she's been missing all night. One of them Middlesbrough coppers what's been drafted in for the Feast took the call yesterday evening but the lazy bastard couldn't be bothered to do much. He took his time passing the news on and we've had the uniforms looking through the night, but there's no sign of her.'

Lorraine turned to Carter. 'Go and talk to the family, find out what yer can . . . or better yet,' she smiled, 'let's put Sara in charge. She wants a case, she's got it – and she'd better not fuck it up, not with a little girl missing. You tell her that from me, Carter. This is make-or-break time for her as far as I'm concerned. And Sanderson, take a couple of uniforms with yer and pay a few of the nonces in the area a visit. And if any of them scream about their rights, just tell them to put it in writing.' She closed the file and put it on her desk. 'Let's pray it's another false alarm.'

'Aye I hope so an' all.' Carter added, 'I know Jacko, so does Luke, and he loves that bairn to bits. Give her the moon if he could.'

When Lorraine entered Christina's room, she was sitting up in bed resting against the pillows and looked exhausted. Deep scratches ran red and angry across her face and the backs of her hands.

For the second time Lorraine clapped eyes on the woman's father and liked him even less than she had the first time. He was sitting next to his daughter wearing a white shirt that looked even tighter than the one he'd had on the previous day, with a totally bored expression on his face, while Luke stood by the window. She also noticed how tired Luke looked. And acknowledged his smile with a brief nod.

'OK, how are yer today, Christina?' she asked gently as she crossed the room and stood at the other side of the bed to Jenkins.

Christina's eyelashes fluttered open and she sighed, tried to smile, then gave up.

Lorraine took her hand. She looked over at the girl's father. 'If yer don't mind, Mr Jenkins, we'd like to talk to Christina . . . alone.'

Jenkins' hackles rose at once. 'Why would that be, like? Anyhow, yer not allowed to interview people without a lawyer, I know that much.'

'Seen it on the telly have yer?' Lorraine asked drily.

'Aye, ah have. So I won't be giving yer any permission to interviewing me daughter without me being present.'

What was he so frightened of, Lorraine wondered, as her own hackles rose.

'Well, Mr Jenkins. First off, we are not interviewing your daughter, merely talking to her. She's a victim, not a suspect. And for that we only need her permission, not yours. Your daughter is well above the age of consent, so I'm pleased to say we do not need you here for the time being. Thank you.'

Defeated, Jenkins stomped from the room after giving Lorraine a look that would have intimidated a lesser woman. Lorraine ignored him.

'Christina,' she started again, as Luke detached himself from the windowsill and came round to stand at the side of the bed Jenkins had just vacated.

Again Christina's eyes fluttered open.

'Try to stay with us, love. We need to find out who done this to yer.'

Christina managed to keep her eyes open and struggled with the tight sheets, trying to get comfortable. She coughed, and gestured for the glass of water on the cabinet beside Luke. He got it for her and held the glass while she sipped.

'He . . .' her voice sounded like she'd been smoking a hundred cigarettes a day for fifty years, though Lorraine suspected she hadn't smoked a cigarette in her life. She rubbed her throat. 'It hurts.'

Lorraine nodded. 'Yes, pet, I bet it does but if yer know something, I need yer to tell us before he strikes again. Please, love. What happened to yer?' Lorraine was desperate to ask if Christina's attacker had tried to strangle her, but knew she had to be careful about asking leading questions.

Christina swallowed painfully. 'I . . . I was coming out of my class. And it was late.' She paused for a moment, remembering. 'The tutor ran on, so we got out late. And I missed the bus.'

Lorraine stroked Christina's hair as the girl spoke – reliving her attack must be terrible. 'Good girl, you're doing really well,' she soothed. 'What did you do once you realised the bus had gone?'

Christina swallowed again. 'I decided to walk. I . . . I was scared to wait by myself at the bus stop in the dark.' A tear ran down her cheek. 'So I set off up towards the woods. I,' she stopped for a moment, clearly sorting things out in her head, 'I heard someone coming up behind me and I was scared, but he walked past me.'

'Yes, we know about him,' Lorraine said. 'It was Allan Greve – you know him, or he knows you. You didn't recognise him because he had his hood up, but he recognised you. It was him who found you.' Poor Greve had been interviewed for several hours after calling in Christina's attack, but it had been fairly clear he wasn't involved. Christina had fought back – there was blood and skin under her long fingernails from where she had scratched her attacker – and Greve didn't have a mark on him.

Christina nodded, understanding. 'So he walked past me and I thought I was safe. But then . . . someone grabbed me from behind.' She coughed, and her hands went up to her throat again. 'His hands were round my neck, and I couldn't breathe.'

'OK, love, that's good,' Lorraine soothed. So it was the strangler again. That made three attacks in just a few days. 'Carry on if you can. Did . . .' she found herself crossing her fingers, 'did you get a look at him?'

Christina nodded and Lorraine felt her pulse begin to race. 'Yes. He was . . . his . . . his face was . . .'

'There's something wrong with his face?' Lorraine looked towards Luke and their eyes met across the bed.

Christina managed a slight nod.

'What was it,' Luke asked urgently. 'Christina, love, can yer tell us? Was it a birth defect like a cleft lip? Or an accident? A scar?'

Christina slowly shook her head. 'Don't know.' Her voice was barely above a whisper now and Lorraine could see she was fast falling asleep again. They'd have to come back later if they wanted to get any more out of her.

'Look, don't try to talk any more, you've done really well.'

'Yes, you have.' Luke smiled warmly at her and Lorraine swore she saw the poor girl blush. Unaware of the effect he was having on her, Luke patted Christina's arm. 'Well done,' he said.

Lorraine watched the slow build-up of the tears in the corner of Christina's eyes, and guessed that the display of emotion had very little to do with what had happened to her.

There's something badly wrong in this woman's life. Something that goes beyond the attack.

And I bet that fucking creep of a father's got something to do with it.

'We'll have to go now, Christina,' she said softly, 'but we'll come back. Is there anything yer need?'

Slowly, Christina shook her head.

They said goodbye to her and a few moments later they passed Jenkins coming along the corridor holding a cup of coffee. 'Finished, are yers?'

'Oh yes, Mr Jenkins,' Lorraine said. 'For the moment.' She stared at Christina's father, and he was the first one to drop his eyes.

14

Heartsick, her eyes red and sore from crying all night, Melanie stared hatefully at the white bandages which bound her ankles together, then at the bandage from the same roll that was wrapped tightly round her wrists.

She hadn't been tied up to begin with – that had happened once she started screaming to get out. To begin with she'd thought it'd be OK – you did think that when someone was nice to you, and stroked your hair, and sang to you – but then things had gone wrong when she had asked to go home. That's when the trouble had started.

Now her voice was all but gone from shouting, and her throat hurt something terrible, but all she'd received for her efforts had been a hard slap on her face, that still stung. It was the first time in her life that Melanie had ever been hit and she was still suffering shock from it.

Being tied up like this made her bad leg really really hurt. But she wouldn't cry any more, even though she was more frightened that ever. When she got home she might tell Suzy how frightened she was, but she wouldn't tell Emma. When her voice came back she'd shout again, oh yes she would. And when Dad and Nana found her, there would be more stinging slaps given, *but not for me. Oh no, Nana will go bloody mad and so will Dad.*

She felt quite brave now that she'd swore, even though it was only in her mind.

She moved her head and looked at the green door. Somewhere out there was home.

A long slow sigh eased from between her lips.

I shouldn't have gone.

Now I'm gonna get wrong again.

And I might miss Houghton Feast altogether.

And I just bet it was a lie and me nana's not even poorly.

Bottom lip trembling, she tore her eyes from the door and looked around the tiny bedroom. The wallpaper was covered with huge old-fashioned pink roses. There was a small white dressing table, and transfers on the drawers mimicked the roses on the walls. The same transfers were on the wardrobe doors.

She hated roses now, and figured she would for the rest of her life. Roses would always remind her of this horrible stinky room, 'cos they were everywhere.

And she was in really big trouble because she'd been out all night, even though it wasn't her fault.

Might be grounded for a whole year.

She became very indignant a moment later when she remembered, *And I didn't even go with a stranger!!!*

Carter, cup of tea in one hand and a slice of newly-baked cheese and onion pie in the other, was listening to Doris talking about Melanie and Jacko – who was at this very moment scouring the streets for his daughter. Half the Houghton force were out searching for Melanie now, checking as much as possible of the fairground and the surrounding area before the Feast began in just a few hours – and Houghton went mental. Those who weren't out on the search for Melanie had been called in by Lorraine, who seemed to have had some sort of breakthrough on the strangler case. Just as he'd turned into Tulip Crescent he'd heard the call on the radio for all available officers to report to Detective Inspector Hunt. At a guess, she must have got something from Christina Jenkins.

'So when exactly was the last time yer saw her, Doris. We need to know pretty much to the minute,' Carter said, putting his pie back on the plate and scrubbing crumbs off his jacket.

'Can't really remember,' Doris said with a worried look. 'I think she was at the gate playing with Jess, the bairn's got an affinity with animals. Cats, dogs, they all love her . . . Or that might have been the day before.'

'She talks to Jess just about every day, sometimes she takes her for a walk,' Dolly Smith put in.

'So if I say she was last seen in the company of a black and white collie, nobody will remember that particular day either.'

'Not really.' Dolly shook her head.

Carter gave a sigh. He was doing everything he could, but with this little information there wasn't exactly going to be much to go on. And he wasn't even supposed to be here – Sara Jacobs was in charge of this case, Lorraine had made that very clear, but Sara was too determined to get herself an in with the murders to concentrate on a missing kid. It made him want to slap her. Then Doris said, eyes alight with remembering, 'I was baking pies and she'd went upstairs, and that's the last I saw of her. So it was after she'd been playing with Jess.'

'Good, so about what time would that be?'

Doris looked crestfallen. 'Don't really know.'

Carter sighed and looked at his empty notebook, then turned to Dolly. 'Can you remember seeing her at all?'

'Now yer come to mention it, I didn't actually see her, but I did hear her.'

'Oh, so how did yer know it was Melanie if yer didn't see her?'

'Cos nobody can sing, "Swing low, sweet chariot", like Melanie can. The bairn's got the voice of an angel . . . And before yer ask it was after dinner.'

'Good.' Carter said as he wrote, 'After Dinner'. Finally they were getting somewhere.

Mr Skillings walked in as Carter was writing. 'No sign yet?'

'No,' Doris said, as she gently stroked around her injury. It was hurting like hell now and it felt as if her whole head was throbbing.

'Here.' Mr Skillings handed her the packet of tablets he'd been to the shop for.

'Want a glass of water with those, Doris love?' Dolly asked.

'No yer all right, I'll take a couple with the last of this tea.'

'Hello, Mr Skillings,' Carter said.

'Hi, son, how yer doing?'

'Not bad at all . . .' But before Carter could get into a deep conversation about his favourite subject, because Mr Skillings was also a member of the history group, Jacko arrived back home.

Striding into the middle of the sitting room, looking totally dishevelled, he faced Carter and demanded, 'So, what the hell are yer doing to find her?'

'Everything we can, Jacko, we didn't get notified until this morning that Melanie was missing. I think the uniforms expected her to turn up behind somebody's settee safe and well this morning . . . But they did still look through the night.'

Jacko shook his head and sat down. He put his head in his hands and dry-washed his face. When he looked again at Carter his one good eye was bright with un-shed tears. 'What am I gonna do, eh? You tell me that. 'Cos I've searched everywhere, mate.'

Jacko went quiet for a moment, then he slowly shook his head again. Every piece of his soul was in his face, as he went on, 'She's not on this estate, and that's a fact. Some black-hearted bastard's got me bairn.' He sniffed and tried hard to swallow the sob that welled up from deep inside.

Hammerman slapped Lance Halliday hard enough for the FUCK OFF AND FLY bird tattoo on his cheek to turn bright red around the edges.

'I told yer to just frighten her, yer fucking moron. Now me name's fucking muck on half a dozen estates, yer fucking crazy bastard.' He grabbed Halliday by his throat, shook him once then pushed him away, shaking his hand as if he'd touched something so foul his own hand would turn black at any minute.

Halliday kept his balance, though the giggle from his sister standing in the corner did not help his temper, nor Hammerman's. He stepped towards Halliday again. Halliday clenched his teeth and shrugged, then spat out the words, 'The old cow's nuts, man. Fucking cheeky bastard, that's all she is, threatened me with her fucking son. Who the fuck's he anyhow?'

'Yer'll find out when he comes looking for the pair of us. Jacko'll not let this go. Eight fucking stitches she's got, for fuck's sake,' Hammerman screamed, his face going as red as the slap marks on Halliday's cheek. 'Yer fucking useless. Nowt but a fucking plastic gangster. You and that mad fucking sister of yours, pair of fucking lunatics, should be locked up in the fucking nuthouse and the fucking key thrown away . . . What the fuck did yer have to cut her for, can yer tell me that even? She's an old wife for Christ's sake.'

'Ah didn't cut her, man.' Halliday was more surely that ever. 'She tripped and hit the cupboard or something. Honest . . . Fucking clumsy crazy old bitch, she fucking well fell.' He spat on the ground.

Hammerman slapped him again, but Halliday shrugged the slap off the same way he'd shrugged off the other ones, then held his hand out.

'Money.'

Hammerman shook his head. 'You've got to be fucking joking. After the job you pulled? Not a chance.'

Halliday started to look agitated. 'Now come on, man, we said fifty. I need that fifty.'

But Hammerman wasn't budging. 'You're lucky I don't have yer kneecapped, yer useless twat. Yer rotten to the core, kid, and that's the truth. Now fuck off, and I don't ever want to see yer again . . . Nor you, yer fucking drug crazy bitch,' he said to Julie who just giggled at him, her eyes glittering with the high from her latest heroin fix, then cracked her chewing gum.

'Till next time,' Halliday said as they walked away.

'I don't fucking think so,' Hammerman muttered to himself.

The Broadway was beginning to fill up. Hundreds of excited kids who couldn't wait to get down to the show field plagued their parents relentlessly, worried they'd miss the opening ceremony.

Vanessa and Sandra stood with Suzy and Emma – Sandra's boys were getting a bit too big to come down the Feast with their mother, Clayton the youngest had informed her. Well, he was nearly fifteen now, but no doubt when Clay's money ran out, he'd sharp find her.

Vanessa looked around, recognising faces she'd never seen for years. Last year, the one before that and probably another two or three before that as well, she'd been too drunk to bring the bairns up to the Feast. Robbie and Kerry had had to do that.

No one knew how many times she'd nearly given in over the last months, but she was getting stronger by the day. To say the cravings had gone would be telling lies, and she'd promised herself no more lies. She did, though, go hours now without thinking about booze, and that had to be progress.

Anyhow, she smiled at the top of Emma's head, she was here now, and her life was back on course with the most important people in it safe and well. That was the main thing.

'Hi, Mam.' Vanessa smiled as Darren, who had shot up during the summer months and now fairly towered over his best friend Kenny, stepped in front of her.

'Heard anything, son?' she said in a quiet voice, so she wouldn't be overheard by Emma and Suzy, who were transfixed by the juggling clowns on stilts.

'Nowt,' he whispered back. 'Jacko's frantic. Our Robbie and Mickey's helping him look again, so's a lot of people. After we've had a look round the shows, we're gonna search the Burnside on our way down. Some of the coppers are helping but most of them's up here at the Feast . . . Ohh,' he rummaged in his pocket and came out with a ten pound note. 'That's off our Robbie for Suzy and Emma.'

At the sound of her name, Emma turned around, spotted the ten pound note and sniffed. Darren threw her a dirty look as he pulled a fiver out of his other pocket. 'And that's off Mickey an' all.'

'Thank God for that.' Vanessa knew the tenner she'd managed to scrape away for the girls out of Kerry's wages would not have lasted five minutes down the show field.

'And look what I've got to meself,' he waved another tenner at her. 'Fiver off Robbie and a fiver off Mickey . . . And I said thank you, before yer ask.'

159

'Good lad, enjoy it.' As she spoke she was feeling in her coat pocket for the two pound fifty she'd put to one side for Darren. 'Here, love, have a good time.'

Darren beamed. 'Thanks, Mam, that's great.'

'I'll give yer a little treat tomorrow, Darren.' Sandra smiled at him.

He grinned back, as Kenny secretly gave a sigh of relief. He had twenty pounds that he would have split down the middle with Darren, but it was much better this way.

'Ohh, I nearly forgot. Mam, I heard some people saying that it was a moneylender what did that to Doris, 'cos can yer remember when they went to Disneyland in Florida . . .'

Sandra gave Vanessa a knowing look. They'd both heard the rumour already and it rang horribly true. Vanessa swiftly changed the subject.

'So, son, is Dolly staying in with Doris tonight?'

'Aye, Mr Skillings is on his way down. He has to take hotdogs and candyfloss back.'

'Ah, isn't that nice of him?' Sandra said.

'Pity they have to miss the show tonight though. We'll pop in and tell them all about it when we get back, eh, Sandra?'

Sandra nodded her agreement as the crowd fell silent waiting for the Mayor's speech.

Samuel Thorenson, grizzled, fat and friendly, had been a member of Houghton pipe band for more than twenty years, but this was the first time he'd had the honour of climbing up the church tower on Houghton Feast Friday to play the bagpipes after the mayor's speech.

His knee had been giving him gyp for a week or more, but he'd never let on to his sister Elsie, who he'd lived with since his saintly wife June had died in her sleep three years ago. Elsie would have taken great delight in finding some way to stop him.

Elsie was under the impression that life had dealt her a raw deal. Samuel knew better: she should have listened to him and June years ago when she was laughing at her son Scott's misdemeanours; he wouldn't be serving ten years for armed robbery now if she'd given him a good clip round his earhole when he'd deserved it. Instead she'd thought most of his antics funny, even laughed when he'd nicked things at six years old. *Boys will be Boys* had been a favourite saying of hers. *He's only a bairn* had been another one. Aye, why that bairn had turned into an undisciplined monster, and an embarrassment to the rest of the family, and Elsie took it out on everybody and anybody rather than face the truth and blame herself.

He'd tried his best with the lad, but Elsie contradicted everything he said. He shrugged and decided to put Elsie and her son – he refused to call him nephew – out of his mind.

Tonight was his night. He was proud to be here and in his heart he knew June was proud of him too.

He managed five steps, then he had to stop for a moment; luckily he was already round the first bend in the clock tower and no one could see him. Terry Smalls was just dying to take his place. Inhaling a couple of deep breaths, he slowly made his way up the stone steps.

It was pretty dark in the tower, and when he reached the top his foot slipped. He grabbed at the side of the wall for balance but his other foot couldn't find a grip, and to his horror he came crashing down, but out of sheer determination he managed to hold his bagpipes aloft with his right hand.

A younger man like Smalls probably wouldn't even have fallen, would have been able to save himself, but at nearly sixty years old one's balance is not as good as it used to be and, resigning himself to the fact that he was going to hurt himself, and dreading the thought that he might let everybody down, Samuel hit the ground. But his landing was cushioned.

Something soft had saved his elbow and hip from serious damage.

Not believing his luck, Samuel scrambled to his knees and looked down at what he'd landed on. He squinted in the poor light, then blinked rapidly, not quite taking in what he was looking at. When the full image hit him, it was far harder than any fall. He gasped, realising at the same time that the sticky stuff on his hand just had to be blood.

Like a frightened crab he scrambled away, scrubbing his hand in disgust until he'd practically scraped it raw on the centuries-old stone, narrowly missing falling backwards down the stairs.

All of his life Samuel had been a strong man, a man to depend on, so his wife had told everybody.

What would happen now if he panicked and ran screaming out of the tower, with gory tales of blood and murder – especially seeing as folks were already het up about the other murders. Houghton had been buzzing for days about it, their phone had never stopped, and Elsie didn't exactly have a lot of friends. He'd already discussed with Smalls the fact that although the Broadway was packed, the people weren't exactly standing on each other's toes like they had been in other years.

If they stampeded and a canny little bairn or two got squashed to death, he'd never be able to live with it on his conscience.

He took a deep breath, and made his mind up. Really, there was only one decent thing he could do: he would play his bagpipes and he would play them like he'd never played them before. He would play for the soul of the poor dead girl he shared the tower with. Then, when the crowd melted away to the show field, he would panic all he wanted, and the vicar and the coppers could take over. Standing up, he stepped carefully over the poor dead girl.

Samuel knew it was a woman, he remembered his landing. A man's body wouldn't have the softness nor the curves that this body had. He took some deep breaths to calm himself, and waited. The Mayor finished her speech and Samuel was as ready as he'd ever be.

The rendition of 'Amazing Grace' that drifted down from the tower that night was perfect. That cold October nght, it had every person, of every generation that stood in the crowd on the Broadway, completely enthralled.

And somewhere, not too far away, a little girl imagined she could hear the lone piper and sobbed her heart out.

Josh had returned at ten o'clock, just as the show field was emptying, and Percy watched him make his way over to the stall. He never said a word of where he'd been – though he'd disappeared last night and been away for a full twenty-four hours now – as he picked up a damp-proof bag and helped Percy pack the teddies away for the night.

The silence had Percy on edge.

Where the hell has he been?

He knew it was a waste of time asking him. Josh told you what he wanted you to know, or he told you nothing. Any badgering just resulted in a heavily-blown fuse.

But Percy was nervous. He'd heard the rumours about a little girl going missing. And the description sounded very much like Josh's little friend Melanie.

Then, sometime after eight, word had gone round the show field with the speed of a dry forest fire, about a woman's body being found in the church tower. All in all, it had been a pretty hectic opening night, and not one to forget in a hurry, especially when the police took the place over and people started going home early. Percy reckoned his takings were easily down by fifty per cent on last year.

He looked at Josh and figured somebody had to break the

ice – and it was always him. With a sigh he said, 'Fancy some nice fish and chips for supper?'

Josh shrugged.

Percy interpreted this as a yes. 'Right then, Josh old son, I'm pretty peckish myself, so I'll pop up the fishy while you finish off here then. OK?'

Again, all he got for his pains was Josh's usual noncommittal shrug. Percy tutted, dropped his bag of teddies, climbed over the side of the stall, stopped a moment to check his wallet for money, then headed off towards Houghton.

The heavy police presence he encountered on his way could not be ignored. He knew that at least half the officers on site were here because of the body in the church tower and were even now combing the grounds for clues. But he also knew that the child's disappearance was at the top of their agenda and that some of the policemen were carrying out a sweep of the entire area.

Was it really Melanie that was missing?

He'd wanted her out of Josh's way, but he'd never wanted her to come to any harm. One hour in the kid's company had been a treasure.

If it's her, the coppers might come after Josh. That tall blonde policewoman who'd interviewed him after he and Tom found the body in the waltzer had seemed rather too interested in Josh . . . but that didn't make sense. Melanie hadn't disappeared then. Percy's head started to spin.

What'll I do if the police come around asking questions?

Strangers in town, we always get it first, and there's plenty of people must have seen her hanging around here. She must have told some of her friends where she was going.

Oh, God, what the hell to do?

Then a moment later he felt guilty and chided himself. I shouldn't even be thinking like this . . . Of course it's not Melanie.

And if it is, though I sincerely hope it's not . . . Then Josh had nothing to do with it. Anybody could see he really likes the kid.

But all the same, no matter how much he tried to convince himself, Percy's heart was heavy with the promise of trouble.

15

Lorraine brushed crumbs off her black trouser suit as she nibbled her toast, and breathed a sigh of relief that yesterday was over. The first day of Houghton Feast was always tough, but throw in a missing kid, a serial killer and on top of all that a body found during the opening ceremony, and you just couldn't make it up! She was shattered.

To make things worse, Clark had insisted they couldn't shut down the Feast so instead of clearing the area, getting SOCO in and getting on with it, Lorraine and her team had had to sidestep a bunch of overexcited kids, hyped up on too much sugar. Fucking useless way to conduct a murder investigation – and Lorraine was fuming.

They'd got a name on the man who was attacked on the bridge the same night Diane Fox was killed – Dave Ridley, of all people. But naturally, with Lorraine's luck the way it was at the moment, he was a notorious drunk and seemed to have disappeared off the face of the earth. So that had so far turned out to be a dead end.

And they'd been making no progress with the only clue

166

they seemed to have – Christina's words about the man having something wrong with his face. That was as much as she could tell them; she just didn't know what she meant as she'd only got a glimpse, but she was adamant that something wasn't right. They'd started off rounding up everyone who fitted the description in the area, but without knowing exactly what they were looking for the numbers were just too high. They'd get some DNA on the murderer from the skin underneath Christina's fingernails, but it took time to get that processed – and unless there was a miraculous match in the database, DNA wasn't much use until they had a suspect.

But she took a deep breath, and forced herself to tune into the chat around the breakfast table. Mavis and Peggy were planning a trip to the Gateshead Metro Centre this morning – how on earth could her mother be so calm, knowing she had to go into hospital next week? Where the end result of the visit could mean losing a breast. Or worse. It took Lorraine's breath away.

As if sensing what was on her mind, Mavis reached over and patted the back of Lorraine's hand. 'Don't worry, Lorry, it'll be all right.'

What could she do in the face of such optimism? Plus Lorraine suspected that Mavis had done her crying, and now there was nothing left to do but wait and hope.

She smiled. 'I know it will, Mam.'

She rose to go. 'Oh, and don't forget, the parade starts at half past two, not three o'clock. Remember last year?'

Mavis smiled. 'Yeah, no need to rub it in.'

'What happened last year, like?' Peggy asked.

'Mam missed the start. Weren't you there? Oh no I remember, you were in Barbados or some such exotic place . . .'

'Yeah so I was, great time an' all.' She nudged Mavis and the pair of them giggled like two schoolgirls, as Peggy went on, 'Yer see, Lorry, it was like . . .'

'Please,' Lorraine held her hand up. 'Spare me the details. I'll see the pair of you later.'

She left Peggy to her reminiscing and went to work.

She was talking to Sanderson when the phone rang. Frowning, she picked it up. 'Yes.'

After a minute or two and once or twice holding the phone away from her ear she said goodbye, put the phone down and called Sara Jacobs into her office.

'Sara, what the hell is going on with the Melanie Musgrove case? That was Jacko Musgrove demanding to know what we're doing about his missing daughter – who, quite frankly, I'm starting to worry about. She is, after all, only eight years old. What's going on?'

'Well,' Sara blustered, 'I knew you'd need help on the strangler case as well, so I . . .' she groped for a way to explain what she'd done without sounding like a complete bitch, '. . . I delegated. Carter went to interview Jacko and his family – he knows them so I thought they'd trust him. And we've had coppers out looking for her all over.'

'But you've made no progress?' Lorraine's voice was like ice.

'Well no, not exactly.' Sara had the grace to at least look embarrassed.

'And yer didn't think to come and check in with me, to give me an update?' *Christ, if only I didn't have a bunch of murders on my hands I could deal with Melanie's disappearance meself. Bloody awful timing.*

'Well, no. I didn't. Sorry.'

'Sorry! Sorry's not fucking good enough. There's an eight-year-old kid lost out there, probably terrified. Have yer forgotten what happened here just a few months ago? Have yer forgotten how close those girls came to dying?'

Sara stood there in silence.

'Well, have yer?' Lorraine raged.

'No, ma'am,' Sara replied at last.

'So what the fuck are yer doing still standing in front of my desk? Get out of here, get over to the Musgroves, and do yer fucking job the way you should have done it in the first place.'

Sara turned to go, but Lorraine stopped her. 'And Sara? I want updates every two hours. You clearly can't be trusted.'

'And the murders?' Sara asked in a quiet voice

Luke chose that moment to walk in, followed by Dinwall. Chuffed that they'd chosen probably the best moment of the day to arrive in her office, Lorraine smiled sweetly as she said, 'Oh, I think we have enough experienced detectives in the room to deal with a few murders, don't you?'

Lost for words and obviously huffed, Sara left the room to go and visit Jacko.

Good, Lorraine thought. About time that madam was brought down a peg or two.

'Ready, Luke?' Dinwall asked.

'Yeah, wheel the first one in.'

Dinwall beckoned to someone, and Luke groaned and said, 'Jesus Christ,' under his breath when Dave Ridley walked into the interview room. 'So they finally found you.'

Dave sat down and grinned at Luke, loving all the attention. 'Hi, Luke old mate,' he said cheerfully.

Dinwall raised his eyebrows. He hadn't known that Luke knew Dave Ridley. Then again, Luke was a friendly bloke and he had grown up in Houghton, so he was bound to know a lot of the folk – personally, he couldn't stand blokes like Ridley. Drain on society, that's all they were.

'Hello, Dave . . . So where the hell have you been? And what on earth happened to yer face?'

With a huge grin, Dave proceeded with great gusto to tell the same story he'd told Mickey a week earlier on the park bench. When he was finished Luke stared at him.

'If yer taking the piss, Dave, I warn yer I'm not in the mood.'

'Honest.' Dave was indignant. 'I swear on me Mam's life. It all happened exactly like that. The social sent out a hit man after me.' The fact that Dave's mother had been dead for five years, and he was swearing on a life that didn't exist, did not seem to occur to Dave.

Dinwall was looking strangely at Dave, but what Luke said next had him swing his head towards Luke in disbelief. Surely he wasn't buying this, anybody could see that Ridley was as mad as a pan of crabs.

'So yer think it was about two o'clock when this attack took place?'

'Aye.' Dave nodded adamantly.

'Yer were jumped on from behind?'

'Aye, I've already told yer, by the hit . . .'

'Let's not get into who beat yer up yet, Dave.' Luke leaned over the table, bringing himself closer to Ridley. 'Now listen, 'cos this is very important, do yer understand?'

Wide-eyed, Dave nodded his understanding.

'Right,' Luke went on. 'I need yer to think real hard here, Dave. Can yer remember seeing anybody else as yer passed the church that night? Anybody at all. I don't care if it was ghosts out of the churchyard or a host of angels out of the church, OK? I need yer to try and remember. It's very important.'

Dave thought hard, making it look painful, and he began to shake his head. Then he stopped, looked at Luke and said, 'Do yer know, I think I did say goodnight to somebody.'

'Who, Dave? Think now, 'cos I really need to know.'

Dave scratched his chin, he was all out of thinking. What

he needed was a drink. 'It's all shadows, man. I can't see his face.'

'Him?'

'Aye, I'm certain it was a man, somehow, but I can't for the life of me see his face.'

'OK, Dave, yer doing good . . . Can yer remember if it was before the attack or after?'

'Before, 'cos . . .' His attention wavered, and he frowned for a minute as he tried to get his thoughts back on track. 'Ohh, it was definitely before.' He nodded his affirmation, then licked his dry lips.

'Right, Dave, well done. Now, think again. What did he look like?'

Dave went silent as he began to think again. And ten minutes later the three men were still sitting in silence.

'Dave? Any ideas?' Luke nudged.

He shook his head. 'No, man, sorry. But what about that friggin' hit . . .'

'Don't worry, Dave, we'll look out for him as well. Can yer remember what *he* looked like?'

Dinwall coughed into his hand trying to get Luke's attention, but Luke ignored him as he stared intently at Dave.

Dave tried hard but it was no good. All that was in his mind now was wave after wave of golden cider. 'Ner.' He shook his head. 'Sorry, I just can't see him right now.'

Luke gave a heavy sigh. 'OK, well keep thinking. We'll probably need to speak to yer again so don't you do one of your disappearing tricks, and in the meantime I want yer to keep on going over everything in your head . . . OK? And as soon as you can see that face in your mind, you give me a call. Right?'

'Yer know the number,' Dinwall said dryly.

'Very funny.' Dave gave him a searing look as he went out the door.

Waiting until Dave was out of earshot, Dinwall said, 'Surely yer not buying that, Luke.'

'Dinwall, don't yer get it? Dave Ridley was at the church – beside the bridge – near enough the same time as Diane Fox. Either his hit man, or the man he said goodnight to, is probably our murderer. Maybe Dave got in his way, or he thought he saw something and tried to kill him. But thank God Dave's stronger that he looks. 'Cos judging by that face he's had a hell of a beating.'

'OK, so Dave Ridley's seen our murderer. Why don't we just keep him here and question him big time?'

'James. The poor sod's mentally ill. We can't keep him, not without a lawyer and a doctor present. Best we do it like this, try for a little bit at a time . . . The boss'll be interested in this, she'll probably want to talk to him herself, and Dave will do anything for Lorraine.'

Dinwall looked extremely surprised. 'Yer mean she knows him?'

'He wasn't always like that, yer know. People aren't born with a bottle of brandy or whatever stuck in their mouths. She went to school with him. And anything else yer want to know yer'll have to ask her.'

Far from happy, Sara Jacobs, mouth pulled into a severe line, knocked on Jacko's door. When he opened it, she stared at him for a moment, her eyes widening as she took in his eye patch and scar. Then her heart started racing.

Noticing none of this Jacko said, 'Ohh, yer better come in.'

Smiling to herself behind Jacko's back, she followed him into the sitting room. Doris, not looking well at all, was sitting beside the fire. Turning her head slightly, she smiled wanly at Sara.

'OK,' Sara said, sitting down across from Doris, where she

also had a good view of Jacko. She took a notebook and pen out of her bag and started to question Jacko.

'Can yer tell me where yer were the night before last?'

'Nice coat,' Doris interrupted. 'I love that deep purple colour, it really suits yer.'

'Heather, it's called heather.' She nodded unsmilingly at Doris, then looked back at Jacko.

'Quiet, Mam.' Jacko gently squeezed Doris's shoulder. 'Can yer say that again?' he asked, wearing a puzzled frown.

'Can you tell me where you were on the night your daughter disappeared?'

'Aye, looking for her, where the hell do yer think I was?'

'Can you confirm that, Mrs Musgrove?'

Doris looked as puzzled as her son. 'I, er . . . I think so.'

'Yer think so?'

'Aye.'

'And last night?'

Doris looked at Jacko. She wasn't sure of what was going on here, but she had a vague feeling that it wasn't good. This woman, whether she knew it or not, kept looking at Jacko in a very weird way. And she had a splitting headache which made it hard to concentrate.

Jacko broke the silence. 'Looking for me bairn again,' he snapped, not liking the way the questioning was going himself.

'Witnesses?'

'Are you mad? The whole friggin' street. And we've already gone through this with Carter who, I might flaming well add, had a better manner than you've got.'

Sara ignored the last sentence and instead asked, 'You were with them the whole time?'

Jacko gritted his teeth, looked her in the face and spat the words at her. 'Well, not exactly, we split up for a while so's we could cover more ground, like. Yer know what I mean?'

'We being who in particular, Mr Musgrove?'

'Mickey, Robbie, me mate Beefy, half a dozen coppers – and like I said before, most of the friggin' estate.'

'Hmm.'

Jacko watched her suspiciously for a minute while she caught up with everything on her notepad.

She looked up at him with a smug expression on her face, 'So, where did yer go when yer were on yer own?'

Enough was enough. Some people have long fuses, some have short, and Jacko's fuse was all burned out. He jumped up and was quite pleased when the smug little bastard in front of him flinched. If she'd been a man he would have flattened her, copper or not. 'Where the fuck is all this going? Yer supposed to be here about our Melanie. Not me. I'm not fucking missing.'

He calmed sightly when he heard Doris tutting. Shaking his head he muttered, 'Sorry, Mam.'

'Really, our Jacko, yer were brought up better than that. Fancy swearing in front of a lady.'

'There's only one lady in this room, Mam, and that's you.'

'Yeah, I know.'

Jacko hid a grin, obviously Doris hadn't lost all her marbles yet. Then his jaw dropped and the grin turned to a look of pure astonishment when Sara Jacobs took out her walkie talkie asked for back-up.

Mickey and Robbie stood with Cal outside of the church. It was nearly half past two, time for the parade. They had spent most of the morning searching the fields near Russel Woods – quite a lot of people had turned up and the police had organised a straight line search. The line had been forty eight people long. It had turned up nothing.

The murders were the sole topic of conversation, whoever anyone met up with that was the first thing mentioned. You could actually see the fear in a lot of the women's eyes on the street, and each face was silently screaming, 'Who's next?'

Cal had Betty, Flo, and Lady Jane in tow, and also Sid who, Cal whispered to Robbie and Mickey, had the hots for Betty, and had attached himself to the group.

'Ge'bye,' Robbie said. 'He's ninety if he's a day.'

'The dirty old sod,' Mickey murmured as he looked Sid up and down. Sid gave him a toothless grin.

Cal laughed. 'He's all right actually, a right good laugh sometimes – he's all there an' all. And the old bugger can move pretty fast.'

'Hi, Sid.' Mickey nodded as Sid sidled up to him.

Cal introduced them, and Sid said, 'Eee, lads, what a time we're having with all these murders, eh? Never known the likes of it. I've told the girls to be careful.' He nodded in the direction of Betty, Flo and Jane.

'Oh, aye,' Mickey nodded, thinking even a murderer had to be hard up to have a go at one of them three.

Then, to the delight of all, the parade, which they had heard making its stately way towards them for ten minutes or more, arrived. First came a pipe band, then a float. The float from the Blue Lion had people dressed as cavemen and cavewomen. Each person held a bucket filled with sweets that they threw at the crowd. Following alongside all the floats were men from the Round Table with more buckets, only these ones they were hoping to fill for charity.

Mickey felt the change in his pocket – about seventy-three pence he judged – and wondered if he moved and stood on the other side of Cal the Round Table man might think he'd already contributed. Too late, he was here. Mickey fished twenty pence from the rest and threw it into the bucket, and at the same time a red lollipop hit him on the cheek. Everyone laughed and Mickey, grinning, opened the lollipop and stuck it in his mouth, determined to get his twenty pence worth out of it.

Then the Seahills float arrived. There were wolf whistles galore, and Mickey's eyes nearly popped out when he saw Claire. Her outfit was pale pink, and she smiled at him as she threw extra sweets in their direction. Suzy shouted 'Hello,' and waved. The space that Melanie had been meant to occupy was empty.

But Mickey was still staring at Claire. 'Jesus,' he whispered to himself. But Old Sid, eyes nearly as wide as Mickey's, heard him.

'Yer can say that again, bonny lad.' He looked at Betty, 'Yer should have gone in for that, Betty love, yer would have stole the show.'

Betty curled her lip at him. 'Fat chance, yer creep.'

Sid smiled at her with adoring eyes. 'Isn't she wonderful,' he said to no one in particular.

After the last pipe band had passed them by, the crowds started to disperse, some heading for the show field but most herding their families towards home, an anxious eye on every family member. Across the road, a tall Rasta and a woman with long raven hair moved off in the direction of the show field. Mickey had stared in fascination at the Rasta, the first one he'd ever seen in the flesh so to speak, and he touched his own bald head, looked at Robbie and grinned.

Cal took his people back to the home for tea, and Mickey walked down to the Seahills with Robbie, calling in at Graswell chippy on the way.

As they passed Dolly Smith's house, Jess came down the path. It was Mickey who noticed she had something in her mouth.

'Hang on, Robbie . . . Here, girl.' Jess stopped, sat down and thumped her tail, but for some reason she seemed reluctant to come any closer.

'What is it?' Robbie asked.

'Here, girl. 'Mickey leaned forward, holding out a chip to encourage her. 'Come here, girl, come on.'

Not the type of dog to miss out on any fondling, wherever it was coming from, or a free treat, Jess slowly crossed the last two or three yards. She dropped what had been in her mouth at Mickey's feet.

'Oh, God,' Robbie said, as Mickey picked the object up and turned it over in his hand.

'It's one of Melanie's, isn't it. Look, Jacko gets one side of her shoe built up.'

With a sinking feeling, Mickey slowly nodded.

16

Carter knocked on the Lumsdons' door, and it was answered a few moments later by Emma.

'What do yer want?' she asked.

'Is yer mam in, Emma?'

'Not telling yer.' Then she actually grinned. 'Aye, man. Do yer want her?'

'Please, Emma.'

'Maaam.' Emma screamed loud enough to deafen anybody as far away as Durham. 'It's that ginger copper.'

Vanessa came to the door. 'Emma!'

'It's all right, Mrs Lumsdon . . . I wonder if I could have a word with Suzy please . . . It's about Melanie Musgrove.'

'Why, aye, come on in.'

Carter followed Vanessa down the passageway and into the sitting room. Suzy was on the settee sandwiched in between her older sisters, Kerry and Claire.

'Hello, girls,' Carter said. All three of them smiled at him and Carter couldn't help but notice the change in them since the last time he'd seen the family. Emma of course was still her usual charming self.

'Come about little Melanie have yer?' Kerry asked.

'Aye.' Carter nodded at her.

Kerry stood up, 'Well, I've got training, so make sure yer tell him everything he needs to know, mind, our Suzy, or else.'

Suzy nodded uncertainly. 'I already told you everything,' she said in a voice not much louder than a whisper.

'OK, Suzy,' Carter said, as he sat down opposite her. 'You were very good when you talked to my friend Sanderson – he told me all about you – but I'm afraid we still haven't been able to find Melanie and we're getting rather worried about her. You're her best friend – everyone says so – and so we're hoping that there might be something you forgot before? We won't mind,' he smiled encouragingly at her, 'everyone forgets things from time to time, and the important thing is that you tell me everything you can remember about the last time yer saw Melanie, pet. Even if yer don't think it's important, tell me everything. OK?'

Suzy looked from her mother to Carter, then dropped her eyes as she shook her head. 'No, don't know nothing,' she whispered.

'Mam, she's hiding something,' Claire yelled.

'Are yer, Suzy?' Vanessa asked, giving her youngest a puzzled look. Claire was usually right about Suzy, but it wasn't like her to keep secrets when her friend might be in danger.

Suzy nodded. 'Aye, but I might get wrong,' she muttered, her head still down and looking at them through her fringe.

'Listen Suzy,' Vanessa said urgently. 'If yer know anything about Melanie at all, yer must tell. I promise yer won't get wrong.'

'I won't miss the fireworks on Monday night?'

'No. Now tell the policeman everything yer know, else yer will get wrong.'

Claire sat forward on her seat in case she missed anything. She nudged Suzy, 'Come on, spit it out, what have yers been up to?'

Emma, who was sitting in the window, looked round the curtain, and stared one by one at everybody in the room. It wasn't often you could hear silence in the Lumsdon household, but this was the quietest moment in months.

'We, Melanie made me promise not to tell – an' I didn't think it mattered, so I didn't, but . . .' she faltered, then carried on again in a stronger voice, 'we went up the show field the other day and the man frightened me.'

'What man?' Vanessa frowned, as Carter followed Claire's lead and moved forward to the edge of his seat.

'The man with the poorly face,' Suzy nodded, as if they all knew who she was talking about.

'What do yer mean, love, poorly face?'

'Only half of it. The other half's all right.'

Carter felt a chill in his bones as he remembered what Christina had apparently said about her attacker. 'How did he frighten yer, pet?' he asked carefully. 'Did he try to hurt yer in any way? If he did yer have to tell us, no matter what he said he'd do if yer did.'

Suzy shook her head. 'No, he just shouted at us, and told us to go. But Melanie laughed at him, and she said he was her friend. I know she went up there to see him a few times and had some rides 'cos she told me.'

'This man, did he belong with the fair?' Carter asked, holding his breath.

'Yes. I remember 'cos Melanie said he lived in the biggest thing there, she went inside. It's got red Indians painted on it. Oh, and I just remembered, Melanie says he has an uncle, he lives with him an' all.'

'Well done. One other thing, Suzy. Did Melanie ever say what this man's name is?'

'Aye, she did . . . Josh.'

'Any other names, pet?'

Suzy thought for a moment then shook her head.

'Good girl, Suzy.' Carter stood up. He shook Suzy's hand and she giggled. 'You've been very helpful.'

Vanessa saw Carter to the door. 'The little so and sos. They know they haven't got to go out of the estate. I don't know how many times they're told.'

But before Carter could answer her, Dolly Smith practically ran up the path. 'Jacko's been arrested,' she said breathlessly.

Melanie refused to eat, even though she was starving, and truly she didn't know how long she'd be able to keep it up. If a bowl of raspberry ripple ice cream appeared again, she just might have to try some.

Just a bit, like.

Her leg hurt and she wanted to go home. She'd said this over and over. But no notice had been taken at all. She'd tried asking nicely.

That hadn't worked . . . Huh.

She might as well be talking to herself, as Nana always said to her and Dad.

But worst of all she'd missed most of Houghton Feast, and that was shocking, 'cos it was only on once a year. It's not like it's all gonna be on again next week.

Nana spent all that time making me costume, and now I'm never gonna get to wear it. She sighed.

And now she was supposed to wear this stupid dress.

It was ancient, and it had a funny smell.

No way.

But her refusal was laughed at. The bandages on her arms

were loosened, with dire threats about what would happen if she tried any tricks – uttered in a don't-you-dare-push-my-patience kind of voice.

Then, to her utter chagrin, she was stripped naked and plunged into a bath that was barely warm. Lifted back out, towelled off with a rough towel, and all to the radio blasting out some daft fiddle music that she'd never heard before.

And didn't like.

And was never ever gonna like if she had to stay here for a thousand years.

So there.

'Please, can I go home,' she begged, as the dress was dropped over her shoulders.

When her face appeared above the dress, it was greeted by a shaking head.

Melanie burst into tears.

Carter radioed in and got Sanderson. He was on his way to the show field to have a talk with this Josh person whoever he was, but he wanted to find out what had happened to Jacko. He didn't want to phone Lorraine in case she thought he was just gossiping. Sanderson had been his best bet but the detective had heard nothing yet and promised to call Carter as soon as he knew something.

Carter drove into the show field and spotted the tourer at once. It could hardly be missed, nor could the young man in the denim shirt and jeans sitting on the steps.

'Jesus Christ,' Carter muttered to himself. 'The poor bastard.' He got out of the car and walked over to the tourer, but the man spotted him and, standing up, went inside slamming the door behind him.

Carter shrugged. Well that certainly wasn't a first. He knocked on the door of the tourer. 'Just a minute,' he heard a deep voice say a moment later.

Then the door was opened by a much older man than the one who had been sitting on the step.

The uncle, Carter presumed . . . That's good, two birds with one stone.

'Hello, I'm Police Constable Carter. Could I have a few words with you and yer nephew about Melanie Musgrove, if yer don't mind.'

'No, no . . . Come in.' A severe look on his face, the man turned, leading the way for Carter to follow.

Inside, he gestured for Carter to sit down as he said, 'I've been expecting you.'

'And why would that be, sir?'

'I think you know as well as I do. A child is missing. A few days ago that child, Melanie, started hanging around here and she made a friend of my nephew.' He shrugged. 'And now of course you are here.'

Carter nodded. There was very little he could add to that, except, 'So, where is yer nephew?' He wondered if the big man would lie and say he didn't know.

The man stood up and went down the small corridor. He paused for a few seconds, then knocked on a door and said, 'Josh, the police are here. Could you come out? They would like a word.' He hesitated a moment then added, 'It's about Melanie.'

They waited. Carter was beginning to think that Josh had climbed out of a window when the door finally opened and Josh, scowling, came out.

'What?' he demanded sullenly of Carter.

'It's about Melanie Musgrove.'

'What about her?'

'She's missing.'

'So, it's got nothing to do with me. Anyhow I hardly know her, she's just some snotty-nosed kid that was hanging around. There's loads of them do that, it happens wherever we go. You chase them and they go, but she wouldn't be told. Isn't that right?' He looked at his uncle for confirmation. Percy nodded.

Carter could see how nervous Josh was, and he figured an innocent man would never be as defensive as this one.

'When was the last time yer saw her?'

Josh shrugged. 'Can't remember.' He walked past his uncle and stood near the door. 'She was just a nuisance. I didn't ask her to come here. I chased her away.'

Carter watched Josh slowly edging his way closer to the door. He had a feeling he was gonna do a runner. He stood. 'I think you'd better come down the station, Josh. We can talk better there.'

He'd barely finished his sentence when Josh turned and bolted for the door – but Carter, prepared, flung himself after Josh and brought him down with a flying tackle. Physically, Josh was as fit as Carter, and he managed to wriggle his way out of the policeman's grasp, but Carter grabbed his ankle. Josh reached for a wooden coffee table and raised it above his head, ready to bring it crashing down on Carter's head.

'Nooo,' Percy shouted.

But there was no need. In a split second the anger left Josh's eyes and he changed direction and brought the table crashing down on Carter's arms.

Carter howled in pain and let go of Josh's ankle. Free, Josh jumped up and was out of the door before Carter could get to his feet.

Carter took chase, but Josh had a good head start. Soon he was lost in the crowds that were mingling around the show field.

The phone was ringing off the hook as Lorraine came back into her office clutching a mug of half-cold part-dissolved instant coffee. Impatient as ever, she'd not been able to even wait for the kettle to boil. She pulled a face as she simultaneously gulped a mouthful and reached for the receiver. It tasted as disgusting as it looked.

'Detective Inspector Hunt here. How can I help yer?'

'Formal, aren't we?' Scottie's familiar voice came down the line.

'About time too. So what yer got for me?'

'Was a time when conversation used to be more civil, Lorraine. You know, simple things like "Hello, how are yer?" and the like.'

'Don't mess me around, Scottie,' Lorraine sighed wearily. 'I can't be doing with it. The Feast is well underway and we've a poor kid what has gone missing, three dead bodies, a badly hurt woman in hospital, an' a murderer we're nowhere even close to finding. Then there's the newspaper reporters practically besieging the station – flaming vultures, the lot of them. Aye, an' as if that weren't enough we've the usual pickpockets and drunks and domestics that always goes hand in hand with the Feast. I'm meant to be the one who protects folk and catches the bad'uns. But is there any sign of it? Not so as yer would notice, there isn't. No way.'

'Sorry, pet. Just trying to lighten the tension a bit. Yer sounded like yer've had enough of it an' all. Yer know, love, yer might not reckon much on what yer mam is always telling yer, but yer do need to try and detach yerself a bit. Yer'll be no use if yer get too involved emotionally, yer know. Yer can only do the best yer can do – I know, I know, yer've heard it all before an' yer've no time for it. But yer know why Mavis tells yer it? Because it's true.'

Scottie broke off. He knew Lorraine of old and even if he hadn't, the stony silence at the other end of the phone told him that he may as well be addressing his words to one of the corpses lying in the mortuary. *Aye, an' they might take a bit more notice of me than she will, an' all.*

185

'I'm sorry to say that there's not much I'm gonna tell yer about the victim that'll be new to yer,' he said, referring to the body Samuel Thorenson had literally stumbled on at the top of the church tower.

Lorraine hadn't been able to find out much either – just that her name was Lizzy Williams and she was definitely one of the travellers, but no one seemed to have known her very well. They all looked a bit vague when Lorraine questioned them: she'd turned up a year or so earlier, clearly running away from something – a violent stepfather was the common assumption – and although she'd mucked in and helped out with everything she'd pretty much kept herself to herself. She'd been a loner by nature, and the chaos of the travelling life gave her an easy way to keep her distance. Until some bastard murdered her. Lorraine gave a heavy sigh. 'OK Scottie, so there's not much. Is there anything you *can* tell me?'

'Strangled, like the others, an' a fairly quick death an' all, thank Christ for small mercies. MO looks identical, down to the thumb prints on the back of her neck, but I can confirm that she was taken there and dumped, bit like our second woman left at the fairground. An' that tells yer that our man had some strength. Aye, either strength, or help.'

'Help?' said a shocked Lorraine. 'Are yer seriously suggesting that there's two of them killing these women? Jesus, Scottie.'

'Hold on, I just said that our fella had to have been fairly strong to have got the body up there. An' quiet, though the church grounds aren't that busy I suppose. Whatever. She was definitely killed someplace else and the body moved afterwards. Forensics are doing their stuff in the hope of finding anything that might tell yer just where he strangled her.'

'There was nothing conclusive from the second girl's body so I won't hold me breath for that, Scottie. But it's interesting that with the first he just dumped the body over the bridge where he murdered her. Whereas with these two he's moved them, an' that makes me wonder why. An' it means we can't rule out that there's a pair of them. Though it makes me fairly sick to think on it.'

'Aye. An' there's one more thing that'll interest yer. I've to carry out more tests to sort the precise timing but I reckon this one was killed before the rest – definitely before the lass that the fair workers discovered on the waltzer.'

'What? Are yer certain, Scottie?'

'Like I just said, I'm waiting on some results to confirm the timing, but yes. It looks like it.'

'Well it fits with the last time anyone was up in that tower,' mused Lorraine. 'I've already checked that out and Samuel's last rehearsal was a good week or more ago.'

'I can't tell yer that the body had laid up there in the tower for that long though, pet. The lividity tells me she'd been lying in one place a while, but at the moment that could also be the place where he killed her, yer know.'

'Yeah, I know. There's not a bloody lot that we do know, is there?' Lorraine retorted, before apologising. 'I'm sorry, Scottie. It's not you I'm angry with. I just want to solve this before the bastard goes after someone else.'

They said their goodbyes and Lorraine put the phone down. Thinking about what he'd told her she absent-mindedly picked up the now practically icy coffee and took a sip.

Fuck it! Cold coffee an' a friggin' cold case an' all. Doesn't that just about say it all.

17

Stella put the finishing touches to her make-up and grimaced: black was a colour that had never been kind to her. She was on the doors later on tonight and as she looked at her reflection the badge on her chest caught her eye making her groan out loud. They weren't just bouncers any more, they were Door Supervisors, for God's sake.

They'd even had to take a test, the Security Industry Authority licence. These days the penalty for working the doors without your SIA was five long years. It was because a couple of Hammerman's heavies had failed their SIA test that she'd been called in to work the doors this evening.

For Christ's sake, the book of rules was ten inches tall and an inch thick – how the hell were people like Gulliver, who was a damn good bouncer, but who couldn't read to save his life, be expected to pass an exam?

Hammerman thought he'd cracked it, though. He'd told Stella that he was going to make them take the test again, only this time he'd fork out for tutors. The thought of Gulliver, an enormous bloke who resembled a great big grisly bear, sitting behind a tiddly little school desk made her laugh.

As she was putting away her make-up, a groaning noise from somewhere close caused her to drop her lipstick. *Damn this old house, fucking noises all over the place.*

She had just straightened up when a loud knocking set her heart jumping. *Shit, I told him I didn't need a lift tonight.*

Stella quickly gathered her things together and took one last look in the mirror. She'd do. As she left the room, she kissed her fingers and placed them momentarily on the picture of her daughter she kept on the sideboard.

As soon as she opened the door Hammerman tried to bustle through. Putting her hand on his chest she smiled and gently eased him back out.

He frowned his disappointment. 'What's up with you then? We've got plenty of time.'

'Later, save it for later. Besides I'm on the doors tonight, remember? I'm all made-up an' I don't want to have to start over. Specially not with the traffic at the bridge getting worse each night.'

The frown still in place, Hammerman allowed himself to be coerced into going back to the car. With huge relief Stella slid in next to him. She knew she'd have her work cut out getting rid of him later on. *Ugly pig. Thinks I'm there for whenever he wants me, he does. Like all bleeding men.*

To distract him she said, 'How's Doris Musgrove?'

'Far as I know the cheeky old git is still alive and kicking. She brought it on herself yer know. Don't think I make a habit of having old women beaten up. That cheeky old cow had something coming somewhere along the line, even if the pair of them went a bit too far. One thing though, she had a go back at him, got to admire her for that.'

'Good for her.'

In all fairness though, she thought, this was the first time something like this had ever happened. Usually if it was women who owed, Hammerman sorted the husbands, who then sorted their wives.

'Aye, but yer name'll be mud now all right, won't it? They'll be calling yer the granny basher next.'

She heard his teeth grinding together and knew that, although she could have pushed it further, she'd said enough. She knew exactly which buttons to press with Hammerman and would often needle away until he was worked into a fair lather. But right now she merely wanted to distract him. With any luck he would stew all night, and likely go back after the tattooed freak who'd done the deed, leaving her alone.

That was Hammerman's nature to the core. Yer took a beating then, when you thought yer were safe and it was all over, the bastard came back again. Hammerman was a stewer, he always went back again, and it was always worse the second time around.

God help Halliday when he reaped the seeds she'd sown tonight.

Carter arrived back at the station to find all hell had broken loose. Lorraine, her face like thunder stood to one side, her hands so tightly clenched that the knuckles stood out stark white.

'What's up?' Carter asked.

'Listen,' she hissed. 'Clark is about to make an announcement.'

Carter faced front and stood open-mouthed as Clark told everyone that, thanks to Sara Jacobs, they had detained for questioning someone who they strongly suspected might be the killer.

Sanderson gave Carter a questioning frown and Carter shrugged in reply. A moment later both their jaws dropped when Clark named Jacko Musgrove as the suspect and announced that he had every confidence of a real break-through in the case within hours. He cautioned them against revealing the identity of the detainee to the public for the moment but said that he hoped they might be in a very different position before the night was out.

Carter turned to Lorraine in stunned disbelief. 'No way,' he mouthed. She nodded her agreement.

Carter turned back to look at Clark who stood alongside the very smug Sara Jacobs.

'Sir,' he said, trying to get Clark's attention. 'Sir.' Clark ignored him.

'I've instructed Sara to let the press know we're questioning someone and to expect an official statement before long. Now that the nationals have got hold of the story, they're making all our lives hell.' He nodded at the room in general, then turned to leave.

While Clark had been talking Carter had quietly filled Lorraine in on what had happened at the show field. Quickly Lorraine ushered him after Clark.

'Sir, sir,' Carter said, catching up with the superintendent.

Clark frowned at him as he kept on walking. 'What?' he said abruptly, obviously not remembering who he was.

'Sir, I think I have a lead on the missing girl, Melanie Musgrove.'

That stopped him in his tracks, Carter could practically see his mind working overtime.

'Tell me, er . . .'

'Carter, sir.'

'Oh yes, Carter. Well what do you mean? A lead on where she is? Or on who took her? Jacobs's theory is that this Musgrove fellow has done something to his daughter as well as the murdered women. The girl's shoe was found near her home as I've been given to understand.'

'Don't know, sir, but it seems to me that one of the travellers knows something,' and he proceeded to tell him everything that had happened on his visit to see Josh.

'Well, the travellers have got their badd'uns, same as any community, so he could have been running from you for any damn reason, but you're right, it's pretty suspicious. Maybe he's even in league with Jacko Musgrove. Well let's put out an All Points Bulletin and pick him up too. Oh, by the way, well done, Cartwright.' He looked over Carter's shoulder to where he could see Lorraine. 'Bright lad you have here, Detective Inspector Hunt. He and Sara Jacobs might make quite a team.'

Lorraine nodded. Inside she was seething. Not at Carter who had done a good and thorough job, but at Jacobs who had gone over her head to Clark claiming that she'd been unable to get hold of Lorraine and it was urgent. Lorraine knew damn well she'd been contactable by radio and by mobile and that Jacobs was simply seeking to ingratiate herself.

Aye, a right sneaky bitch that one. I should've trusted me instincts.

Carter turned to Lorraine with a look of pure horror on his face. 'Me an' Sara Jacobs, boss? No way.'

'Don't worry, Carter. It ain't gonna happen.'

Not flippin' likely when I'm gonna do me best to get cow-face transferred outta here first chance I get.

'Do yer think it is Jacko then, boss?' Luke asked as he joined them.

'What I think is that it's all a bit too quick and a bit too heavy-handed for my liking,' Lorraine answered. 'Jesus, we've only just found out who the girl in the tower is. We've not even ruled out the possibility that there might be two of them killing and not only one. I'm not saying I don't think he did it for certain like – but I'd've preferred a quieter, less official chat with him first. Aye an' maybe on his own turf where he'd've been more at ease than he's gonna be where he is.'

Luke and Carter nodded their agreement.

'Any road, for the time being I want everyone to carry on with both investigations. If it isn't Jacko – and like I say, my instinct's telling me it isn't – then the killer's still out there. An' so far the only real info we have is Christina's claim that whoever attacked her has got something wrong with his face.'

'So has this Josh bloke too, Boss,' Carter broke in.

'That's right, so get onto getting him picked up pronto will yer, Carter. An' let's not forget,' Lorraine shook her head wearily, 'we've still got this poor lass missing. If Jacko is innocent then we've banged up a grieving father and the press'll flaming well hang us for that, for sure.'

A traumatised Jacko looked round at his surroundings. The holding cell was very small – one cot bed nailed to the wall and one toilet, just below the tiny window. The place reeked of vomit, sweat, urine and a cheap disinfectant that failed abysmally to cover the stink.

Obviously I haven't been given the de luxe suite.

There was graffiti on every available surface. He lost count of how many times 'Dan was here' decorated the walls. Whether it was the same Dan or not was impossible to tell. If it was, he must have spent all of one night signing his autograph. *Aye, or been locked up every night for God knows how many years.*

Whatever, he sighed, there was no way of telling. And he didn't care that much one way or another.

There were other names, some ancient, some recent, that he recognised, but he soon lost interest.

He was in deep shit this time all right.

He put his head in his hands. Many a time he'd been in a bad situation – good God, in his circle, he didn't know many who hadn't. And sometimes he'd been that far down, there had seemed to be no way out. But he'd managed one way or another and each and every time he'd clawed himself back up. *Aye, man. But never ever anything this bad.*

No, never anything this bad.

Fucking hell. Suspected of murder.

Jesus Christ.

What the fuck have I ever done to deserve this?

Fuck me, what about Melanie? What about me kid?

The thought of Melanie filled him with despair and frustration.

What the fuck could he do?

How the hell can I find her in here?

Like a quick swinging shuggy boat ride at the show field, his emotions swung from despair to anger and he pounded his fist on the thin mattress.

Melanie going's got to have something to do with that bastard Hammerman. He's lost the fucking plot and taking it all out on me and mine.

It's got to be that bastard, I know it has. First me mam and now me bairn.

The anger boiled over into rage. He jumped up and began pacing the floor. Four paces, then his nose touched the wall and for a brief moment he stood and stared at the cracks, running every which way like the webs of a demented spider. Then he spun round and paced the other four back.

Over and over he paced. In his mind's eye he saw Doris, blood running down her face. Then Melanie.

Ohh, God, Melanie.

Melanie laughing, Melanie crying. But Melanie only ever cried when the pain got too bad. Mostly she laughed, and mostly she sang.

He could hear her now.

Could see her walking down the street, then spotting him and trying to run in that funny hop-a-long, leg-dragging way she had. Spotting him and grinning all over her face. Her dad!

But what if it wasn't Hammerman – what if the real murderer had taken her?

Ohh, Jesus, no!

He sobbed then and, unashamed, let the hot tears run down his face.

His Melanie loved him, loved him when half the world looked down on him. He knew what they thought, them in their fancy suits – them that had chances which had been denied to the likes of him. He'd seen the way some of them stared at him, thinking he was no good.

Well let them walk in his shoes where the shit was knee deep.

But his own sweet Melanie saw in him what they in their blinkers missed. And where was he when she needed him the most?

He punched the wall, the webs multiplied.

Stuck in this bastard dump.

He turned to the bed and with one angry heave tore it from the wall and threw it at the door. Metal vibrated against metal and when the sound died down, running feet could be heard in the corridor outside.

When the door was opened a few seconds later, the burly policeman found Jacko on his knees with his forehead touching the floor.

He reels from the churchyard, oblivious to the traffic as he crosses the road.

A week, a whole week she's been dead. He is lost without her. Mother.

Slowly, shuffling like an old man, he walks the half mile or so to the Broadway. Spotting an empty seat, he claims it for his own. Most of the people passing by ignore him. Ignore the big fat tears that fall onto the pavement almost as if he is invisible.

But that's all right. They've done that most of his life anyhow.

The two or three who do stop, hastily move on when he won't answer them.

Then one stops who has his heart beating so fast he wants to get up and dance.

'Hi,' she says. She smiles. 'Sorry to hear about yer mam.'

He nods: everything that could be said has already been spoken. They are only words and meaningless now that Mother is gone.

She perseveres, lending him her hankie, and gradually he begins to respond. They chat for a while – longer than she has ever spoken to him in all the years he's known her. She tells him things about herself he has to pretend he doesn't know already and when she finally nods her goodbye he feels his spirits plunge. His angel, gone.

As he watches her walk away he is slowly rubbing the angel's handkerchief against the top of his thigh: by the time she reaches the corner it is in his pocket, safely hidden away.

18

Josh woke to a chorus of birds, some already in full song, some sounding as if they were just waking up from a long hard night on the town. For a moment he hadn't the faintest idea where he was. Then the smell of damp earth very close to his nose brought everything back. He was in Newbottle Woods, hiding out in the witch's cave.

Sitting up, he yawned as he brushed a few red and gold leaves and – with extreme distaste – one or two fat brown spiders from his legs. Last night he'd been terrified nearly to death at the thought of trying to sleep in the cave and though he had managed to shut his eyes for a couple of hours, he didn't feel that happy about it this morning. Local legend had it that way way back there had been a coven on the site and that the witches still haunted the cave. Looking around him at the spooky shadows he could just about believe it. He knew deep down that the story had probably originated as a yarn to frighten the kids away, because it was dangerous and so hard to get to, but all the same . . .

Josh shivered. But then he reminded himself that that was

why it was such a good place to hide: scary, remote and inaccessible. Except he'd forgotten how hard it actually was to reach the damned place, and he'd narrowly missed breaking a few limbs on the way.

He knew why he was really shivering: the cave was damp with all the recent rain they'd had and he had no matches for a fire, nor warm clothes. He hadn't had time to bring anything.

He sneezed once, then twice. There was a moment's dead silence then a scrabbling sound came from the back of the cave.

'Oh, my God,' he muttered. What the hell had he spent the night with?

He didn't really want to know, his legs were urging him to get out of there, and fast. His heart was banging against his ribs, but he couldn't stop himself from slowly turning around.

Fearfully he peered into the deep darkness behind him and though his body was preparing for flight, on another level he was thanking God that he hadn't heard the noise in the middle of the night. *I'd've pissed myself.*

At first he couldn't see anything. Then she moved.

'Wow, you frightened the life outta me!'

The fox showed her teeth.

'OK, you don't want to be friends. That's fine by me.'

She snarled and Josh scuttled to the side of the cave, giving her an easy exit. She took her time about it, nervously sniffing the air as she sidled past him, then in a quick dart she was gone, and it was as if she'd never been there.

'Jesus.' He looked out into the woods wondering if she was watching him from the bushes.

They think I've hurt Melanie. The thought came so abruptly that he actually winced.

Even Uncle Percy was giving me odd looks.

The thought that his Uncle Percy could be thinking on the same lines as the police upset him. He curled in on himself, trying to keep warm. Remembering all the rubbish the little nuisance had spouted.

At first he'd thought her family were rich, what with her babbling about Disneyland and the collection of fancy dolls she had. She even had names for every one of them. The dolls had hurt because his youngest sister had also collected them and he'd found himself picturing their plastic faces melting in the intense heat which had destroyed their owner.

Shaking his head as if trying to dislodge all thoughts of his family – like you could shake an angry bee away – Josh concentrated on Melanie, going over each time he'd seen her and every word he could remember her saying, hoping that something might prove the solution to the mess he was in.

People had been locked up for years for things they hadn't done and he wasn't going to be the next one. Not when he was innocent. Never mind what dirty nasty things people might think, he hadn't hurt Melanie and he never would have. He liked the kid, was that so hard to understand?

She made him want to laugh.

Had made him laugh.

Was that such a bad thing?

Eventually he'd found out that Melanie's family weren't loaded at all. Her dad just worked himself silly providing everything she wanted. She wasn't spoilt though – as kids go, Melanie was all right. He'd actually found himself liking her.

How could that be bad?

But where was the kid? Had she run off? No, too happy and excited about the Feast happening. Surely not murdered like the other poor girls? Another shiver ran through him. But then again, she was only a kid whereas they were all fully grown. If only he could think who it was that Melanie had gone home with the last time he'd seen her at the fairground.

Not her grandmother, and certainly not her father.

But what was the point. If the police got hold of him and he told them – swore to them – that he had nothing whatsoever to do with her going missing, would they believe him?

Probably not. They would take one look at him.

Think gypsy.

Damaged gypsy.

Guilty.

Case solved.

There's only one thing to do, he thought with sudden determination. *Find Melanie myself.*

The cell door opened and Carter came in carrying a mug of tea.

Jacko sighed and said, 'Thanks, mate,' as he reached for the mug and Carter handed it over.

'No bother, mate. Manage to get any sleep did yer?'

Jacko gave a hollow laugh. 'Oh yeah, tons of time for sleeping when you lot've been friggin' well interrogating me all night.' He took a drink of the tea before going on. 'No, none at all. An' even if there was a chance of catching some kip in this shithole, how the hell can I? Our Melanie's out there, with God alone knows who, and me stuck in here. I tell yer, man, me own bairn and I can't do nothing. But I reckon I'm well past time for yer either to charge me or let me go. And when I finally do get out . . .'

Carter nodded. God help whoever had Melanie Musgrove, 'cos Jacko wouldn't rest until he found her. He tutted his sympathy.

'Yer don't think I'm the murderer do yer, Carter? I ask yer, me a fucking murderer, yer know me better than that, man. And where the fuck's Luke, he's gotta know it's not me.'

'He's been doing his own interviewing all night. Him an' Inspector Hunt. Following up on stuff to do with the lass the piper found up in the tower. But if it's any consolation I know he doesn't think it's you, in fact he was quite adamant it wasn't you. Told Clark himself it wasn't. Anyhow, the boss isn't certain it's you either.'

'So what the fuck am I still in here for then! Jesus.'

'Cos we have to check out everything, Jacko, yer know we do. An' Sara Jacobs has made a pretty strong argument, what with yer not being able to account for where yer were, an' yer having a patch on yer eye, an' the rest.'

'Yeah, well Sara Jacobs has made one big fucking mistake. The bloody murderer is still out there, while I'm bloody well stuck in here.'

Carter nodded, then said, 'Well yer right on one thing, they can't keep yer much longer an' they can't charge yer.'

'Yer sure about that, man?'

'Yeah, there's no real evidence and it's not like yer've confessed to anything even though they were trying for it half the night.'

'So I'll be out before long?'

'Aye.'

'So why didn't yer tell me as soon as yer came in, yer friggin' dolt.'

'Yer didn't give us much of a chance, Jacko.'

Jacko's eyes shone. 'Thank Christ. I canna wait to get out of here and back out looking.'

'Yer'll have to watch yer step though, no plans to visit Orlando in the near future. Cos yer'll not be allowed to leave Tyne and Wear for a while.'

'Howay, man, what're yer on about?'

''Cos Jacobs is still convinced it's you. An' she's busy ferreting out everything she can about yer.'

'Well I think if I was in the habit of murdering folk there

202

would be no need for them to do any friggin' ferreting. It'd be public knowledge.'

'Aye, but yer have been known to, er . . .'

'Defend meself once or twice. Is that what yer getting at, Carter?'

'Aye, ah suppose.'

'Yer know as well as I do, the twice it got to court it was proven self-defence. Anyhow, both of them were drug dealers so they got what they deserved.'

'I know yer a pussycat an' so does Luke. But on paper, in black and white, well, it just doesn't have the same ring, if yer know what I mean.'

Jacko nodded, he knew what Carter meant all right.

Both of them looked up as the duty officer came to the cell door. 'Let's be having yer, Jacko, yer can go now.'

Jacko jumped up, spilling the remains of his tea in his haste as he said a heartfelt, 'Thank God.'

Lorraine stared at the scowling faces as they drove into the Seahills.

Big mistake, they should have used an unmarked car. If I wasn't so flaming angry I would have known that. *So why didn't Luke think of it?*

She looked sideways under her lashes at him thinking how good he looked in jeans and a navy sweatshirt. Then shook that thought away and opted for the safer route of feeling disgruntled at him and at the world. They'd spent the night carrying out further interviews at the fairground, the theory that a traveller might have carried out the murders strengthened by the revelation that the girl in the tower was one of their own. She'd apparently gone missing soon after arriving in Houghton, but the bloke on the dodgems who she'd lived with claimed that he'd assumed she'd run off and that she'd done it before. He'd had a strong alibi for the nights of the other murders and nothing at all wrong with his face which was their only concrete lead on the killer for the moment. It was starting to feel as though they were back at square one.

Lorraine was dog tired and irritable. She'd only had time to call in at home for a quick shower before coming out again and she'd had Luke wait whilst she pulled on a change of clothes. In contrast to her he looked as fresh as he always did – Mavis had lent him a razor and you'd scarce know that he'd been up all night. Lorraine had come down to find him all cosied up in the kitchen.

Yeah, an' wasn't he fairly sucked up to me mam and the Rock Chick, an' them feeding him bacon sandwichs an' the rest. He's got the bloody pair of them thinking he's the best thing since sliced bread. I bet they'd even lick the bloody crumbs up for him an' all.

Ohh, they're all the same.

She turned her mind back to the present. For a Sunday morning, the place was buzzing. People stood around in clusters and if animosity had a colour you would have been able to see it radiating off them in waves.

They pulled up across the road from Jacko's house planning to have a quiet word with Doris whilst she was on her own, Carter having radioed the news that her son was about to be let go. On the facing pavement four teenage boys lounged in regulation tracksuits, their caps shoved back on their heads in the latest fashion, holding up the Musgroves' garden wall.

Lorraine, her hair caught in a neat ponytail and in jeans and a pink top, got out and turned to lock the patrol car. She ignored the wolf whistle which in any case soon stopped when Luke glared at the boy responsible.

'There's nobody in,' the boy who looked like he had Chinese ancestry called, his large round face never changing expression.

'Are youse two coppers?' asked another, his white track-suit looking slightly the worse for wear.

Lorraine looked at him. 'Yes, why?'

'Bloody coppers. Waste of space me dad says. Can't even find a missing kid, can yer. But yer locked her dad up. Huh, like Jacko's a murderer.'

The front door behind the boys opened and a small grey-haired woman with thick-rimmed glasses peered out. 'Shoo, go get yerselves away from here. I'm sick of telling yers, get a bloody job. Hanging around all day, just courting trouble the whole lot of yer.'

Slowly the boys peeled away from the wall and started heading up the street. The only one Lorraine heard make a comment was the one who'd mouthed off at her. 'Nosy old goat,' he muttered to his friends.

'Pssst.' Lorraine looked over the road. 'Pssst.' The old woman was waving them over. Shrugging, she gave Luke a half smile, and the pair of them crossed the road. There was nothing they liked better than a willing gossip. Lorraine had discovered long ago that if they approached you, then yer got to know things that any amount of questioning wouldn't drag out of them.

'Bloody kids. Nowt to do. That's the problem. My Ronny predicted this, so he did. When they closed the pits he said as how it'd make for problems. Kids that age twenty years ago would have been right out of school, and into the pits where they belong. Heritage, see, no chance to get into bother,' she clicked her tongue. 'My Ronny was right, he always said there would be trouble with the youth. Anyhow, if yer've come to see Doris she's over at the NHS Emergency place in Sunderland. Trevor took her and Dolly up about half an hour ago. She's complaining about headaches now. Bleedin' disgraceful it was what they done to her. No wonder that she's got headaches, eh, the poor bugger. Have yer found little Melanie yet, is that what yer've come about?'

Lorraine shook her head. 'No, sorry . . .'

'Aww, shame. Bad time Houghton Feast. October yer see, bad month, always brings the worst outta folk. My Ronny passed over in October yer know. An' you'll've heard of that October Revolution that 'appened way back, tho' I'm blessed if I rightly recall what it was.' At this, Lorraine and Luke exchanged wry grins: there was gossip and then there was pure wittering on and it looked as though there was no stopping this one now she'd started. 'Aye, I'll tell yer summat else, that there bomb that nearly did for our Mrs Thatcher down in Brighton was in October. What d'yer think of that then?'

'Yes, well –' Lorraine tried to interrupt the old woman but she might as well have saved her breath.

'An' it was October if me memory serves me right when that poor wee lass Amanda died in that dreadful crash. That was awful that was. What a waste, eh. Canny kid, Amanda. Well, sometimes like, 'cos yer don't like to speak ill of the dead, do yer. To tell yer the truth she could be a nasty spiteful little bitch at times. Her mother though, wouldn't have a wrong word said about her. I'm pleased she moved away. A lady bouncer, whoever heard of such a thing. Couldn't bounce a ball if yer ask me . . .'

'Well, thank you it's been nice to talk,' Lorraine got in quickly. 'We'll come back later and catch Mrs Musgrove. Goodbye then.' She and Luke turned away and started back across the road, barely able to stifle their giggles.

'Aye, ta-ra.' Looking disappointed, the old woman closed the door.

'She never stopped once to draw breath!' Luke laughed. 'I was watching her.'

'Yer right there. Jesus, I'd even put money on her out-talking Mam and Peggy an' that's saying something. The October Revolution for Christ's sake! The only thing wrong with October round here is what the flippin' Feast always brings with it. Fun for the kids but a pain in the bloody neck for the rest of us. But while she rattled away I was thinking back on last year, Luke, an' I'm wondering if yer shouldn't take another look at that poor lass what got attacked to see if there might be a link. If I remember rightly she'd come over from Silksworth for the fireworks but her address'll be at the station. Call in to Carter and ask him to look it up. It's a long shot an' she gave a full statement at the time but let's try it.'

'OK, boss. Are yer coming with me?'

'No, yer can drop me at the station to pick up a car. I want to go an' check on Doris. I still want to talk to her about Melanie 'cos I just don't trust Sara Jacobs to have made a proper enough job of it. If I know her she's more likely to have put the old woman's back up and got nowt from her.'

'D'yer think she knows more than she's letting on then?' Luke asked, looking at Lorraine as they got into the car.

'Aye, just a hunch.'

He's doing it again.

Why does he look at me like that?

And why the fuck do I get goose pimples all over every time he does?

'Shit.'

'Sorry?'

'Nowt. Just phone Carter like I told yer.'

Mickey and Robbie were waiting outside the police station when Jacko walked out.

Mickey gave him a high five. 'Great to see yer, mate!'

'Aye, and youse two bald bastards an' all,' Jacko replied as he nodded at Robbie. 'Heard anything, lads?'

207

'No. We've still looked though, even when yer were in here, Jacko. Us and the rest of the lads, and some off the Homelands and the Burnside. Beefy stayed up all night looking. He says he'll catch yer later.'

Robbie shifted about as he answered, not wanting to tell Jacko about Melanie's shoe that they'd found and handed in to the police. God knows the poor bloke had enough to worry about already.

'I appreciate it, mate, yer know I do. God am I glad to get outta there. Another five minutes and they'd have had me in a bloody straitjacket. Anyhow, it's good of yers to meet me, but I've gotta go somewhere.'

'Where?' Mickey asked. 'We'll come with yer.'

'No lads, it's best yer don't get involved.'

'But –'

Jacko frowned at Mickey. 'This I've got to do by meself. I'll not drag anybody else into me own trouble. Good of yer to offer, but no.' Then he turned and hurried away.

Watching him, Mickey said, 'We shoulda went with him.'

'It's enough that he knows we were here for him, and that Beefy spent the night doing what he would have done.'

'Yer probably right. Anyhow I've got to go up home, some family thing. Aunts and Uncles coming for the community hymn singing in the Broadway tonight.'

'Is it still on, like? Cos me mam and Sandra were wondering earlier?'

Mickey shrugged, 'I don't think something as simple as a murderer would keep Aunt Mabel away.'

Robbie had met Mickey's Aunt Mabel. 'Aye, she's awesome, isn't she.'

They laughed, then Mickey headed up to Hall Lane while Robbie made his way to the Seahills.

Mickey nearly reached safety, he was actually turning into his gate when Fran shouted, 'Good God! Is that you, Mickey?'

Bloody hell.
Twice in a week.
She's stalking me.
What to do? What to do?
Pretend I didn't hear her and bolt for the door?
Pretend I'm me cousin Adam?
Like that's gonna work on eagle eye.
Too late, she was close enough to touch.
And I bet me bloody scalp's bright red.
'Erm . . . hi, Fran. How yer doing?'

'Aye, I'm just great, lad, but I was wondering what yer might be doing later? Only yer see Mickey, ever since yer've shaved yer head I've started to see yer in a totally new light.'

'What?' Mickey practically jumped for joy he was that excited. His wildest imaginings seemed to be turning true.

'Well, er, I'm meant to be seeing relations but I can get out of it, I know I can –.' He broke off as he caught sight of Fran's skinny friend Kelly trying to hide behind her and realised the pair of them were killing themselves trying to stifle their laughter. Mustering what little dignity he had left Mickey gave the pair a hard look saying, 'Aye, very clever girls, very clever. An' I'm the one to have fell for it.' Then turning, he stalked through the gate.

'So yer telling me that yer think this Hammerman's the one what had yer beaten?' Once Lorraine had heard that Doris had been given the all-clear by the emergency room, she felt like bashing the old woman's head against the surgery wall for not telling the police about Hammerman before. But she kept her cool: after all, that's what Doris was. An old woman. Sighing, she repeated slowly and calmly, 'Yer think it was Hammerman, don't yer, Doris?'

'Well, I can't say for sure, can I? But he'd been round that morning collecting, him an' that Stella woman. An' I wouldn't put it past him 'cos he's a wrong 'un through and through. An' she's no better than she ought to be since she lost that kid of hers. I feel for her like, but what's she want to be picking on folk like me for, eh?'

'But did yer not consider that this bloke might've had something to do with Melanie going missing? That he could be holding her as some kind of ransom if yer owes them all that money? Yer may have lost us valuable time Doris by not saying this before.'

Sensing Lorraine's suppressed anger, Doris's face crumpled and she suddenly sagged from the middle. 'I would've done,' she sobbed, 'if that police lady had given me half a chance. But she were so intent on poor Jacko that she wasn't listening to nothing, an' then when she took him in an' it all went sideways I must've forgot what I was gonna say.'

As Lorraine helped Doris to a chair to a chorus of tuts from Dolly she was already reaching for her radio. 'I want the identity and whereabouts of someone who terms himself Hammerman,' she told a startled Carter. 'Aye an' find out what yer can about his sidekick an' all, someone called Stella who used to live local.'

'Sure thing, boss.'

'An' Carter.'

'Yes, boss?'

'Keep Jacobs out of it for the moment.'

Aye, an' the useless bitch'll be out of a job soon an' all if I have my way . . .

'No,' Melanie yelled. 'No, no no.' She'd seen the needle before she'd seen anything else. In her imagination it grew and grew, blotting everything else out as it seemed to float in mid-air from the doorway across to her bed.

Needles were for druggies. And this was the fourth time she'd had it.

210

She was a druggie.

Please, Jesus, I don't want to be a druggie. Please Jesus, send me me dad.

'Please, no. Please let me go home!' she pleaded.

'Now yer know it doesn't hurt.'

'I won't scream honest. I won't try to escape. Please!' she sobbed.

Her captor tutted. 'Don't be such a crybaby.'

'Just let me go home. I want me dad. Please, I want me dad.'

'No yer don't.'

'I do! I do!' Melanie wriggled as much as she could. 'I do too. And he's bigger than you, he'd stop you.'

'Now stop acting up, I have to go to work. And this is your home now. Really I don't know why yer going on like this, yer never used to before.'

Terrified, Melanie tried her hardest to pull away but she was tied too securely. She could do nothing but watch in horror as the needle was plunged into her arm delivering the liquid Diazepam.

In seconds the pink roses were shedding their petals and blurring into one as she drifted off to sleep.

19

The loud knock on the door startled Stella. 'Hammerman
. . . Shit.'

Quickly putting on her coat, and taking three deep breaths
to calm herself, she went to the door. She was surprised on
opening it to find two detectives standing there.

'Stella Naysmith?' Lorraine asked. Luke stood by her side.
He'd had a wasted trip to Silksworth as the woman had gone
to London for the Feast weekend to escape her memories of
the previous year's attack.

'Yeah, that's me. What's wrong?' Stella asked, horribly
reminded that the last time there had been police on her
doorstep it was to inform her that Amanda was dead.

Lorraine, antennae on full alert as usual, picked up a
nervous undertone in the other woman's voice, but kept her
voice light and easy. 'Can we come in?'

'Well I'm just on me way out, like.'

'It won't take long.'

Obviously not liking the idea, Stella shrugged. 'Well I
suppose so.'

Inside Lorraine looked around. Despite the house's age the decor was fantastic with what looked like the latest and the best of everything.

'Had a pay rise, Stella? I guess your boss – this Hammerman as they call him – is pretty generous with other people's money?'

Stella was immediately on the defensive. 'I save a lot. And since when was it a crime to like nice things?'

Lorraine shook her head, 'Never has been, Stella. Not if they're legitimately come by.'

'Yeah, well, they are that. An' therefore I canna see how it's any concern of yours.'

'It's yer boss we've come about, Stella. We've been hearing quite a bit about this Mr Hammerman lately an' we thought as how yer might want to have a little chat with us seein' as yer seem to know him so well.'

'I just work for him is all. An' I would've thought you lot would have more important things on yer hands than bothering the likes of me. What about these horrible murders, eh? An' there's that little wee girl what's gone missing an' all. Have yer found her yet?'

Lorraine, a master at changing the subject herself, easily picked up on Stella's poor effort and to Stella's shock replied, 'That's what we're here about.'

'What?'

'Aye, I believe you and this Hammerman were on the Seahills the day Melanie went missing, paying a little call on her poor granny.'

'Yeah, an' what if we were?'

'So did either of yers see anything?'

'No.'

'Yer seem pretty sure about that. Noticed nothing at all did yers? No strange cars, no strange people?'

'I already said.'

'So yer did, Stella. But it seems mighty strange to me that one minute yer was coming on strong to poor old Doris an' the next little Melanie is gone. Are yer sure there's nothing more yer want to tell me? Fancy a little blackmail did the pair of yer? No chance yer holding her to ransom on account of not getting yer money? 'Cos if yer are, then I'll be throwing the flippin' book at the pair of yers, an' make no mistake about that.'

'She's a gob on 'er, yer boss, ain't she?' Stella said to Luke, not in the least fazed by Lorraine's accusations. 'Well mebbe she should go an' yap somewhere else 'cos she's fairly in the wrong here.'

'Pretty girl your Amanda, wasn't she?' Luke said, staring at the photo of a girl with long dark hair on the sideboard.

Stella looked shell shocked by the sudden change of direction. Quickly she gathered her thoughts. 'Aye. She was the best thing that ever happened to me an' all.'

'Drink-driving wasn't it?' Luke asked casually, having been thoroughly briefed by Carter.

'She was never that daft!' Stella exploded angrily. 'She was a good girl my Amanda an' I tell yers, she never would have taken a drink an' then drove.'

'Yeah, I heard tell that yer were saying so at the time. And since. Yer seem convinced that it wasn't an accident. Do yer still feel the same?'

'Aye, nowt's changed on that score. And nothing you nor anybody else can say will make me change me mind. I know that youse lot are covering up something, an' yer can be certain that one of these days it'll come out. An' then we'll see who's asking the questions, eh?'

'OK, Stella,' Lorraine broke in. 'That's enough of that. So yer know nothing about the kid, is that right? An' yer've not seen any strangers or anything untoward when yer were doing your rounds?'

Stella shook her head. 'Sorry.'

Yeah, yer look it. Lorraine thought, but said, 'Right then, if yer can't help we'll not keep yer any longer and we'll be on our way. But yer know we'll be keeping an eye on yer, don't be in any doubt of that. Isn't that right, Luke?'

Without waiting for Luke to answer, Lorraine went on, 'Goodbye then. For now.'

Stella nodded, trying hard not to look too eager to get rid of them. 'I, er, if I do remember anything, or hear anything at all, I'll give yer a ring.'

'You do that, Stella.' Luke smiled, as they turned away from the door.

On their way to the car Lorraine was trying to dissect the uneasy feeling she had. She was also wondering why Luke had smiled at Stella the way he had as they left.

No different to any of them.

They'll smile at anything in a skirt, just for the bloody sake of it. Men. Who needs them.

She rummaged in her pocket for a pencil.

Where the hell is it. That's the trouble with jeans, no room for nothing. She finally found it tucked in the corner, just as they reached the car.

'Where now, boss?' Luke asked, sensing her mood.

'Back to the Musgroves'.'

Wondering why she was being so abrupt, Luke was quiet for the rest of the drive to the Seahills.

Jacko had coerced Trevor into giving him a lift to the hospital. A short detour to Sunderland's Mowbray Park, so that Jacko could 'borrow' a few flowers, had cost them a mere ten minutes.

'Are yer coming up, Trev?' Jacko asked while they were trying to find a parking space which was proving nearly impossible, even on a Sunday.

'No, no. I'll just wait here.'

Noticing Trevor's nervousness, Jacko said, 'What for?'

'Why man, she doesn't want both of us up there. The poor lass is very ill from what I hear.'

'Why, aye, she will, man. Ha'way.'

If the truth was known Jacko didn't look forward to the visit himself. He wasn't blind – Christina was a damn good-looking lass. Though he'd never let on to anybody, least of all his mam 'cos she'd have the banns up in the church before he'd even said hello to the girl, he'd quite fancied her for some time and dreaded seeing what some bastard had done to her. Not that anything would ever come of it. *Aye, she'd probably have a heart attack or something if I asked her out. And that's only if I ever got past that twat of a father of hers.*

But Trevor was adamant. 'No, I'll just hang here, yer not gonna be that long anyhow are yer, I mean Christina's not noted for her conversations, like, is she?'

Jacko managed a hollow laugh. 'Why that makes a pair of yer then, doesn't it?'

Jacko took the lift thinking that Trevor was worse than he was where women were concerned.

He knew his way around the hospital from his visits with Melanie and had no trouble finding Christina. He looked into her room and saw that she was alone, staring out of the window at the sky. A portable television entertained itself in the corner of the room.

Feeling relieved that at least she was on her own, Jacko knocked lightly on the open door. Christina turned and he watched her pale face change colour as she saw who it was.

Knowing how shy she was, and sensing her near to panic, Jacko crossed the room quickly. 'Hello, Christina, I brought you these.' He put the bedraggled flowers on the bed and Christina's blush deepened.

She mumbled a barely audible thank you and looked at the flowers with unconcealed amazement.

Jacko wanted to take hold of her hand – she seemed so sad and vulnerable, and the scratches on her face were terrible to see.

Dear God, looks like she's been whipped with barbed wire.

He knew, though, that making any sudden moves towards her would probably scare her even more, so instead he said, 'Christina love, I need yer to tell the coppers that it wasn't me what attacked yer. It's important, else I wouldn't have bothered yer knowing how poorly yer are, like, pet. Only it's our Melanie, yer'll have heard that she's missing, and there's these two coppers what are determined to pin the murders and your own attack on me. So please girl, I need yer help on this one. Can't find our Melanie without it. They're gonna keep on after me and maybe take me back in again if yer don't tell them that it weren't me.'

She lifted her head slowly and, although Jacko's heart was very badly bruised right now, when she smiled at him he felt it quicken.

'So if yer could . . .' He broke off, and waited anxiously for her reaction.

What if she's not sure?

What if she does think it was me?

He felt his pulse race as anxiety grabbed hold of him and began to squeeze.

Slowly Christina nodded.

'Ohh, great, yer don't know how much that means.' Jacko nearly collapsed on the bed with relief. 'Emm, shouldn't there be a copper here, on guard like?' He didn't want to frighten her but he thought it strange, unless there'd been someone outside and he'd missed them? He quickly moved to the door and looked up and down the corridor: empty.

'Tea,' she said, when he looked back at her.

'Eh?'

'He's gone for some tea.'

'Oh, OK. Right then, pet, I'd better be going.' He moved to the door but then stopped and asked, 'Would yer like me to come back and visit? When things is sorted like?'

It seemed to take for ever for Christina to answer, then slowly the hint of a barely seen smile played on her lips and she said, 'Yes. I would like that. Please.'

Jacko nodded, then turning he quickly headed back towards the lift.

Samuel Thorenson was considered by more than a few to be a hero because of his cool head on Friday night. Tonight he led the community hymn singing and sang with more gusto than ever. Usually the Broadway was packed to overflowing with even the people who never set foot in the church from one year to the next enjoying the open-air service. But tonight the crowd was sparse and there was not one unaccompanied female to be seen.

Jacko stood at the back searching the faces in the gathering one by one. Would the person who had Melanie be here?

Was she still alive?

These thoughts and many more haunted him, as with shoulders hunched he left the Broadway to the sound of 'Abide With Me'.

What a fucking depressing hymn.

He shook his head as he passed the Blue Lion and, looking in the window, saw people enjoying themselves.

Didn't they know that he could never enjoy himself again? Never. Melanie was gone – for days now! – and not a sign of her anywhere. It was as if the last eight years had never existed. He watched his past self walking out of the hospital all those years ago. This time no little blanket-covered bundle in his arms.

Nothing. Nada.

By the time he reached the Seahills the tears were flowing thick and fast.

Beefy was the first person he bumped into and he took one look at Jacko and sighed.

'Come on man. It's not over yet.'

He put his arm around his friend. 'Come back to our house for a bit, eh? Come on, yer need to chill a bit. I've got a couple of cans here an' we'll share them, eh?'

'No. Can't have a drink. Gotta think straight.' Jacko wiped his face with his sleeve. 'I'm gonna look for Hammerman 'cos I think he's got Melanie.'

'What makes yer think that creep's got her?'

'Stands to reason, he had me mam cut.'

'I've heard that she was just supposed to be frightened, only it sort of got outta hand. Apparently Hammerman's already given the kid what done it a good clouting.'

'I'll give the bastard more than a good clouting –' He looked at Beefy. 'Who is he? Yer know who hurt me mam, don't yer. Why the fuck didn't yer tell me who it was?'

He grabbed hold of Beefy's denim jacket by the lapels. 'Why?' he demanded.

'OK, mate. Chill. I didn't tell yer 'cos yer've got enough on yer plate as it is. Time enough to sort the creep out later. He'll keep. Besides, I've been looking out for him meself.'

Jacko let go. 'Sorry, mate.'

'That's OK. Come on, we'll go back to mine.'

'No, I'm gonna look for Hammerman. Ha'way man, I've gotta be doing something, can yer not see that?'

'Aye, I can that.' Beefy nodded, feeling desperate for his mate.

'Have yer got any dosh? Trev'll need petrol money – I already owe him for today. And I swear the fucking petrol gets dearer every time we go into a garage.'

'I've got a tenner.' Beefy pulled the note out of his pocket. 'But we'll have to get the bus. Trev went straight back out when he brought yer back from the hospital an' I ain't seen him come back yet.'

'We?'

'Yer don't think for one minute I'd let yer go by yerself? Friggin' hell, Jacko. Newcastle, why yer'll get eaten alive, yer daft bugger. Two of us, we stand a better chance.'

'Yer a good mate, Beefy.'

'Only doing what you'd do for me. What about the kids, Robbie and Mickey? And Cal, he's got a car. Big bastard an' all, he could come in handy.'

'Ner, leave them outta this, they're good lads. No need for them to get into trouble on my account.'

Beefy nodded, then together they turned and headed for the bus stop.

20

Lorraine sneaked a look at Luke. He smiled and she hastily swallowed a piece of half-chewed steak to smile back at him. Thanking God in the process that she hadn't choked on it. They were sitting opposite each other at her mother's dining table, of all places. A further visit to Doris had elicited nothing more and after a brief trip to the hospital where they'd learned nothing new from Christina save that she was sure it wasn't Jacko, she'd told Luke to drop her at home for a long overdue break. But she'd reckoned without the terrible twosome.

Damn the pair of them.

'Are you stopping for supper, Luke?' said Peggy in her most sugary sweet, wheedling voice. Any thicker and treacle wouldn't have got a look in.

'We have far too much food.' Mavis smiled at him.

Then the pair of them suddenly get a phone call and both of them have to run out: a sick friend?

My arse. They'll have dragged me uncle Harry in on the act.

Jesus.

If there's too much food, then where the hell's theirs? Seems to me there weren't never going to be more than two portions.

How embarrassing can yer get. It's not as if Luke's slow or owt. For God's sake.

I swear I'll be the one up for murder tomorrow.

Yer wouldn't think she was in danger of losing a breast. She should be thinking about herself, not about fixing me up.

As if I need your intervention in any case, thank ye, Mother.

Lorraine thought about what what Peggy had told her that morning. Mavis fully believed Dr Mountjoy and that was that. Until somebody told her otherwise she had a tiny lump that was going to be whipped out and that'd be the finish to it. End of story. And that kind of thinking was the only way she, Mavis, could function. So Lorraine had to stop worrying because Mavis wasn't, and neither was Peggy.

Right. OK, back off and chill out. I get the message. Still an' all it was one thing to say it . . . Lorraine frowned at where her thoughts were taking her.

'Everything all right, Lorraine?' Luke asked.

'Yeah, fine.'

The bloody pair of them were right in one respect though, Luke was bloody gorgeous.

Stop it.

How do I get rid of him?

Say I'm going to bed? Lorraine actually blushed – Good God, no. He might get the wrong idea.

The supper had been all right so far, but what happened when they finished eating?

However, what Luke said next threw all thoughts of bed, or anything else, right out the window. 'Shocking what Clark said, isn't it?'

Damn, what the hell did he remind me for? Clark's censure on the night Jacko had been taken into custody still smarted.

Lorraine had tried to point out that they were jumping to conclusions – *more like flamin' hurling themselves to conclusions if yer ask me* – but Clark had been dismissive.

'Shocking, that's not the word. How dare he suggest that I'm jealous of the little bitch. What'd he say, was I worried that Jacobs was stealing my glory by solving the case? Bloody hell. For one, she's totally wrong. The pair of them are off the planet to even entertain the suspicion that Jacko could be the murderer.'

'I agree with yer.' Luke, obviously full, put his knife and fork down. 'But what can we do, for now it feels like he won't hear a word said against her.'

'Only a fool like Clark would fall for the little cow's imaginings and I'm telling yer, it'll go nowhere. He's always been soft on women what suck up to him and by Christ, Jacobs'd give a friggin' Hoover a run for its money. I tell yer, Luke, I've watched her an' the way she is makes me sick to me stomach.'

'Aye, boss. An' have yer noticed yet what's goin' on between her an' Dinwall? Everyone is talking about it down at the station.'

This was sticky ground and Lorraine was starting to think that perhaps she wasn't being very professional in discussing Sara Jacobs so openly with Luke.

'Yeah, well, the point is that the real murderer is definitely still out there to my mind. We've got to crack this one, Luke, and find him before that fool locks the wrong man up again. And before another woman loses her life, 'cos this one's on the rampage, no mistaking.'

Luke nodded, 'I know, boss, but doesn't seem like we're getting any closer, does it?'

'Feels to me, Luke, like we're missing a piece of the jigsaw. I reckon there's something linking the murders that we're just not getting right now. It's a bit slim, but I keep thinking about

Diane Fox's heel which is still missing even though we've searched the whole area. Maybe there's a link with Samantha Dankton's earring? Oh, I dunno, maybe there's not.'

As she finished speaking Luke sat up straighter. 'Boss, I didn't mention it as it didn't seem important, but yer know that when her dad went through Christina's stuff she was missing a glove? He reckoned as how she'd either lost it in the ambulance or when she was admitted – either way, it was the hospital's fault and bye, didn't he kick up about it, but d'yer think that might be linked an' all?'

'It could be,' mused Lorraine. 'Or it could just be that it's just missing, if yer know what I mean. Given the violence at each crime scene, it's not surprising that stuff got pulled off or snapped. We'll do a check on the other woman's belongings tomorrow, but I'm pretty certain that there was nothing gone insofar as we could tell. Oh I dunno, Luke, I know it seems daft but yer know the only other thing I can see as they all have in common is the way they look. It came to me earlier when yer were looking at that picture of Stella's daughter, but it's a bit of a long shot.'

'Go on, boss.'

'Probably nothing, but if yer think about it each of them so far has had long dark hair which two have been wearing loose on the night of the attack.'

'That's true enough, boss. Do yer reckon he has something against dark-haired women then?'

'Seems unlikely, doesn't it? But yer know it keeps nagging away at me. Also –' she fished around in her pockets for a pencil. Why was the craving always worst when she'd had something to eat? 'Just out of curiosity, can yer remember what that girl looked like that was attacked last year?'

Luke chewed on his thumbnail then his face lit up with recognition. 'I can, because at the time didn't Leanne Walker dye her hair very much the same colour?'

Well, trust him to remember Constable Leanne Walker of all people! She tutted.

'Pardon?'

'Nowt. Just wondering how Leanne's doing in Canada. It's been about six months now, hasn't it.'

'Fine, she's been promoted already.'

Yeah, great, so how the hell does he know that?

As if reading her thoughts Luke went on, 'She talks pretty often to Sanderson, isn't he like an uncle or something?'

'Oh, yeah.' Lorraine tried not to show her relief. 'Her mother is a half-cousin of his. Anyhow to get back to the girl who was attacked last October, I think we should look at the records again if yer sure there's no way of getting hold of her until she's back from London. Last year just might have been the start of all this.'

Luke nodded, then for a long silent moment they were looking at each other.

Lorraine realised that he had the softest darkest brown eyes she'd ever seen. Her gaze travelled downwards to his mouth; he smiled, and she was practically mesmerised by the glint of gold. She felt herself weakening, wondering what it would be like to kiss him. Luke moved towards her and she felt her skin start to tingle in anticipation. Just as she felt sure he was going to touch her the spell was suddenly shattered as Luke's arm caught the edge of a glass of water and it tumbled, the contents running across the table and splashing into her lap.

'Oh, God! I'm so sorry, Lorraine! Er, I mean, boss.' He quickly passed her a napkin.

'It's fine. It's fine. Just a bit of water.' The bit of water had soaked right through her jeans.

'Look, yer need to change, so I'll go now, and see yer in the morning. OK?'

'Yeah, great. Whatever.'

'I'll just see meself out.'

Lorraine waved her hand in reply, unable to quite meet his eyes. When she heard the front door close behind him she breathed a heavy sigh of relief then muttered, 'I'm fairly gonna kill Rock Chick and the Hippy. That was far too close.'

Josh shivered and hunched over the tiny fire. He'd cadged the matches off two kids who had climbed into the cave and nearly died of fright when they saw him. The pair had been just about to light up a couple of spliffs when he'd stepped out of the shadows.

The girls only looked about twelve years old and so he'd promised not to grass them up in return for a Mars bar and a box of matches. They had gone quietly, leaving behind them the spliffs that one of them had nicked out of her brother's pockets. After the lecture Josh gave them it was unlikely that either would ever want to touch drugs again.

Josh had no use for the stuff, and thought anyone who did stupid. But God knows, there were plenty of stupid people about and so he put them in a safe place at the back of the cave thinking that if he had to, he could use them to barter with.

Other than the surprise visit by the girls it had been a long lonely day for Josh. The vixen had appeared twice and each time he'd moved to the side to give her room. But she was a timid creature, easily startled, and despite Josh's murmured reassurances she refused to come in.

His excitement at the thought of being the one to find Melanie and prove his innocence had fast evaporated. The whole day had been spent going over and over events in his mind. For the last hour, and for the umpteenth time, he'd been wrestling as hard as he could with the memory of when he last saw her.

Josh sighed. He felt there had to be something he was

missing. Had to be, else what chance did he have? Once more he started at the begining of the day, moved through early morning, then on to dinner time. Dissected the row he'd had with Percy, and again stormed over to the hot-dog van.

They had gone into the trailer where Melanie had sung along to his collection of CDs. Mostly the Bee Gees, which really belonged to Percy. A little soft metal and some dance music had been more to Josh's taste.

It was thinking about music that finally made Josh remember. He'd offered to walk Melanie home and he could suddenly see himself alongside her, smiling at her antics as she sang 'Stayin' Alive' and pretended to hold a microphone. She'd had to stop when a bout of giggling interrupted her performance, but just then somebody had pulled up in a car she recognised. Melanie had hurried to the car, said something to the driver, then turned and given Josh a wave, saying she would see him in the morning.

But he hadn't got a proper look at who was driving. The car had stopped a few yards in front of a bus stop and Melanie had run on ahead so he couldn't actually see whoever it was behind the wheel. He remembered that Melanie had been smiling though. She seemed quite happy, and surely she wouldn't have got in if she didn't know who it was.

Would she?

No, I haven't known her long, but she's not that daft.

'I should have got the number,' he muttered as he shook his head at his own stupidity. 'It's my fault. Letting Melanie get in a car with somebody – why ever didn't I think? Probably a flaming kidnapper on the loose and I blew it.'

Once he'd started remembering, the whole thing flooded back to him and he knew without a doubt that if he saw the car again he would know it. But then again, maybe all this meant nothing. Could be that the car was one of those red herrings they always went on about in those afternoon mystery movies he and Percy sometimes watched on TV? And maybe it wasn't even then that Melanie had gone missing?

Josh groaned out loud. He was sunk. He knew he was. And no way out of it.

His stomach rumbled, adding to his misery. One Mars bar had not gone a long way towards filling it. Tomorrow he would just have to risk sneaking back to the tourer. There was nothing else he could do. He desperately needed some proper food and drink for a start. And no way could he count on kids turning up every day for a sly smoke – why the next lot could be half a dozen strapping boys and what chance against them would there be?

Monday afternoons were usually heaving and surely he could make his way through the crowd without being spotted. If he kept his hood up and his head down – and his cool – he bet he could make it through. There were plenty of people around these days who covered their faces with hoods.

For a brief moment hope soared in him at the thought of hot food and hot water back at the tourer. But then the thought of what might happen if someone saw his scarred face came into his mind. He'd be recognised right away, that was certain.

Yeah, an' that would be sodding that.

Locked up for life. For something he hadn't done.

No one would believe him about the car. They would say he'd made it up.

Feeling completely isolated and convinced he didn't have a friend anywhere, Josh lay down. His long years as a loner and his distorted sense of the world caused by the accident meant that even considering going back and simply telling the truth wasn't an option. The whole universe was against him in his mind, and that was that. He didn't know who he hated the most, himself or other people.

Through the day Josh had collected as much soft grass as

he could to make a bed and at first he thought that at least he would have a fairly comfortable night. But within minutes of lying down it compressed and he could feel the stony ground underneath him.

Jacko and Beefy walked along Newcastle quayside. They had popped into a few bars, but knew better than to ask for Hammerman on his home turf. If they did, then word was going to spread like lightning and they'd have zero chance of success.

Their lead finally came when Beefy resorted to his mobile. He had a few friends from this neck of the woods and one or two thoroughly detested Hammerman. Beefy had phoned around and called in a few favours, and finally they'd found someone who'd been only to happy to tell them where Hammerman could be tracked down.

The quayside had gone through some dramatic changes over the last few years and now it rivalled any city in England. They passed the Millennium Bridge which had been designed in the form of a blinking eye, so that when it blinked it let river traffic flow underneath it. On the Gateshead side, across the river, the Sage building in the shape of a gigantic glass caterpillar stole the skyline from the more sedate Baltic art gallery which was once a flour mill.

'Canny good here now, isn't it?' Beefy asked, as they neared the nightclub they'd been directed to at the very far end of the quay.

Jacko shrugged, the last thing on his mind was the sights and sounds of Newcastle, but begrudgingly he admitted, 'Aye, ah suppose.'

They reached Hammerman's club with two clear plans in mind. Plan A was to pay to get in like any ordinary customer. Get Hammerman on his own, beat the shit out of him, and find out where Melanie was.

Plan B had one significant difference. To run like hell if they were disturbed.

Both plans went right out the window when they found out just how much it cost to get in.

'What're we gonna do?' Jacko asked. 'What the fucking hell are we gonna do?'

'Don't panic.' Beefy pulled Jacko around the corner into the shadows. 'Listen, Jacko, yer not thinking straight because of all the stress – and I don't blame yer – but wanting to barge in there like a bull in a china shop isn't gonna get us anywhere. Except maybe the bottom of the Tyne. So just follow my lead, OK?'

Jacko sighed, 'Right, OK, but what fucking lead?'

'First we scout round the building. His office must be round the back somewhere. The window could be open an' then we'll climb in and nab him.'

'Yeah, just like that.'

'Got a better plan?'

Jacko shook his head.

'I thought not. So, come on.'

Slowly they made their way around the building. At the back which looked out onto the river there were two rooms with lights on. Jacko was slightly taller than Beefy and the added few inches allowed him to see into the rooms. The first one was obviously some sort of storage facilty with grey file boxes on one wall and black file boxes on the other. It was deserted and Jacko silently gestured for Beefy to move on. They edged their way carefully along to the next window. Jacko eased up the wall until his eyes were over the plastic window sill, moving very slowly in case a sudden movement caught somebody's eye and gave them away. In one swift glance he took in the contents of the room, pausing long enough to count the people in it, then he slid quickly back down to face Beefy.

'Well?'

'There's a whole pile of them in there. About six easily, I reckon. The two in the corner, big bastards both of them, are counting money like there's no tomorrow. The others seem to be arguing the toss about something, including Hammerman who's pacing about like a friggin' caged lion.'

'Shit. Not much we can do against six, is there? Especially if that twat gets his hammer out.'

Stumped for the moment, they both leaned back and rested their heads against the wall.

A few minutes later Jacko snapped his fingers. 'I know! We can't follow him home 'cos we haven't got a car. But in one of your former lives weren't you a car thief.'

'You asking me to break the law, Jacko?'

'Yeah, like yer now squeaky clean, Beefy? Come off it.'

'But what's the great idea, then? Stealing Hammerman's car, where the hell's that gonna get us.'

'I'm not asking yer to steal it, man. No, we just break into it and then hide. Then when he goes home, we jump him.'

Beefy's face lit up. 'Sounds good to me. I know his car an' all. I probably helped pay for the frigging thing with the amount of interest the greedy bastard charges. But what if he ain't going home on his own and there's people what get into the car with him?'

'Do yer want to help me or not, Beefy? I'm sick of yer thinking up obstacles all the time. What am I meant to do? Sit on me arse an' just hope me daughter comes home?'

'Sorry, Jacko, didn't mean it like that, did I?' Beefy knew that his friend was desperate and that he'd take any risk if it meant there was a chance of getting Melanie back. 'Yer know that I'm right beside yer, mate. Whatever.'

'Yeah, I do', said Jacko, calming straight down. 'Right, round to the car park – and pray it's pretty dark where his car's parked.'

Beefy bent down and picked a heavy stone up. 'No probs, Jacko old son, we'll just put the light out. Bloody kids, nowt but a nuisance these days, they friggin' well get everywhere, don't they?' Beefy grinned. 'Little bastards.'

The car park was where Jacko had predicted it would be and the kids had already been there. Shards of glass littered the paving and there were three lights already out – wonder of wonders, two of them directly beside Hammerman's car. It looked like things were definitely going their way.

But Jacko held his breath; things were never this easy, not for him, something was bound to happen.

For once his luck held and within seconds Beefy had the bonnet up and the alarm disconnected. It didn't take him much longer than that to break into the car.

When Hammerman bought the dark green people carrier he hadn't dreamed, couldn't have guessed in a million, just what a favour he'd be doing for Jacko a year down the line. The tinted windows made it practically impossible to see inside the car making it unlikely that Beefy would be spotted from the outside, and the seat rows provided more than enough space for him to crouch down. Jacko, on the outside, nodded to Beefy to crank the window and for the next two hours the old friends talked quietly through the gap. Twice Jacko broke down and started to cry but Beefy's reassurances that Melanie was safe somewhere calmed him. He had to believe it was only a matter of time.

At two o clock, when everyone had gone home, the club lights went out covering everything with pitch darkness. Jacko froze where he was, hidden from view. To their horror, when Hammerman came out Stella was with him. In the dim moonlight Jacko could see that Hammerman had his hand on Stella's back and was trying to usher her towards the car.

'Damn,' Beefy whispered.

Jacko's heart beat so fast he thought he was going to have a heart attack.

A moment later he breathed easy when it looked like Stella was having none of it. A taxi pulled up and she quickly kissed Hammerman on his cheek, then just as quickly jumped into the cab which sped off even before she'd properly closed the door.

'Thank God for that,' Beefy's voice whispered in the darkness.

Jacko was staring at Hammerman, his blood pounding so loudly in his ears that he didn't hear a word Beefy said. All he was thinking over and over was: *Soon, soon I'll have her back, and this bastard's gonna be dead.*

Hammerman put his key in the lock, momentarily pausing when the interior lights didn't come on. Shrugging, he got into the car and reached for the seat belt. He was just about to put the key in the ignition when he was grabbed from behind.

Unable to shout out because of the hands round his throat, and with his whole body filling up with fear, he closed his eyes tight, trying to deny that this was happening at all. A moment later though his eyes flipped open when he heard the passenger door open and felt someone get in beside him. He suddenly realised that there were two of them, and that he wasn't going to get out of this. No way could he even attempt to close his eyes now, they were bulging with terror.

'Answer every question he asks. Try taking the piss an' he'll kill yer,' a voice said in his ear. He tried to nod and felt the hands relax, and the pressure ease on his throat.

'Where is she?' the man who had got in the passenger door demanded.

'Jacko?' Hammerman whispered. He wanted to rub his throat to try to ease the pain but the hands had dropped to the top of his arms where their grip was like a pair of hard metal bands.

'Aye, it's me. Now where is she! And don't give us any shit. I want me bairn and I want her now, an' I don't give a fuck if I have to kill yer to find her.'

'Melanie? Are yer on about Melanie? What makes yer think I've got her. Jesus Christ.'

Despite his pain, Hammerman's fear was overtaken by amazement. Jacko could hear it in his voice. Either that or he was a damn good actor.

'I've got two bairns of me own, for fuck's sake. One of them's even the same age as Melanie.'

Jacko grabbed Hammerman's chin and his grip was even more fierce than Beefy's. 'Where the fuck is she? I swear I'll fucking kill yer, so I will. Where is she, yer fucker!' he demanded, becoming more frantic by the minute.

Hammerman struggled but Jacko's grip tightened. 'Where the fuck is she?' He was nearly screaming now, and shaking Hammerman's chin like a terrier shakes a rat.

'Jacko. Jacko.' Beefy placed his hand over Jacko's. 'He can't answer while yer've got that kind of grip on him. Ease off, mate, OK. Ease off, Jacko, come on mate.'

Beefy's voice finally penetrated the red mist in Jacko's head and he let go of Hammerman.

Hammerman gently touched the sides of his face. He was in agony, certain his jaw bone had snapped in at least two places. The pain, like white hot fire, was horrendous and he moaned quietly.

'Where is she?'

Hammerman stared at Jacko. 'I haven't got her. I swear.'

'Yes yer have, yer took her 'cos I owe yer. Just like yer had me mam cut. Yer fucking low-life bastard.' He raised his fist to smash Hammerman's face but Beefy grabbed it with both hands and wrestled Jacko's arm down.

'Give him a chance, Jacko. Let him speak.' Beefy was beginning to believe Hammerman.

'Why would I want to kidnap the bairn, Jacko? I swear on me own bairns' lives. I haven't got Melanie, I haven't. What would be the point?'

Jacko looked at Beefy who shrugged, then nodded. 'Sounds good to me.'

'Yer cut me mam.' This was a statement, not a question, and Jacko's eyes burned into Hammerman's.

'No! Honest, Jacko. The stupid little fuck was just supposed to frighten her. An' I've already had him sorted.'

'I believe him, Jacko,' Beefy said. 'I told yer I'd heard that the freaky bastard had been sorted.'

Slowly Jacko relaxed. He half believed Hammerman himself. Still, he'd deserved what he'd got – even if he hadn't ordered Doris to be cut, it was through him that she had been.

He reached out and flicked Hammeman's jaw. Hammerman moaned in agony. 'That's for Doris Musgrove. A damn good woman. One way or another, you were responsible.'

He got out of the car followed by Beefy, and as they walked away they could hear Hammerman moaning.

'Wow.' Beefy said, then five minutes later as they were striding across Newcastle bridge, 'Wow.'

He has been sat outside her house waiting for what seems like for ever. He can tell by the light upstairs that she is at home. He knows which one is her bedroom and he imagines her dressing for the evening: standing in front of the mirror in her bra and panties as she does her make-up, then draping her beautiful body with the softest of clothes.

At first he was content to sit and watch and try to keep his growing excitement under control. She likes him – he knows she does. And she is so lovely. Not one of those dirty girls Mother warned him about, the sort he used to see down at the beck. But now he is growing impatient. He needs to see her. Perhaps he should be brave and just go and knock and maybe even ask her if she'd like to go out?

At that moment the front door swings open and he hears her call out cheerily, 'Ta-ra, Mam. Won't be late.' He finds he is holding his breath as she trips down the path and through the gate and before he knows it, he's almost missed his chance.

He scrambles out of the car, losing all dignity in his haste to intercept her, and stands in front of her blocking her route.

'Oh! God, you frightened me!' She giggles then, tossing her dark hair back as she speaks. 'Are yer going in to see me mam? She's at home, yer know.'

'Nnn- No. It was you I wanted to see.'

He leans forward and rests his hand on her shoulder. 'I wanted to thank yer for yer kindness to me.'

She looks puzzled. 'What kindness? Listen, I can't stop, really sorry, but I'm late already.' And she starts to move away from him. To leave him behind.

But as she removes his hand from her shoulder she holds it for the briefest of moments and he is sure he feels her squeeze his fingers gently – it's almost a caress. Suddenly, in that moment – with that soft but firm touch – he knows then that she feels about him the way he felt about her, and sheer joy surges through his veins. She loves him too!

Smiling, happy in his confidence that this is what she wants – what she's been waiting for – he gently touches her breast.

'Ohh . . . yer cheeky, bastard creep!' she yells, hitting him with her bag so that he has to put both hands up to protect his poor face.

'Sorry,' he mumbles, stepping back in shock. But she is yelling so loudly she doesn't hear him.

'Go on, piss off, yer dirty twat.'

'No, no, yer wrong.' He can't understand what's gone wrong. This is what she wanted. Why is she turning on him now? He has to make her understand –

'Pervert. Ugly little creep!'

Face burning with humiliation, he gets back into his car and drives away.

That night his dreams are haunted by the encounter. Her voice taunting him over and over again.

Somewhere towards dawn he wakes up. Getting out of bed he moves to the window, on the way collecting his binoculars from the chair.

21

Lorraine wore her black suit with a cream blouse. She decided to leave her hair down today and brushed it thoroughly. Then, out of sheer frustration at the way things were going, brushed it some more. Finally knowing she was simply putting off facing Mavis, she placed the brush on her dresser.

The smell of bacon wafted along the passageway and her stomach revolted. 'Jesus, not every day.'

'Hi,' Peggy said as Lorraine entered the kitchen. 'Breakfast's on, pet.'

'Thanks, Peggy, but no thanks. This morning cornflakes will do.'

'Oh.' Peggy looked disappointed for a moment, then she grinned, 'I wonder if Luke –?'

'No.'

'Ohh.' She put her head on one side, smiled at Lorraine like a mischievous child, and said, 'Carter?'

'Peggy, why don't yer go and feed the homeless, I'm sure they'd gobble yer bacon sandwiches up as fast as yer can turn them out.'

Peggy shrugged. 'I've done me share for the homeless. I married two men and suffered a third, didn't I.'

As tense as she was, Lorraine had to smile. Shaking her head she took her mobile out and phoned Carter and then Luke. She blushed when she spoke to Luke and didn't miss Peggy raising her eyebrows at her.

When she put her phone back in her bag Peggy said, 'So he is coming over, then? And Luke an' all.'

'Yeah, Peggy, but I think they'll both have had breakfast, don't you.'

Lorraine checked she had everything she needed then handed Peggy her car keys because Peggy was borrowing it to take Mavis to the hospital. 'Phone me the minute yer know something. I'd be there, but these two cases are driving me round the bend an' me time's not me own.'

'Yeah, an' it's better than you sitting there driving me round the bend.' Peggy walked over and kissed Lorraine's cheek. 'Don't worry. She's gonna be fine.'

Lorraine nodded, 'I'll just pop in.' She walked along the passageway and knocked on Mavis's door.

'Come in.' Lorraine noted that her mother sounded cheery. *Perhaps there's nothing to worry about.*

'Hi, Mam,' Lorraine said as she walked in. 'All right?'

'I'm fine, pet. And I must say, you're looking particularly lovely this morning. I do love your hair down.'

Lorraine flicked her hair off her shoulder. 'Yeah, but sometimes it gets in the way.'

Lorraine and Mavis had a very good relationship and were normally quite comfortable with each other but right now Lorraine felt awkward and clumsy. It was perhaps the first time with her mother that she'd had to think up something to say. She still couldn't get her head round the fact that Mavis didn't seem worried and though she longed to talk to her about what was going to happen later that morning, at the same time she felt she couldn't. That Mavis didn't want her to.

'Has Peggy made breakfast yet?' Mavis asked brightly.

'Just about.'

Mavis forced a smile. 'There's one big advantage to having surgery today: Peggy can't force me to eat breakfast, though I'm sure she thinks bacon and eggs is a cure for everything.'

'Oh, Mam, how yer feeling? Are yer worried about today?' Lorraine asked, feeling that the mention of cures paved the way. 'If only –'

'Yeah, well let's not get into "if onlys", pet, 'cos that could take all of the week up. Yer know my feelings, I trust Dr Mountjoy's diagnosis and this time tomorrow I'll have the all clear. So don't yer fret about it, pet.'

Lorraine backed off. 'Course I won't, Mam. I've got to go now 'cos Carter's outside, but I'll be waiting for a phone call from Rock Chick so make sure yer remind her.'

'OK. So go do yer job and find that canny little bairn – and quit worrying about me, d'yer hear?'

Lorraine sighed, nodded, and kissed her mother. 'See yer, kiddo.'

Mavis waved.

After Lorraine had gone the smile melted away. She lay back on the pillows and sighed. The truth of the matter was that she was really worried sick, and it had her worn out. Worried sick and half frightened to death. She couldn't help but think of the other women in the family who had had breast cancer, even though Dr Mountjoy said that a lot of progress had been made since her mother had died.

She didn't think that Lorraine had seen through her though and she was pleased for that. Lorraine had enough on her plate, what with murderers on the loose and a little one missing, not to mention working with a back-stabber like Sara Jacobs.

240

But Mavis guessed that her best friend knew how she really felt.

A moment later Peggy bustled in. 'Nearly time for us to be getting on our way, love. What yer wearing this morning?' Peggy stood at the wardrobe door ready to get out anything Mavis asked for. And not for the first time Mavis thanked God for such a good friend.

Melanie, groggy from last night's injection, ate the porridge that was being spoon-fed to her, even though every mouthful hurt as it went past the huge lump in her throat.

She stared at her jailer with angry eyes. She would eat, 'cos she had to.

But she didn't have to speak and she didn't have to sing.

No matter how many times the horrible red dress was put on her and she was stood on the old wooden stool and expected to sing a stupid song she hadn't ever heard before.

She wouldn't do it.

No way!

Her eyes shone bright with the rebellion her anger had fuelled as she forced down another mouthful.

She had a plan.

Lorraine, Luke, and Carter had a pile of files in front of each of them. It was Luke who found the one about the previous year's attack. Excitedly he handed it to Lorraine. 'Look, look at her photograph, boss.'

'Bloody hell,' Carter said, looking over Lorraine's shoulder. The photo showed a young, attractive woman, her straight dark hair cascading down over her shoulders.

Lorraine nodded. 'I'll bet me life there's a connection. Five women, all dead ringers for each other. Three dead, two still alive – only by chance, mind yer. All of them attacked from behind. The method of murder or attempted murder in each case has been strangulation.'

She looked at the two men. 'What does that tell yer?'

'Coward?' Carter ventured.

Lorraine nodded. 'Could well be. Whoever he is, he didn't want to confront his victims face-to-face. An' don't forget what Christina said about the bloke having something wrong with his face. Maybe that's why it's from the back too.'

'Do yer still think there might be two of them, boss?' asked Carter.

'No, I think it's unlikely,' Lorraine replied. 'Christina didn't see anyone else an' though that don't mean anything given how little she did take in, I think this murdering bastard is acting alone. What d'yer think, Luke?' Lorraine looked at him.

Jesus, how can he look better each day?

She mentally shook herself: she was concentrating on the case – she had to.

'Yeah, I agree, boss. An' I reckon the way he does them – only going for women on their own in out-of-the-way places, an' each time picking ones what match his tastes, shows that he's a planner. He's setting them up carefully if yer ask me.'

'Yer right, Luke. This isn't some crazy, this is somebody who's managing to function. The people around him may be noticing small changes, but not enough to tie him to murder.'

'Weird that last year's was at Feast time too, isn't it,' wondered Carter. 'An' then nothing, so far as we know, happening in between. D'yer think there's something that happened, historic-like? Maybe a curse that's been passed down over the years, or a devilish legacy or the like.'

'I'll give yer all the cursing yer want, yer idiot,' Lorraine said, heartily sick of Carter's local history classes. 'That's ignorant superstition is all, Carter. Yer as bad as that bloody old woman wittering on about October –'

Lorraine suddenly stopped as a thought came to her, then jumped to her feet. – 'Just a hunch, well, more like a long shot, but dig Stella's daughter's autopsy report out, will yer, Carter.'

Carter nodded and went next door where the filing systems were kept. Leaving Lorraine alone with Luke. Luke got up from his chair and came to stand by Lorraine at the window. *Woah there, boyo*, she thought, but he'd scooped up the case file of the girl who was attacked last year and only wanted more light to study it. She didn't quite know whether she was disappointed or pleased.

'Yer know yer could be on to something, boss. Amanda did look the same as the others. In fact I'd say that Amanda and this one could almost be sisters.' Luke tapped the girls photograph. 'Stacey Keeton. Twenty six years old.' He looked at Lorraine, seemed to suddenly realise just how close he was standing to her, and moved away slightly.

'She's due back today. Has to be worth paying her a visit.'

'Can't do any harm,' Lorraine replied off-handedly

Been all the same if I had kissed him last night. Seems like today he doesn't even want to stand near me. Huh.

Carter arrived back with Amanda's case file. 'Here yer go, boss.'

'Thanks.'

The three of them pored over the pages in the case file, but it didn't tell them anything they hadn't known before. It had certainly been an horrific accident: Amanda's car had hurtled over a cliff edge and the drop had been so steep there'd been no chance she'd survive. After blood tests the coroner had concluded she'd been driving under the influence of alcohol and recorded a verdict of death by misadventure.

Amanda's build was similar to that of the other victims,

and she did have dark hair which she wore loose, but instead of being long in the autopsy photo her hair was cut very short. The crash had happened around the time of Houghton Feast, but there was nothing here to suggest that her death was anything but a tragic accident and that she was yet another fool who thought they were able to drink and drive.

After half an hour they gave up although Lorraine shook her head at Carter when he made to put the file back and instead tucked it into her bag.

'There's nothing as I can see here, not at first glance any road. We'd best be getting on. Luke, you go to Silksworth and see if yer can grab some time with Stacey Keeton. Try to get her to remember everything she can. Go over it in depth – sometimes things come back to yer long after the event.' She turned to Carter. 'Carter, you go back to the Lumsdons and go through it with little Suzy again. Then go back to the show field and give this Josh's uncle a thorough grilling an' all. I'm off to see Scottie.'

She looked at her watch, 'We should all be back here by, say half past one. OK?'

Luke and Carter nodded. Lorraine picked up the keys for the patrol car she had at her disposal and was the first out of the door.

Doris sat staring at the fire. Mr Skillings had just been in and made her a cup of tea. Then he'd gone up to Newbottle post office with Dolly to draw all three of their pensions.

As she sat alternately sipping her tea and dunking a ginger snap biscuit, she watched her son. Jacko was gently snoring on the settee. She shook her head wondering what time the poor soul came in last night.

He looked exhausted. Poor sod.

But neither of them had hardly slept a wink since Melanie had disappeared. It was Jacko who needed it though, he was tramping all over the place and not eating properly. Without even looking in the oven she knew that the mince and dumplings Dolly had made yesterday wouldn't be touched.

Such a shame with half the world starving.

And a body could only take so much before it caved in on itself.

She'd tried to wake him up at first, to send him to bed where he could get a proper sleep in between nice crispy sheets, but it had proved nigh on impossible.

God knows how long he'll sleep for now he's practically collapsed on there.

Good job Sandra came along and did the Hoovering yesterday.

Damn good of her an' all it was.

She sighed, her thoughts drifting from her son to her granddaughter. She remembered the day Jacko had brought her home. So proud he was. Not another bairn like Melanie in the world. And not a prouder father neither.

Ohh, dear. *Please God, I know yer very busy and all that. But if yer listening, please send our Melanie home before this good man wakes up. 'Cos we miss her something terrible, God, and the pain's unbearable.*

Not knowing's the worst.

Doris shook her head and turned back to the fire. In the last three days she'd aged ten years or more. She was too tired to wipe away the fat tears that ran down her wrinkled cheeks. Unheeded they fell onto the hearth.

And if it's my fault, God, and I've done something to offend yer, please take me now and send our Melanie back to her dad where she belongs.

22

Josh had brushed as much of Newbottle Woods off his clothes as he could. But grass and mud tended to cling and he knew he looked a mess. There was no disguising it: he looked like what he was, that is someone who'd spent more than one ill-prepared night in the great outdoors.

The vixen had appeared at first light this morning. He knew that this was her home and she considered him the interloper, but she seemed perfectly prepared to wait him out. Shrugging at her, he'd moved out of the cave, then walked ten yards away from the entrance to stand and watch. He'd judged that a good twenty minutes went by before she moved back in and reclaimed her territory.

Josh had given her a wave before setting off and despite his hunger and tiredness it didn't seem any time at all before he was on the verge of Newbottle, heading to God knew what. They weren't gonna lock him up though, that much he knew.

Not when he'd done nothing wrong.

Slowly, head down, and avoiding any eye contact at all with the few people on the street, he walked by the converted farmhouse, down on past the post office, then turned left and moved towards Grasswell.

His plan was to cut across as much green belt as he could until he reached the show field. If he went through the Burnside to the beck, he could then double back to where he wanted to be. The only problem being he would have to pass the police station. The thought of that made him actually quiver and he wasn't quite sure whether he'd have the guts to do it or not.

He passed Grasswell fish shop and quickened his pace, aware of the looks he was getting which were making him steadily more and more nervous. He didn't really have a clue where he was heading but as he neared the entrance to a caravan site the thought came to him and he stopped dead.

'Bloody hell,' he muttered, 'the aunts.'

In an instant his plan changed. Quickly he turned in through the entrance and, ignoring an Alsatian cross which came sniffing around his legs, he tried to get his bearings. As far as he could remember the aunts' caravan was at the back. He cut through the first row and came out at the top where there was less chance of him being seen, although if he guessed rightly he'd probably already been clocked by somebody – especially with that damned dog still following him. It could obviously smell the fox.

Reaching the last row he spotted the caravan immediately. It hadn't changed much since the last time Percy had made him visit. Two-toned cream and brown, it was one of the oldest on the site. It was the bright yellow checked curtains edged with white lace that he remembered more than the caravan, though. He'd gone with his mother to buy them as a present for the aunts. That was the time his youngest sister got lost in Sunderland's Woolworths. Her screams soon helped them to find her though, and he remembered his mum's fright turning to anger. She wasn't really cross, not deep down, she wasn't really that sort. More likely to cuddle you than to clout.

Shaking his head, he pushed past memories to one side and hardened his heart. He needed a clear head. Because he had to do something to help Melanie, one way or the other, no matter how frightened he was. She was a little girl, and probably a lot more scared than him.

He knocked on the door. Waited a moment, then knocked again.

'OK, coming.' Josh recognised Aunt Matilda's voice. Good, she was the more helpful of the two. He remembered his mother used to say that it was disgraceful the way Patty had Matilda running around after her.

The door finally opened and Matilda, now with two walking sticks, looked out at him. At first she pulled back and Josh could read the fear in her face, but before he properly got the words, 'Aunt Matilda' out she'd recognised him, and her face broke out in smiles.

'Josh! Oh, Patty,' she turned and looked inside the caravan. 'It's Josh, Patty. Josh has finally come to see us. Come in, son, come in.' Josh thought she must be wary of a broken hip or something, the way she slowly moved to the side.

Josh stepped in and Matilda reached out to cuddle him, but immediately dropped her arms. 'Ohh, Josh.'

'Sorry, Aunt Matilda.' *God I must stink to high heaven.* 'I'll explain.'

'Don't you think it would be better if you bathed first? Has Percy got no hot water in that mountain of a caravan?'

'It's a long story. Can I?' Josh pointed to the shower door.

'Yes, yes of course. Pass your clothes out while you are in there – we have a washer and a dryer, you know. I suppose you'll be wanting food?'

'God, yes please,' Josh said, his hunger momentarily outweighing his need to get clean.

'Shower first,' Matilda told him. Josh ducked into the bathroom, stripped, and handed his clothes out. As he was closing the door he heard Patty's whining voice.

'You know what the police said. If he came around, we had to phone them at once.'

'Shh, Patty, give the boy a chance. We should hear his side first. Besides, he's family. Since when did we start handing our own into the law.'

'Plenty times, if they've got bad blood.'

'Well we don't know that. Not until we hear what the boy has to say.'

'What if he wants to stay, have you thought of that? He might murder us in our beds, did you ever think of that?'

Matilda already had a frying pan in one hand and an egg in the other. 'For Goodness sake, Patty, don't be silly. Like I said, we have to give the boy a chance. He made friends with a little girl who's gone missing, that doesn't make him a murderer. It's, it's just circumstances.'

With a sinking heart and a deep sense of betrayal, Josh quietly closed the door. Only one person could have sent the police here. And that was Percy.

'This wasn't one of mine, Lorraine.' Scottie had fished out Amanda's autopsy report from the case file and was glancing down the pages.

'Give me a look at that.' Edna put the test tube down, literally dropped off the high stool she'd been sitting on, and came over to the bench.

Scottie handed it over. After a moment Edna said, 'Aye, I thought so. I remember this one 'cos there was a hell of an argument between the boyfriend and the mother. Big as him she was, looked like she could take a man down with one punch.'

'Can yer remember what about, Edna?' Lorraine asked.

'Near enough. Emm . . .' Edna thought for a minute or so, then went on. 'The boyfriend got here first and made the formal identification. Fairly breaking his heart he was. Then the mother arrived and she went ballistic. Tore the identification sheet out of Tobias's hand.' She looked at Scottie, 'Yer had yer yearly dose of flu, if yer remember.'

Scottie tutted. Ignoring him, Edna went on. 'Denied that it was her daughter, she did. Called the boyfriend every name under the sun that yer can think of, and then some more.'

'Does that happen often?'

'Yer mean denial?' Scottie put in. He shrugged. 'I've known it before but statistically, I haven't a clue.'

'Hmm.' Lorraine looked back at Edna.

'Aye, but this one fairly freaked out. Started belting into the lad, gave him the works. He just stood there poor soul and took it.'

'Weird. What was her problem, then? Was she blaming him for the girl dying? She was meant to be on her own when she crashed.'

'Don't know,' said Edna. 'All I do know is that it took a couple of us to hold her down. She wasn't making much sense but I reckon grief will do that to you, every time.'

Lorraine turned back to Scottie. 'So will yer take a look at the autopsy report then, Scottie?'

'I'll go through it and come back to yer.'

'Thanks for that. It'll probably get us nowhere but there's just something nagging away at me. It's a bad case, this one. Lots of things involved which don't seem to make no sense. What do yer reckon to them all looking very much alike then, Scottie. D'yer reckon there's anything to it?'

'I would say that's no stranger than some poor mother denying that her daughter was dead, pet. Could just be coincidence. But here's something that'll freak yer out. Says here that Amanda's hair was dyed.'

'Shit. You serious?'

'Yup.'

'Yeah, but then again, not everybody's gonna know that she dyed her hair. D'yer see what I mean? She could somehow still be linked to our murders.'

'That's true enough.'

Lorraine sighed. When was she going to get a breakthrough? 'OK, thanks, keep up the good work.' She looked at her watch. 'I need to be getting back, but I'll talk to yers later.'

As Lorraine passed the rectory field she could see that the fair was still in full swing. A fine day had certainly helped, but how long would the crowds stay out?

Once the ox was roasted they would probably all go home. She'd heard that the people who owned the rides were complaining about serious losses this year.

Well what did they expect: people weren't coming out, and who could blame them?

Most of the population were terrified.

She was pleased to see Luke and Carter's cars were already in the car park. As she went through the door Clark and Jacobs were on their way out. Jacobs gave Lorraine a smug look.

For two pins I'd claw the tart's eyes out.

Clark stopped. 'We're on our way to Durham. Sara found out that they had a spate of killings a few years back that seem to match our own.'

'We know about them, sir. They are quite different. Most of the victims were male, and they were suffocated and not strangled.'

'I don't agree,' Jacobs said. 'They could be linked, you know. The ages were all about the same for one thing –'

'Well it won't hurt to look into them again,' Clark said

hurriedly. Lorraine knew he wouldn't want to lose face in front of Jacobs and before she could say anything else, the pair were off.

'Bye then, sir,' Lorraine said to Clark's back as he and Jacobs sped off down the path.

She was still smiling when she entered her room. Luke and Carter looked at each other.

'Good news, boss?' Carter asked.

'Depends which way yer look at it. Clark and Jacobs have gone haring off to Durham. Seems they've found similar cases, just a few years old.'

Carter burst out laughing.

Puzzled, Luke said, 'Share the joke, then.'

'We already looked into that. The murders were in 1909, only a misprint on the system makes it look like 1999.'

Luke grinned. 'Serves the pair of them right.'

'Didn't yer tell Clark that, boss? Aren't yer worried?'

'Didn't get the chance, Carter. Wouldn't listen.' Lorraine didn't give a toss what Clark's reaction would be on his return. He was too keen by half on that little bitch Jacobs, and maybe next time he'd think twice before backing her up on yet another mistake.

'Anyhow, enough of that. We've got a murderer to find, and a kid still missing. Yer know something, if Melanie had black hair I would have said for some reason she'd fallen foul of him an' all. Yer know, wrong time, wrong place.'

Luke nodded. 'Yeah, but I feel that it's not related at all.'

'Well, I'm worried to death for the bairn but for the moment we've got some good guys on it. And yer know Jacko's due on the television tomorrow morning to make an appeal. That's if Clark and his pig-headed sidekick don't find a reason to throw him back in jail.'

Carter shook his head. 'Shame, poor Jacko's going off his head with worry. Also boss, there's no trace of Josh Quinn

252

at all. It's like he's gone up in a puff of smoke. The uncle hasn't cast eyes on him. Dinwall visited some aunts of his what live local first thing this morning. Seems they haven't seen him for a few years though.'

'Aye, but that doesn't say he won't head there if he's got nowhere else to go,' Luke put in.

Lorraine agreed with Luke as she opened her desk drawer. She found a pencil almost at once.

'So, Luke. Did yer talk to Stacey yet?'

'Yeah, boss. Felt right sorry for her, nervous little thing. Afraid of her own shadow. Though likely as not it'll have been what's happened to her that has made her that way. Nothing really new there, though. Same pattern as this year's attacks for certain. Grabbed from behind like the others, an' she says she would've been dead for sure if a bloke from the fair hadn't come along and frightened him off. She doesn't know the name of the guy who rescued her, reckons he just vanished, but she doesn't think he'd've seen anything 'cos he was a fair way off when he started yelling.'

'In a lonely place an' at night-time?'

'Yeah, boss. Just like these ones. But I should tell yer that I asked her whether she noticed anything missing like, afterwards, and she said that it was funny that I should ask because she'd lost her shopping.'

'What do yer mean, her shopping?'

'She'd bought some –' here, despite his blackness, Luke's skin seemed to take on extra colour, 'new underwear, boss, and it was missing. She says she only noticed the bag had gone later, at the hospital, and she reckoned some scally at the fair had had it away.'

Lorraine shook her head. It seemed likely that the case was linked, but it was like the other – the missing objects could have a perfectly innocent explanation and knowing the opportunistic thieving that went on during the Feast it was just as likely that Stacey's shopping was nicked. It wasn't really giving them any new clues.

She turned to Carter. 'How about you? Did yer find out anything at all about Amanda's boyfriend?' Lorraine had phoned him as soon as she'd left the morgue.

Carter opened the file he'd been carrying and every sheet of paper came tumbling out. 'Sorry, boss.' He scrambled around on the floor picking them up.

'That's a damn lot of files on the boyfriend of a supposed accident victim, Carter?'

By now he had everything on the table and was busily trying to sort it out. 'Er, some of it's me local history papers, boss. We've a meeting coming up.'

'Oh, how very interesting, Carter.' Lorraine's voice was heavily tinged with sarcasm but Carter took her at her word.

'Yes, boss, an' tell yer what, it is really interesting an' all. Did yer know that Barnard Gilpin was responsible for the first ox-roasting? He used to roast it and give it to the poor, an' that's why the first sandwich which comes off the ox on Houghton Feast Monday is free. It's tradition like. And I bet yer didn't know that Queen Mary, when she heard about it, ordered him to London to be beheaded. Anyhow, when he was on his way he fell off his horse and broke his leg. An innkeeper took him in and he was to stay there until his leg healed. Then he had a stroke of luck while he was waiting for it to mend.' Carter paused for effect. 'Queen Mary died.' Carter nodded at Luke and Lorraine. 'And guess what?'

Lorraine looked ready to throttle him. She'd already heard most of these stories from Mavis and in any case, this was scarcely the time.

Luke seemed interested though. 'No idea, Carter, what?'

'Queen Elizabeth the First only went and pardoned him.'

'Well bloody good for her,' Lorraine said. 'An' are we now finished with today's history lesson, Carter?'

Luke, even though Lorraine threw daggers at him, couldn't resist saying, 'I'm surprised people round here don't say "He's got the luck of Barnard Gilpin," yer know, like they say, "He's got the luck of the devil."'

Carter grinned, 'Aye, yer right, Luke.'

'When yer ready, guys,' Lorraine said, looking from one to the other, her eyes finally resting on Carter. 'What have yer got?'

'Well, me and Sanderson checked the electoral roll an' he wasn't registered anywhere in Tyne and Wear.'

'Shit.'

'So we tried DVLA using his previous car reg and he's moved.'

'Never. Will you get on with it Carter, yer turning into a bloody drama queen.'

Luke feigned a cough to hide his smirk as a deeply frustrated Lorraine bit a lump out of her pencil.

'Sorry, boss. He moved to Morpeth sometime last year.'

'Morpeth.'

'Aye.'

'Get yer coat on, Luke.'

'What, we going there now?'

'It's only,' she looked at her watch, 'forty minutes at this time of day.'

'OK, boss.'

'Carter, I want you to go and see if yer can get hold of this Hammerman. I don't think that he has much to do with it but we need to check. An' when you've done with that yer to go and visit Jacko again. Tell him we're doing everything we can to find Melanie. Reassure him. But at the same time see what yer can find out about Doris. She's keeping quiet for some reason an', who knows, the person who cut Doris could have Melanie. Aye, an' ask Hammerman if he knows anything about the attack on Doris, an' all.' She shrugged. 'It might be connected in some way. If yer still can't get anything out of either of them, then put feelers out, talk to some narks.'

'OK, boss.'

As Carter left, Lorraine took out her mobile. She stared at it for a moment, as if willing it to ring.

'Something the matter, boss?' Luke asked, shrugging into his black leather jacket.

'Just waiting for an important call that should have come a while ago.' She stood, collected her bag and headed for the door. 'Come on then,' her eyes flicked to the desk, 'and don't forget the address.'

Mickey was hanging around the show field, doing a damn poor job of looking interested in his surroundings. He was here for two reasons: one checking the place out for signs of Melanie for word had sharp spread that the coppers were looking for a traveller. The second reason was the wonderful smell that was drifting over the place. His mother had parted with some of her hard-earned cash – as she like to call it – and he was waiting for an ox sandwich.

He'd spent some time talking to the candyfloss girl who he'd gone to school with and, flipping heck, what a beauty she'd turned out to be. He hadn't recognised her at first. Two years ago she'd worn thick glasses and had mousey hair: now she was golden blonde, with big brown eyes that had been hidden for years.

Amazing.

She'd told him that she'd thrown the glasses away and bought contacts. She was now high on his list of most fanciable babes in Houghton.

In spite of his banter with candyfloss girl, he was keeping a close eye on the ox-roasting pit. As the time grew closer and the delicious smell of roasting ox grew stronger, he'd said goodbye to the girl, whose name he couldn't remember, and slowly began moving from stall to stall, each move bringing him closer to the pit.

He was about fifteen yards away when out of the corner of his eye he spotted Dave Ridley entering the field. Just at that moment an old woman quickly overtook him.

No way. He knew exactly where they were heading.

He hadn't hung around this long to be pipped at the post. He broke into a sprint, passing half a dozen others who had the same idea as he did. He reached his goal just a split second before the mayor cut the first slice.

'Yeah!' he said, spinning round and grinning in Dave Ridley's face.

'That's not fair,' Ridley complained.

'Tough, Dave. Anyhow, how do yer mean it's not fair?'

Ridley shrugged. 'I've waited all day.'

'Cheers, mate.' Mickey grinned, his mouth watering as the first sandwich was handed to him.

'Anyhow, Dave, yer a bloody liar,' Mickey said, before taking a huge bite out of his sandwich and walking away.

On his way down to the Seahills he kept his eyes open in case he saw Melanie, not one net-covered window escaped his scrutiny.

Yer never know, he said to himself, they reckon the best way to hide something is in full view.

He was halfway through the Burnside when he bumped into Mr Skillings.

'Hello, son, queue gone down yet for the sandwiches?'

'Ner, it's halfway round the field.'

'Bloody hell. I bet there's nowt left when I get there. I've got to get four. One each for me, Doris, Dolly, and Jacko.'

'How are they?'

'Not good, son, not good. The life and soul's gone out of the pair of them. And the weight that's dropped off Jacko already is something shocking.'

'Me and Robbie's going over when I get down, see if there's anything more we can do.'

As they talked neither of them noticed the man in the grey sweatshirt, with his hood pulled up so that his face was all but invisible, pass them by.

Peggy had read every magazine in the place. Drunk five cups of what had to be the most putrid coffee in the whole world. Listened for an hour to a screaming kid who just wouldn't shut up, no matter what his poor harrassed mother – who wasn't much more than a kid herself – did for him.

Closing her eyes, she rested the back of her head against the cool wall and tried to tune him out. She thought of Mavis; they had been friends since the first day of school. Had hit it off right away and been, as her own mother used to say, 'thick as thieves' ever since.

What she would do if Mavis did have cancer just didn't bear thinking about. They had helped each other through everything. Knew everything about one another that there was to know.

Mavis knows things about me that no one, not even Lorry, will ever know, and vice versa. Why aye, an' doesn't she know more than any of those blokes I was fool enough to marry ever did?

She thought then of Lorraine's father who Lorraine thought was dead. If something happened to Mavis, would I have to tell her the truth?

Or leave it as it is?

She bit hard on a sob at the thought of Mavis dying. But cancer wasn't always the end, not these days. Not always anyhow.

Still screeching, the little boy chose that moment to run past and in doing so stood right on her toes. Peggy gritted her teeth and smiled at the mother with a death head grin.

She was just about ready to pull her hair out when the doctor finally showed up.

'Mrs Margaret Monk? Is there a Mrs Monk here?'

Peggy started, unused to hearing herself called Margaret. 'Yeah, that'll be me.'

'Could you come with me please,' he asked.

'My God, what's wrong, what d'yer want me for?' But the doctor was already disappearing down the corridor even as Peggy quickly got to her feet. She rushed after him and followed him into to his office. He was tall, broad with thick dark hair.

Silently he pulled out a chair for her, then went round his desk and waited for Peggy to sit down before he seated himself.

By, but they do things different when yer go private.

Lorraine had insisted that Mavis go private, whatever the cost, if it meant that things would be sorted that little bit quicker.

He looked up from his notes and met her eyes.

Lorraine and Luke made good time to Morpeth, a pleasant market town, a fairly short drive up the A1 from Newcastle.

'Which street is it?' Lorraine asked, as they pulled off the motorway and entered the town.

Luke glanced at the address, '147 Hillary Street.'

It took a further ten minutes to get through the heavy traffic, then they were both standing outside the red door of the house.

Luke knocked, and a moment later the door opened. A fair-haired man of medium build, who Lorraine thought was probably somewhere in his late twenties, stood in the entrance. He frowned at them before saying, 'Can I help yers?'

'Police,' Lorraine said, showing her badge. 'Do yer mind if we come in for a chat?'

'Well – What – I haven't –'

'It's all right, sir, it's nothing you've done. We just want to ask yer some questions about a previous girlfriend. You are Andy Brown, aren't you?'

'Oh. Yes of course, come in then.' He stepped to one side to allow Lorraine and Luke to enter.

They walked down a passageway, and he showed them into a small, but very neat, sitting room at the front of the house. The decor was modern with lots of silver, and lots of modern art pictures on the walls. Lorraine's quick glance took in at least three small tables scattered about the room and a big armchair alongside a settee which was blue with white tasselled throws.

On the main wall above a gas fire was an oil painting of a beautiful raven-haired girl in a green dress.

'Very good likeness.' Lorraine said. 'It's Amanda, isn't it?'

Andy's smile was sad. 'Yes, I got it painted from a photograph. A local artist. Good, isn't he?'

'He is that,' Luke agreed

Lorraine nodded, 'Right, we won't keep yer long. As yer probably remember, we didn't have anything to do with the accident when it happened.'

I was on my honeymoon at the time.

Damn and blast.

Quickly she pulled herself together. 'I'm afraid that I can't tell yer why I need to ask yer to do this, but could yer please go through it with us? We'd like yer – in yer own words – just to tell us what yer can remember. Any little details, no matter how small.'

'Yer have it all on file, yer know?' Andy said gruffly. But then couldn't resist the opportunity to talk about the woman he still loved. He shrugged. 'Well, they said it was drink-driving, but I never believed it and neither did her mam. Amanda was no shrinking violet, but neither was she daft enough to drink-drive. She was dead against that kind of thing, always had something to say about the idiots what did that. No, we took turns: if she was having a drink I drove, and vice versa. Or we got a taxi.' He paused, looking at the portrait. 'Hard to think she's not here any more. We were gonna get married, yer know. Had it all planned. We even had the rings, matching ones an' all. White gold.'

Andy sighed and shook his head sadly before going on. 'I had to identify her, yer know. Stella, her mam, wouldn't. She sort of freaked out, if yer know what I mean.'

'Do yer keep in touch with Stella at all? Like meet up and visit the churchyard, maybe?' Lorraine asked.

'No, never. That's one of the reasons I changed me job and moved here, to keep out of her road. At times it was as though she still wouldn't accept that Amanda had gone. She'd call me at my old place an' ask if she could speak to Amanda and I hated having to keep saying to her that she was dead. Other times she'd ring and say nothing, just cry and cry, though I suppose that were more normal than when she'd pretend that Amanda was still alive. Sometimes she'd talk like she'd just gone to the shops or something, and she'd be back for tea any minute. I bet if yer were to check her cupboards yer would find Amanda's favourite grub in there. She's still got all of Amanda's things, yer know, everything since Amanda was born. All of her clothes, which is unhealthy if yer ask me.'

Lorraine glanced up at the portrait thinking that keeping your dead fiancée on your sitting-room wall could scarcely be called healthy. And what the hell did new girlfriends think if they had to sit on the sofa with the ex staring down?

'And I don't think she's ever been to the churchyard. Not even once,' Andy continued. 'She passed out at the funeral, yer know. Screamed that it was all my fault and then collapsed in a heap.'

'Oh, dear. Must've been pretty dreadful.' Luke sounded genuinely upset and Andy warmed to him.

'It probably sounds a curious question, Andy,' Lorraine said, 'but in this portrait and in all the photos Amanda's got long hair. Did she get it cut?'

'Yeah. Just before she died. She regretted it straight off. Said it made her look ugly, but nothing could've done that. She was beautiful my Amanda. Loads of fellas made passes at her. But she just ignored them. It was me she loved. Only me.'

He fell quiet for a moment and Lorraine let him be. This one was a talker and if yer just let talkers babble then sooner or later, if guilty, they hung themselves. Or innocently divulged vital information they didn't even know they had.

A minute later Andy went on. 'Aye, but there was one man made a pass a few days before she died. She told me all about it and d'yer know, I'd like to meet up with him even now. I'd like to get all those fellas together who used to ogle her and I'd say, "Yer made her life a misery, yer little shits. And yer know what, now she's dead – how d'yer feel about that?" Yeah, I would. And that one bloke, the one just before her accident, why I'd spit in his eye, I would. Right in his eye, an' then see how he gets on ogling women like Amanda. Why he led her a hell of a dance, he did. Just wouldn't take no for an answer she told me, and half put the fear of God in her the way he went on. Bit of a creep if yer ask me, something wrong with his face. Aye, I'll bet he couldn't get a woman the normal way so he had to come on all strong and heavy, like.'

'What?' Lorraine, who had been looking around the room and only keeping one ear on the conversation, picked right up on Andy's reference to something being wrong with the man's face. 'What did yer say? Something was wrong with his face?'

'Aye.'

'Do yer know exactly what? A scar, an eyepatch maybes? A burn, or a birthmark?'

Andy shook his head, 'Don't really know. When I said I was gonna have a few words with him, she said to leave it alone, she'd known him all her life and she felt sorry for him.'

'Did she say how she knew him? Was he a work colleague, or a neighbour?' Lorraine asked. 'And,' inwardly she held her breath, 'do yer have any idea where he might live?'

'I've always thought he must've been a neighbour for her to say she'd known him for ever. Aye, an' afterwards, I drove round a couple of times, just to see if I could see him, yer know, but I never did.'

'Can yer remember exactly what it was that was wrong with his face? This could be very important, Andy, please try hard.'

Andy tried his best but in the end shook his head. 'No, she never said, I'm sure she didn't. But I know it weren't an eyepatch 'cos she did say that compared to this bloke, Jacko Musgrove had it lucky an' was a picture.'

Lorraine and Luke exchanged a glance at the mention of Jacko's name.

Andy looked imploringly at them. 'Does this mean yer've found something out about her accident, then? If yer have, yer must tell me. Maybe if I only knew what she was doing out on that road and with drink in her I'd be able to properly put her to rest.'

'I can't tell yer anything yet, lad,' Lorraine spoke gently, feeling truly sorry for this man who – like Amanda's mother – seemed unable to let go. 'It might be something, it might be nothing. But I can promise yer that the moment I find out anything then I'll be straight back in touch. You've been a great help. Thank you.' Lorraine shook his hand and Luke did likewise, then Andy saw them out.

In the car Lorraine was valiantly searching for pencils. She looked at Luke, 'If Amanda's death is connected – and the more I hear, the more likely it's looking – then seems like Jacko's definitely in the clear.'

'I told yer, didn't I? Jacko's just not the serial-killer type.'

'Yeah, I know. But it's Clark we need to convince. Sanderson told me that the stupid old fart still thinks Jacko might be in the picture for it. Get the blue light out Luke, and get us home just about as fast as you can.'

23

Peggy decided that although she liked the doctor's manners, she certainly didn't like his miserable face.

For fuck's sake smile, yer ugly rat. Me bloody heart's going like the clappers here.

'Well, are you and Mavis very good friends?' He asked, with a slight twitch of his lips that may, or may not, have been an attempt at a smile.

'Oh aye, Doctor. Very good friends, since for ever. So close, we might as well be joined at the hip.'

What the hell has that got to do with anything, who needs the rabbiting, just get on with it, will yer. Jesus!

'Well it's more usual to talk first to a close relative, but the nurses tell me that you've been pestering them non-stop. And there's a file note saying that Mavis has said that in the absence of next of kin you're the one to talk to.'

'Oh I am, Doctor. I am that.'

Next of kin? Oh Christ, no. Was it bad news then? Put me out me misery, will yer, yer bastard man.

The doctor took a deep breath before launching into a

long monologue full of hospital jargon that Peggy simply didn't understand.

For God's sake, I wouldn't like this bloke to yank me intestines out, it would take for ever to tell the tale and I'd still never know what was wrong. If this is what going private means, yer can keep it.

Peggy had had enough: it seemed like he was saying the same thing over and over again. 'Look, Doc,' she interrupted him, 'just give us the bare bones, will yer. Has me best mate got cancer or not? 'Cos if she has, I've got to contact her daughter right away. She'll be worrying herself sick. And she's got an important job, yer know. A Detective Inspector, our Lorry is.'

Shit, now I'm rabbiting on as much as he was.

'Well,' he shook his head, 'I've just explained it all to you, haven't I?'

'No yer haven't, yer've babbled on for five minutes and I've never understood a word yer've said. So just bottom-line it. Please.'

'For goodness sake, woman. No. Your best friend does not have cancer. Is that clear enough for you? And she'll be ready to go home later today.'

'So why the hell didn't yer say so! And what's took so bloody long?' Peggy just stopped herself from adding, *Yer toffee-nosed twat.*

'It took a while for Mrs Hunt to come round from the anaesthetic. Some people do take a little longer and until patients are fully aware of their surroundings and all is normal we are reluctant to –'

'So she's fine? Is that what yer saying?'

'Yes.'

'Thank Christ!' Peggy pulled her mobile out of her bag.

'I'm sorry but that should be switched off whilst you're inside the hospital.'

'I'm only phoning the Detective Inspector. Who is seriously worried about her mother, as you might expect.'

'Well you'll still have to go outside, Mrs Monk. Hospital policy.'

Peggy watched his face and was amazed at the way his eyebrows drew together to emphasise every word as he proceeded to give her a detailed description of what her mobile phone could do to every machine in the hospital.

'Right-oh, OK, Doctor,' she said, when he was finally finished. 'That's no bother to me, man.' Jumping up, she quickly made her way to the door. Turning, she gave the doctor who was watching her with a bemused expression a little wave. 'Bye, Doc, it's been nice knowing yer. Oh, and thanks for everything.'

A minute later she was in Mavis's room. Mavis, looking pale but splendid in a flowing light blue kaftan-style dressing gown, smiled serenely at her. 'I told yer all along there was nothing to worry about, didn't I. Didn't I tell yer that.'

'Aye, yer did that, mate. I always said yer had a bit of witch in yer.' Peggy smiled.

A moment later Mavis's serenity changed to puzzlement. 'Whatever are yer doing?' she asked, as Peggy quickly crossed the room, opened the window wide, and managed after a supreme effort to get the top half of her body out of the window.

'Phoning our Lorry. The poor lamb will be going spare, wondering what's happening. And old happy face, back there, says I can't use the bloody mobile in the hospital. I don't want to be responsible for some poor sod dying while he's wired up to a machine that these things interfere with.'

In Mavis's slightly woozy state it seemed to make perfect sense that her best friend was hanging out of a hospital window six storeys above ground.

'Of course,' she smiled.

*   *   *

Lorraine and Luke were crossing the car park when Lorraine's mobile rang. She stopped walking, quickly pulled her mobile out, and a moment later her face was covered in smiles. 'Yes! Yes! Yes!' she shouted.

She put her mobile away, grinned at Luke, then in her happiness impulsively flung her arms round him. 'It's me mam, Luke. Everything's great! It's just a cyst, like old Dr Mountjoy said.'

Luke liked Mavis very much and was truly pleased to hear that she was going to be all right. But he was even more pleased to find himself standing with Lorraine's arms around him. 'Oh, that's great news, boss. About time the cards fell your way.'

He wished he'd never opened his mouth because as soon as he spoke, Lorraine seemed to realise what she was doing. She dropped her arms at once and moved away. Their eyes met for a long long moment, and Lorraine tried to fight the blush she could feel spreading over her face. Mentally shaking herself she finally looked away from him. 'Aye, it is an' all. Mind you, me and Peggy were always more worried than she was. Although Peggy said it was all an act, an' that Mam was really terrified in case she was going to lose a breast.'

She knew she was babbling to cover her embarrassment.

For God's sake, why the hell did I have to do something stupid like that?

Fancy grabbing him in the flaming car park. Of all the bloody places.

And I just bet there's plenty of prying eyes watching, an' all.

Lorraine stepped away from him, tugged her jacket straight and went on, 'So let's go and see if we can make them fall right for Jacko, eh?' Quickly she turned away and strode on.

Luke tried not to show his disappointment as he nodded his agreement and followed her.

A few minutes later they were facing Clark over his grand

oak desk. He'd yet to fully forgive Lorraine for letting him go off on a wild goose chase to Durham and his face was stern as he listened. She might be his best officer – with Luke a damn good runner-up – but by, she took some controlling.

Lorraine went in to bat explaining that this latest development made it even more unlikely that Jacko could be a suspect, but even as she talked she could see that Clark wasn't fully convinced.

'It's inconclusive, Lorraine,' he said when she finished, with an adamant shake of his head. 'I've not heard enough to entirely rule Jacko Musgrove out in my mind. We have to still consider him a potential suspect.'

Lorraine thought that she'd like to take a swing at the smug know-it-all bastard and could barely hold her temper in check. 'Nonsense!' she snapped.

Clark raised his eyebrows and Lorraine added, 'sir.'

Mollified, he shrugged and asked, 'But why are you so certain? It seems to me that the facts can just as easily be argued another way and it would be downright dangerous for us to rule him out. Jacobs was saying to me only this morning –' He caught Lorraine's glare at the mention of Jacobs's name and went on, 'Yes, well. Give me evidence, girl. And then I'll listen.'

'I agree there's no hard evidence, sir. But I know the man. He wouldn't do it. He wouldn't hurt a hair on that kid's head, and as for being our serial killer, no way.'

'Oh, come on now.' Clark rose, his knuckles resting on the desk and his Adam's apple moving up and down with every word that he spoke. 'How many times have people said, "Because I know he wouldn't." Eh? You can go back hundreds of years and people have been saying the same thing over and over. For Christ's sake, woman, do you think Jack the Ripper's best friend believed it was him?'

'Erm . . . No, sir. I'm sure he didn't.'

Clark did not miss the note of sarcasm in Lorraine's voice but chose to ignore it. 'OK, D I Hunt, you have twenty-four hours to come up with some hard evidence. After that, Mr Musgrove comes back in for questioning. Understand?'

'Thank you, sir.' Moving quickly in case she finally triggered his anger, Lorraine turned and walked out with Luke close on her heels.

After picking up Carter who had been hovering in the corridor they went to her office and Lorraine closed the door with a mighty slam. 'Jack the Ripper? Jack the flaming Ripper! Is that bloody man for real, or what?'

Luke burst out laughing as a puzzled Carter looked from one to the other. He grinned after Luke explained, then said earnestly, 'Which Jack the Ripper, boss? Cos yer know there was two of them. I've been learning all about it.'

For an answer Lorraine threw a dozen pencils at him and was about to tell him just what she thought of his history classes when the phone rang. It was Scottie and Lorraine greeted him cheerily: despite their lack of progress with the case, Mavis's news made her feel that this too would come right in the end.

'It's about that autopsy report yer asked me to look at,' Scottie replied when Lorraine asked him why he'd rung.

'Yes, go on,' Lorraine said impatiently, thinking that perhaps this was the long-awaited breakthrough.

'Well, it's not a straightforward one, that I can tell yer. It's always hard, interpreting another pathologist's findings, but as far as I can see there was no real reason to rush to the conclusion that the poor lass was drunk. The blood tests did show traces of alcohol, but there's a reason, Lorraine, that I'm using the word "trace". Yer see although there was a lot of alcohol in her throat an' it was all over her clothes according to my report, the actual alcohol content of her blood was pretty minimal.'

'Well that doesn't make sense. Why wouldn't it've come out at the inquest?'

'I don't rightly know, Lorraine. I'm not saying there was no drink at all 'cos by all accounts there was booze all over her. Just that the level in her blood stream left her well under the limit.'

'There was no mention of there being a bottle with her in the car or anything, Scottie. So seems unlikely that she'd just started drinking as she drove along and it spilled?'

'Not unless she took a couple of swigs then threw it out the window or something. But they'd've checked all that at the time, yer know.'

'More likely they might've checked than they definitely would have, Scottie. Yer know as well as I do that things don't always happen like they should. Not that I really think that's likely. What about the death itself, anything suspicious?'

'She was pretty badly broken up by all accounts. Looks as though her head went through part of the car windshield when the car landed – must've fallen slightly onto its side. She wasn't wearing a seat belt, not that it would've saved her in this instance. Anyhow. Covered in cuts and abrasions, and from what I can make out her head was near severed by the glass.'

'Dear God.' Lorraine shuddered at she thought of the photo and portrait she'd seen of a beautiful smiling young woman, her hair cascading round her neck.

'The rest of the autopsy photographs were missing from the case file, otherwise I might have been able to tell yer more. Edna reckons they'll have gone to central filing by now and is gonna put in for them, on the off chance.'

'Thanks, Scottie. I owe yer.'

Lorraine lowered the receiver and looked at Luke and Carter who had been listening to her side of the call. 'Did yer get all that? Seems that Stella and Andy might be right, an' that Amanda didn't drink and drive. But if she wasn't drunk, then why did she lose control of the car and send it over the cliff edge? Wasn't a wet night or anything, and no skid marks anywhere on the road.'

Neither man could offer an answer and Lorraine shook her head, all her tiredness flooding back. 'Just what we need, eh? Another bleeding mystery. We're meant to be solving them, guys, not discovering even more!'

Josh had made his way back to the woods after leaving the aunts' caravan that afternoon. He had a sleeping bag now and once he'd remade his bed of grass, he'd eaten two pork pies from the stash of food he'd been given. He might be clean and fed, but God, he still felt completely miserable.

He'd watched the Monday night firework display from the top of the cave. He'd always been fascinated by fireworks and the Houghton Feast display, which was supplied by the Showman's Guild, was always splendid. However it had been cold comfort because when it was all over he'd had to climb back down into the darkness of the cave. No sign of the fox, though. He guessed the fireworks would have scared her.

He kept going over his confrontation with Uncle Percy who had turned up at the aunts' caravan just as Josh was shovelling the best bacon and eggs he'd ever tasted in his life down his throat. His uncle's utter shock at seeing him had been perfectly clear on his face. And was Josh imagining it, or had it taken quite a while to convince Uncle Percy that he was innocent?

Josh frowned at the small fire he had going.

'He did . . . In the end, I know he did believe me,' he muttered, nodding his head as if to convince himself. His Uncle Percy was a decent man. *He wouldn't've helped me if he thought I'd done something bad.*

'And he was right in saying that if I refused to give myself

272

up I should come back to the cave in case the police are still watching the show field. Why would he have told me that, if he didn't care?'

He sighed. He was lonely with no one for company, except for maybe a reluctant fox who probably didn't trust him either. But what was he to do? He just knew that the police wouldn't believe him when he told them he was innocent. Percy had promised that when the fair closed on Wednesday he'd come and pick up Josh and they'd leave the area together. But he was stuck here till then with only his thoughts for company.

And what if they still come after me? He wondered. What then? He couldn't expect Percy to join him on the run for the rest of his life. Should he slope off on his own, had he already done Percy and the aunts enough damage? God, what was the point of any of it for someone like him?

'I've gotta have a plan, here,' he told himself.

But what?

Fucking hell! I'm the only person I know that this could happen to.

Josh stirred the embers of the dying fire with the stick he'd snapped from one of the trees and admitted, deep down, that he hated being alone. He'd been wrong for all those years to claim that that was what he wanted: being entirely on your own just had to be the most horrendous thing in the world. He knew now that each of those times he'd locked himself in the trailer he'd never really been truly alone. There were always people within calling distance, always the sounds and smells of the fair.

Out here, a whole lot of nothingness. Nothing but the damp smell of dew on the grass and the frenzied feeding sounds of night creatures.

And, he nodded his head, for once in complete agreement with himself, it was no good him just hanging around waiting for Melanie to simply show up. 'Cos that was never gonna happen.

Think. Think. Got to think, damn it. Do I definitely not know whose car it was she got into? If it was me what found her then I'd be a hero, and maybe never on my own ever again.

He put his head in his hands as if that gesture would send all the cogs in his head whirring faster. But it only made his head ache with the stress of it all. He was sure he'd not seen the car before, and what earthly use was it to anyone for him to keep thinking that at least he'd know it if he saw it again. Tons of cars passed through this area. Hundreds and hundreds each day. What was he going to do? Stand watching at the side of a road and wait for it to go past him? Huh, fat chance there was of that.

He pounded his knee out of sheer frustration. He was useless, he was. Always had been and always would be. They should have left him to die with his family in the fire and then none of this would be happening.

He felt full of self-pity until he thought of Melanie and what terror – if she was still alive – she might be going through.

You're pathetic, you are. What about her, eh? She's just a little kid. That's all. A nice kid.

A special kid who had made him wake up when nobody else had been able to. A kid who hadn't given a damn what he looked like. Meeting her had brought him back to the world after what seemed like a long, miserable, pointless sleep. She'd made him realise that he should have stopped feeling sorry for himself years ago and how was he repaying her? By being sorrier for himself than ever, and even wishing he was dead.

Josh's expression changed from self-pity to determination.

One way or another I'll find her, no way can I let that girl down.

Snapping the stick in half, he threw it on the nearly dead fire.

'Wherever you are, Melanie, I'm gonna find you.'

Standing, he shook the heavy-duty sleeping bag out, then climbed in. It was pure luxury after trying to sleep on the hard ground and in moments he was fast asleep.

Although in his own bed, Jacko was finding it impossible to sleep. He turned over and over restlessly, completely exhausted but almost too tired to drop off. Just the idea that he'd been thought a murderer had drained him dry. And if that wasn't enough, he was also suspected of doing something to his own daughter – little Melanie, missing now for the best part of a week. He knew the cheeky bastard coppers still thought that he had something to do with it, especially that rotten little black-haired thing.

Every moment of every hour he dreaded a knock on the door signalling that they were back to take him in again. And he knew he couldn't stand it if they did.

He grabbed the pillow and punched into it. 'Bastards. Bastards. Bastards.'

On the fourth punch one of Doris's little lavender sachets shot out and landed on the window sill. Such a small thing, but the sight of his mother's hand-sewn sachets calmed him almost at once. Reaching over he retrieved the sachet and put it back under his pillow.

Sighing deeply, he lay back down and stared at the moon through his window. Thinking back on today's gossip that the coppers were looking for a bloke from the fair. A fucking traveller. It was the talk of Houghton. A bloke with a badly-scarred face.

The bastard'll have no face when I catch up with him, that's for sure.

Beefy – who always managed to find out whatever was

going down before it even happened – had said that the bloke was on the run. In Beefy's mind that alone was enough to show he must be guilty.

'Yeah, well I'll go with that. An' I'll make sure I catch him before the coppers. Fuck Luke and his "Leave it to us." It's my Melanie what's missing and I'm leaving it to nobody.'

He sat up again before getting out of bed and going to the window. The night was cold, a sure sign that winter was coming. He remembered how much Melanie loved the snow. He'd made her a sledge three years ago and it had hardly snowed since.

'Maybe this year,' he muttered, deciding he might as well go downstairs and make a cup of tea.

Ten minutes later, tea in hand, he went into the sitting room. He'd forgotten to draw the curtains earlier and the moon shone as brightly through the window as it had upstairs.

Jacko glared at it. 'Bastard moon.'

Sitting down with his back to the window, he took a drink of his tea. He was barely halfway through the cup when his eyes started to close and a moment later he was sleeping the sleep of the truly exhausted. The cup gradually slipped from his fingers, its contents spilling down his bare leg. Jacko didn't feel a thing and gently snored away the rest of the night.

They'd not known it, but Jacko and Josh had finally fallen asleep at much the same time. Nor did they know that that was exactly when, not so many miles away, little Melanie had woken up.

The sound of the front door closing had woken her. Eyes wide, she stared with fear at the ceiling and tried to shrink into herself, to go back into the dark. Tried to get away from the glaring night bulb that burned day and night up above.

She'd found a place inside herself to go to: a warm, safe place that felt like home. A place Dad and Nana shared with her, and sometimes her new friend Josh. But tonight, no matter how hard she tried, she just couldn't get there.

The door opened with its familiar creak. It made the same noise at exactly the same place every time someone entered and Melanie had grown to dread the sound.

Her body trembled and although she tried to stop shivering, she couldn't. She'd wet the bed earlier on – not for the first time either – and it was starting to smell. The only change of clothing she'd been offered was that awful red dress and she simply couldn't bear to think of putting it back on.

'Hello, little one,' the dreaded voice said.

Melanie, unable to escape for all her planning had come to nothing, hungry, sore, cold, and frightened, gave in. She couldn't take any more. The effort she had put in had been heroic for an eight-year-old but she had finally reached a state of utter despair.

Not caring what happened next, she said the words the voice had endlessly demanded to hear. 'Hello, Mam.'

He waits outside, sinking into the shadows cast by the huge October moon. He knows she's in there. In that hellhole The Blue Lion. He knows where she is most of the time.

'Oh,' he catches his breath and squeezes further back, his shadow all but disappearing. Here she is. Alone. She's cut all her beautiful hair off and for a moment he feels anger surging within him. But then he calms. He knows that she's done it thinking to make herself prettier for him.

Silently he follows her, hood up and head down, waiting for his chance. Then he remembers, smiling to himself as he crosses the road and takes a different street, reaching the Seahills before her.

The corner house of the street has huge poplar trees that provide plenty of cover. He's hiding behind the third one as her heels, tap tap tapping, announce her presence. She's singing and the last words of her song turn into a frightened squeal as he steps out in front of her. She tries to sidestep him but, as if they are sharing some macabre dance, he keeps in time with her.

'What do yer want?,' she demands bravely, although her voice trembles.

Finally he speaks.

'I know yer want me.'

'What do yer mean, I want yer. I want nothing to do with yer, more like.'

'No. You squeezed me fingers an' I felt yer touch me leg, an' all. There's only one reason why a woman touches a man's leg.' Despite everything, he's still stunned by her denial.

'It was an accident, yer great big idiot. I'd be some kind of idiot meself to fancy somebody who looked like you do. For *fuck's* sake, give us a break will yer.'

He steps towards her, hurt by her words but desperate to make her understand.

'You *cut* your hair for me, didn't you!' He moves closer and reaches out to touch it.

'Hey, what do yer think yer doing? Yer horrible, yer are. Yer disgust me yer ugly-looking creep.'

She's nervous, but not terrified yet. She's known him all her life.

'Fuck off, will yer,' she pushes his chest. 'Fuck off,' she echoes herself as she sees the look on his face. He's seething now, almost at boiling point, and when she sees just how much anger is in his eyes, the fear hits her. She opens her mouth to scream but, desperate to stop her, he seizes her throat and squeezes hard.

She struggles, her heels kicking backwards at his ankles and her arms flailing. A branch bends as, still strangling her, he drags her backwards into the trees.

'You're mine. Why won't you understand? Why won't you –' His body is so tense now it almost feels as if he's in spasm, his hands tightening of their own volition, clutching her neck harder and harder. Then, all of a sudden, the branch *snaps forward again and lashes his face and the stinging hurt brings him to his senses.*

Too late: she's dead. He lifts her face to his and kisses her, claiming when she's dead what she owed him in life. Minutes pass and he finally stops himself. As he looks down at her poor broken body he knows he has to hide what he's done.

Quickly, making sure that there is no one to see him, he throws her over his shoulder and carries her the few streets to where her car is parked outside her house. Plucking the car keys out of her bag he throws her in the passenger seat and jumps in the driver's side.

Twenty minutes later and with only the shortest of stops at his own house, he reaches the coast. He has a plan: the cliffs are pretty high near Souter lighthouse and as he pulls over he is already reaching for the bottle of whisky he's taken from home. Cradling her head he eases her lips open and pours as much as he can into her mouth, then splashes the rest of the alcohol over her body and the inside of the car.

'What a dreadful accident. But drinking and driving are full of peril, aren't they, pet? Easy to crash over the cliffs and onto the rocks.' He takes one last kiss, then spits out the whisky and climbs out of the car.

24

Josh woke to the sound of pouring rain and the smell of wet grass and sodden trees. A whole curtain of raindrops fell from the mouth of the cave making it almost impossible to see outside.

'Must've been raining most of the night,' he muttered, as sitting up he stretched, yawned, then rubbed sleep from his eyes. 'Well, don't matter to me whether it's wet, dry or some-place in between the two. Not gonna let a little water put me off.'

He was as determined this morning to go looking for Melanie as he had been the previous evening. He had to do something, he couldn't just sit around in a cave and wait for things to happen to him. *Or to her.*

Disentangling himself from the sleeping bag, he nodded his confirmation. He had to go looking for that car. He plucked an apple out of his rucksack as he ran the whole scene through his mind. No one had spotted him going to the aunts and back yesterday, he was sure he could scout around a bit without being seen. He bit into the apple, quickly finishing it off and then folded his bedding, hiding it in the corner behind a medium-sized rock. The last thing he needed was a bunch of local kids coming in and trashing the place for the fun of it.

He'd actually slept quite well last night, maybe due to exhaustion. Although without the sleeping bag he knew that he'd have been in for another dreary night awake, stone after stone digging into his kidneys. One thing he'd learned about stones over the past few nights was that when you got rid of one, there was always another two – or even three – waiting to take its place. Stones had a particular breeding pattern all of their own.

He hadn't seen the fox since the firework display, even though he'd kept an eye out for her. And she didn't seem to be about today. He hoped the smell of humans hadn't put her off this cosy den for ever, especially if she ever had cubs.

The climb from the cave was very steep and the rain had made the pathway quite treacherous. He made it to the top intact, although he was covered in mud up to his knees. But thankfully the rain had stopped by the time he left the woods and a watery sun was in charge of the sky.

He noticed the boy with the tattoos at the same time as the boy noticed him. Josh couldn't actually tell whether he was a boy or a fully-grown man, there was so much ink on his face. But he didn't miss the nudge the girl standing beside him gave with her elbow, nor her sly grin.

Sensing trouble, he hesitated and wondered whether he should cross the road to avoid the pair. He looked up and down the street but it was completely deserted, even the little post office wasn't open yet. He didn't quite know whether he wished there were people around or not. It would increase the chances of him being spotted, but these two looked like they could be a problem for someone who was on his own.

Josh was no coward, it had never been an issue for him.

But he'd never felt the need to prove he belonged with the apes either. He just didn't like fighting, full stop. If you fought with someone you had to touch them, and touching was something Josh hadn't done for years. Living the life he did meant that confrontations with drunken yobbos late at night in the show field happened fairly often. Usually he gritted his teeth and just walked away. He might cringe inside at the names shouted after him and even fret for hours afterwards, but walking away had always seemed the better option.

Lance Halliday moved fast, but his sister moved faster. In moments Josh had one in front of him and the other behind.

'Tip it up,' Halliday growled.

Josh actually felt like laughing and, against his will, a small grin appeared on his face. Tip what up, he thought.

'You laughing at me? Yer ugly bastard.' There was a touch of amazement in Halliday's voice.

Josh knew he was courting danger. He could see it in the pale staring eyes of his tormentor, ringed round with the hideous tattoos. But too much had happened in the last few days for him to keep his usual cool. He was wanted by the police for the first time in his life, and for a charge so vile it turned his stomach. He'd had to live like an animal in a cave, with only a fox for company. And the only friend he'd made in the last ten years, little kid or not, had gone missing. Deep down he was seriously pissed off.

'I might be,' he shrugged.

Lance looked taken aback for a moment. 'Yer a cheeky twat, I'll give yer that.'

'Yeah, and you're an ugly tattooed twat. An' I'll give you that, and all.'

What the hell am I saying? Josh thought to himself in horror. I've got to keep a low profile to go to search for Melanie, and I'm pissing about arguing with a retarded ape.

A moment later he saw the punch coming and ducked

quickly, but not in time to stop it glancing off the side of his head. Recovering his balance and before the older boy had a chance to strike again, Josh threw an uppercut that caught Lance fair and square on his chin. Lance rocked back on his heels and it seemed like Josh had the advantage but just then something that felt like a plank of wood caught him right behind his knees. He hit the ground with a thud that knocked the wind out of him.

Halliday seized the moment and began to kick Josh as he lay on the ground. He started in on Josh's body but before long moved up towards his head. If Josh had been a true fighter, or had any real practice at the skills of self-defence, he might have been able to hold his own with Halliday. As it was, he just about managed to curl up into a ball and cover his head with his hands before Julie joined her brother, the pair of them raining down blow after savage blow. The brutal kicking rendered Josh entirely helpless, little Melanie his last conscious thought.

Lorraine took Mavis's breakfast in on a tray. As she was fussing over her mother rearranging the pillows, she heard a voice from the kitchen call out, 'Ohh, is this for me?'

She smiled. 'Yeah, Peggy. Enjoy it.'

'Thanks, pet,' came the reply, the words were muffled by Peggy's first mouthful of bacon and egg.

'Oh, yer shouldn't have, love. It looks lovely.' Mavis beamed up at Lorraine.

'Yes I should. Now you just rest up today, right. I mean it, Mam.'

'OK,' Mavis laughed. 'But do yer honestly think for one minute, pet, that with the Gorgon on guard out there it's likely I'll be able to do anything else?'

'Yeah, well just make sure the pair of yers don't cook something up between yers.'

'Whatever do yer mean?'

'Yer knows exactly what I mean, Mam. Me love life is me own, an' I don't want you two anywhere near it.'

'What love life's that then?'

Lorraine ignored her mother's question and Mavis patted her daughter's hand. 'Yer a good girl, Lorry. The best. Now just get yerself off to work and catch some villains, and don't worry about me.'

'OK, but I mean it, Mam. Make sure the pair of yers behave yerselves.'

'Oh we will,' Peggy, looking like a bell tent with legs in her cerise dressing gown, said from behind her.

Lorraine was wearing an identically coloured blouse with her charcoal grey suit and thought for a moment about going and changing before deciding she simply didn't have the time. Shaking her head, she tried to hide a grin as she grabbed her bag and headed for her car.

Luke had beaten her to the station and already had various case files spread out across his desk. 'How's Mavis?' he asked with a wide smile revealing a glint of gold.

I wonder if he realises just how sexy that makes him look, Lorraine thought as she pulled up a chair. 'Both the Hippy and the Rock Chick are doing fine,' she answered.

Luke laughed.

Lorraine rummaged for a pencil. Course he knows. Probably practises smiling in the mirror. I can just see him now, grinning this way and that way.

'So,' she pulled one of the files towards her, 'how far on are yer?'

Luke was re-examining all the files they'd pulled when they'd first interviewed Christina. To their surprise there had been quite a few men who had had some kind of facial deformity and a criminal record, although quite what constituted a 'deformity' seemed to vary hugely from case to case. Lorraine remembered Carter getting the giggles when he read of some poor bloke who'd apparently had 'excessive facial hair'. And Lorraine had come across one where the man had one blue eye and one brown – scarcely flipping deformed.

'Well I've managed to eliminate quite a few already on the grounds of where they've lived for the last fifteen years or so. Amanda told her boyfriend that she'd known this bloke since she was a kid. She was twenty when she died and that was three years ago, so no one who moved into the area recently can be in the frame. Nor anyone who didn't live somewhere round her way when she was growing up. Now I'm throwing out the ones who are just too young to be included.'

'So is this . . . ?' Lorraine tapped the remaining files with her fingernail.

Luke nodded. 'The main suspects.'

Lorraine flicked through the files but after a few minutes she shook her head. 'We're gonna have to get all six of them in. I know we checked them out and dismissed them when Christina got hurt, an' I know the Amanda thing might be nothing. But we don't have any option, Luke.'

'Yeah, yer never know.'

'Pass their names to Carter then, he can round them up. An' tell him we want them a.s.a.p.'

'Sure, boss.' Luke left in search of Carter.

Lorraine rose and went to the window where she stared out at the courtroom steps for a minute or two. Something was niggling at her, but she couldn't quite pin it down. She thought how strange it was that after three deaths in quick succession it had been quiet for a few days, although they couldn't let themselves believe that the killings had stopped. Luke came back and was about to say something when Lorraine spun round.

286

'Yer know, Luke, I really think it must be Houghton Feast where the answer lies. It's just too much of a coincidence that all this is happening at the same time of year. It's pretty certain that Stacey was one of his, an' now this year it's escalated. And all the killings happening in the run-up to the Feast. Aye, an' Christina was obviously meant to go the same way. I keep thinking that there must be some kind of clue to the timings that we're missing. It just doesn't make any sense.'

'But what could it be about the Feast, boss?' Luke asked, watching Lorraine pace the length of the room and back and fighting to keep the admiration out of his eyes. 'Yer surely don't think anything of Carter an' his curse?'

'No, course I don't. But I do know that our fella's on a spree this time. He's got it all worked out and, by God, I think he's enjoying it.'

'Aye, he is that.'

'But what sets him off in the first place? The fair must be some kind of trigger. He's a loner this one, I know it, but it's scarcely gonna be just 'cos he hates crowds. What the hell sets him off?'

Lorraine continued pacing as her mind worked. She knew it could be one of the travellers who was the killer. After all, they turned up at the same time every year. Knew too, that there was one on the run who could've matched Christina's description – and why would this Josh have gone walkbouts if he had nothing to fear? Despite this, every instinct told her that the murders were too planned and too personal for it to be a traveller. And wasn't Mavis always telling her just how important instincts were? No, she was convinced it was someone local, the more so given how thoroughly they'd grilled every man at the show-ground.

'What if, Luke, what if it really is connected with Amanda? That it's her dying at Feast time that's led to all this? It'd make sense of them all looking the same, wouldn't it?'

'Yeah, it would, boss. But we know it's not her fiancée, don't we? Even if he had the strength, which he doesn't on account of being such a weedy sort, he wasn't even in the country at the start of last week.'

'No, it's not Andy. But it could be the mother, for instance. Scottie said it had to have been a man who did the crimes, but let's face it she works as a flipping bouncer. Yer have to be pretty strong to do that. She might have the motive – remember Edna saying she was crazed with grief and Andy on about her not accepting Amanda was dead? But then again,' Lorraine contradicted herself, 'she doesn't have a bloody mark on her face, does she.'

This brought her sharp back to the present and she wearily picked up the files of the six men Carter was bringing in. 'Tell yer what though, Luke, when Carter's done rounding up our lads then yer might as well get him to double-check Stella's whereabouts on the nights of the murders, eh.'

Mr Skillings had walked up the bank to Newbottle on his weekly visit to see his sister Verity who lived in Cathedral View. He had crossed the main road and was nearly at the post office when he noticed a bundle of red rags in the gutter.

He tutted. 'I don't know, people these days. No pride in the place, that's what's missing with most of them. A nice little village like this. Disgraceful. Whatever will they be dumping next.' He tutted again, then his heart nearly stopped when the bundle of rags seemed to move. He leaned forward to look closer and stifled a gasp.

'Oh my God!' Mr Skillings realised that the red colour was blood and that the bundle of rags was in fact a young man. 'What the hell happened to you, son?'

Josh slowly rolled over and just as slowly started to get to his feet. He steadied himself with one hand against the wall, the other holding his right side. The pain was so severe that he was certain there had to be at least two ribs broken and he could tell that his face was covered in blood.

'Eh, bonny lad, are yer all right?'

Josh, his left eye swollen shut, squinted at Mr Skillings with his other eye and sighed from the heart. Thinking that even a blind man would be able to see that he was far from all right.

'Can I help yer?'

Josh shook his head to say no.

'I'll phone the police, shall I? An ambulance? I think yer need to see a doctor at least.'

'No!' Josh panicked. If the police got their eager hands on him he'd never get loose and there'd be no chance he could help Melanie.

'No, thank you. I'm fine really. I'm all right.' He straightened up, gritting his teeth to cover the groan that was trying to force its way up from his toes. He knew that by the time it reached his throat it would have collected so many pain signals from all over his body that it would become a full-blown pain scream.

Yeah, an' once I start, I might never stop.

He took a careful step and Mr Skillings watched, feeling a mixture of concern, amazement and not a little admiration.

Not bad, Josh thought, taking another step. His left ankle twinged slightly but it held his weight. He'd make it.

Muttering his thanks once more to Mr Skillings he slowly started his journey down towards the Seahills.

Mr Skillings fought down his instinctive urge to help the young man and watched as Josh made his faltering and painful way down the road. He found himself praying that whatever it was that was so important to the lad, would happen.

He'd seen that kind of brave confidence before, in the trenches and on the beaches. He turned away, knowing that this lad was going to get to wherever it was he wanted so badly to go.

A bus arrived and deposited half a dozen people on the pavement just as Josh passed the bus stop. Of the six people who got off only two noticed Josh limping past: an old woman, who shrank away with a fearful look on her face, and a young mother with two toddlers who, although her hands were full, went to try to help. Josh said no to her kindness, and she too watched with a kind of strange fascination as he hobbled on his way.

Lorraine tapped her fingers on the desk out of sheer frustration as she watched Luke interview the third suspect Carter had brought in. The first bloke had had a huge mark covering half his face but the poor sod was pushing seventy and practically blind. She doubted that he'd have been able to find his own neck to tie a scarf round it, let alone wrap his gnarled old fingers round anyone else's. Number two was another birthmark and on compassionate leave from the navy as of three days before. He swore he had half of Her Majesty's fleet to give him an alibi and a quick phone call proved him right.

Why the hell hadn't Carter weeded these two out? Lorraine shook her head. Sometimes she actually felt like putting him up against a wall and shooting him herself.

She leafed through the file of the man Luke was now questioning. Oh, Jesus. Married for fifteen years, a bank clerk for twenty. Three kids, a fucking mortgage, all the trappings of an ordinary life. Whilst this didn't always mean the person was a saint, in this case both the kind of disfigurement he had and his whereabouts on the nights in question seemed to rule him out. His was purely and simply a case of really bad acne, leaving him with terrible scarring all over. In fact, Lorraine thought, he'd give the Elephant Man a run for his money, wonder was that some woman had gone and married him. Then was cross with herself for having such nasty thoughts.

Whatever his problem, he and his family had been at home on the nights in question, and given there were also neighbours round for a card night on one of the evenings, it wasn't likely that he was making it up. His 'criminal record' had also turned out to be nothing. Three unpaid parking tickets and a speeding fine. And even they'd turned out to be for a car he no longer owned.

What a waste of bloody time.

She signalled for Luke to terminate the interview and watched as the hugely relieved man hastily left the room.

Once he'd gone, Luke stretched and slowly rolled his neck from side to side trying to get the stress kinks out of it. Lorraine watched him through half lowered lids.

He's doing that on purpose. The bastard.

Aye, an' I'll bet he practises that in front of the mirror an' all. Bloody men, vainest creatures on the planet.

She still felt the sting of embarrassment she'd experienced when she instinctively flung her arms around him on hearing her mother's good news.

It had felt good though.

Luke's voice broke into her thoughts, 'What now, boss?'

She focussed on him, blew air upwards disturbing her fringe and shrugged. 'Beats me. I guess we'll just have to carry on with the interviews. Though I've got a strong feeling looking through this lot,' she flung a very thin handful of files across the desk, 'that the bastard we want's not amongst them.'

Josh wasn't sure that he could go on for much longer. His ribs were killing him and the twinge in his ankle had turned into a stab which bit in with every step. He allowed himself to take five minutes' rest on the kerbside, promising his poor body that afterwards it would feel OK. He knew he was kidding both his body and himself though, he was never going to feel OK again. And instead of creeping about the place keeping a low profile, he'd gone and made himself into the biggest spectacle there was. The only good thing was that the blood and the bruising covered over the scarred part of his face but, all the same, everyone who passed by was now having a good look.

'Fuck off, why don't you?' he muttered angrily, seeing yet another vehicle slow down as it went past. 'You never heard of the walking wounded, you vulture –'

He broke off as he looked at the car driving past him. 'Yes! Thank you, Jesus!' It was the selfsame car that he'd seen Melanie get into. He knew it was, he'd have recognised it anywhere. From the bashed-in front wing and cracked side mirror to the sticker for Center Parcs in the back window, this was the car he'd done nothing but picture every night in the cave.

This time he'd got a good look at the driver. And, even better, he knew just where he'd seen them before.

25

Doris and Jacko sat in front of the blank television, despair etched on their faces. With each hour that passed, the chance of Melanie's safe return seemed to recede and neither could settle to anything knowing that she was somewhere out there.

Doris had tried to get Jacko to talk.

'I wonder how Christina's getting on in hospital. She's a lovely lass. Don't yer think so, Jacko?'

'Aye.'

'Yer could do no better, yer know. When she gets out and is on the mend, like. An' I won't be around for ever. Little Melanie'll need a mam.'

'How can I be thinking of that, with my Melanie still missing? Shut it, will yer, Mam. Now's not the time.'

'I'm sorry, pet. I thought it might take yer mind off things, like. She is a lovely lass an' I know for a fact that father of hers treats her something awful. Dolly reckons that 'cos the Mam was out shopping for a present for Christina when she got killed, he blames her, like. Reckons he knocks her around a bit an' all.'

Jacko sighed. He did have feelings for Christina. And God knows, he'd have loved to have rescued her from that old bastard. Aye, and if he was laying a figure on her then he'd lay one on him, and all.

But how could he think about anything but Melanie right now? He couldn't. Everybody else in the world could be heading towards meltdown and he wouldn't care. Only one thing mattered: Melanie.

Please God, please God. Let me have her safe back.

Weary and aching all over, Josh finally reached the Musgroves'. His elation at seeing the car and its driver had long vanished and he half dreaded what was to come. Once he'd seen the car the only thing he could think of doing was going in search of Melanie's dad. He thought that if he could reach him safely – and get his story out before the man throttled him – then he might have help.

He stood outside the house for a moment, remembering back to walking Melanie home here after one of her trips to the showground. That felt an awfully long time ago to Josh, seemed like a million things had happened to him since.

As he stared at the door he felt his throat dry up and his heart begin to pound. Despite the news he had for the family, he was nervous of the reception he might get. As far as Melanie's folks knew, he was the one who had their girl. Her father would probably finish the job that that ink-faced idiot had started.

He stood as straight as he could which, given the hellish state of his ribs, was anything but straight, then took the final step to the door. He knocked, hesitant at first, then when no one answered with a slightly firmer hand.

The door finally opened and an old woman with deep black circles under her eyes stared out at him. One eye was also swollen up with a huge great shiner and she looked so full of sorrow it made Josh's almost want to cry. He rightly took her to be Melanie's grandmother and was about to take all his courage in his hands and introduce himself when she let out a cry.

'Ohh, dear me, what on earth –'

Doris's mouth hung open in shock at the sight of him and Josh cursed himself for not thinking what a picture he must make.

'Jacko, Jacko, there's a strange lad at our door and he looks like he's bloody well bleeding to death. I think yer better get an ambulance. Hurry up, son. Hurry up.'

'No, please. No ambulance.' Josh held his hand up. 'I'm fine, really I am. If you'll just give me a few minutes . . . I really need to talk to you. It – it's very important.'

'Yer look anything but fine to me,' a deep voice said and Jacko stepped into the doorway as Doris moved over. 'What do yer want?' He eyed Josh suspiciously.

'The lad needs help, Jacko. Yer can see that.'

'What do yer want?' Jacko repeated, ignoring Doris.

Josh swallowed hard. 'I know who took Melanie,' he mumbled, every second expecting a blow to come his way.

'Yer what?' Jacko had only heard Melanie's name but it was enough for him to grab Josh by his throat and haul him over the front step. He shook Josh as though he were no heavier than a feather. 'What did yer say?' he demanded, his face close up in Josh's own. But Josh barely heard the end of the question as he slumped forward in a dead faint.

'Jacko,' Doris put a restraining arm on her son, 'the lad's passed out. For God's sake, carry him into the house. Hurry up will yer, man. He seems to know something about our Melanie.'

Jacko scooped Josh up and carried him through into the sitting room where he none too gently dumped him onto the settee. Doris ran quickly through to the kitchen and filled a bowl with water.

As she knelt down to bathe Josh's face, Josh moaned softly.

'Throw the water over him,' Jacko demanded impatiently. 'That'll wake him up.'

'Don't be silly,' Doris replied, carefully washing the blood from Josh's face.

'Christ! Here's me thinking I was an ugly bugger on account of me eye patch!' Jacko said when Doris had finished.

'Jacko, that's not nice. The poor lad's obviously been burned or something. Dreadful for the lad an' he's only a kid. Thank God these cuts seem mainly superficial, most of them any road. The face always bleeds heavily yer know, makes it look a lot worse than what it is.'

'The poor bastard's still had a hell of a beating though. Look at that boot mark on his brow.' Jacko pointed to the hairline mark on Josh's forehead.

The poor bastard chose that moment to open his eyes. He struggled to sit up but when Jacko put his arm round his back to help him, Josh yelped and clutched at his side.

'Ohh, I bet yer've got a couple of broken ribs there, mate.' Josh nodded. 'I think so.'

'Yeah, well if yer haven't I guarantee yer will have if yer don't spill yer guts about our Melanie.'

Josh swallowed hard. There was only one way to tell it and he knew he'd better be quick. Melanie's dad looked like he meant business and in his current fragile state he felt as though another beating would finish him off for good. Taking a deep breath he blurted out, 'I'm Josh, from the show field.'

'I thought as much when I saw yer scar, yer cheeky bastard. Get the coppers, Mam, before I kill him.'

'Please, no,' Josh sobbed. 'I can't taken any more. If you just listen to me, I think I know who took Melanie away.'

'Well who? Yer bastard, talk will yer?' Jacko was yelling

so loudly his face had turned a livid red. 'So help me, if yer pussyfoot around much longer then I'll finish the job some other bastard started.'

'Jacko!' Doris shouted nearly as loudly as her son. 'Will yer calm down an' give him a chance to say his piece?'

Jacko, nostrils flaring, glared at Doris and then at Josh. 'Right. Yer've got five. Spit it out.'

Josh struggled to turn sideways on the settee in order to ease the pressure on his ribs while Jacko, breathing heavily, stood menacingly over him.

It took Josh a moment or two to find a position which lessened the pain his ribs were causing him, then he said, 'It was a woman.'

'A woman?' Jacko and Doris said in unison, utter disbelief showing on their faces.

'What woman?' asked Doris.

Hesitantly, and stopping for frequent breaths, Josh told his tale. When he explained how he'd seen Melanie get in a car and why he'd not told anyone about it, Doris had to almost physically restrain Jacko from going back on his promise and knocking the boy into the middle of the following week. This brought a fresh flood of tears from Josh and it was several more minutes before they could get him to go on with his story. Minutes which to Jacko felt like years.

'But who was in the car then, man? Yer not making yerself bloody clear, yer bloody little idiot, are yer?'

'I didn't know that, did I? Not till I saw it again today.' Josh told them of setting out to look for the car that morning and how when he suddenly saw it, it felt like a miracle had come true.

'And I could see the driver and all this time, couldn't I? I don't know her name but I've seen her before right here in your street.'

'In our street? Who is it, man?'

'I told you. I don't know her name. But it was when we were short of help up at the fairground and Uncle Percy and a couple of the other men came to see if any of the lads round here wanted jobs for the day. I was sitting in the van –' Josh moved slightly and gasped with the pain of it. He paused, waiting for the twinge to disappear, but Jacko was not in the mood for patience.

'And?' he urged.

'She was with some man. I'm not certain, but I think they were collecting money.'

'The bastard!' Jacko yelled, punching his left palm with his right fist. 'I knew it all along. Hammerman.'

'Is that her name?' Josh asked.

'Ner, the woman's name's Stella.'

'The car that picked Melanie – which was the one I saw the woman in this morning – wasn't the same car as the woman and man were in when they were collecting money, though.'

'What d'yer mean? Explain yerself, yer little creep.'

'Ha'way, Jacko, give him time, will yer,' interrupted Doris. 'The lad's doing his best.'

'Well the car I saw when I was in Uncle Percy's van was a brand newish Ford Galaxy. A big kind of bottle green thing that you take people around in, you know?'

Jacko, thinking back to the recent visit he and Beefy had paid Hammerman, knew exactly.

'This one is different,' Josh went on. 'It's a red Volkswagen Golf. The old sort, must've been at least ten or twelve years old.'

'That's Stella's car, that is,' volunteered Doris. 'I've seen her in it when she's brought pop and sweets for the bairn.' She looked at her son with a knowing frown on her face.

'Get away, yer wouldn't know a Volkswagen Golf if it were written all over it in big letters, yer wouldn't, Mam.'

'Yer, I would an' all. It's what Mr Skillings had before he had to give up driving on account of his eyesight getting so poor.'

Doris seemed pretty sure of herself and Jacko knew that it was her memory for recent things rather than for the past that was the problem. He also knew that he couldn't afford to ignore what the boy was telling him and he nodded slowly as he made up his mind.

'Right. Get him an ambulance will yer, Mam. I'm gonna go and check this out. She moved to Gateshead, didn't she?'

'Aye, son. A while back. But don't yer think yer ought to tell the police, Jacko? Yer surely not thinking of going over there yerself?'

'By the time they've come an' with all the explaining it'd take we'll have lost valuable hours, Mam. They're a bunch of stupid twats, an' all. Most of them probably still think that it's me what did it, yer know they do. And,' he looked sternly at Josh, 'I can't tell yer that I one hundred per cent believe this little creep's story. No, I'm gonna check it out for meself.'

Doris tutted. 'I wish yer wouldn't, Jacko.' She was moving across to the phone when Josh caught hold of her arm. Tears now streaming down his face he begged her, 'Please, no ambulance. Please don't ring for one. They'll send the police, I know they will, and I'll end up in the nick.'

Jacko frowned down at Josh. 'Aye, an' maybe that's the best place for yer. How do we know that yer not making this up to throw the scent off yerself?'

'Look at the flaming state of me!' Josh's tears turned to an indignant anger. 'For God's sake, do you know how long it took me to get down that damned bank?'

Jacko grudgingly nodded. 'Get him some painkillers, Mam. If he's right, then we owe him big time.'

'Won't he need strapping up or something? If his ribs are

broken, Jacko, then the poor lad needs some proper medicine for it.'

'They don't do that nowadays, Mam, I'm telling yer.' He stared at Josh who, although Jacko didn't want to admit it, had given him hope. 'I'm away to sort this. I've a good idea who'll know where she's moved to. And if he's wrong,' he turned to Josh, 'or yer stringing me along to protect yerself, then God help him when I get back.'

'OK son. But take care of yerself, yer hear me.'

'Aye, yer've no fear of that. An' I'll send Mickey and Robbie over to keep an eye on him whilst I'm gone, Mam.'

Doris nodded. 'I still think he needs a doctor, though.'

Josh carefully eased himself up from the settee. Wincing with the pain that moving caused he looked straight at Jacko. 'I swear to you that I never harmed a hair on Melanie's head. I love her like she was my own sister.'

Josh held Jacko's gaze, willing him to hear the truth in his voice. Jacko nodded and turned for the doorway, grabbing his jacket as he hurried out. Sinking back onto the cushions Josh was glad that he hadn't voiced the other thought running through his mind: *Yeah, and now I've looked at you I know why Melanie wasn't frightened or disgusted by my face.*

Scowling, Lance Halliday sat across the table from Lorraine and Luke, his grimace adding to the ugliness of his heavily-inked face. He was furious at being hauled into the police station but his earlier ranting about his rights and wanting a lawyer had quietened down to a sullen silence.

Carter had been on his way to bring in another of the men they wanted to question when he'd spotted Halliday and his sister chucking bricks at a poor cat in the park. He knew that Halliday was actually far too young to be a serious candidate for the interviews they were currently conducting, but on the grounds that his face fitted the brief he thought he would bring him in. Lorraine's initial exasperation with Carter disappeared when she caught sight of Halliday's knuckles and saw how bruised and bloody they were. This guy had definitely been in some kind of fight, and from the look of it a pretty serious one too. God knows if it was related to all this, or just Halliday up to his usual badness. But she pitied the poor bloke at the end of his fists because it looked like the punishment he'd doled out had been severe.

I hope to fuck it was a bloke an' not some poor woman. I wouldn't put it past this creep to go for a girl. He's a bully, an' like all bullies, a friggin' coward who'll only take on folk that are weaker than themselves.

Lorraine despised men who beat up women and, God knows, she'd seen plenty of it since she'd joined the police. Not that she approved of any kind of violence.

Not unless it's me that's giving it out.

She had to clench her own hands at the thought how much she'd like to clout the little idiot seated across from her and as she turned her attention back to him she noticed that Luke looked to be thinking along similar lines.

'Listen to me, yer little scumbag. I've just about had it to here with yer wasting my time. If yer don't tell me what yer've been up to then, I promise yer, I'll throw the flaming book at yer, so I will.'

But continued silence was the only reply.

'Right. That's it, Luke.' Lorraine's exasperation got the better of her. 'Take him down and charge him with withholding information, will yer? I can't stand to breathe the same air as this vermin any more.'

She saw Halliday startle when he heard this and hid a smile. This guy was only out on probation: it would be no more difficult to send him back inside than to blink. Within minutes he was singing louder than a choirboy and though his version had a bloke attacking him for no reason, Lorraine didn't believe for one second that his injuries were purely self defence. However when it became obvious that, however bad the fight, it wasn't related to the current investigation, she signalled to Luke to wind things up and let him go.

She was just about to leave Luke to it when something the now babbling Halliday said caught her ear.

'What was that you just said?' she demanded.

'I didn't do nothin'. I tell yers, it wasn't me.'

'No, what yer just said about the bloke you claimed started hitting yer.'

'I didn't do nothin', I tell yer. He just started in on me. Huge, he was, like a great bloody brick shit house. An' pug ugly. A great big bleedin' burn all over one side of his face –'

Lorraine and Luke looked at each other, knowing immediately that this had to be the traveller who had run off from the fair. They were going to be enjoying the pleasure of Mr Halliday's company for just a little bit longer.

Aye, an' let's see if I can get through it without taking a swing at the creep.

Jacko had practically begged Trevor to take him to Gateshead. At first he'd claimed that he had no idea where Stella lived, but Jacko had told him that he had the address and that he knew the way. Then Trevor said that he was having car trouble but Jacko had known right off that he was lying for he'd seen him out in it less than two hours ago. In the end he'd had no choice but to threaten him. He didn't like bullies but this was about Melanie and he was prepared to use every trick in the book to get him where he wanted to be. Time enough to feel sorry later: telling Trevor he'd burn him out of his house had perhaps been a little extreme.

Now they were stuck in a damn traffic jam, right outside McDonald's. About a mile and a half to go to the bridge and they'd been stationery for twenty minutes at least.

Jesus!

Jacko fretted while a stubbornly silent Trevor stared out the windscreen. He began to tap on the dashboard, little caring when he saw how much it was getting on Trevor's nerves.

Why did he lie to me?

Could be the lazy bastard just didn't want to help.

Aye why, he'll be even more upset when he finds out I haven't got a fucking penny to pay him with.

Jacko tapped louder and perversely found himself almost grinning when he saw Trevor grinding his teeth.

Suddenly, and for no apparent reason that Jacko could see, they started moving again. Once they'd gone twenty yards and turned the corner the cause of the hold-up became clear. A car had gone into the back of a bus and there were so many rubber-neckers that the traffic had been forced to a standstill.

'I guess it's not just the people on the Seahills that are nosy bastards, eh, Trevor.'

Trevor grunted an answer that Jacko took for a yes. Then at long last they were pulling into Gateshead.

A few minutes later Jacko stood outside Stella's house: Trevor had opted to stay in the car.

'Turning into a right miserable bastard, he is,' Jacko muttered as he pressed the doorbell.

Within seconds it was opened by Stella who seemed momentarily stunned at the sight of Jacko standing on her step. But she recovered herself quickly and beamed at him. 'Hello, Jacko, love.' Still smiling she stepped back from the door. 'Come on in, will yer.'

'I, er.' Now that he was here and faced with a welcoming Stella, Jacko didn't know quite what to say. He'd been ready to shout and demand entrance, but she was practically dragging him into the house. She definitely didn't look like she was hiding anything, in fact she looked like she'd never put a foot wrong in her life.

Jacko followed her along a white painted hallway and into a sitting room which he thought looked as though it had come straight from the set of *Gone with the Wind*. Velvet cushions, frilly curtains and lots of fancy lace everywhere, it was so totally feminine that he half wondered why she didn't have a sign up saying, 'Males not allowed'.

'Haway, lad. Sit yerself down.' Stella patted the cushions on the plush white sofa as Jacko shuffled his feet on the sheepskin rug which lay just inside the door. He felt that even his clothes were carrying dirt into this pristine house and that he wouldn't dare sit down on anything even if he were stark naked.

'It's all right, Jacko. Everything's stain proof,' Stella said, almost as though she knew what he'd been thinking. 'It's amazing what they can do these days, isn't it? Come on, sit down and rest yer feet.'

Rather than joining her on the sofa where she'd indicated, Jacko went instead to the slightly plainer chair across the other side of the room. He'd known Stella for a long time but he'd never known her to be this friendly. Wasn't she usually demanding money off him with menaces? And now this. It was certainly strange.

'How's Christina? I heard yer had a soft spot for that one. It must have been right shocking for yer to hear that what happened to her.'

'Fine, thanks. She's still recovering in hospital.'

'Good. So how come yer've ended up on my doorstep of all places?'

Suddenly Jacko felt like a fool. He had to be here on a wild goose chase. And when he got back that clown would never know what hit him. They'd need more than an ambulance to pick up all the parts.

'Er. Well me and Trev were just passing through. An' he said as how this was where yer were living now, so I thought I'd pop in to say hello, like.'

'Oh. OK. That's nice of yer. Cup of tea, then? An' how about Trevor, will he want one? Where is he anyhow?'

Jacko felt horribly uncomfortable. Both at being in this unnaturally white house and because of why he had come. With every minute that passed the idea that Stella knew where Melanie was seemed more and more daft.

'He's still in the car. And no to the tea, thank you. I really ought to be getting back before long.' He took a deep breath and plunged into it. 'Yer'll have heard that our Melanie's gone missing, have yer? It's been all over the news for days.'

'Never! Oh my God, Jacko. That's dreadful, that is. You poor soul, yer must be beside yerself with worry.'

'Aye. Yes, yes, I am. Yer know the bastards even locked me up for it, can yer believe it. Her own dad, an' they thought I could've been involved.'

'They didn't! Dear me, no.'

'Yeah. Not sure they don't still suspect me an' all. They keep saying they want me to go on the telly to do a broadcast but then it keeps on being put off.'

'Oh, Jacko, love. I'm so sorry. Is there anything that I can do?'

Stella had given Jacko his opening and he seized it. 'Well the thing is, Stella. The thing is that someone said they thought they saw you giving her a lift.'

'Well when was this, Jacko? I did give the poor lass a ride a few days ago but she's never been missing that long, surely? It must have been right at the beginning of last week. I was driving along and I saw how much trouble that poor leg was giving her, so I just dropped her off home. Surely Doris said?'

Jacko's heart sank. Stella didn't know anything. And if his

mother had had her full set of marbles she might have remembered when Stella had brought Melanie home and saved him from this wasted trip.

He got to his feet awkwardly and said, 'Oh, well, I'm sorry to have wasted yer time.'

'Think nothing of it, Jacko. I only wish that I could do something to help yers. I'll tell yer what, don't even think about that money yer owe Hammerman whilst all this is going on. I'll make it all right with him, just leave it to me.' As she ushered Jacko towards the doorway she added, 'Actually I'm glad yer came, 'cos what happened to Doris has been playing on me mind.'

'Now I want yer to know that we in no way hold yers responsible, Stella.'

'I did try to stop it happening. And in all honesty Hammerman didn't tell them to work her over the way that they did.'

'Yeah, well. The bastard did though and trust me, he'll get his come-uppance. Same as Hammerman did.'

Stella smiled. She'd known all along that Jacko had been behind what happened to Hammerman, even though the liar had denied that Jacko had had any involvement at all. Fallen down the stairs drunk! A likely story.

'Now you'll let me know if there's anything I can do for yer, Jacko?'

'Yeah, I will.'

Jacko heard the door close behind him and with a heavy heart returned to Trevor's car. Getting into the passenger seat he turned and growled at his driver, 'Get me home. An' double quick.'

'So run that past me again. Where were yer the two days leading up to Houghton Feast?'

'The nuthouse.' Derek Laverton, tall, slim, thirty years old, and fast heading for the title 'Attitude King of the Year', curled his lip and stared sullenly back at Lorraine.

Those same lips had been slashed and carved into a permanent smile. What had prompted him to mutilate himself in such a way was beyond Lorraine's comprehension but she did know that it hadn't made him a sweeter person, that was for sure. She stared back at him, heartily sick. She'd managed to keep her cool during all those hours with Halliday but she knew that this one just might make her snap.

Sanderson was out combing the streets around where Halliday had claimed he'd last seen Josh and she'd returned to the job of interviewing the suspects Carter had been rounding up. But this one promised to be just as useless as the others.

'Enjoy it, did yer? Yer stay in the nuthouse.'

'Are yer fucking daft, or what?'

'No, you're the fucking one what's been in the fucking nuthouse, not me.'

Slightly taken aback that Lorraine, instead of reading him the riot act about his language, had simply given back as good as she got, Laverton paused for a moment. Then said, 'Very funny. I can walk out of here any time I want, yer know.'

'Can yer, now.'

'Aye.'

'Try it, mate. This is my nick, an' while yer in it yer'll do what I say. OK.'

'Who the fuck are you, like.'

'Any more shit from you an', trust me, yer'll find out,' Lorraine snapped at him. Laverton glowered at her.

Ignoring him, Lorraine flicked through his file. Petty burglary, one attempted garage hold-up, two attempted video shop hold-ups.

Must've had a bad video out, to do it twice.

In each case he'd been caught before he'd managed to take anything. Also, Lorraine chewed the inside of her lip as she read the next sentence: Detainee has a habit of using threatening behaviour towards the opposite sex.

'Found anything interesting in there yet?' he smirked.

'Nothing I haven't seen before. Men like you are two a penny.'

Closing the file she put it on top of the others.

'See? Files like this? Two a penny.'

That had him bristling. Probably thought he was unique.

'Rather pathetic, aren't yer.'

'What do yer mean?' he snarled.

'What I mean is, yer nowt but a great big motor mouth, aren't yer. Up to frightening the poor folks in Shadley Moor Mental Hospital. An old saying: "In the Kingdom of the blind, the one-eyed man is King." That's your scenario, eh? Get yer kicks out of being king of the hill, don't yer. Pretending yer mentally ill to claim extra benefit. Getting yerself signed into hospital, and while yer at it leading the other patients a merry dance. Nice one.'

Laverton jumped out of his chair. 'Who the hell do yer think yer are?' He folded his arms in front of his chest. 'I'm saying nowt more until I have a lawyer.' His lower lip jutted out in a pout, making him look like a spoilt brat.

'Why? Yer haven't done anything.'

'So why the fuck are yer questioning me, then?'

Lorraine shrugged. 'Routine.'

'Bloody routine, yer bastard. Cos yers haven't got a clue, have yers? Yer'll just haul anybody in off the street. Makes yers look good, like yer doing yer job. Fucking coppers.' He towered over her, his carved smile fighting the hatred in his eyes.

Lorraine sighed and shook her head. 'Get him outta here, will yer.'

Luke took hold of Laverton's elbow but he pushed him off and said, 'One day, bitch.'

'Open yer mouth once more and I'll have yer in the cells, double quick.'

Luke took his elbow again and none too gently escorted him out of the door and down the corridor. When he came back Lorraine was standing by the window. Shafts of pale sunshine came through the side window, highlighting her hair.

God, she's lovely.

Should I ask her now?

Dinner, a film, what?

Deciding that the moment had come to finally take the plunge, Luke stepped towards her. He was just about to speak when, 'Next one, boss?,' came from behind. Lorraine turned round and looked at Carter, entirely missing the longing on Luke's face.

'Yeah, guess so. Who is it?'

'Trevor Mattherson. Dinwall has gone to pick him up.'

'I'm fed up with this.' She turned to Luke, 'Feels like we're getting nowhere. An' Trevor's scarcely the Mr Big of the criminal underworld, is he?' Lorraine gestured towards his file. 'Shoplifting when he was twelve and squeaky clean ever since. Yer just know it's going to be another waste of time.'

'Do you want to call it a day then, boss?'

'Nah. We gotta do it. Even if it does look like this might've been a false lead. Carter, call me when you've got Trevor here at the station. And in the meantime can yer find out how Sanderson's getting on.'

'Course, boss.' As Carter left the room Luke looked at Lorraine enquiringly. He had a feeling that she was already planning the next step. 'So what's on yer mind, boss? Do yer want to talk about it?'

'Not yet, Luke. Let's concentrate on Trevor. But if nothing comes out of that then yes, I have been thinking of a plan.'

Like silent water with a long way to fall, he flows over the garden wall. Stealthily because he feels sure he is being watched. He's had that feeling for a few nights now. A creepy, hairs-on-the-back-of-your-neck kind of feeling. Shuddering slightly he opens the door and slips into his house.

Inside though, his mood changes. Angrily he shucks off his shoes and kicks them against the wall.

'Bastard!'

'Bastard!'

He stares at the sideboard where his trophy boxes live now that they no longer have to be kept in his bedroom. Nothing to put in them.

'Nothing!' He screams into the dark room.

How could I make such a stupid mistake?

Five more minutes and he would have had her, but her stupid bastard friends had turned up and he knew that he couldn't touch anyone in a crowd. She'd smiled at him, he knew she had. Her long dark hair flying around and that look in her eyes telling him that she'd come back, just for him.

Damn them. Damn them all to hell. Hearts as black as their hair, every one of them. He should have known she'd never stay dead but would keep coming back to haunt him. Haunt him and taunt him, that dirty come-to-bed look on her face.

Minutes pass and he gradually grows quieter. He makes his way across to the sideboard after peeking through the window at the silent street outside. He breathes easy: he's seen no one, no twitching curtains. His neighbours are all with the sandman.

Unlocking the sideboard, he lifts out one of the smaller boxes and takes off its lid. Very gently he pushes the collection of objects in there to one side and takes out the broken heel.

As he walks into the kitchen he fondles the heel. His smile growing wider with each step, he opens the cupboard door.

Tuna tonight. Tuna and sweetcorn. Mother had hated the smell in the house and it had taken him a long while to dare to buy a can.

A few minutes later he sits in his chair and takes a bite of his sandwich, the broken stiletto lying safely in his lap.

26

Jacko jumped out of Trevor's car saying, 'I'll sort yer out later, mate. OK?'

'Aye,' Trevor said as he pulled away.

Watching him drive off Jacko frowned. Trevor was a tight twat, always had been and normally it was always money up front. Sometimes he'd wait a day or two if yer were lucky, but today he'd never even asked for any petrol money. Granted, Jacko had made him go to Gateshead by threatening him, but even so, it was pretty strange.

'And where the hell's he going?' Jacko's frown deepened as Trevor drove past his house and headed on down the street without stopping.

Jacko shrugged. He had enough with his own problems which were slowly driving him out of his head.

Walking into the house he found his mother, Mickey, Robbie and Josh in the sitting room. When he saw the little liar dining on egg, beans and chips he couldn't control his fury.

'What the fucking hell do yer think yer doing?' Jacko

demanded. 'He's a bastard liar, and yer feeding him! I don't fucking believe it.'

'Jacko Musgrove! I will not have that language in this house. And you'd better fucking well believe it. So there.' Doris put her knife and fork down.

'Have yer forgotten what's happened to our Melanie, Mam? Have yer? And a fucking creep like this comes to the door with a blown up tale about nowt. Nowt – do yer hear me? Just so as to save his own skin, aye, an' with the flaming neck to try to get us to help an' all. Jesus. And, yer not only believe him, but yer letting him fucking feed his face!' By this time Jacko was shouting and seemed on the verge of completely losing control.

Josh rose painfully, his hands clutching his ribs. 'I told you what I know and what I saw.'

'Yer a liar. A damn twisted liar. I've been there and Melanie's nowhere in sight. Stella didn't even know that she was missing, for Christ's sake. I could kill yer, yer lying little bastard.'

Doris tutted.

'She got in the car with that woman, I saw her.' Josh was edging towards the door.

'Yeah, she did. Yer right. But yer know what? That was flaming well days ago, yer stupid little twat. Stella admitted she gave her a lift home. An' where the hell do yer think yer going?' He moved menacingly towards the retreating Josh.

'It wasn't days ago. Honest it wasn't. I did see that car stop and Melanie get in –'

'Jacko, mate,' Mickey stepped in front of Jacko. 'We've been listening to him – me, Robbie and yer mam. The kid's got nothing to do with Melanie going, yer know, he really likes her and he was really trying to help.'

'Outta the way.' Jacko went to push Mickey to one side.

Robbie stood. 'Yer should listen, Jacko. We all believe him. He's had a really rough time.'

'Then yer all a bunch of friggin' idiots. Dafter than I ever thought yers was.'

Josh made a sudden break for freedom and Jacko lunged after him, determined that he shouldn't get away. Mickey dove on top of Jacko's back while Robbie hit the floor and grabbed hold of Jacko's legs. Doris sidestepped her son and bustled Josh down the hallway and out of the door. Slamming it shut behind him she stood, arms akimbo, in front of it. She knew the lads wouldn't be able to hold Jacko for long and she also knew she had to talk some sense into him before he really hurt someone, guilty or not, and ended up in prison. Jacko had been a gentle giant all his life with a long long fuse but once that fuse blew, there would be no holding him back.

'Bastards!' Jacko screamed from the floor. Then he was up, with Mickey still clinging to his back. Once on his feet he shook the younger man off easily, as if he were no more than a troublesome midge.

'Jacko, son.' Doris held out her hands and tried to placate him, 'Please, please let him go. He's a good lad what's had a raw deal most of his life. Yer can identify with that yerself, surely yer can. He's done no harm to Melanie – trust me, yer know I know people an' can tell what they're like. The lad wants the same as we do. Please, Jacko.' Doris started to cry as she saw that her pleading wasn't having any effect. Jacko's eyes were fixed and staring as he marched down the hallway towards her with a murderous look on his face.

Melanie lay staring at the familiar spot on the ceiling, her mouth sore from the gag stuffed into it. Her head was aching and she was incredibly thirsty: lunch had been tomato soup which she hadn't wanted, but had been forced to eat. She asked 'Mam' if she could have some water to drink but 'Mam' said that it only made her wet the bed and that she would have to wait.

The pain in her leg was really bad today, so bad that she thought she might pass out. She knew that without the daily exercises her father made her do, her bad leg was gradually getting much worse. She'd tried to do the exercises for herself at the beginning, but it was just too difficult to do them without any help. Perhaps she would end up in a wheelchair like those other children who had what she had.

She tried to close her mind to the pain and to concentrate on something else. But she didn't want to think about her dad or her nana as it would only make her cry and then 'Mam' would be really cross with her.

Melanie was starting to believe that she was never going to leave here. Never see her friends or her family again. At first she'd prayed that this was some kind of nightmare she'd soon wake up from, but she was starting to wonder if perhaps it was her other life that was the dream. It was starting to seem impossible that she'd ever sat on the settee cuddling her nana or been swung shrieking in the air by her dad.

Melanie's fighting spirit was slowly being eroded and although a small flame still burned deep down, it seemed likely that before long it would be entirely out.

Cal had just drawn up outside the Musgroves' when the door flew open and Doris bundled Josh out. Mickey had phoned him earlier so he knew just who the boy was.

From the speed with which Josh was moving, Cal guessed that Jacko's trip to Gateshead hadn't met with success. The lad was managing a fair trot, despite having to hang on to his ribs.

Throwing open the passenger door he called out, 'Over here, mate. Come on, get in.' Josh looked very doubtful until Cal added, 'It's all right, yer can trust me. I'm a friend of Mickey and Robbie's.' Then muttered as Josh hobbled towards him, 'An' let's face it, yer haven't got much choice.'

As soon as Josh got in the car Cal revved the engine and spun up the street. They drove in silence for several minutes until they'd gone a distance sufficiently far enough away from the marauding Jacko for Cal to judge that they were probably safe. Pulling to a halt, Cal looked across at Josh, 'Jesus, Mickey said that yer were a bit of a mess.'

Josh nodded and looked more miserable than ever.

'Weird isn't it, that the prick what done that to yer was the same twat what worked poor Doris over?'

'Yes. And I think Melanie's dad would've liked to have finished the job off, and all,' Josh answered.

'Well, yer can't blame him, mate, can yer? I'm guessing on account of the way that yer were racing out the house that Jacko had had a wasted trip over to Stella's? He must've been beside himself I should think.'

'He was. Something awful. But I know I'm right. She did take Melanie. And it was right when she went missing, it was. I tell you I'm not a liar. I'm not. And I never touched Melanie, you've got to believe me, I just want to find her like everybody else. I swear I never hurt her in any way.'

'All right, mate. Calm down. I believe yer.' Cal still thought it a bit weird that a bloke Josh's age should have made friends with such a little girl but Mickey and Robbie had vouched for him. 'So what are yer gonna do now?'

'I'm going to go there myself and ask this Stella person. I'll show you all who's right, I will. You wait and see if I don't.'

'I told yer, I believe yer. Well come on then, let's be off.'

'What, are you going to help me then?' Josh could scarcely believe that someone he'd only just met would not only take his word for things, but was also going to go out of his way to help.

'What d'yer think I'm gonna do, man? I want to see little Melanie safe as much as you.'

Cal had a good idea where Stella lived and headed out towards Washington for the Gateshead road. She was the second cousin of a third cousin, or something like that. He knew the connection went way back but that his parents hadn't ever counted her as real family.

They were driving past the Galleries Shopping Centre when Cal braked suddenly and said, 'Hey, look at that.' He pointed across the road to where Trevor was being helped into a police car before remembering that Josh wouldn't have a clue who Trevor was. Josh in fact was busy sliding down in his seat for fear of being spotted by the policeman so Cal quickly speeded up again. He figured that it couldn't have been much because Trevor didn't seem particularly worried from the expression on his face.

Josh groaned as he pulled himself back to an upright position and seemed to be having difficulty breathing. 'You all right, mate?' Cal frowned, glancing quickly across.

'Yeah. Don't worry about me, I'll be fine. Ribs mend eventually.'

'Aye. Been there, done that. But until they do mend yer just want to hold yer hands up and beg to be shot. Man, is it painful.'

Josh nodded and gave a deep sigh.

'Ten minutes and we'll be there, that's if the traffic's all right. Usually is at this time of day, like.'

Cal knew he was making small talk, evading the question he was really dying to ask. Shrugging, he decided to come right out with it, 'So, how come you and Melanie are friends?'

Josh winced. ''Cos we are.' His voice was gruff until he looked at Cal's open friendly face and realised there was no malice there, only curiosity. He knew that he didn't have to justify his and Melanie's friendship to anyone but he felt a sudden need to talk. It felt as though his mouth had decided to unhinge after years of silence, or maybe it was his mind realising that the whole world wasn't against him. There were people like Cal and Mickey and Robbie who would do things for you without expecting anything in return.

'It sort of happened, you know, the way some things do. Nobody planned it. You probably hung around the show field when you were a kid.'

Cal nodded. As a kid his big obsession had been the dodgems and he half felt that that was where his love of driving first came from. And it wasn't that long ago that he was still helping on the coconut stall.

Taking frequent shallow breaths Josh went on, suddenly wanting to tell Cal exactly what he'd told Doris and the other two boys. 'I – I – I chased her away at first. Who the hell wants nuisance kids hanging around. But she wouldn't listen, she just kept coming back. Like a fucking toothache, she was. Then I heard her singing . . .' Josh smiled a moment before asking Cal, 'Have you ever heard Melanie sing?'

Cal, keeping his eyes on the road, grinned. 'Oh, aye, man. She's got a great voice for such a little kid.'

'Well we just sort of got talking from there on, and I just really like her. It – it's as if I've known her for ever, if you know what I mean. And she never once got freaked out by my face, or nothing, and I can't tell you what that meant to me. Anyhow, I can't really explain it but suddenly she was really important to me. I can't really explain it any other way. And I know how it must look to other people – Uncle Percy pointed that one out. But –' He shrugged and fell silent then. All out of words, all out of energy.

He just hoped that if Melanie was where he thought she was, he'd have the strength to help her.

Trevor smiled at Lorraine when Carter ushered him in. Luke stood in the far corner with the *Sunderland Echo* in his hands, the murders and the missing child dominating the headlines.

318

'Hello, Detective Hunt,' he said, sitting in the chair indicated by Luke.

Lorraine smiled back at him. She remembered Trevor from the Lumsdon case when he'd been a great help to Kerry and the rest of her family.

'Hi. It's just a formality, Trevor. I hope yer don't mind helping us with our enquiries?'

'Not at all, officer. Fire away.'

'When was the last time yer saw Melanie Musgrove?' Lorraine asked, wanting to disguise the real reason for getting him in.

Trevor shrugged. 'Sometime last week, I suppose. Can't remember which day, though. Her and one of the Lumsdon girls were playing with an old skipping rope. Can't remember seeing her since. Shame she's missing, such a nice kid. She limps, yer know, sometimes really bad, an' all. I've watched her playing in the street. They have a rope, her and Suzy, but Melanie can't really jump over it. Suzy sort of holds it and lets it flop on the ground. Together a lot the two of them are.'

'Uh, huh.' Lorraine nodded before quietly asking, 'And Christina Jenkins? When did yer last see her?'

'Who? What? Oh, aye, Christina. Couldn't think who yer meant for a minute. Is she, er, is she all right, like?'

'She's gonna be just fine. No thanks to the bastard who attacked her though.'

'Shocking that young women can't walk the roads in safety these days.'

Again Lorraine nodded her agreement.

'I, er, I thought it was Melanie yer was questioning people about?'

'Yer, but . . .' Lorraine let the 'but' slide.

After a few moments and noting that Trevor was becoming slightly agitated Lorraine asked, 'So when was the last time yer saw Christina Jenkins, Trevor?'

'Don't know. Can't remember.' He spoke quickly, looking down at his feet.

'OK. Fair enough.' Lorraine let that one go and another few moments passed before she asked, 'Did yer ever know a girl called Amanda then, Trevor? A few years back this would've been.'

Trevor looked incredibly startled by her question but his reply when it came was emphatic, 'No. No, I never did.'

'Are yer sure about that, Trevor? Do yer want to take a bit longer to think about it? Only seems a bit odd to me given that she lived in the same road as you.'

'Amanda, yer say. No. Not that I can remember, like. But yer know I don't know everyone round our way. I like to keep meself to meself, not like some.' Trevor shifted from one buttock to the other in his seat. Then with a sly glint in his eye looked directly at Lorraine. 'Why, does this lass say she knows me, then?'

Lorraine knew full well that Trevor remembered Amanda and that he knew there was no way a dead girl had been talking to Lorraine. Deciding not to push him on the subject she changed tack and, after offering him a coffee which he accepted, quizzed him as to his whereabouts on the nights of the murders. According to Trevor he'd been at home watching telly every night last week. She couldn't fault him on the programmes which was in itself suspicious: most people would have to think for a while to remember what they'd watched but listening to him you'd almost believe he'd swallowed a TV listings magazine.

Half an hour later Trevor's story was still the same. He didn't know any Amandas, he hadn't seen Christina in ages, and he'd been home alone with only the telly for company.

'OK. Yer can go now, Trevor.' Lorraine said wearily, knowing that she was unlikely to get much more out of him. 'We're finished with yer for the moment.'

Trevor's relief was obvious as he quickly scrambled to his feet but he looked less happy when Lorraine called as he was leaving, 'Finished for the moment, I said, Trevor. Don't go far, eh? Never know when we might need yer again.'

Once the door had closed behind him Lorraine and Luke looked at each other, both thinking the same thing.

'Bit strange, boss. He must've known Amanda, surely?'

'Yeah, course he did. An' yer have to ask why he wasn't owning to it. And I didn't believe that stuff about the telly programmes an' what he watched an' what he didn't for a moment. No one keeps chapter and verse like that in their heads.'

'So what do yer reckon, boss?'

Lorraine thought for a moment. 'We keep an eye on him, for now. Give him twenty-four hours an' then just when he thinks we've moved on, we'll pull him back in. There may be some other reason for him being so shifty like, and yer cannot arrest a bloke for pretending that he's watched TV. But it's like it was with Jacko Musgrove, there's no hard evidence against him at the moment.' Lorraine eyed the now empty cup of coffee on the table before adding, 'Although there could be.'

'What's that then, boss?'

'Why d'yer think I offered everyone we interviewed coffee, Luke? Out of the goodness of me heart? No way. I want yer to get that off to the lab sharpish, and have it tested for his DNA. I just hope to God there's enough uncontaminated saliva on it to get a clean profile.'

'Good one.' Luke looked at Lorraine admiringly.

'Yeah. But we'll have to wait a while for the results to come back an' even if it did match the DNA we took from Christina, it won't prove anything on the other murders. We can't wait that long, Luke. No, I want to move on to Plan B.'

Luke listened intently as Lorraine outlined the plan to him,

321

nodding vigorously as he saw how it might work. It was dangerous – some would say foolhardy – and Lorraine was keen to keep the details between the two of them in order to make sure nothing leaked. But he was proud and glad that she trusted him enough to make him part of it and determined to look out for her.

Even if she does think she can look out for her flipping self.

Melanie lay very still. The long red dress was hot and heavy. Because she'd finally agreed to wear the horrible rag, she'd had her gag removed and been at last allowed some water. Mam told her that she was a good little girl and like all good little girls she could go to the bathroom herself.

Slowly, and with Mam watching every move, Melanie swung her legs over the side of the bed and tried to ignore the pain as they touched the floor. She made to stand but her bad leg simply wouldn't support her and she collapsed on the carpet as if she'd been thrown there.

'Really, Amanda.' Mam hurried over and helped her to her feet. 'All this was totally unnecessary. If you'd done as yer were told in the first place, then Mam wouldn't have to help yer now, would she?'

'Thank you, Mam.' Melanie murmured as her mind started to believe that she really was Amanda. Mam slowly guided her through the door to the bathroom and although the walk was pure agony for Melanie, she didn't cry out once. Mam wouldn't have liked that at all.

When she came back out of the bathroom she needed more help to get back to her room. Her leg hurt so much she couldn't wait to lie down again and when she reached the bed she sank gratefully down.

But Mam was having none of it. 'Now come on, Amanda, you've lain in that bed far too long. Yer've just had the flu, that's all. Come on, sit up. I know, we'll do one of your jigsaws, eh? Then Mam will give yer a nice bath, and brush yer hair till it shines. OK?'

Mam smiled at her little girl. 'We'll do the one with castles. That's your favourite, isn't it?'

'Yes Mam,' Melanie, becoming Amanda, replied.

27

Jacko faced his mother, his fists clenched at his sides. For a long moment he stared at her as though she was a stranger, then his mood broke and he gave a deep sigh. He gently reached out and moved her to one side, away from the door. As he did so tears started to slide down his face.

'I love yer, Mam. But I've gotta find me bairn,' Jacko said, with a barely controlled sob.

'Going after Josh won't help anything, son. He had nothing to do with it. Please listen to me. Please. Before yer do something yer'll regret for ever.'

'She's right, Jacko,' Mickey added, getting to his feet from the floor. 'Just listen for once, will yer.'

At this Jacko's misery turned to anger and he spun round to face Mickey. Even though he knew what a maddened Jacko was capable of doing to him and could feel himself trembling inside, Mickey courageously stood his ground. 'Just wait a minute till yer calmer, Jacko.'

'No!' Jacko shouted. Grabbing the door and nearly wrenching it loose from its hinges, he ran outside just in time to see Cal's car disappearing down the street. He could tell from the shape of his passenger that he had Josh with him and in a flash realised that the lad had escaped. He turned back to the doorway where Doris, Mickey and Robbie stood watching him and literally shook his fist. 'You bastards. Traitors, that's all yer are. Nothing but rotten treacherous bastards. For fuck's sake, how can yer have let him go? The bastard's got our Melanie hidden away somewhere, I know he has. Are yer fucking blind, or what. I'll never forgive yer for this, Doris Musgrove. Yer no longer me mam, d'yer hear me? I no longer own yer as mine.' He looked with disgust at Mickey and Robbie, 'And neither of youse two are me friends any more.'

Doris started to cry with huge sobs that shook her whole body. 'Sorry son, I'm sorry.'

Jacko's head went down, the pain of his betrayal by the ones he trusted most harshly etched in every line of his face. He shoulders heaved then he dropped to his knees on the pathway. 'Fuck you, God. Just fuck you,' he yelled.

His cry brought neighbours out on their doorsteps, their concern obvious as they gazed at this great hulk of a man who had been literally brought down. Dolly Smith walked over and put her arms around Doris who was sobbing as loudly as her son.

Mr Skillings went to Jacko and put a hand on his shoulder hoping to comfort this broken giant he'd known since boyhood, only to have it shrugged off. He looked awkwardly about for help but no one knew what to do. Mickey, dashing tears from his own face, said, 'Maybe I should go an' get Beefy? He might be able to handle this?' Robbie nodded his agreement as he went to help Dolly who was trying to get Doris to go inside the house.

Mickey was back in minutes with Beefy close behind him, his training shoe laces flying every which way. 'Jesus fucking

Christ,' groaned Beefy at the sight of Jacko who now lay prostrate in the middle of the path. He went quickly over to his friend muttering, 'Come on, lad. Come on. We'll sort it,' as he tried to pull him up.

Moments later, a car came roaring into the street. It pulled up with a screech of brakes outside the Musgroves' and two police officers leapt out. Beefy stood up from where he'd been kneeling next to Jacko and looked puzzled. 'What do you lot want, then?' he asked, but neither officer answered him. 'Ha'way, what do yer think yer doing?' Beefy shouted when the small dark-haired policewoman came over and stood astride Jacko, then tried to turn him over onto his back. As he felt himself seized, Jacko struggled and one of his arms caught the officer at the side of her leg. She staggered slightly, then recovered herself.

'Right that does it.'

Ignoring Beefy's protests, the policewoman slapped a pair of handcuffs on the now motionless Jacko's wrists. To everyone's astonishment she began to read him his rights. 'Jacko Musgrove, you are under arrest for causing a serious breach of the peace. And also for assaulting a police officer. You,' she broke off to crouch down next to him and speak right into his face, 'are gonna go down for this, do yer hear me? And for a very long time an' all.' As Sara Jacobs straightened up and continued her caution, a loud scream pierced the air.

Doris threw off Dolly's restraining arms and ran back to her son, 'Leave him alone, will yer? He hasn't done anything, he didn't hurt yers. Yer can't take him back in, it'll kill him, d'yer hear me?' Dolly added her voice to Doris's protests and even Mickey chimed in telling them that they could see by the state Jacko was in that he wasn't a threat, but it was hopeless. Jacobs and the other policeman hauled the dazed Jacko to his feet, dragged him over to the car and bundled him into the back seat. A minute later they were driving away, the road fairly lined with stunned neighbours none of whom could believe that any of them would have called the police to report a disturbance.

Beefy was the first to get his wits together although the half brick he threw at the police car only bounced harmlessly in its wake.

Lorraine arrived home at five to six. She planned a hot soak, leaving herself plenty of time to dress for the evening. But when she came in through the back door which opened directly into the kitchen, the smell of mince and dumplings made her reconsider her plans.

'Ohh, Mam. That smells great.'

'Yeah, ready in five, pet,' Mavis said, mashing potatoes and turnip as she spoke.

'Good, 'cos I'm starving,' Peggy said from the doorway, her hair wrapped up in a pink towel and her voluptuous body draped in a matching pink dressing gown.

'Yer always are,' Lorraine retorted. She grinned at Peggy to show she didn't mean it although she privately thought to herself that Rock Chick would have more to worry about than whether she was going to get fed or not if there was no hot water left in the system.

Going over to the TV in the corner of the kitchen Lorraine asked Mavis, 'Mind if I put this on, Mam? Jacko'll be doing his appeal on the local news tonight.'

'Course not, pet,' Mavis replied. 'I just hope it does some good, love. Doesn't bear thinking about that poor little girl still missing. Me heart goes out to Jacko, the poor lad.'

The three sat round the kitchen table and listened to the news whilst they ate the delicious meal that Mavis had prepared. But to Lorraine's surprise, the only mention made of the missing child was that officers were still carrying out a house-to-house search in the immediate area. A local MP's criticism of the police for failing to arrest the man who the media had dubbed 'The Houghton Feast Strangler' took up much of the programme, and this was followed by a brief statement from a grim-faced Superintendent Clark denying that the case had gone cold. Clark ended with a warning to all local women not to go out on their own at night unless they really had to.

'Fat chance of finding a fella round here to escort a lady, eh?' Peggy joked, but one look at Lorraine's thundery face told her that she wasn't in the mood to hear it.

'This is plain bloody daft, this is,' she muttered to herself, pushing her plate to one side and reaching for the phone. Within seconds she had Carter on the line and listened with horror as he told her that rather than sitting in a television studio, Jacko was once again sitting in a cell.

'I was just about to ring yer, boss. I'm right worried about him, an' all. Dead quiet he is. There's something not right.'

Telling Carter that she wanted to talk to Clark as soon as he'd returned to the police station she rang off and turned to face a puzzled Mavis and Peggy. Before she'd even started to tell them why Jacko hadn't made his broadcast her mobile shrilled and Sanderson came on the line.

'Yer not gonna like it, boss.'

'Yeah, I've a feeling I won't. Well come on then, tell me the flaming worst.'

'I pinned Dinwall down, boss. It seems that Sara Jacobs has never given up thinking that Jacko Musgrove is guilty. She only went behind yer back and got permission from Clark to keep an eye on him, an' she interpreted this to mean that she could more or less trail him wherever he went.'

'What!' Lorraine exploded. 'Yer friggin' well telling me that the bitch hasn't been following up on finding Melanie like she's meant to be doing?'

'Aye. Dinwall says that she reckons the Melanie case is linked to the murders which is linked to Jacko. Anyhows, today they drove over to the Musgroves' and were gonna sit in the car watching from up the street, then kind of watch him from the distance when he went out, like.'

To Mavis and Peggy's alarm, Lorraine's free hand was softly punching the chair cushion by her side. Ignoring their concerned looks she interrupted Sanderson, 'Get on with it, will yer.'

'Yes, boss. Well just as they drove up and parked at the top of the Musgroves' road, Jacko came racing out of the house and started yelling at this other car what was just driving off. Dinwall said that Jacobs was onto it like a shot, said as how he was making a disturbance and that they had the right now to take him in.'

'But if no one had complained or anything, what was she gonna charge him with?'

'Dinwall reckons she didn't care. Says as how she thought once she had him back in she'd be able to break him and do him for the murders. I think the pair of them might've had some kind of falling out over it 'cos he was quick to let me know that he didn't necessarily agree with her. But there's more.'

The chair cushion by now resembled a pudding taken out of the oven long before it was ready: completely flattened, it looked unlikely that it would ever regain its former shape. Peggy tutted at the sight until Lorraine gave her a warning glance.

'Yeah, I thought there flaming well would be.'

'Dinwall says he didn't see it, but Jacobs claimed Jacko assaulted her. Reckons she's a huge bruise on her leg an' that she can barely walk.'

'She'll get a bruise on her arse from my foot when I get hold of her. I just don't believe it. That evil little cow shouldn't be wearing the –' Lorraine stopped herself, aware that her outburst was unprofessional.

'Listen, Sanderson, I can't come back into the station immediately and Luke's not around for a while so I need you an' Carter to sort this one out. I want yer to get the duty doctor in as soon as possible an' have him – or her – take a look at Jacko. And when that's happened they can have a look at Sara Jacobs's injury, an' all. I don't want Jacko charged with anything before I get there, d'yer hear me? I'm bloody well waiting for Clark to ring me, an' all.'

Sanderson promised to take control of the situation and Lorraine rang off. She took her still half full plate over to the sink, all appetite gone, then turning, told Mavis and Peggy that she was going upstairs for a quick change.

Peggy, about to launch into her favourite tirade about starving people the world over, wisely chose to keep quiet when she saw the expression on Lorraine's face.

Cal watched Josh as he slowly made his way up Stella's path. He didn't know him that well but he had to admit the guy had guts. He'd felt the agony of broken ribs himself, courtesy of a school rugby game, and he remembered taking to his bed for days rather than face the repeated hurt of moving around.

Cal had spent the rest of the journey trying to find out just what Josh thought he was going to do when he got to Stella's but he soon realised that the younger boy had no plan. Cal had tried to persuade him that going to the house was just plain stupid: Stella was a strong woman and she could fight as good as any man. And in any case, hadn't Jacko already tried going there and discovered nothing. In Cal's opinion, Josh should bring in the police and there was no two ways about it. But Josh was adamant. He was as certain as he'd ever been of anything in his whole life that they wouldn't believe him. He'd be locked up for sure, and when he finally got out it might be too late.

To Cal's mind, if someone felt that strongly about something, yer went with the flow.

Josh reached the front door and paused, a little daunted by the solid wood in front of him. He knocked once and could hear it reverberate through the house. His heart pounded as he waited to confront her with the fact that he personally had seen Melanie get into Stella's car on the day she went missing. He knew at the back of his mind that there was a possibility that Stella didn't have Melanie – it was feasible that she had, as she had claimed, just given Melanie a lift home and someone had kidnapped her after that – but his gut told him she was lying. After all, he knew she was lying about the timing as it had definitely been the day Melanie disappeared so surely there was a good chance she was lying about everything else. And in the end, she was his only hope.

He didn't know what he'd do once she opened the door, but he hoped something would come to him. If she tried to punch him out he knew Cal would help him. But more likely she'd invite him in, like Jacko. Only he wouldn't fall for her lies – he'd make her tell him the truth. And that was that. He shrugged. Nothing else to do.

He knocked again. Still no answer.

The longer he waited the more certain he was that Stella wasn't at home. Giving one final rap on the door, he limped back up the pathway to the car.

'There's nobody in, Cal. I'm gonna go round the back an' try an' find a window, or something. It's dark enough now for me to be able to look in an' not be seen.'

'I'll take yer,' Cal said. 'Get in.'

'No, that's OK. You've done enough getting me here.'

'Don't be friggin' stupid, man. It's in the middle of a bloody terrace. Yer'll need to go right up the length of the street an' back round the other side if yer gonna get through. And look at the state of yer.'

Josh nodded and climbed back in the car, hiding a yelp of pain as he put the seat belt across his chest. Cal drove slowly round to the back where they had to count the houses as they passed them because the high green painted fences had no numbers to tell you where you were. On the first attempt they couldn't decide just which house was Stella's and Cal had to reverse back up for another try. When they found the one they wanted they sat, engine idling, and Cal asked Josh for the umpteenth time what he thought he was gonna do next. Josh, staring up at the house, pointed out a faint light in one of the windows. 'I bet she's in there,' he muttered, then loudly and with the utmost conviction: 'She's in there, I know it.'

'Who, Stella?'

'Melanie, man. She's there. I just know that she is.'

It was on Cal's mind to ask how the hell he could be so certain. But he'd seen hunches pay off before for no apparent reason other than complete and utter faith.

'Look, if yer really serious about this, Josh, then I reckon we should go an' get Robbie an' Mickey. We're gonna have to get over this fence yer know, an' I can't see me climbing on yer shoulders or nothing, the state you're in.'

Josh's face fell at the thought of yet another delay but then he nodded slowly. 'Yeah, you're right. But I'm gonna stop here, Cal. Stella might come back, or she might try an' move Melanie or something. And I couldn't bear it now we've got this close if we lost the chance.'

'OK, that makes sense. But d'yer promise me that yer not gonna do anything daft? I'll be there and back before yer know it, but I'm not going if yer not gonna give me yer word.'

332

'Look at me, will you? Do you honestly think I'm going to suddenly grow wings and fly over or something? I just want to keep watch – I'll go mad if I have to drive all that way there and back with you.'

Cal took one last look at the high fence at the rear of Stella's garden and then one last look at Josh before reluctantly agreeing to this plan. Once Josh had got out, Cal drove to the end of the street and then paused, looking in his rear mirror. When he saw Josh ease himself down onto the wall opposite Stella's garden with every appearance of being content to sit out the wait, he revved his engine and tore off, determined to beat all records for getting to Houghton and back.

28

Stella was happy. It was so obvious from her beaming smiles and cheerful banter with the punters that Hammerman just had to ask her what the reason was.

She smiled sweetly at him. 'Amanda's back,' she said. Then with a zippy spring in her step that Hammerman had not seen for a long time, she left to check that the recently employed pole dancers had all reported for work.

Hammerman stared after her. 'Amanda's back?' he repeated to himself, with a puzzled frown.

'Sorry, boss?' One of the bouncers passing on his way to take his turn at the door stopped alongside him.

'Amanda's back,' Hammerman repeated, without thinking.

'Oh, aye, where's she been then?' the bouncer asked, not having a clue who Amanda was.

'In the fucking grave.'

'Oh, right.' Looking at Hammerman as if he might be slightly odd in his head, the bouncer went to his post by the double doors of the club where a long queue of people stood waiting to get in.

Stella was helping one of the girls on with her costume when a horrible thought hit her.

Shit. Did I lock the flaming back door?

She froze. Had she?

Ohh, God. She'd been so flustered by Jacko's visit before she'd left for work, she just couldn't be sure.

Heart pounding with the uncertainly of it she dropped the turquoise sequinned garment that, when worn, left nothing at all to the imagination. Then to the amazement of the half-dozen girls getting themselves ready, she simply ran from the dressing room.

The club was nearly full but the crowds scarcely slowed Stella. Her eyes fixed and almost frantic with fear she barged her way through, nearly pole-axing one punter who stood in her way.

The Rasta propping up the bar at the nightclub in Houghton was no stranger to the place. Although he turned up at odd intervals, Stew Axel, the barman, knew him only as Mac. A slightly seedy, slightly run-down place compared to Hammerman's establishment, the club had been open for about fifteen years and Stew had worked there for ten of them. He liked his job and, in the main, liked the customers. Most were happy to chat as they propped up the bar and Stew had got to know the life stories of many of them. The huge black man was pretty reticent though and Stew knew little about his past, or even his present, come to that.

But what he did know is that he seemed to score with the best-looking chicks nearly every time he came to the club. Dressed all in black it was sometimes quite hard to see him on the dance floor if the swirling spotlights weren't on him. But when they did shine on him he was invariably with some glamorous woman who would have eyes only for him.

'Freshen that drink for yer, Mac?'

Mac looked into his drink and frowned. 'Yeah, why not.' He swallowed the last mouthful and passed the empty glass over to Stew.

'She's a right smasher, isn't she?' Stew gestured with his head in the direction of the raven-haired beauty who Mac had been watching for the past ten minutes as he passed a fresh half of lager over.

Mac's smile was slow and lazy as he nodded his head.

Over in the far corner five or six women were noisily celebrating a divorce. The dark-haired woman left the couple she'd been talking to and moved over to the divorce party where she was welcomed like a long-lost sister. The man she'd just left gazed after her approvingly whilst the look of his blonde companion, who was showing more skin than clothes, carried a more hostile emotion.

There were more eyes on her than Stew's, the Rasta's, and those of the man and his jealous partner. Across the room, half hidden in the shadows, someone else watched the scene unfolding, a small smile playing on his lips.

Once Cal's car had disappeared Josh carefully got to his feet. When he was certain that the coast was clear he crossed over to the rear of the houses and quietly broke off the rotten piece of fencing at the very corner of the plot. It hurt, but within minutes he'd gained entry and he paused, half expecting a light to come on in the kitchen window which was a mere five yards from the fence.

Once he realised that the entire ground floor was in darkness and that this showed no sign of changing, he relaxed slightly. Slowly, almost on tiptoe, he crept up to the kitchen door, not entirely sure what he was hoping for but having a vague thought of somehow being able to pick the lock like you saw on all the films. When he tried the handle and the door swung silently open, his breath caught in his throat.

That means there must be somebody in.
What to do?
Knock?

He stepped over the threshold only to find that it was darker inside the house than it had been outside. Hesitatingly he took a step towards what looked like a door at the far side of the kitchen.

No. He stopped.

Better shout. At least I can't get done for breaking and entering if I let them know I'm here.

'Hello,' he shouted, not knowing whether he felt nervous or stupid, but realising that it was probably both. He paused, his foot hovering a few inches above the floor. What if Stella really had dropped Melanie off back at her own house, as she'd claimed to? He'd look a right fool then. He placed his foot down, then shook his head. No, she had her, and that was that.

He waited for a moment, then louder and with more conviction, 'Hello, is anybody in?'

Still no answer. He moved forward until he was standing in the doorway which opened onto a passageway that fed the rest of the house. The heavy wood front door was at the end of the corridor, the street light outside offering a weak illumination through the panel of glass at the top of the door. On the left a door led to what he assumed would be a sitting room: on the right a staircase led upstairs.

'Hello,' he tried again, straining to hear something. Anything that might tell him whether the house was occupied or not. He hadn't realised he was holding his breath until a sudden pain caused a wave of dizziness. Clutching at the handrail he made his way along the passage until he reached the bottom of the stairs where he gently eased his aching body down. He promised himself a few minutes, that's all, just a little time until the pain in his chest started to wear off.

* * *

337

The happy divorcées were happy no longer. The row that had broken out at the end of the club seemed to have been caused by the raven-haired woman and she was now being told, seeing as how no one had invited her to join them in the first place, to please sling her hook.

'Aw, fuck off the lot of yers,' she said, tossing back her long loose dark hair. Grabbing her tiny clutch bag off the table she staggered towards the exit, but halfway there an arm blocked her way. She followed the arm from the wrist up, past the elbow, then the shoulder, and looked into a pair of dark-brown eyes.

'Want a lift home?' the man asked.

'Piss off.'

He laughed. 'I've had worse refusals.'

'Have yer now.' She set herself, hands on her hips, and snarled, 'So who the fuck do yer think yer are, Brad fucking Pitt?'

He held his hands up in submission. 'Just asking, pet. Chill, eh.'

'And I'm just telling. All the same the fucking world over. I've had enough of yers. Bastards yer are, the whole fucking lot of yers.'

She turned and stomped out of the nightclub.

A few people had turned to watch the scene, frowning to themselves as she made her unsteady exit. An exit of this sort was scarcely an unusual sight in a club like this and shrugging, they turned back to their drinks. No one seemed to notice the shadows stir in the corner, nor the man who slithered out of his booth and followed her through the door.

At the bar Mac finished his drink and said goodnight to Stew.

'Early night?' Stew asked, more out of boredom than any real interest.

'Yeah, something like that,' Mac answered as he walked away.

Outside the club the woman crossed the Broadway, her tapping heels on the road the only sound in the silence of the night. When she reached the church archway she paused a moment, rubbing her bare shoulders in a futile attempt to keep warm. Then she tottered forward again, almost stumbling against the ancient gravestones lining the path.

She seemed oblivious to the dark shadow creeping along behind her, matching her step for step but making no noise on his rubber soles. Minutes passed and it looked as though she would soon be through the churchyard and into relative safety, but when the sudden lunge came it was made with practised ease. Before she could even cry out strong fingers had circled her throat and locked together, completely closing off any access to air.

Lorraine used one of the very first karate moves her Sensi had taught her. Seizing her attacker's little fingers she quickly yanked outwards and was instantly rewarded with the satisfying crunch of dislocated bones.

Trevor screamed, his hold on Lorraine's neck immediately broken. Holding his arms to his chest he screamed again when Lorraine pivoted round and delivered a karate chop to his chest which brought him down.

Luke, his Rasta outfit flapping, arrived a moment later and knelt on Trevor's shoulders to still his agonised writhing so he could get the cuffs on.

'Got yer. Yer bastard,' Lorraine said gruffly as she pulled her mobile out of her hip pocket and pulled off her wig.

'Get a car over to the church right now, Carter. We've got the bastard.' Smiling at Luke she held the phone away from her ear as Carter yelled a jubilant 'Yes!'

Only then did Lorraine massage her throat gently. Trevor was much stronger than he looked and she knew that the bruising was going to be pretty bad. Thank God she'd had Luke as back-up, and thank God too for her Sensi: his lessons had paid off, and not for the first time in her career.

Josh had rested far longer than he had planned to. It took a strong effort of will to haul himself upright and he felt his body protest as he got to his feet. 'Got to get a move on,' he told himself, trying to ignore the pain as he almost crawled up the stairs.

He made slow progress but finally reached the landing where he saw there were three rooms, each with the door closed. The first opened onto a fairly spacious bathroom with pink and white tiling on the walls, vivid pink towels and an equally pink bathroom suite.

Closing the door he faced what he guessed were the bedrooms. 'Hello?' he tried once more, then held his breath when he fancied he'd heard a noise from the room on the right. 'Hello?' He waited, his heart beating rapidly, but this time there was nothing. Shaking his head in disappointment he edged along to the first bedroom and very very slowly opened the door.

Jesus Christ.

It was as though there were flowers in full bloom everywhere. On the walls, on the furniture – even the carpet looked like it had been planted in the Spring. Whoever had decorated this place had gone way over the top with their floral motif and with the bright light overhead it seemed like a garden gone mad. He looked at the bed expecting a ghastly flowery bedspread, then froze, his mouth agape with disbelief.

'Melanie!' he gasped. 'Melanie, I've found you!'

He'd rarely felt such jubilation in his life before: he'd been right all along and here Melanie was, safe and alive.

Thank you, God. Thank you.

He moved towards the bed, his face wreathed in smiles.

'Melanie, I'm here now. I've come for you, love. It's me, it's Josh, Melanie.'

The little girl shook her head. 'No,' she murmured, moving further away from him.

Josh stopped. She looked terrible: black circles under her eyes, her face far paler than it ever should be, and the old-fashioned red dress she had on draining her colour even more. It pained Josh to look at her. The once vibrant little girl was a wreck of her former self.

'It's me, Melanie. Josh – remember? Everything's gonna be all right, I've come to take you home.'

'No.'

Why, what the hell was wrong with her?

'Nn – no – not Melanie . . .' she hesitated, struggling with herself as if she wasn't sure who she was, then, 'Amanda.'

Josh moved to the foot of the bed. What had that woman done to her? Frantic, but desperately trying to keep a lid on it in case his panic transmitted itself to her, he adopted a gentle tone before going on. 'No. No, you're not Amanda.'

Whoever the hell she might be.

Josh took a deep breath, hurting his ribs enough to make him slightly light-headed but knowing that he had to keep calm so as not to frighten her more.

'Listen, Melanie. Please listen to me,' he begged. 'You are Melanie. Do you understand me? You are Melanie. I don't care what she's done or said, you are Melanie. Melanie Musgrove. Your dad's called Jacko – he has a patch over his eye, remember? And your nana's name is Doris. You told me that, Melanie, remember? You told me that in the park.'

He saw doubt on her face and quickly went on, 'Sing, Melanie, sing. Sing "Sweet Chariot" like you used to. Come on, Melanie, love, sing it for me.'

She shook her head, 'Amanda can't sing.'

Was her voice a little stronger? He dared to hope. 'But

341

Melanie can,' he told her. 'And you are Melanie. Sing, Melanie, you know how much you love to sing.'

She stared at him, her lovely dark eyes seemed to carry a look of the lost who would never be found. But he had found her and she was going to be all right – she had to be. He was wasting valuable time here, what she needed was a hospital and doctors who could treat this. His job was to get her to safety and right now.

'Come on, Melanie. Come home with me.'

She hesitated, but Josh sensed her wavering. 'Come on,' he held out his hand. 'We have to go now, lovey. Let's go home, shall we.'

Slowly she began to edge her way to the side of the bed and as she slid across he was certain he could hear her begin to hum the 'Sweet Chariot' refrain. His heart soared.

'Home. Daddy. Nana,' she whispered, but as her legs slipped over the side of the bed she gave a little moan of pain.

Josh wished with all his heart that his ribs were all right as then he might have been able to carry her, but he knew that that was impossible and there was nothing he could do except encourage her to move at her own speed. 'Come on then, love. There's a good girl – you can do it.'

Melanie's face contorted with the awful hurt of her leg but she moved slowly forward and Josh swallowed a lump in his throat as he saw that deep down, her courage was intact. 'That's it. Well done. Come on now,' he murmured, trying to support her as she dragged her poorly leg behind her and started to limp across the floor.

She nearly smiled. She was going to smile, he knew she was. Then suddenly she froze, the unborn smile never materialising on her face. Staring over his shoulder the light went out of her eyes and, too late, Josh got the message.

He tried to turn, but he wasn't quick enough, and he screamed in agony as the knife plunged into his back.

29

The media circus had shown up even before the car carrying Trevor arrived back at the station, making Lorraine wonder just who had tipped them off. They bundled Trevor inside under the cover of a blanket and five minutes later Clark came out and read a hastily prepared statement confirming that yes, a very strong suspect had been taken into custody. Clark sidestepped the journalists' questions as best he could, promising more details later, but had to admit that the missing child's father who they'd questioned earlier was now entirely in the clear.

Fortunately for Clark, a bewildered and still stunned Jacko had been released on Lorraine's instructions before she and Luke and carried out their sting. He'd gone home to Doris with Sanderson's assurance that the police wouldn't be prosecuting. Privately Lorraine thought that if Jacko hadn't been wholly taken up with worrying about Melanie, he might have realised that he had a case for wrongful arrest.

The duty surgeon had given Trevor a cursory examination and after binding up his fingers gave them the go-ahead to begin their interrogation. Lorraine was straight in there, Luke close behind her, without even taking the time to change out of her nightclub gear.

'Well, yer pathetic little creep. What have yer got to say for yerself?' she started, before she was even properly in the room.

Luke assumed a protective stance behind her, her fast blackening throat reminding him of how close she'd been to getting seriously hurt. He'd have liked to have been able to have a proper go at the man he'd had to stand by and watch attacking her, but Lorraine had warned him that they were going to play this one entirely by the book.

Lorraine fully expected Trevor to start bleating on about wanting a lawyer, but to her huge frustration by way of answer Trevor slid off his chair onto the floor. He huddled there, his face hidden by his bandaged hands, then came a muffled muttering which neither Lorraine nor Luke could properly make out.

'What's he on about, Luke?'

'Dunno, boss.' Luke bent over and forced Trevor's hands down and then listened with horror to the torrent of madness that came forth.

'Little bitch, yer asked for it. Didn't I tell yer, Mother? I told yer Amanda was asking me to do that thing to her and yer just made me wash me mouth out with soap. She wanted it, she did an' all. But she's a dirty hoor, so she is. But I didn't touch her, Mother. I only wanted to stroke. Lovely long hair, flying out. But then she went and cut it all off. An' I only wanted to stroke. I killed yer, yer know that. But yer still want me an' yer keep coming back to me, don't yer? But yer shan't take my collection, yer shan't yer know. Come to me then, Amanda. Yer know yer want to. I'll show yer my collection, so I will. Dirty rotten hoor.'

Lorraine signalled to Luke and they both left the room,

then instructed the desk sergeant to get the psychiatrist on call over to the station as soon as possible.

'Do yer think it's genuine, Lorraine? Er, I mean, boss?' Luke asked. 'Or is he putting it on, planning to plead insanity?'

'I don't know yet, Luke. But it's strange that the moment we have him he's turned nutty as a fruitcake, isn't it? Any road, I'm not gonna hang around waiting – get Carter to get a search warrant for his house and let's see what we can find out.'

Cal's car squealed to a halt outside Stella's and he started to climb out. He'd first driven to the back of the house with Robbie and Mickey but found no sign of Josh. Cal was pretty certain he'd grown impatient of waiting and left the others to look for him whilst he came back round the front to see if there was any sign of him there.

Before he was even halfway out of the car he noticed the red Volkswagen parked halfway up on the pavement, the car door hanging open as if someone had deserted it in a hurry.

'Shit!'

Quickly he ran up the pathway and was pushing his way through the front door which had also been left open when he heard Josh scream. Hairs standing up on the back of his neck he took the stairs three at a time, practically bouncing from one wall to another in his haste. He burst into the room, taking in the awful scene at a glance. Melanie, in a weird old dress, lay slumped half on the bed and half off it, whilst to the side Stella stood over Josh. She had a bloody knife in her hand which she had just pulled from his back and was ready to plunge in again.

'No!' Cal yelled, grabbing a vase from the dressing table and flinging it at Stella's arm. It hit just as the knife stabbed through Josh's shoulders, deflecting the blade's pathway away from his heart but puncturing his left lung. Stella let out a cry of frustration and heaved the knife back out to try again but already Cal was on her, holding tight to her arm. With her lips pulled back in a feral snarl she turned, this time aiming for Cal's chest.

Quickly he sidestepped, then grabbing her hair pulled her head back before slamming it into the wooden bed post. She still fought so he brutally slammed it against the post again. This time she lost consciousness and slumped over Josh's prone body and Cal was faced with the horrible choice of whether to try to help Josh or to get Melanie out. Fortunately at that moment Robbie and Mickey burst into the room having discovered Josh's route into the house from the back.

Robbie grabbed Melanie who lay with her eyes tight shut, not making a sound. While Cal and Mickey went to Josh's aid he ran out of the house with her tucked under his arm and gently lowered her onto the lawn. Checking first that she was breathing and seeing that there was little more he could do for her, he ran to the nearest house and practically knocked the door down to get to a phone.

Within minutes there were police cars and ambulances at the scene. Cal and Mickey, having been hustled out of the bedroom by the worried-looking paramedics, stood with Robbie on the pavement and watched Josh carried out on a stretcher. The first ambulance tore off with siren blaring and lights flashing: the second, carrying Melanie, was not far behind. Stella was the last to be brought out, conscious now and raving. She lunged at Cal as she was taken past him and would have had him had it not been for the two burly policemen who managed to pin her down.

Lorraine took the call from her Gateshead counterpart on her way to Trevor's house with a search warrant and she diverted the car to the Musgroves' house knowing that this news took precedence over the man they already held.

* ` * *

Percy had reached the hospital seconds before Jacko and Doris were brought in by Lorraine and Luke. He knew nothing of what had gone on as he paced the floor outside the operating theatre where they were working on his nephew, only that Josh was critically ill and that the doctors feared the worst. Percy had glimpsed Josh as he was taken down to theatre and seen that the skin surrounding his livid burn was a contrasting deathly white. They were already pumping blood into him as they tore down the corridors and one nurse ran alongside the trolley squeezing a device which was pushing air into his one working lung.

Jacko had the car door open even before Luke screeched to a halt outside the Accident and Emergency entrance, and was out and running before he'd turned the engine off.

'Where is she?' he yelled to a porter. 'Where is she?' Guessing who he was the porter pointed to a side door, then stood back to give Jacko a clear passageway into the room. When Jacko burst in he found Melanie sitting on the examination table with a cup of orange juice. She was smiling shyly at the doctor standing with his stethoscope at the end of the bed, whilst the huge black nurse who held the cup for her looked as though she was finding it difficult not to simply cuddle the child to her breast.

'Melanie. Oh, Melanie,' Jacko sobbed.

Melanie pushed the cup to one side and held her arms wide: 'Daddy! My daddy!'

Pushing his way through, Jacko lifted her up and enveloped her in a hug, sobbing unashamedly in his relief at the sheer feel of her. Burying his face in her hair he squeezed her tight and promised himself that he was never going to let her go.

Doris stood back and waited her turn, her own tears spilling over when Melanie looked up from Jacko's shoulder and grinned her usual mischievous grin. 'Wasn't my fault,

Nana. Honest.' Melanie wriggled her arms free and held them out to Doris.

Standing in the doorway Lorraine felt the back of her own eyelids prickle with tears. Luke was similarly overcome and in the emotion of the moment put his arm around Lorraine's shoulders and pulled her to him. Lorraine stood there for a second relishing the warmth and comfort of his embrace but then pulled away.

'Daddy, where's Josh?' Melanie asked.

Jacko looked at the doctor who shook his head and then looked away.

30

Lorraine rose early the following morning and had left the house before either Mavis or Peggy had stirred. She'd stayed late at the hospital the previous evening and then gone on to Trevor's house, but they'd both waited up for her having heard on the local radio the news that little Melanie had been found. They'd heard about Trevor's arrest too, or rather, the arrest of someone strongly suspected of committing the crimes. Tongues were already wagging locally and by the time Lorraine arrived home, utterly exhausted, two people had already phoned to pass on the gossip about who the murderer was.

Mavis took one look at Lorraine who still wore her club get-up under her overcoat and knew at once that her daughter had had a difficult night. As she shrugged off her coat the bruises ringing her throat stood out like an emerald and sapphire necklace and, listening to Lorraine's brief version of how she'd trapped Trevor, Mavis shivered to think how close her daughter had come to death. Much as she wanted to question Lorraine more closely, with a mother's instinct she knew that now wasn't the time and silencing Peggy's eager chatter with a glare she made Lorraine a mug of hot milk before guiding her up to bed.

Lorraine had spent a largely sleepless night going over and over the case in her mind. She'd left her mobile on as the station had instructions to call her once Trevor came round from his sedated sleep. She'd also left a message at the hospital and as she drove into work she comforted herself that the lack of a call at least meant that Josh was still clinging onto life.

Luke must have also had problems sleeping because when Lorraine arrived he was already there.

'Cuppa tea, boss?' he asked, already half out his chair and on the way to fetch it.

'Yeah. Thanks, Luke. No news from the hospital then?'

'No. Josh's still in a critical condition but to be honest, it doesn't sound good. Melanie had a good night's sleep though, from all accounts, an' they reckon they'll let her go home later on today. Doctor said that Jacko wouldn't be parted from her, an' I don't blame him. Spent the night on a chair just holding on to her hand.'

Half an hour later the rest of the team started to drift in and Lorraine called them all together for a debrief. She revealed that forensics had already found fibres in Trevor's car suggesting that he'd used it to transport the bodies, together with some bloodstained clothing in the boot. And their search of the house the previous evening had turned up more bloodstained clothing together with a gruesome collection of objects spanning several decades. The missing items from his victims were found carefully wrapped and labelled and seemed to be taking pride of place. She ended by cautioning them not to say anything to the media for the time being and as she spoke glared across at Jacobs who she knew for a fact had tipped the journalists off the night before, though she couldn't prove it.

350

Yet. But I will. Yer can bet on it, yer lying little cow.

Turning her thoughts back to the team of officers in front of her she dismissed them, asking Carter and Luke to stay behind.

'So do yer think Trevor is mad then, boss?' Carter asked. 'An' that he couldn't help what he was doing, like?'

'No one in their right mind is gonna be going around murdering, are they?' Luke interrupted. 'But I reckon there's some of it that he's just putting on.'

'Aye, I agree with yer, Luke,' Lorraine answered. 'He's fairly disturbed, that's for sure. But he's been carrying on with his everyday life without any problem – look how he was when we had him in for questioning. I want one last go at him an' then I'll hand him over for his psychiatric evaluation or whatever it is that they call it nowdays. I wanna talk to him about when it all started 'cos there's something about the way Amanda died that still just doesn't seem right to me.'

Five minutes later Lorraine and Luke were inside the cell where Trevor was being held, with Carter waiting outside on the door. It was the selfsame cell where Jacko had spent his long night in custody but someone had at least supplied Trevor with a blanket and a pillow for his bed. He'd stirred as they'd come into the room but on seeing them had turned over to face the wall.

'Yer can't question me. I'm poorly, I am. An' I'm not answerable for my actions,' he muttered, adopting the legal speak he'd heard a million times on telly.

'Not answerable, eh? Well that's a pity, Trevor. 'Cos yer know me an' Luke here have come to have a word. An' it sure as hell isn't gonna be a one-sided conversation, this word we're having, yer creep yer.'

Lorraine strode over to where Trevor was lying and with Luke's help, forced him to sit up. 'That's better, isn't it, Trevor.

351

Didn't that mother of yers ever teach yer any manners? Dead rude of yer to just lie there when yer've got visitors. Eh, Luke, don't yer think so.'

'Yeah, boss, dead rude.'

'Now what do yer do, Luke,' Lorraine continued, 'when yer've got visitors coming to see yer?'

'Why aye, boss. First of all yer shake their hand.'

'Like this, Luke?' Lorraine seized Trevor's wrist and took a tight hold on his still bandaged finger, then shook it vigorously, ignoring his high-pitched screams.

Within thirty minutes Trevor was talking and had made a full confession – from faking Amanda's fatal car crash three years ago, to attacking Stacey Keeton two years later, and then to murdering first Lizzy Williams then Diane Fox then Samantha Dankton this year – and doing his best to strangle Christina Jenkins as well. He begged and pleaded for forgiveness, claiming that he was ruled by an uncontrollable urge which meant that he couldn't really be blamed. He did seem to truly believe that Amanda kept returning from the dead to haunt him and his attacks on the women had been his attempt to keep returning Amanda to her grave. When Trevor moved each woman after he'd killed her it had been an attempt to replicate the way he disposed of Amanda, but each time he had driven out to Souter lighthouse he had found cars parked up by courting couples and had been unable to carry out his plan. And they were right in thinking that Dave Ridley had interrupted him when he was dealing with Diane Fox. He'd returned from the coast intent on leaving her by the roadside but when Dave had turned up he'd had no choice but to throw her over the bridge.

Some elements of his story were still a bit confused, but it slowly became clear that he'd had a thing for poor Amanda for a long time – probably since she hit puberty. When Stella and Amanda had been living in Houghton Trevor had spent a lot of time watching her, and fantasising about her, but it wasn't until his mother's death pushed him over the edge that he actually lost control enough to approach her. His mother had passed away just a few weeks before that fateful Houghton Feast when Amanda died, and the bereavement did seem to be the original trigger. And then although he'd managed to hold himself back most of the time since, Houghton Feast brought it all back with a vengeance.

As Lorraine left the room she turned back to look at Trevor who once again lay huddled on the floor. She wondered if she ought to feel pity for him, he was certainly pathetic. But no, what she felt was total disgust.

Percy sat by his nephew's bed with a bowed head and slumped shoulders, finding it impossible to believe that Josh was going to pull through. He'd spent most of the night watching the numerous monitors they'd hooked Josh up to, convinced that at any moment they'd start bleeping away signalling the end. The doctors had told Percy that Josh had lost four pints of blood and that his heart had stopped twice on the operating table. They'd re-inflated his lung and he was breathing for himself again, but if the coma didn't lift in the next seventy-two hours then his long-term chances were slim.

He'd had a policeman fetch the aunts around midnight as he knew that they'd want to say their goodbyes. They'd cried when they saw Josh's poor broken body and in truth Percy was glad when they'd finally gone. He couldn't cry and he half-wondered if it was shock that was numbing him – after all the lad had gone through with the fire, and his family dying, and after all he'd been put through at the burns unit, it wasn't fair that he should end up like this.

Around five a.m. Percy had found himself praying, praying to a God in whom he only half-believed. 'Please God, don't let the lad die, I beg of you. He's suffered enough.' Whether it was God's doing or not, Josh had made it through to the morning and for a short time Percy had allowed himself to hope. But the consultant's face was grave when he came to examine him and he again told Percy to prepare himself for the worst.

When Lorraine and Luke arrived at the hospital they found Jacko hurrying back to the ward clutching a bagful of Melanie's clothes. The red dress she'd arrived in had been taken as evidence and in any case he was determined that she would never see the wretched garment again. They went with him to her room where they saw for themselves that she was pretty much back to normal, eating a massive breakfast as quickly as she could get it down her and cheeking her nana who sat beside her bed.

At Doris's bidding Melanie thanked Lorraine and Luke for believing in her dad. But her thoughts were still full of Josh and she was soon back asking when she could see him. 'Not yet, pet. Not yet,' Jacko answered, now knowing that it was Josh who had saved his daughter and feeling terrible about the way he'd treated the boy.

'I'll go and find out what I can,' Lorraine said quietly to Jacko, before slipping out of the room. She was back in minutes and gestured with her head for Jacko to come outside into the corridor. Gently he disentangled himself from Melanie whose hand he'd seized as soon as he'd come into the room.

'It's not good news I'm afraid, Jacko. He's right poorly. In fact –' Jacko stared at her, silently urging her to go on. Lorraine sighed. 'In fact Josh is not expected to make it. The doctors have told his uncle that he isn't even trying, it's like he almost wants to die. I'm sorry, Jacko.'

Jacko leaned back against the wall. Why did everything

good that ever happened to him have to have a downside. He shook his head then said, 'Melanie's gonna want to see him.'

'I guessed that. His uncle's with him at the moment and he said it would be fine for yer to take her in.'

Jacko nodded then dry washed his face before turning back into the room. 'Melanie, would yer like to go and see Josh now?'

'Yes! I would, Daddy!' Doris helped Melanie into the wheelchair at the side of the bed and then Jacko, warning her that Josh was asleep and wouldn't look too good, pushed her to the lift and up two floors to intensive care.

As they walked into Josh's room Percy looked up at them. Jacko could see that he'd been crying, and felt a lump forming in his own throat. He pushed Melanie over to Josh and at first she seemed in awe of the machines and all the tubes going in and out of her friend. Then biting her lip she carefully stroked his arm, saying in a quiet voice, 'Is Josh going to die?'

Percy sighed heavily. He liked kids and he didn't believe in lying to them. He looked once at Jacko who nodded his assent then, with his eyes fixed on hers, gently said, 'Yes.'

Melanie's lips quivered and her eyes filled up. Nudging the tears away with her knuckles she held tight to his arm. For a full five minutes there was not a sound to be heard in the room save for the throbbing of all the machinery, then in crystal clear tones came Melanie's voice, 'Swing low, sweet chariot . . .'

She sang the whole song through and when she was finished peace settled over the room. Percy, who was holding Josh's other hand, fancied he felt a slight movement but then it went again. No, he'd imagined it.

A couple of hours later, when the consultant returned to check on Josh, he found the three of them still sitting there in a tranquil silence, Melanie still holding on to Josh's hand with her eyes tightly closed.

He read Josh's chart, and then checked some of the monitors. Then he frowned and, looking at Percy with raised eyebrows, said, 'I don't want to get your hopes up, but both his heart rate and his pulse have improved.'

'What does that mean?'

'It means we wait and see. All I can say is – tentatively – that his condition has certainly improved.'

Percy felt his own heart start to race and he impulsively hugged Melanie to him. 'You've done it, love! You've done it. You've brought our Josh back, you really have!'

Lorraine and Luke left the hospital. Melanie had refused to leave Josh, and Jacko and Doris had said they were fine to let her stay on a while. At first they drove silently, each lost in their own thoughts, then as they passed the Penshaw Monument Luke said, 'Do yer think the jury might take pity on Stella?'

Lorraine blew air out of her cheeks. 'Well we don't know for sure that she won't be up for murder yet, Josh isn't out of the woods. But if he does make it, God knows they might. She hadn't planned to hurt Melanie, just to turn her into her dead daughter. She'll probably get time for attempted murder though, even if Josh does survive. Plus it is kidnapping when all's said and done, so she could be looking at a good long stretch. As for Trevor, I hope they'll throw the bloody key away. If it hadn't been for him killing Amanda in the first place, then Stella wouldn't have done what she did.' She sighed. 'It's harder to hate a mother driven mad by grief, isn't it.'

Luke nodded. 'And it's amazing that Trevor's lived there all these years an' entirely gotten away with his perverted habits.'

'Aye. Just goes to show, doesn't it, that yer never can tell.'

356

Although at least there shouldn't be any problems convincing a jury of Trevor's guilt. Even without his confession, they had enough evidence from the DNA test – which was a perfect match for the DNA taken from under Christina's nails – to put him away for a long time.

Luke nodded. 'Clark, of course, has come up smelling of roses. Carter heard him tell someone that our little dressing-up game to catch the killer was all his idea.'

'Yer don't say,' Lorraine groaned. 'I'd love to hear him explain his tactical decision when he probably doesn't even understand how we ended up in the right place at the right time.'

Luke smiled his agreement. Following Trevor from home to make sure they were in the right club, rather than picking one he'd been seen at before and hoping for the best, had been a smart decision on Lorraine's part. Actually, it had been the only option – time had been running out. 'What about Sara Jacobs?' he changed the subject.

Lorraine laughed at this, 'Oh, she's on lollipop duty for a good time to come.'

Luke joined in Lorraine's laughter, then for another few moments they were quiet.

As they pulled into the station yard Luke looked across at Lorraine's profile. *This is as good a chance as I'm gonna get.*

He turned to her and took the plunge. 'Emm, Lorraine, what do yer reckon to –'

'Boss! Boss!'

'What, Carter?' Lorraine said, smiling at Luke as she climbed out of the car.

'There's been a shooting incident at Newbottle and Clark wants all hands on deck.'

Lorraine got back into the car. 'OK, Newbottle it is then, Luke.'

He sighed – his question would have to wait – and turned the key in the ignition.

357